THE MEN ALARMED HIM. It was odd to see six well-dressed men outside a wood in the middle of nowhere. Each of them wore a sword in a well-kept leather scabbard, belted over the good cloth of their coats, and Moril did not like the way the hilts of those swords looked smooth with frequent use. But the truly alarming thing about them was that they had an air of purpose, all of them, which hit Moril like a gust of cold wind and frightened him.

"My father won't be back for ages," he said, hoping they would go away.

"Then we'll wait for him."

Also by
DIANA WYNNE JONES

Stopping for a Spell

A Tale of Time City

The Time of the Ghost

Unexpected Magic: *Collected Stories*

Warlock at the Wheel and Other Stories

Wild Robert

Witch's Business

Year of the Griffin

Yes, Dear

THE WORLDS OF CHRESTOMANCI

Book 1: Charmed Life

Book 2: The Lives of Christopher Chant

Book 3: The Magicians of Caprona

Book 4: Witch Week

Book 5: Conrad's Fate

Mixed Magics: *Four Tales of Chrestomanci*

The Chronicles of Chrestomanci, Volume I
(Contains books 1 and 2)

The Chronicles of Chrestomanci, Volume II
(Contains books 3 and 4)

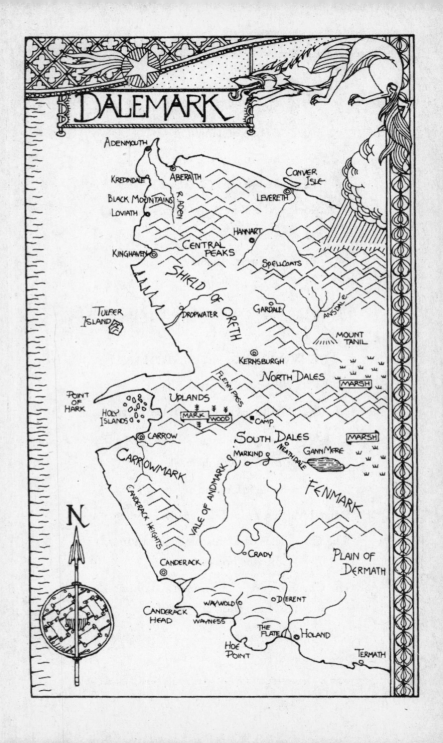

DIANA WYNNE JONES

The Dalemark Quartet

· VOLUME ONE ·

CART AND CWIDDER
 AND
DROWNED AMMET

A GREENWILLOW BOOK

eos

An Imprint of HarperCollinsPublishers

Eos is an imprint of HarperCollins Publishers.

The Dalemark Quartet, Volume 1
Copyright © 2005 by Diana Wynne Jones

Cart and Cwidder copyright © 1975 by Diana Wynne Jones
First published in Great Britain in 1975 by Macmillan London Ltd.
Published in 1993 by Mandarin, an imprint of Reed Consumer
Books Ltd.
First published in the United States in 1977 by Atheneum.
Published in 1995 by Greenwillow Books.

Drowned Ammet copyright © 1977 by Diana Wynne Jones
First published in Great Britain in 1977 by Macmillan London Ltd.
Published in 1993 by Mandarin, an imprint of Reed Consumer
Books Ltd.
First published in the United States in 1978 by Atheneum.
Published in 1995 by Greenwillow Books.

Map by David Cuzic

Library of Congress Cataloging-in-Publication Data
Jones, Diana Wynne.
   The Dalemark quartet, volume 1 / Diana Wynne Jones.—1st Eos
ed.
   p.   cm.
   ISBN 0-06-076369-8 (pbk.)
   [1. Fantasy.]   I. Title: Cart and cwidder.   II. Title: Drowned
Ammet.   III. Title.
PZ7.J684Dak 2005   2004024824
[Fic]—dc22

Typography by Christopher Stengel
❖
First Eos edition, 2005
Visit us on the World Wide Web!
www.harpereos.com

· CART AND CWIDDER ·

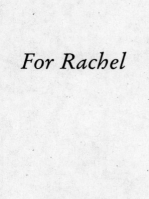

For Rachel

1

"Do come out of that dream, Moril," Lenina said.

"Glad rags, Moril," said Brid. "We're nearly in Derent."

Moril sighed reproachfully. He had not been in a dream, and he felt it was unfair of his mother to call it that. He had merely been gazing at the white road as it wandered northward, thinking how glad he was to be going that way again, and how glad he would be to get out of the South. It was spring, and it was already far too hot. But that was not the worst of the South. The worst, to Moril's mind, was the need to be careful. You dared not put a foot, or a word, out of place for fear of being clapped in jail. People were watching all the time to report what you said. It gave Moril the creeps. And it irked him that there were songs his father dared not sing in the South for fear of sounding seditious. They were the best songs, too, to Moril's mind. They all came from the North. Moril himself had been born in the North, in the earldom of Hannart. And his favorite hero, the Adon, had once upon a time been Earl of Hannart.

"You're dreaming again!" Lenina said sharply.

"No, I'm not," said Moril. He left his perch behind the driving seat and climbed hastily into the covered back of the cart. His mother and his sister were already changed into their cheap tinsel-trimmed show dresses. Lenina, who was pale and blond and still very beautiful, was in silver and pale gold. Brid, who was darker and browner, had a glimmering peacock dress. Lenina hung Moril's suit above the rack of musical instruments, and Moril squeezed up to that end to change, very careful not to bang a cwidder or scrape the hand organ. Each instrument was shiny with use and gleaming with care. Each had its special place. Everything in the cart did. Clennen insisted on it. He said that life in a small cart would otherwise become impossible.

Once Moril was changed, he emerged from the cart as a very flamboyant figure, for his suit was the same peacock as Brid's dress and his hair was red—a bright, wild red. He had inherited Lenina's paleness. His face was white, with a few red freckles.

"You know, Mother," Brid said, as she had said before every show since they left Holand, "I don't think I like that color on Moril."

"It makes people notice him," said Lenina, and went to take the reins while Clennen and Dagner changed in their turn.

Moril went to walk in the damp springing grass on the roadside, which was rough-soft under his toes, where he could have a good view of the cart that was his home. It was painted in a number of noticeable colors, principally pink and gold. Picked out in gold and sky blue along the sides were the words *Clennen the Singer.* Moril knew it was garish, but he loved this cart all the same. It moved softly, because it was well sprung and well oiled, and ran easily behind Olob, the glistening brown horse. Clennen always said he would not part with Olob for an earldom. Olob—his real name was Barangarolob, because Clennen loved long names—was harnessed in pink and scarlet, with a great deal of polished brass, and looked as magnificent as the rest of the turnout. Moril was just thinking that his mother and Brid on the driving seat looked like two queens—or perhaps a queen and a princess—when Clennen stuck his head out of the canvas at the back.

"Admiring us, are you?" he called cheerfully. Moril smiled and nodded. "It's like life," Clennen said. "You may wonder what goes on inside, but what matters is the look of it and the kind of performance we give. Remember that." His head popped back inside again.

Moril went on smiling. His father was always giving them odd thoughts to remember. He would probably want this one repeated to him in a day or so. Moril thought about it—in the dreamy way in which he usually gave his attention to anything—and he could not see that their turnout was like life. Life was not pink and gold. At least, some of theirs was, he supposed, but that was only saying the cart *was* life.

He was still pondering when they came under some big trees covered with pale buds, and the canvas cover went down with a bit of a clatter, revealing Clennen and Dagner dressed in scarlet and ready for the show. Moril scampered back and climbed up with them. Clennen smiled jovially. Dagner, whose face was tight and pinched, as it always was before a show, pushed Moril's cwidder into his hands and Moril into the right place without a word. He handed the big old cwidder to Clennen and the panhorn to Brid, and took up a pipe and a long, thin drum himself. By the time they were all settled, Olob was clopping smoothly into the main square of Derent.

"Ready," said Clennen. "Two, three." And they struck up.

Derent was not a big place. The number of people who came into the square in response to their opening song was not encouraging. There was a trickle of children and ten adults at the most. True, the people sitting outside the tavern turned their chairs round to get a better view, but Moril had a vague feeling, all the same, that they were wasting their talents on Derent. He said so to Brid, while Lenina was reaching past him to receive the hand organ from Dagner.

"All your feelings are vague!" Lenina said, overhearing. "Be quiet."

Undaunted by the sparse crowd, Clennen began his

usual patter. "Ladies and gentlemen, come and listen! I am Clennen the Singer, on my way from Holand to the North. I bring you news, views, songs and tales, things old and things new. Roll up, draw up chairs, come near and listen!" Clennen had a fine rolling voice, speaking or singing. It rumbled round the square. Eyes were drawn to him, for his presence matched his voice. He was a big man, and not a thin one, though the scarlet suit made his paunch look bigger than it really was. He had a good sharp curl of ginger beard, which made up for the bald patch at the back of his head—now hidden by his scarlet hat. But the main thing about him was his enormous, jovial, total good humor. It seemed to fetch people by magic or multiply those there out of thin air. Before his speech was over, there were forty or fifty people listening to it.

"So there!" Brid said to Moril.

Before the performance could start, however, someone pushed up to the cart, calling, "Have you got any news from Holand, Clennen?" So they had to wait. They were used to this. Moril thought of it as part of the performance—and it certainly seemed to be one of their duties—to bring news from one part of Dalemark to the others. In the South particularly, there were few other ways in which people could get to know what was happening in the next lordship, let alone the next earldom.

"Now, let's see," said Clennen. "There's been a new earl invested for the South Dales—the old one's grandson. And they tell me Hadd has fallen out with Henda again." This surprised nobody. They were two very quarrelsome earls. "And I *hear*," said Clennen, stressing the *hear*, to show that he was not trying to stir up trouble, "I *hear* the cause of it had something to do with a shipload of Northmen that came into harbor at Holand last month." This caused confused and careful muttering. Nobody knew what to make of a ship from the North coming into Holand, or whether they were breaking the law to think of it at all. Clennen passed on to other news. "The Earl of Waywold is making new money—copper and goodness knows what else in it—worth nothing. You get more than two thousand to one gold. Now the price on the Porter—you've all heard of the Porter, I suppose?" Everyone had. The Porter was a notorious spy, much wanted by the earls of the South for passing illegal information and stirring up discontent. Not one of the earls had been able to catch him. "The price on the Porter's head now being two thousand gold," said Clennen, "it's to be hoped that he's not taken in Waywold, or you'll have to collect your reward in a wagon." This caused some cautious laughter. "And the storm last month carried off the lord's roof in Bradbrook, not to speak of my tent," said Clennen.

Lenina, by this time, had sorted out the strips of paper on which she had written messages from people in other places to friends and relatives in Derent. She began calling them out. "Is there someone called Coran here? I've a message from his uncle at Pennet." A red-faced young man pushed forward. He confessed, as if he were ashamed of it, that he could read, and was handed the paper. "Is there a Granny Ben here?"

"She's sick, but I'll tell her," someone called.

So it went on. Lenina handed out messages to those who could read, and read them out to those who could not. More people hurried into the square, hearing there was news. Shortly there was a fair throng of people, all in great good humor, all telling one another the latest news from Holand.

Then Clennen called out: "Now I'm putting my hat on the ground here. If you want a song of us, too, do us the favor of filling it with silver." The scarlet hat spun neatly onto the cobblestones and waited, looking empty and expectant. Clennen waited, too, with rather the same look. And after a second the red-faced Coran, grateful for his message, tossed a silver coin into it. Another followed, and another. Lenina, watching expertly, muttered to Brid that it looked like good takings.

After that the performance began in earnest. Moril did not have much time even for vague thinking. Though he did not do much of the singing, his job was to play treble to the low sweet notes of his father's big cwidder, and he was kept fairly busy. His fingers grew hot and tingly, and he leaned over and blew on them to cool them as he played. Clennen, as he had promised the crowd, gave them old favorites and new favorites—ballads, love songs, and comic songs—and some songs that were entirely new. Several of these were his own. Clennen was a great maker of songs. Brid and Dagner joined him for some of them, or played panhorn, drum, and third cwidder, and Lenina played stolidly on the hand organ. She played well—since Clennen had taught her—but always rather mechanically, as if her mind were elsewhere. And Moril fingered away busily, his left hand sliding up and down the long, inlaid arm of his cwidder, his right thrumming on the strings until his fingertips glowed.

Every so often Clennen would pause and send a cheerfully reproachful look toward his hat. This usually caused a hand to come out from the crowd and drop a small, shamed coin in with the others. Then Clennen would beam round at everyone and go on again. When the hat was more than half full, he said: "Now I think the time has come for some of the songs out of our past. As you may know, the history of Dalemark is full of fine singers, but, to my mind, there have never been two to compare with the Adon and Osfameron. Neither has ever been equaled. But Osfameron was an ancestor of mine. I happen to be descended from him in a direct line, father to son. And it was said of Osfameron that he could charm the rocks from the mountains, the dead from their sleep, and the gold from men's purses." Here a slight raising of Clennen's sandy eyebrows in the direction of the hat called forth an apologetic penny and a ripple of laughter from everyone. "So, ladies and gentlemen," said Clennen, "I shall now sing four songs by Osfameron."

Moril sighed and leaned his cwidder carefully against the side of the cart. The old songs only needed the big cwidder, so he could have a rest. In spite of this, he wished his father would not sing them. Moril much preferred the new, full-bodied music. The old required a fingering which made even the big mellow cwidder sound cracked and thin, and Clennen seemed to find it necessary to change his deep singing voice until it became thin, high, and peculiar. As for the words—Moril listened to the first song and wondered what Osfameron had been on about.

"The Adon's hall was open. Through it
Swallows darted. The soul flies through life.
Osfameron in his mind's eye knew it.
The bird's life is not the man's life."

But the crowd appreciated it. Moril heard someone say: "I do like to hear the old songs done in the right way." And when they were over, there was a round of applause and a few more coins.

Then Dagner, with his face more tight and pinched than ever, took up his cwidder. Clennen said, "I now introduce my eldest son, Dastgandlen Handagner." This was Dagner's full name. Clennen loved long names. "He will sing you some of his own songs," said Clennen, and waved Dagner forward into the center of the cart. Dagner, with a grimace of pure nervousness, bowed to the crowd and began to sing. Moril could never understand why this part was such a torment to Dagner. He knew his brother would have died rather than miss his part in the performance, yet he was never happy until it was over. Perhaps it was because Dagner had made the songs himself.

They were strange, moody little songs, with odd rhythms. Dagner made them even odder, by singing now loud, now soft, for no real reason, unless it was nerves. And they had a haunting something. The tunes stuck in your head and you hummed them when you thought you had long forgotten them. Moril listened and watched, and envied Dagner this gift of making songs. He would have given—well—his toes, anyway, to be able to compose anything.

> *"The color in your head*
> *The color in your mind*
> *Is dead*
> *If you follow it blind,"*

Dagner sang, and the crowd grew to like it. Dagner was not remarkable to look at—he was thin and sandy-haired, with a large Adam's apple—and people expected his songs to be unremarkable, too. But when he finished, there was applause and some more coins. Dagner flushed pale purple with pleasure and was almost at ease for the rest of the show.

There was not much more. The whole family sang a few more songs together and wound up with "Jolly Holanders." They always finished with that in the South, and the audience always joined in. Then it was a matter of putting away the instruments and replying to the things people came up to say.

This was always rather a confused time. There were the usual number of people who seemed to know Clennen well; the usual giggly girls who wanted Dagner to tell them how he composed songs, a thing Dagner could never explain and always tried to do; the usual kind people who told Moril he was quite a musician for a youngster; and the usual gentlemen who drifted up to Lenina and Brid and tried to murmur sweet nothings to them. Clennen was always very quick to notice these gentlemen, particularly those who approached Brid. Poor Brid looked older than she was in her show clothes—she was really only just thirteen—and she did not know how to deal with murmuring gentlemen at all.

"Well, you see, my father taught me," Moril explained.

"They come into my head like—er—ideas," Dagner explained.

"It is Lenina, isn't it?" murmured a gentleman at the head of the cart.

"It is," said Lenina.

"I didn't quite hear what you said," Brid said rather desperately to another gentleman.

"I don't go to Hannart. I had a little disagreement with the Earl," said Clennen. He swung round and, with one comprehensive look, disposed of the man Brid could not hear and also the one who thought Lenina was herself. "But I'm going through Dropwater and beyond," he continued, turning back to his friends.

Lenina had collected the money and was counting it. "Good," she said. "We can stay at the inn here. I fancy a roof over my head."

Moril and Brid fancied it, too. It was the height of luxury. There would be feather beds, a proper bath, and real food cooked indoors. Brid licked her lips and gave Moril a delighted grin. Moril smiled back in his milky, sleepy way.

"No. No time," said Clennen, when at last he was free to be asked. "We have to press on. We're picking up a passenger on the road."

Lenina said nothing. It was not her way. While Brid, Moril, and even Dagner protested, she simply picked up the reins and encouraged Olob to move.

2

"Where are we picking up the passenger?" Brid inquired when they were three miles or so beyond Derent and her discontent had worn off somewhat. She was back in her everyday blue check and looked rather younger than she was.

"Couple of miles on. I'll tell you where," Clennen said to Dagner, who was driving.

"Going North, is he?" Dagner said.

"That's right," said Clennen.

Moril, in the ordinary rust-colored clothes he preferred, and in which, to Brid's mind, he looked a great deal nicer, trotted along beside the cart and hoped vaguely that the passenger would be agreeable. They had taken a woman last year who had driven him nearly crazy with boredom. She had known a hundred little boys, and they were all better than Moril in some way, and she had at least two long stories about each boy to prove it. They took someone most years, going North. Since North and South had begun their long disagreement, very little traffic went between. Those who had no horse—and to walk meant the risk of being taken up as a vagrant and clapped into jail—had to rely on such people as the licensed singers to take them as paying passengers.

The disagreement had begun so far in the past that not many people knew its cause: The North had one version, the South another. But it was certain that three kings of Dalemark had died, one after another, without leaving a proper heir to the throne. And almost every earl in the land had some kind of claim to be king. Even before the last king ruled from Hannart in the North, there had been quarrels and wars, and the country showed signs of breaking up into two. And when the Adon, who was the last king, died, his heirs were not to be found. Civil war began in earnest.

Since then the only rulers of Dalemark had been the earls, each in his own earldom, with the lords under them. No one now wanted a king. Keril, the present Earl of Hannart, said publicly that he had no claim to the throne. But the disagreement ran deeper than ever. The men of the North claimed that half the land was enslaved, and the earls of the South said the North was plotting against them. The year Brid was born, Keril, Earl of Hannart, had been proclaimed a public enemy by every earl and lord in the South. After that the only people who dared travel between were accredited traders and licensed singers, and they had to prove that their business was harmless or they might be arrested anywhere in the South.

Moril had met some of the traders and quite a few of the singers. Clennen did not speak highly of any of them, except perhaps the singer Hestefan, whom Moril had not met. But Moril had never heard any of them complain of having to take passengers. He thought they must all be very patient people.

"What about payment?" asked Lenina.

"You wait and see," said Clennen, with a laugh.

"That's all very well," said Brid, returning to her discontent. "But why do we always have to take someone? Why can't the stupid North make friends with the silly South?"

"You tell me," said Clennen. And after Brid had stammered for a minute, he laughed and said, "Would *you* make friends with someone you knew would stab you in the back if he got the chance? Remember that. Mind you, there was a time when the South was as free a place as the North. Remember that, too."

This was a bold thing to say in the South. The last rebellion had been stamped out very harshly indeed, and the strict laws were still in force. You did not say anything that suggested you were discontented with the ways of the South. The countryside was known to be full of spies and informers, watching and listening to give warning of rebellious thoughts.

That was why, when Clennen spoke of North, South,

and freedom in the same breath, Moril saw Lenina look round the hedges to make sure no one was listening. He found himself doing the same.

But the hedges, though the leaves were already dusty, were still thin enough to see through. Nothing moved in them but birds. The only people they saw, for the next mile or so, were in the distance, planting vines on a hillside, until they came to where a road branched off to another vineyard. There, on the triangle made by the turning, a man was waiting. At his feet he had a huge round bottle half encased in a straw basket. He waved, and Dagner drew up. Olob turned his head and looked at the huge bottle with evident misgiving.

"Evening, Flind," said Clennen. "Is that our payment there, by your feet?" The man nodded. He seemed disinclined to smile, though Clennen smiled broadly at him. "I hoped it was," said Clennen. "Where's the passenger?"

Flind jerked a thumb. The passenger, probably in an attempt to keep out of the sun, was sitting behind the bottle in its shadow. He looked very hot, very untidy, rather discontented, and rather younger than Dagner.

"Help him into the cart," Clennen said to Moril.

Moril did his best, but the passenger shook off his helping hand. "I can get in by myself," he said, "I'm not a cripple." He climbed in very nimbly and sat on the floor. The canvas cover was half up, and he seemed glad of its shade. Moril looked vaguely after him and hoped it was the heat that made him feel so disagreeable. He knew from bitter experience that someone around Dagner's age could make life very unpleasant if he was steadily disagreeable for some hundreds of miles. This could be worse than the woman last year. He looked at Brid, who made her squeezed-lemon face back.

Clennen and Flind, meanwhile, were heaving the huge jar through the tailgate of the cart. It took a good deal of effort, and a lot of space once it was in. Olob almost laid his head backward over his shoulders in an attempt to show his strong disapproval of it.

"Are you really taking our payment in wine?" said Lenina.

"Can you think of a better one?" said Clennen. "My dear girl, there's only beer to drink in the North! Count your blessings. We'll broach it this evening, shall we? Or would you rather wait until we're going through Markind?"

"Oh—this evening," said Lenina, smiling a little.

Clennen latched the tailgate, waved to Flind, and they went on. Olob made a very expressive business of getting the cart under way again. Brid was quite sorry for him, straining in front of all that extra weight, but everyone else knew that the cart was so well sprung and greased that Olob could hardly feel the difference. Dagner made no bones about flicking him with the whip.

"What a lazy horse!" exclaimed the passenger.

"They're often the wisest ones," said Clennen.

The passenger, realizing he had been snubbed, put his chin on his knees and sighed gustily. Brid and Moril took turns at eyeing him through the gap in the tailgate. He was burlier than Dagner, though he was younger, and much the same height. But he was more remarkable-looking, because he was a queer combination of dark and fair. His hair was tawny-fair, and there was a lot of it, like a lion's mane, only rather more untidy, and his eyes were a pale blue-green. But his eyebrows were thick and black, and his skin very brown. His nose put them in mind of an eagle. He still had that fed-up look, which they decided must be due to more than the heat.

"Perhaps his grandfather's dying, and they sent for him, and he doesn't want to go," Brid speculated. Moril was content to leave it vague. He simply hoped the passenger would not vent his annoyance on them.

A mile or so farther on Clennen said: "We haven't got your name, lad. There's a lot in a name, I always think. What is it?"

"It's Kialan," said the passenger. "With a *K*."

"Even with a *K*, it's not half long enough for me," said Clennen.

"Well, what do you expect me to say? It's really my name!" the passenger protested.

"I like longer names," Clennen explained. "Clennen's too short for me, too. Lenina—my wife's name—is too short. But my children all have good spreading names, because I could choose them myself. The lad driving is Dastgandlen Handagner, my daughter is Cennoreth Manaliabrid, and the one with the red hair is Osfameron Tanamoril."

Moril ground his teeth and waited for the passenger

to laugh. But, in fact, he looked rather awed. "Oh," he said. "Er, do you call them all that when you want to speak to them?"

"And the lazy-wise horse is Barangarolob," Clennen added, perfectly seriously, as if he were simply anxious for Kialan to know. Dagner gave a little whinny of laughter, which might have come from Olob. Kialan looked piteous.

"Take no notice," said Lenina. "They're Dagner, Brid, and Moril for short. And the horse is Olob."

Kialan looked relieved. He gave another gusty sigh or so and took off his coat. He must have been hot in it, because it was a thick coat, of good cloth. Brid whispered that it must be his best one, but Moril had lost interest in Kialan by then and did not care. Kialan folded the coat— not as carefully as such a good garment deserved—and used it as a pillow while he pretended to go to sleep. Brid knew he was only pretending, because he started up every time any travelers passed them and looked through the opening of the cover to see who they were.

There was not much traffic on the road. Mostly it was slow wagons, which Olob trotted past without any difficulty, sending spurts of white grit from beneath the cartwheels, until Moril, trotting in the rear, seemed to have hair the same color as Clennen's. But there were a few horsemen, and these overtook Olob as easily as Olob overtook the wagons. Once, quite a group of riders came past, raising a whirl of white dust, and were scanned by Kialan with great interest. One of the group seemed equally interested in them. He craned round in his saddle as he passed to get a good look at the cart.

"Who was that fellow?" Clennen said to Lenina.

"I couldn't say," she answered.

"Funny," said Clennen, "I seem to have seen him before." But since the man was a perfectly neutral-looking person, neither dark nor fair and neither young nor old, Clennen could not place him and gave up the attempt.

Shortly after that, as the sun was getting low, Olob left the road of his own accord and jolted the cart among gorse bushes into a heathy meadow. He stopped near a stream.

"Olob thinks this'll do," Dagner said to Clennen. "Will it?"

"You don't really let your horse choose where to stop!" Kialan exclaimed.

"He doesn't often let us down," said Clennen, surveying the meadow. "Yes, very nice. Horses have a gift for stopping, Kialan. Remember that."

The fed-up look settled on Kialan's face, and he watched, a little scornfully, while Dagner unharnessed Olob and led him off to drink. He watched Moril wiping the dust off the cart and Brid collecting firewood.

"Don't offer to help, will you?" Brid muttered in his direction.

While Lenina was cooking supper, Clennen fetched the big cwidder down, polished it, tuned it carefully, and beckoned Moril. Moril came reluctantly. He was rather in awe of the big cwidder. Its shining round belly was even more imposing than Clennen's. The inlaid patterns on the front and arm, made of pearl and ivory and various colored woods, puzzled him by their strangeness. And its voice when you played it was so surprisingly sweet and quite unlike that of the other cwidders. Clennen took such care of it that Moril still sometimes thought—as he had when he was little—that this cwidder was an extra, special part of Clennen, more important than his father's arm or leg—something on the lines of a wooden soul.

"Let's have that song of Osfameron's," said Clennen.

Moril liked the old songs so little that he was making very heavy weather of learning them. Clennen corrected him, made him go back to the beginning, and twice stopped him in the middle of the second verse. To make matters worse, Kialan came over and stood himself in front of Moril, listening. Moril, in self-defense, went into a dream between two notes, and stopped. He was with the Adon, on a green road in the North.

"Do you really need to teach him?" said Kialan.

"How else," asked Clennen, "do you think he'd learn?"

Kialan seemed a bit confused. "Well—I sort of supposed they picked it up—from giving shows," he said.

"Or it grew naturally, along with hair and finger-nails?" Clennen suggested.

"No—I—Oh, that's silly!" said Kialan, and to Moril's relief, he drifted away. But he drifted back when

Moril had finished and Brid took his place. Kialan caught Moril's sleeve. "I say, you all know all this music, but I suppose you can't even read and write, can you?"

Moril removed his sleeve. "Of course I can," he said. "My mother taught us." Before Kialan could ask any more impertinent questions, he scurried off among the gorse bushes to the stream. He stayed there, lost in vagueness, watching the bright water hurry over the different brightness of the stones beneath, until he heard Brid shouting.

"Supper! *Wash*, Moril!"

Supper was not very good, and what little bread they had was stale. "I say, this tastes peculiar!" Kialan said, pushing his share about on his plate.

Lenina's face, which never had much expression, went quite blank. "I meant to buy bread and onions in Derent," she said. "But there was no time."

There was a heavy pause. Then Clennen said, "Look, lad, we've got to travel more than a hundred and fifty miles together, you and us. It needs a little give-and-take, don't you think? I'd hate to have to break a good cwidder over your head."

The sun was setting then, and the light was red. But Moril thought that this did not entirely account for the color of Kialan's face. Kialan, however, said nothing. He silently accepted some of the wine and drank it, but he did not speak again until much later. By then Clennen had become very jolly with the wine. Beaming in the firelight, he leaned back against the wheel of the cart and said to Dagner, "Give us that new song of yours."

"It's not quite ready yet," said Dagner. But, since this was not a performance, he willingly fetched his cwidder and picked out a sketch of what Moril thought was a very promising tune. And without a trace of nervousness, he half sang, half spoke the words.

> *"Come with me, come with me.*
> *The blackbird asks you, 'Follow me.'*
> *No one will know, no one will know,*
> *Wherever you go, I shall go.*
> *Come with me. Morning spreads,*
> *Clouds are high in milky threads,*
> *The moon looks like a white thumbnail,*
> *Larks are singing up the dale.*
> *The sun is up, so follow me.*
> *I'd like us to go secretly*
> *Along the road, across the hill*
> *Where water runs and woods are still."*

"And then I think the first four lines again," Dagner said, looking up at Clennen.

"No," said Clennen. "Won't do."

"Well, I needn't have them again," Dagner said humbly.

"I mean the whole thing won't do," said Clennen.

Dagner looked very dashed. Kialan seemed unable to stop himself saying indignantly: "Why? I thought it was going to be a jolly good song."

"The tune's all right, as far as it's gone," said Clennen. "But why spoil a tune like that with those words?"

"They're jolly good words," Kialan insisted. "I liked them."

"It's the words I seem to want," Dagner said diffidently.

"I see," said Clennen. "Then in that case don't utter them again until we're in the North—unless you want us taken up for rebels."

Dagner tried to explain. "But I—it wasn't. I was just trying to say how much I liked traveling in the cart and—and so on."

"Were you?" said Clennen. "And haven't you heard the songs the freedom fighters used to sing here the year of the rebellion—oh, it'll be sixteen years ago now, the year you were born? They never dared say a thing straight out, so it was all put sideways—'Follow the lark' was one, 'Free as air and secret' another went, and the best known was 'Come up the dale with me.' The lords here still hang a man on the spot for singing words like that."

"And I do think that's ridiculous!" Kialan burst out. "Why can't people sing what they want here? What's the matter with everyone?"

Brid and Moril looked at his firelit face with interest. It began to seem as if Kialan might be a freedom fighter. They felt they could forgive him much if he was. Clennen, however, simply seemed amused.

"I hope there's not someone behind the gorse listening to you," he said. Kialan's head jerked round toward the nearest looming bush. "See?" said Clennen. "That's why, in one easy lesson, lad. No one can trust anyone anymore. It comes of uneasy rulers paying uneasy men to make the rest uneasy, too. It's not always been like that, you know. Dagner, what did I say outside Derent?"

Dagner's mind was woefully on his unsuitable song. "Oh—er—something about life being only a performance, I think."

"I knew I could trust you to get the wrong saying—and the wrong saying wrong," Clennen said tolerantly. "Anyone?"

"You said the South was once as free as the North," said Brid. "You said it to me, really."

"Then remember it," said Clennen.

3

After one night attempting to share the smaller tent with Kialan and Dagner, Moril took to creeping into the cart along with Brid and the wine jar. As he told Brid, even the wine jar took up less space than Kialan, and it did not have knees and elbows. Moril had woken up three times to find himself out among the guy ropes in the dew. He resented it. He resented Kialan, and he wished Dagner joy of him. It was hard to tell if Dagner got on with Kialan or not, because he was such an untalkative person. Dagner was like Lenina in that way. It was quite impossible to tell what Lenina thought about Kialan—or, indeed, about anything else.

Kialan, in spite of Clennen's rebuke, seemed unable to stop making outspoken remarks. "You know, that cart is really horribly garish," he said, on the second morning. Perhaps he had some excuse. It was standing against the dawn sky, as he saw it, and Moril's red head was just emerging from it. The effect was undeniably colorful, but Brid was keenly offended.

"It isn't!" she said.

"I expect you're too young to have much taste," Kialan replied. Brid swore to Moril that she was Kialan's enemy for life after that one.

What Moril resented most—apart from Kialan's elbows and the fact that Kialan never made the slightest attempt to help with any of the chores—was the superior way Kialan stood by and listened in whenever Moril had a music lesson. Unfortunately he had them fairly frequently in the next few days. They were taking—perhaps for Kialan's benefit—a more direct route to Flennpass and the North than usual. It meant that they did not pass through any large towns and only two villages. Lenina bought supplies in the first, but they did not perform in either. Clennen took the opportunity to grind away at the old songs with Moril, to keep Brid hard at the panhorn, and to rehearse a number of songs with all of them.

Kialan stood by and put Moril off continually. Moril came so to resent it that he took refuge in more than usual vagueness. He would sit on his perch behind the driving seat staring up the white road unreeling ahead between the gray-green slopes of the South, basking in the hot sun—which never tanned him however long he sat in it—and dream of his birthplace in the North. It always saddened Moril that his father would never go to Hannart because of his disagreement with Earl Keril. He longed to see it, and he had built up in his mind a complete image of what it was like. There was an old gray castle in it, rowan trees, and blue hills of a certain spiky shape. Moril saw it clearly. He saw the whole North with it, spread over the gray-green southern landscape as if it were painted on a window: dark woods and emerald dales, the queer green roads from olden days which led to places that were not important any longer, hard gray rocks, and the great waterfall at Dropwater. In it lived all the stories of magic and adventure that seemed to go with the North. The South had nothing to compare with them.

Hearing Kialan talking behind him, Moril thought that the North had one new advantage. Kialan would leave them there.

"I've said that six times now," Kialan said. "Do you spend *all* your time a thousand miles away?"

Moril was annoyed. His family could accuse him of dreaminess if they wanted, but Kialan was a stranger. "You've no right to say that," he said.

It was possible Kialan did not realize how annoyed Moril was. "You see," Brid explained to him later, a good long way behind the cart, "even when you're angry, you always look so sleepy and—and *milky,* that he probably didn't even notice you were attending. Not," she added tartly, "that he'd have noticed anybody's feelings but his own, mind you."

What Kialan had replied was: "Oh, good grief! I know you're the fool of the family by now, but you don't have to be rude as well as stupid!"

"And the same to you!" Moril retorted, and took Kialan completely by surprise by butting him in the stomach. Kialan fell backward heavily—and painfully, Moril hoped—onto the wine jar. Whereupon Moril found the prudent thing to do was to hop out of the cart double quick and scud off down the road behind it. And for the rest of the day he was forced to walk well in the rear for fear of Kialan's vengeance.

But it was Clennen who took the vengeance. When they camped for the night, he beckoned both Kialan and Moril up to him. "Are you two going to make up and apologize?" he inquired. Moril looked warily at Kialan, and Kialan looked most unlovingly back. Neither answered. "Very well then," said Clennen, and banged their heads together. Nothing seems harder than another person's head. Moril could only hope that Kialan had seen as many stars as he had. He was rather surprised that Kialan did not say anything to Clennen. "Next time, I'll do it harder," Clennen promised. Then, as if nothing had happened, he went on to give Moril a lesson. And to Moril's annoyance, Kialan stood by and listened just as usual.

The following day they reached a market town called Crady, and it came on to rain—big warm drops that seemed like part of the air and very little to do with the moist white sky. The raindrops made dark brown circles in the dust of the road and raised a delicious smell of wet earth. But it meant everyone crowding into the cart to change in great discomfort. Moril was not surprised that Kialan got out.

"I'm not really interested in your show," he said to Clennen. "I'll meet you on the other side of Crady, shall I?"

"If you like, lad," Clennen said cheerfully. Brid and Moril exchanged seething glances in the hot dim space under the cover and wondered why Clennen did not box Kialan's ears for him. But the only thing which seemed to perturb Clennen was the rain. "We shall have no audience in the open," he said. "I'll see what I can do. We'll go in with the cover up."

It was lucky that they did. By the time they came to the marketplace, the rain was coming in white rods and bouncing up off the flagstones. Olob was wearing his most long-suffering expression, and there was not a soul in sight. But Clennen had friends in Crady, just as he had everywhere else. Half an hour later they were installed under the great beams of a warehouse on the corner of the marketplace, and a crowd, damp but interested, was gathering into it.

They gave an indoor kind of show. After Clennen had told everyone about Hadd and Henda, the Waywold money, the price on the Porter's head, and the cost of corn in Derent, and the usual messages had been handed out, they sang songs with a chorus that the audience could join in. Dagner did his part early. Then, when good humor and attention were at their peak, Clennen told one of the old tales. This pleased Moril highly. He always felt rather too hot indoors, and playing the cwidder made him hotter still. But during a tale he was only needed once or twice. All the stories had places where there was a song. For the rest of the time Moril could sit on the dusty chaff of the floor with his arms wrapped round his knees and drink the story in.

Clennen chose to tell a branch of the story of the Adon. It had to be only a branch because, as Clennen was fond of saying, stories clustered round the Adon and Osfameron like bees swarming. The songs which came in where the story needed them were the Adon's own, or Osfameron's. Moril always thought the old songs sounded rather better set in their proper stories, though he still wished the silly fellows had tried to sing more naturally. But their doings made splendid tales. Moril listened avidly to how Lagan wounded the Adon and the wound would not heal until Manaliabrid came out of the East to him. Then came the story of the love of both Lagan and the Adon for Manaliabrid, and how the Adon fled with her to the South. Lagan followed, but Osfameron helped them by singing a certain song in the passes of the mountains, so that the mountains walked and blocked the way through. And Lagan was forced to turn back.

Here Clennen lowered his rich voice to say: "I shall not sing you the song Osfameron sang then, for fear of moving the mountains again. But it is true that since that day the only pass to the North is Flennpass."

The Adon for a time roamed the South with

Manaliabrid, singing for a living, until Lagan found where they were. Then he stole away Kastri, the Adon's son by his first wife, and the Adon followed. But Lagan was something of a magician. He made Kastri invisible and took on the shape of Kastri himself. And when the Adon came up to him, unsuspecting, Lagan stabbed him through the heart.

Here came Manaliabrid's lament, which Moril was supposed to sing. He took up his cwidder for it, glancing as he did so into the warm blue-gray depths of the barn at the attentive audience. To his surprise, Kialan was there. He was standing at the back, very wet and draggled, listening with as much interest as anyone there. Moril supposed he had decided he preferred a performance to a soaking after all. And he was annoyed with Kialan for coming. His head was full of grand things, journeys, flights, fighting, and the magic North of once-upon-a-time. Kialan was the everyday world with a vengeance. Moril felt as if he had a foot on two different worlds, which were spinning apart from one another. It was not a pleasant feeling. He took his eyes off Kialan and concentrated on his cwidder.

Then Clennen went on to how Manaliabrid asked Osfameron for help. Osfameron sang, and made Kastri visible. Then he took up his cwidder and journeyed by a way that only he knew, to the borders of the Dark Land. There he played such music that all the dead crowded in multitudes to hear him. Once they were gathered, Osfameron sang and called the soul of the Adon to him.

And—this part always gave Moril a delicious shiver—Clennen once more lowered his voice to say: "I shall not sing you the song Osfameron sang then, for fear of calling the dead again."

Osfameron led the Adon's soul back and restored it to his body. The Adon arose, defeated Lagan, and reigned as the last King of Dalemark. He was the last king because Manaliabrid's son, who was to have been king after him, chose instead to go back to his mother's country. "And since that time," said Clennen, "there have been no kings in Dalemark. Nor will there be, until the sons of Manaliabrid return."

Moril gave an entranced sigh. He had hardly the heart, after such a story, to join in "Jolly Holanders," and he only managed to sing with an effort. After it he crept away to the other end of the barn to avoid the usual crowd, and sat under the cart, brooding, while Clennen greeted his friends and Dagner failed to explain how he made up songs. If only such things happened nowadays! Moril thought. It seemed such a waste to be descended from the singer Osfameron, who knew the Adon and could call up the dead, and to live such a dull life. The world had gone so ordinary. Compare the Adon, who lived such a splendid life, with the present-day Earl of Hannart, who could think of nothing better to do than to stir up a rebellion, so that he dared not show his face in the South. Or you only had to think of the difference between that Osfameron, Moril brooded, and this one, Osfameron Tanamoril, to see how very plain and ordinary people had become lately. If only—

Here the plain and ordinary life interrupted in the person of Lenina, carrying the chinking hat to the cart. She was followed by the usual kind of murmuring gentleman. "And it must be sixteen years now—" this gentleman was murmuring.

"Seventeen," Lenina said briskly. "Moril, come out of that dream and count this money."

Moril unwillingly scrambled out from under the cart. As he did so, Clennen turned his head, and his voice boomed across the barn. "No, I didn't care for him at all, last time I was in Neathdale." With his voice came a look that caused the murmuring gentleman to wither away into the crowd. Moril watched him wither, a little puzzled. He seemed to be the twin of the murmuring gentleman in Derent.

The takings were not bad, which pleased Lenina. And Clennen was in good humor because an old friend of his had made him a present of a beefsteak. It was beautifully red and tender and wrapped in leaves to keep it fresh. Clennen stowed it carefully in a locker. He talked jovially of supper as they drove through Crady in the slackening drizzle. Kialan, to Brid's contempt, was waiting for them under a tree just beyond the town.

"Huh!" said Brid. "Not interested in our shows, isn't Mr. High-and-Mighty! Did you see him, Moril? Drinking in every word!"

"Yes," said Moril.

While the red steak fizzled over the fire, Brid said

mock-innocently to Kialan: "Father told one of the Adon stories at the show. Do you know them at all?"

"Yes. And a dead bore they are, too," said Kialan. "All that magic!"

"You *would* say that!" said Moril. "I saw—"

"Silence!" said Clennen. "You're interrupting the steak. Not another word until it's ready to eat."

The steak was certainly worthy of respect. Even Kialan had nothing to say against it. They went on again after supper. In his carefree way, Clennen seemed to be quite as anxious as Moril to see the North again. He refused to let Olob choose them a meadow until the sun was nearly down and the sky ahead and to the left was a mass of lilac clouds barred with red.

"Imagine *that* over the peaks of the North Dales," he said. "But even in the South, Mark Wood is fine at this time of year. There's nothing to beat a tall beech in spring. And do you know the Marsh at all, Kialan?"

"A little," said Kialan.

"If we'd time, I'd take you through it just for the flowers," said Clennen. "But it's too far east, more's the pity. The ducks there make your mouth water."

"There are rabbits in the South Dales," Dagner suggested.

"So there are," said Clennen. "Look the snares out tomorrow."

By the end of the following day the landscape had begun to change. The rolling gray-green slopes gave way to higher, greener hills, and there were more trees. It was like a foretaste of the North. Moril began to feel pleasantly excited, although he knew that they were only entering the South Dales. Tholian, Earl of the South Dales, was reputed to be a tyrant fiercer even than Henda. It was still a long way to the North. Beyond these green hills lay the Uplands and Mark Wood, before they came to Flennpass and the North at last.

Nevertheless, budding apple trees made a pleasant change from rows of vines. The nights were slightly cooler, and rabbits were plentiful. Every night Dagner went off to set snares round about the camp, and to Moril's surprise, Kialan made his first helpful gesture and went with Dagner.

"It's only because he likes killing things," Brid said. "He's that type."

Whatever the reason, Kialan was surprisingly good at catching and skinning rabbits, and Lenina was good at rabbit stew. Since they had wine as well, they fed very well for the next few days. Moril was almost grateful to Kialan. But Brid was not in the least grateful because every time they stopped in a town or village to give a show, Kialan would put on his act of not being interested and announce that he would meet them outside the town. And every time, unfailingly, they would see him among the audience, as interested as anyone there.

"Two-faced hypocrite!" Brid said indignantly. "He's just trying to make us feel small."

"That wouldn't do you any harm," Lenina said, in her dry way. Brid was more indignant than ever. It was becoming clear that Lenina rather approved of Kialan. Not that she said anything. It was more that she did not say any of the things she might have done. And when Kialan tore his good coat in the wood, Lenina mended it for him with careful neat stitches.

Kialan seemed far more surprised than grateful when Lenina handed him the mended coat. "Oh—thanks," he said. "You shouldn't have bothered." His face was red, and he seemed actually a little scornful of Lenina for doing it.

"Nothing to what I am!" said Brid. "He can go in rags for all I care."

The day after this they entered the part of the South Dales which was the lordship of Markind. They never gave shows in Markind. Brid's dislike of Kialan came to a head while Olob was patiently dragging the cart up and down the steep little hills of this lordship. The reason was that Clennen, who never disdained an audience, began to explain to Kialan exactly why he always hurried through Markind without giving a performance.

"I took Lenina from here, you see," he said. "From the very middle of Markind, out of the Lord's own hall. Didn't I, Lenina?"

"You did," said Lenina. She always looked very non-committal whenever Clennen told this story.

"She was betrothed to the Lord's son. What was his name? Pennan—that was it. And a wet young idiot he was, too," Clennen said reminiscently. "I was asked in to sing at the betrothal—I had quite a name, even in those days, and I was a good deal in demand for occasions like that, let me tell you. Well, no sooner did I come into the hall and set eyes on Lenina than I knew she was the woman for me. Wasted on that idiot Fenner. That was his name, wasn't it, Lenina?"

"He was called Ganner," said Lenina.

"Oh, yes," said Clennen. "I remember he reminded me of a goose somehow. It must have been the name. I'd thought it was his scraggy neck or those button eyes of his. Anyway, I thought I'd rely on my looks being better than his and deal with Master Gosler later. For the first thing, I concentrated on Lenina. I sang—I've never sung better, before or since—and Lenina here couldn't take her eyes off me. Well, I don't blame her, because I don't mind admitting that I was a fine-looking man in those days, and gifted, too—which Flapper wasn't. So I asked Lenina in a song whether she'd marry me instead of this Honker fellow, and when I came up to get my reward for my singing, she said yes. So then I dealt with him. I turned to him. 'Lording,' I said, most respectful, 'Lording, what gift will you give me?' And he said 'Anything you want. You're a great singer'—which was the only sensible thing he said that evening. So I said, 'I'll take what you have in your right hand.' He was holding Lenina's hand, you see. I still laugh when I think of the look on his face."

While the story went on—and it made a long one, for Clennen went over it several times, embroidering the details—Brid and Moril walked by the roadside out of earshot, watching the fed-up look settle on Kialan's face. They had both heard the story more times than they could remember.

"I suppose the thing about being a singer is that you like telling the same story a hundred times," Brid said rather acidly. "But you'd think Father would remember Ganner's name by this time."

"That's all part of it," said Moril. "I always wonder," he added dreamily, "what would happen if we met Ganner while we were going through Markind. Would he arrest Father?"

"Of course he wouldn't," said Brid. "I don't suppose it's true, anyway. And even if it did happen, Ganner must have grown into a big fat lord by now and forgotten Mother ever existed."

Since this was Brid's true opinion of the matter, it was a little unreasonable of her to be so angry when she found Kialan shared it. But one is seldom reasonable when one dislikes someone. They stopped for lunch, and Clennen, thoroughly in his stride, went on embroidering the story.

"Lenina's a real lady," he said, leaning comfortably against the pink and scarlet wheel of the cart. "She's Tholian's niece, you know. But he cast her off for running away with me. And it was all my fault for playing that trick on Gander. 'Lording,' I said to him, 'give me what you have in your right hand.' Oh, I shall never forget his face! Never!" And he burst out laughing.

Kialan had heard this at least three times by then.

Moril had rarely seen him look so fed up. While Clennen was laughing, Kialan got up quickly to avoid hearing any more, and stumped off without looking where he was going. He nearly fell over Moril and Brid and became more fed up than ever.

"Blinking bore your father is!" he said. "I'd be quite sorry for Ganner if I thought there was a word of truth in it!"

"How dare you!" said Brid. "How *dare* you say that! I've a good mind to punch your nose in!"

"I don't fight with girls," Kialan said loftily. "All I meant was I'm sick of hearing about Ganner. If your father remembers it that well, why on earth can't he get the poor fellow's name right?"

"It's part of the *story!*" screamed Brid, and threw herself at Kialan.

Kialan, for a second or so, tried to keep up his claim not to fight girls, with the result that Brid punched his nose twice and then boxed his ears in perfect freedom. "You spiteful cat!" said Kialan, and grabbed both her wrists. It was in self-defense. On the other hand, he squeezed her wrists so painfully that he hurt Brid rather more than if he had hit her. She lashed out at his legs with her bare feet, but finding that made no impression on Kialan, she sank her teeth into the hand round her wrists. At this, Kialan lost his temper completely and punched Brid with his free hand.

Dagner never let people hit Brid. He surged up from

his seat in the hedgerow and fell on Kialan. Moril, since Dagner seemed to be doing his best to strangle Kialan, thought he had better get Brid out from between them and entered the fray, too. They made a grunting furious bundle. Brid would not unfasten her teeth and Kialan would not let go of Brid. Clennen heaved himself up, strolled over, and wrenched Dagner away from Kialan and Kialan away from Brid. Everyone, including Moril, fell with heavy thumps, this way and that. Clennen might have been fat, but he was also strong.

"Now stop!" said Clennen. "And if you've anything more to say about my story, Kialan, say it to me." He looked cheerfully down at Kialan, angrily sprawled on the roadside sucking his bleeding knuckles. "Well?"

"All right!" said Kialan. "All *right!*" Moril could see he was nearly crying. Brid was crying. "You can keep on saying you'll never forget Ganner—or whatever he's called—all you like," said Kialan. "I don't believe you've even met him! You wouldn't know him if he came walking down the road this minute! So there!"

The cheerfulness died out of Clennen's face. It was replaced by a very odd look. Kialan noticeably tensed at it. "Do you know Ganner then?" Clennen said.

"No, of course I don't!" said Kialan. "How could I? I don't suppose he exists."

"Oh, he exists all right," said Clennen. "And I'm sure you don't know him. Yet you're right. I've seen Ganner three times this month and not known him till this minute." He laughed again, and Kialan relaxed considerably. "Not a face that stands out in a crowd," he said. "Eh, Lenina?"

"I suppose not," agreed Lenina, and continued calmly slicing cold sausage.

"*You* knew him though, didn't you?" Clennen said. "In Derent, and on the road, and again in Crady?"

"Not till he said who he was," Lenina said, quite unperturbed.

There seemed suddenly to be a situation ten times worse. All through lunch Clennen looked at Lenina in a tense, troubled way. He seemed to be expecting her to say something and, at the same time, carefully not saying all sorts of things himself. And Lenina said nothing. She said nothing so positively and obviously that the air seemed sticky with her silence. It was hateful. The rest of them picked awkwardly at their food, and no one spoke much. Kialan did not say anything. It was obvious, even to Brid, that he was kicking himself for causing the situation—as well he might, Moril thought.

When the food was finished and the cart packed again, they went on, still in the same heavy silence. At last Clennen could bear it no longer.

"Lenina," he said, "you're not regretting all that, are you? If you want that kind of life—if you'd rather have Ganner—just say the word and I'll turn Olob toward Markind this moment."

Moril gasped. Brid's mouth came open in her tear-stained face. They looked at Clennen and found he seemed quite serious. Then they looked at Lenina, expecting her to laugh. It was so silly. Lenina was as much part of their life as Olob or the cart. But Lenina did not laugh, nor did she say anything. Not only Brid and Moril, but Dagner, Kialan, and Clennen, too, stared at her in increasing anxiety.

They came to a fork in the road. One branch led west, and the milestone said MARKIND 10. "Do I turn here?" asked Clennen.

Lenina gave herself an impatient shake. "Oh no," she said. "Clennen Mendakersson, you must be a very big fool indeed to think such a thing of me."

Clennen burst into a roll of relieved laughter. He shook the reins, and Olob trotted past the turning. "I must say," he said, laughing still, "I can't see how you could prefer Ganner to me. He couldn't have made the songs I've made to you, not if his life depended on it."

"Then why did you think I did?" Lenina asked coldly. The trouble was not over yet.

"Well," Clennen said awkwardly. "Money and all that. And it's what you were bred to, after all."

"I see," said Lenina. There was silence again for quite half an hour, except for the plopping of Olob's hooves and the light rumble of the cart. Kialan was unable to bear it. He got out and walked ahead, whistling the "Second March" rather defiantly. The others sat with their heads hanging, wishing Lenina would make peace. At last she said, "Oh, Clennen, do stop sitting there watching me like a dog! I'm not going to take wings and fly, am I? It's lucky Olob has more sense than you, or we'd be in the ditch by now!"

Then the trouble seemed to be over. Clennen was shortly laughing and talking again. And Lenina, if she was silent, was silent in her usual way, which everyone was used to. Brid and Moril got out of the cart, too, though they did not go near Kialan. Brid was still too angry with him.

4

That night they camped in one of the many little valleys Markind abounded in. There were woods up its steep sides and a meadow in the bottom, containing a small peaceful lake full of newly hatched tadpoles. Dagner and Kialan went off to set their snares. Lenina put herbs on the fire against the midges, and the fragrant smoke streamed sideways and settled across the lake in bands. Brid and Moril, quite unworried by insects, waded into the shallows of the lake and tried enthusiastically to collect tadpoles in an old pickle jar. Moril had just lost most of them by accident when he looked up to find his father watching them.

"You want a bigger jar," Clennen said. "And both of you want to remember what I said to Kialan about give-and-take."

"*He* doesn't remember it," Brid said sulkily.

"He's never had to learn it before," said Clennen. "That's his trouble. But it's not yours, Brid. A fight takes two."

"Did you hear what he said?" Moril demanded.

"I'm not deaf," said Clennen. "He's entitled to his opinion, like everyone else. And it wouldn't hurt you to find some opinions of your own instead of borrowing Brid's, Moril. Now get that slime off your fingers before you touch my cwidder."

While Moril was having his lesson, Kialan came out of the woods and into the lake, where he tried to teach Dagner to swim. The sight of them splashing about was a great distraction to Moril. It grew worse when Kialan tried to persuade Brid to learn to swim, too. Brid claimed to be afraid of leeches. Nothing would induce her to go above her knees in water, but she agreed to learn the arm movements. Moril could hear her laughing. It looked as if Kialan were trying to make friends.

Moril became more distracted than ever. Perhaps, after all, Kialan was not bad at heart—only tactless. Moril tried to decide what he thought. It really rankled with him that Clennen believed he borrowed Brid's opinions. Moril considered that he thought long and deeply—if rather vaguely—about most things. But he knew he had agreed with Brid, quite unquestioningly, both about Kialan and about the Ganner story. And it looked as if Brid had been wrong about both. Moril did not know what he thought.

"I suppose I ought to be used to you being up in the

clouds by now," said Clennen. "Do you want to swim, too?"

"No," said Moril. "Yes. I mean, is that story about Ganner true then?"

"Word of honor," said Clennen. "Except it's the fellow's face I seem to have forgotten, not his name. I may embroider a detail here and there, but I never tell a story that isn't true, Moril. Remember that. Now go and swim if you want to."

Clennen was clearly very relieved that Lenina was not leaving for Markind. He drank a great deal of the wine that night to celebrate. The level in the huge bottle was almost down to the straw basket when he finally rolled into the larger tent and fell asleep. He was still asleep next morning when Dagner and Kialan went off to look at their snares. When Brid and Moril got up, they could hear him snoring, though Lenina was up and combing out her soft fair hair by the lake. Brid attended to the fire, and Moril tried to attend to Olob. Olob, for some reason, was tetchy. He kept flinging up his head and shying at shadows.

"What's the matter with him?" Moril asked his mother.

Lenina's comb had hit a tangle. She was lugging at it fiercely and not really attending. "No idea," she said. "Leave him be."

So Moril left off trying to groom Olob and turned to put the currycomb back in the cart. He found himself looking at a number of men, who were pushing their way through the last of the wood into the clear space by the lake. They were out almost as soon as Moril saw them, six of them. They stood in a group, looking at Moril, Brid kneeling by the fire, Lenina by the lake, the cart, and the tents.

"Clennen the Singer," one of them said. "Where is he?"

Olob tossed his head and trotted away round the lake.

"He's not here," said Brid.

Moril thought he would have said the same. The men alarmed him. It was odd to see six well-dressed men outside a wood in the middle of nowhere. They were very well dressed. They wore cloth as good as Kialan's coat, and all of them had that sleek look that comes from always living in style. Each of them wore a sword in a well-kept leather scabbard, belted over the good cloth of their coats, and Moril did not like the way the hilts of those swords looked smooth with frequent use. But the truly alarming thing about them was that they had an air of purpose, all of them, which hit Moril like a gust of cold wind and frightened him.

"My father won't be back for ages," he said, hoping they would go away.

"Then we'll wait for him," said the man who had asked. Moril liked him least of all. He was fair and light-eyed, and there was an odd look in those eyes which Moril did not trust.

Lenina evidently felt the same. "Suppose you give me your message for Clennen," she said, coming forward with her hair still loose.

"You wouldn't like it, lady," said the man. "We'll wait."

"Moril," said Lenina. "Go round the lake and fetch your father."

Moril thought that was clever of her. It would deceive the men, and Dagner and Kialan might be some help. He tossed the currycomb into the cart and set off at a trot. But Clennen chose that moment to crawl out of the tent like a badger. He stood up, with his eyes red and blinking inside a tousled frill of hair and beard.

"Somebody call me?" he said sleepily.

Moril stopped, helpless. Everything went so quickly that he could hardly believe it was happening. The six men pushed forward in a body, overwhelming Lenina for a moment, and then leaving her in the open, clutching Brid. Their swords caught the pink early sun. The group round Clennen trampled a bit. Clennen, sleepy as he was, must have put up something of a fight. A man stumbled sideways into the lake. Another fell in with a splash. Then the six men, swords sheathed again, went running away from the lake in a group. One glanced into Clennen's tent and then the smaller one. Another took a quick look into the cart as they passed.

"Nothing here," he called.

"Look in the woods then," said the fair one. And they were gone.

Clennen lay where he had fallen, half in the lake, with blood running out of him into the water.

Before Moril could move, there was a thumping of racing feet. Dagner shot past him round the lake and surged onto his knees in the water beside Clennen. "Have they killed him?"

"Not quite," said Lenina. "Help me move him."

Moril stood where he was, some distance away, and watched them heave his father out of the calm sunny water. Brid's face was grayish white, and her teeth were chattering. Dagner's mouth kept twisting about. Moril could see his hands shaking. But Lenina was quite calm and no paler than usual. As they turned Clennen over, Moril saw a cut in his chest. Bright red blood was gushing from it as fast as the river ran in Dropwater, steaming a little in the cold air over the surface of the lake.

At the sight, the bright trees, the lake, and the sunny sky dipped and swung in front of Moril. Everything turned sour and gray and distant. He could not move from the spot. Up in the woods behind him, he could dimly hear the six men crashing about and calling to one another, but they could have been on the moon for all the fear and interest Moril felt. His eyes stared, so widely that they hurt, at the group by the water.

Lenina, without abating her calm, tore a big strip from her petticoat, and another, to stop the bleeding. "Give me yours," she said to Brid, and while Brid, shaking and shivering, was getting out of her petticoat, Lenina said in the same calm way to Dagner, "Get the small flask from the cart."

Moril stared at his mother working and telling Brid

what to do. The only sign of emotion Lenina showed was when her hair trailed in the way of the bandages. "Bother the stuff!" she said. "Brid, tie it back for me."

Brid was still trying to get a ribbon round Lenina's hair when Dagner scudded back with the flask. "Do you think you can save him?" he asked, as if he were pleading with Lenina.

She looked up at him calmly. "No, Dagner. The most I can do is keep him with you for a while. He'll want to have his say. He always did." She took the flask from Dagner and uncorked it.

Moril desolately watched her trying to get some of the liquid from the flask into Clennen's mouth. It was not fair. He felt it was not fair on his father at all, to die like this, first thing in the morning, miles from anywhere. He ought to have had warning. Dying was a thing someone like Clennen ought to do properly, in front of a crowd, with music playing if possible.

Music was possible, of course. Moril found himself beside the cart, without quite knowing how he had got there. He scrambled up and seized the nearest cwidder. It happened to be the big one. In the ordinary way, Moril would not have chosen it. But being inside the cart made him feel sick and queer, so he simply took what came first to hand and backed hastily down with it.

While he was getting its strap over his back, he realized that Clennen's eyes were open. And it was clear that Clennen shared Moril's opinion. Moril heard him say, rather thickly, but quite strongly, "This came out of the blue, didn't it? I'd have preferred to have notice."

Moril put his hands to the strings and began to play, very softly, the weird broken little tune of "Manaliabrid's Lament." The cwidder responded sweetly. The old song seemed more melodious than usual, and because of the water, it carried out across the lake until the valley seemed full of it. Moril heard its echo from the woods opposite.

His ears were so full of the sound that he did not hear much else of what Clennen said. Clennen's voice became weaker, anyway, after that first remark, and he spoke to Lenina in what was only a murmur. Then he spoke to Brid for a while, reaching out to hold her hand, which made Brid cry. After that, it was Dagner's turn. Clennen was very weak by then. Dagner had to put his head right down near his father's face in order to hear him. Moril played on, as softly as he could, watching Dagner listening and nodding, and wondered vaguely at the amount Clennen seemed to have to say. Then Dagner looked up and beckoned to Moril.

"He wants to talk to you. Quickly."

Moril did not dare take off the cwidder for fear of wasting time. He hurried over to Clennen with it bumping at his thighs and knees, and hoisted it away sideways as he knelt down. Clennen's face was paler than Moril had ever seen a face before. His eyes did not seem to reflect the sky, or Moril bending over him, though it was clear he could see Moril.

"Got the big cwidder, have you?" Clennen said.

Moril nodded. He could not manage to speak. "Keep it carefully," said Clennen. "It's yours now. Always meant to give it to you, Moril, because I think you've got the ability. Or will have. But you have to come to terms with it, and with yourself. Understand?" Moril nodded again, though he did not understand in the least. "You're in two halves at present," Clennen went on. "Often thought so. Come together, Moril, and there's no knowing what you might do. There's power in that cwidder, if you can use it. Used to be Osfameron's. He could use it. Handed down to me. I couldn't use it. Only found the power once, when I—" Clennen paused for breath. Moril waited for him to go on, but nothing happened. Clennen stayed as he was, with his eyes open looking at Moril, and his lips parted. After a while, Moril realized that this was all there would be. He got up and carefully, very carefully, put the cwidder back in its place inside the cart.

Brid was crying loudly. Lenina was standing very upright beside the lake, as calm as ever. Dagner seemed to have frozen into the same sort of calmness, facing her. And Kialan was coming slowly toward them round the lake with a bundle of dead rabbits.

When he reached them, Kialan stopped. He looked at Clennen and, for once, seemed not to know what to say. "I'm—terribly sorry," he said at length.

"It was going to happen sometime," said Lenina. "Will you help us dig a grave, please?"

"Of course," said Kialan. "Here?"

"Why not?" said Lenina. "Clennen never had a home

after he left Hannart, and we can't take him there."

"Very well," said Kialan, and he laid the rabbits down and unhooked the spade from its clips beneath the cart. Dagner went and fetched the pickax, and the two set to work. Lenina watched and seemed ready to take Kialan's advice, as if, in some odd way, Kialan were in charge just then. "I think we should mark the spot," Kialan said as he dug.

"How?" said Lenina.

"Is there a spare board in the cart?" Kialan asked.

"Find him one, Moril," said Lenina.

Moril managed to work free one of the spare boards Clennen always carried under the floor of the cart, and on Kialan's instructions, he sawed off a piece about three feet long. Then he relieved Kialan at the digging for a while. Kialan took out his sheath knife and carved away at the board, quickly and competently, as if this were another thing he was good at. When he had finished, the board had letters deeply and neatly cut into it. CLENNEN THE SINGER.

"That do?" said Kialan.

"Very well," said Lenina.

When the grave was ready, Kialan, Dagner, and Brid put Clennen into it. Moril did not like to see his father topple into the hole. Nor did he like to see the earth going in on top of Clennen's face and clothes. Rather than watch, he fetched his own cwidder and stood back a little, playing another lament, a newer one that had been made for an earl of Dropwater killed in battle. He went on playing while Brid put the turf back in place and Kialan trenched his board in until it was standing upright at the head of the grave, as it should. And now that there was nothing but a grave to be seen, Moril began to feel that something was missing. They should all be feeling and doing something else. They should be angry. Clennen had been murdered. They should be trying to bring the murderers to justice. But none of them thought of it. It was out of the question, here in the South. The six men had been far too well dressed.

"There," said Kialan, wiping his hands on his coat.

"Thank you," said Lenina. "Now I must change. This dress has blood on it. And you, too, Brid. Kialan, I think it would be a good idea if you changed your coat for Dagner's old one."

Kialan agreed to this, although Moril did not think Kialan's good coat was more than a little earthy. When everyone was changed and cleaned, Lenina told Dagner to catch Olob and harness him to the cart. Kialan picked up his bundle of rabbits.

"Leave those," said Lenina. "We don't need them."

"Well, I don't fancy them at the moment, either," said Kialan. "But —"

"Leave them," said Lenina. Kialan did as he was bid. Now Lenina seemed to be definitely in charge. It was she who took the reins when Olob was ready and drove out of the valley.

Brid and Moril looked back. It was a very beautiful valley. Probably, Moril thought, it was a good place to be buried, if one had to be. Brid cried. Dagner did not look back. He had sunk into a silence as profound as any of Lenina's. He did not look at anything, and no one liked to speak to him.

Lenina drove northward for a mile or so, until she came to a road that turned off to the left. Then, to Moril's surprise, she swung the cart into it.

"Hey! Where are we going?" said Moril.

"Markind," said Lenina.

"What? Not to Ganner!" demanded Brid, halting in the middle of a sob.

"Yes. To Ganner," said Lenina. "He said he would have me and mine if ever I was free, and I know he meant it."

"Oh, but no! You can't!" said Moril. "Not just like that!"

"Why not?" Lenina asked. "How do you think we shall live, without a singer to earn us money?"

"We can manage," said Moril. "I can sing. Dagner can—Dagner . . ." His voice tailed away as he thought of Dagner and himself trying to perform as Clennen did. He just could not see Dagner doing it. He did not know what to say, so he stopped, fearing he might be hurting Dagner's feelings. But it looked as if Dagner was not listening. "Father wouldn't like us to go to Markind," Moril asserted. He was sure of that, at least.

"I can't see that your father has much say in the matter now," Lenina answered dryly. "Get this clear, Moril. I know well enough that your father was a good man, and the best singer in Dalemark, and I've done my duty by him for seventeen years. That's half my lifetime, Moril. I've gone barefoot and learned to cook and make music. I've lived in a cart in all weathers, and never complained. I've mended and cleaned and looked after you all. There were things your father did that I didn't agree with at all, but I never argued with him or crossed him. I did my duty exactly in every way, and I've nothing to reproach myself with. But Clennen's dead now, so I'm free to do as I choose. What I'm choosing is my birthright and yours, too. Do you understand?"

"I suppose so," Moril mumbled. He had never heard Lenina say anything like this before. He was frightened and rather shocked to see that she must have been *not* saying it for longer than he had lived. He thought it was wrong of her, but he could not have said why. He thought she was altogether wrong, but he could not find any words to set against her. All he could do was to exchange a scared, helpless look with Brid. Brid said nothing either.

It was Kialan who spoke. He sounded rather embarrassed. "It's not my place to object," he said. "But I do have to get to Hannart, Lenina."

"I know," said Lenina. "I've thought of that. You can pose as my son for the moment, and I'll find someone to take you North as soon as I can, I promise. Hestefan's in the South, I know, and Fredlan may be, too."

Kialan looked exasperated as well as embarrassed.

"But Ganner must know how many children you've got!"

"I shouldn't think so," Lenina said calmly. "People who haven't got children themselves never bother to count other people's. If he wonders, I'll say you've been ill and we'd left you at Fledden."

Kialan sighed. "Oh well. Thanks, anyway."

"Remember that," Lenina said to Moril, Brid, and Dagner, and Moril felt very queer, because "Remember that" was such a favorite saying of Clennen's. "Kialan's your brother. If anyone asks, he's been ill in Fledden."

Olob plodded toward Markind. He did not look happy either, Moril thought, looking at the droop of Olob's head. Moril was so miserable himself that he could almost hear it, like a droning in his ears, and he could not hide away in vagueness, much as he tried. He felt vividly and horribly attentive to everything, from the leaves in the hedge to the shape of Kialan's nose. Kialan's eagle nose was so different from Dagner's, Brid's, or Moril's that surely anyone could tell at a glance he was no relation? Why did he have to be a relation, anyway? And had Clennen known he wanted to go to Hannart? Clennen would not have gone there because he never went to Hannart. And why had the six men killed Clennen? Who were they, and what were they looking for in the wood? And why, why, why above all, had Clennen given Moril a cwidder he did not want in the least?

I shall never play it, Moril thought. I'll polish it and

string it, and maybe tune it from time to time, but I don't want to play it. I know I should be grateful, because it must be very valuable—though it *can't* be old enough to have belonged to Osfameron; he's long ago in a story—but I don't like it and I don't want it.

Markind came into view at the other end of a valley. Without meaning to, Moril looked at it as he always looked at a new town. Sleepy and respectable, he thought. Bad takings. Then he remembered he was supposed to be going here to live, not to sing, and tried very hard to look at the pile of yellowish gray houses with interest. He found he was more interested in the villainously freckled cows which were grazing in the small green meadows outside the town.

Lenina looked at these cows with pleasure. "I remember I always liked those speckles," she said. She encouraged Olob to trot, and the gray and yellow houses approached swiftly. Moril's heart sank rather—and he had thought it was low enough before.

Soon they were winding up a gravelly street between quiet old houses. The houses were tall and cold and shuttered. There were very few people about. Even when they came to the main square and found a market going on under the high plane trees, there were still very few people, and these all sober citizens who looked at the gay cart with strong disapproval. Lenina drove past the stalls looking neither to right nor to left, and drew Olob up in front of a round-topped gateway in a massive yellow wall. Two men who seemed to be on guard at the gate peered round it at the cart in evident astonishment.

"Had you business here?" one of them asked Lenina.

"Certainly," Lenina answered haughtily. "Go and tell Ganner Sagersson that Lenina Thornsdaughter is here."

They looked at her in even more astonishment at that. But one of them went off into the spaces behind the thick yellow wall. The other stayed, frowning wonderingly at Lenina, the cart, and her family, until Moril scarcely knew where to look.

"What's the betting we get a message back to say, Not Today Thank You?" whispered Brid.

"Be quiet, Brid!" said Lenina. "Behave properly, can't you!"

Brid would have lost her bet. The man who had gone with the message came back at a run, and they could hear a number of people behind the gate, running too. The two halves of the gate were flung wide open.

"Please drive in," said the man.

Lenina smiled graciously and shook the reins. Olob plodded forward, disapproval in every line of his ears and back, into a small deep courtyard lined with interested faces. Ganner was standing in the middle of it, smiling delightedly.

"Welcome back, Lenina!" he said. "I never thought I'd see you so soon. What happened?"

"Some men killed Clennen this morning," said Lenina. "They looked like the pick of somebody's hearthmen to me."

"Not really!" exclaimed Ganner. Then he looked a little worried and asked, "Does that mean it happened in my lordship then?"

"Yes," said Lenina. "At Medmere."

"I'd better send some hearthmen over to investigate," said Ganner. "Anyway, come down and come in. Are these your children?"

"My three sons and my daughter," said Lenina.

"What a lot of them!" said Ganner, looking a little daunted. But he smiled gallantly at all four. "I'll do my best to look after you all," he said. Moril could not find it in his heart to dislike Ganner, much as he had intended to. It was so plain he meant well. If, to someone who had been used to Clennen, he seemed a very ordinary person, then that was hardly Ganner's fault, Moril supposed.

"He doesn't look much like a goose," Brid whispered, in some disappointment. Kialan had to bite his lip. Moril looked at Ganner gallantly helping Lenina down from the cart and smiling at her in a way that showed he adored her. Apart from that smile, he really seemed perfectly normal and ungooselike.

"Oh dear, oh dear!" Ganner exclaimed, as they all got down. "Shoes! Boots! Can you only afford one pair of boots?"

Lenina glanced along their line of bare feet, interrupted by Kialan's scuffed boots. "We don't usually bother with them," she explained. "But Collen has tender feet."

"I must make sure you all have shoes this instant!" Ganner exclaimed distractedly.

"You know, I think he may be a goose after all," Brid said, with considerable satisfaction.

5

By that afternoon Moril was wondering if it was only that morning they had left Clennen buried by the lake. It felt like last century. There had been so many changes. After a good breakfast, followed by the attentions of a tailor, a bootmaker, and Ganner's old nurse, followed in turn by an astonishingly good lunch, Moril scarcely knew himself. He looked in a mirror—it was a thing he seldom had the chance of doing, so he looked long and often—and he saw a smoothly combed red-haired boy in a suit of good blue cloth and a pair of soft rust-colored boots. The boots, to tell the truth, pleased him enormously. But he did not look in the least like his idea of himself. Dagner and Kialan had become spruce, gentlemanly figures in the same kind of blue clothes, and Brid a young lady in bright cherry color. They were all four behaving very soberly and politely, not because Ganner insisted on it—because he did not—but simply because Markind was the sort of place where you could behave in no other way.

The biggest change was to Lenina. She was splendidly dressed, too, and she had done her hair the way ladies did. Her cheeks were pinker than usual, and she laughed and chattered and hurried about with Ganner on a hundred errands. Moril had not often seen her laugh, and he had certainly never seen her so talkative. She was like a different person. That troubled him. It troubled him far more than learning she was going to marry Ganner that same evening.

Moril quite liked Ganner. Ganner told Moril he could do just what he liked and go anywhere he wanted, and obviously meant it. He was a very good-natured man. Moril quite liked the other people in the house, too. He liked Ganner's old nurse specially. She fussed rather, and she said rather too often that she had always known Lenina Thornsdaughter would come back to them, but she called Moril "my duck" and said he was a "blessing." And while she was dressing him, she told Moril a story about a lord of Markind who had been outlawed. Moril had not heard the story before, and he drank it up. But he felt strange. Everything felt strange.

Moril took Ganner at his word and explored the house. He found two gardens and the kitchens. He looked at the cellars and the small rooms under the roof, but in between each exploration he found himself drifting into the stableyard. The cart had been put away in a coach house there, just as it was, wine jar, cwidders, and all, down to the string of onions under the driving seat. It was just the same, yet somehow it already looked smaller and dustier and a little faded. Moril spent a lot of time talking to Olob, who was standing dejectedly in a stall nearby and seemed glad of his company. Moril stole sugar for him from the kitchen, which was easy to do because everyone there was in a great bustle, preparing for the wedding feast. Olob ate it politely, but he looked sad, and he was sweating rather.

"Poor fellow," Moril said sadly. "I'm hot, too. It's being in a house."

As the afternoon drew on, Moril became hotter still. Being between walls so oppressed him that he wondered whether to go out and walk in the town. But Markind had not inspired him with any wish to see more of it. He wandered to the stableyard and then into one of the gardens. Brid was there. She was feeling much the same, for she had taken off her cherry-colored boots and was sitting with her feet in one of the goldfish ponds.

They exchanged sad, polite smiles, and Moril went on into the second garden. Behind him he heard Ganner's voice.

"My dear little girl! You'll catch your death like that! Do please dry your feet and put your boots on. You'll worry your mother."

Moril felt sorry for Brid. Then he suddenly felt even more—desperately—sorry for himself. He needed to be somewhere else, out in the open. He looked round wildly, upward, everywhere. And a sturdy creeper growing up the thick yellow wall of the house gave him an idea. He slung himself onto it and started to climb.

It was extremely easy, except for the last bit, which needed a long stride and a heave across some crumbly stonework. Then he was on the wide, leaded roofs. It was splendid. Moril looked round, into the town, out across the valley, and over to valleys beyond. He turned north and looked at the misty blue peaks there, where he had so longed to go, and Kialan—lucky Kialan!—was going soon. But that made him sad. So, presently, Moril began to patter about across the leads and among the chimneys. He skirted courtyards and looked down into the gardens. Then he ran along a narrow part to another wing and looked down into another court.

And there was Ganner, horrified and gesturing below. "Come down! Come down at once!"

Moril looked. There was a lead pipe and an easy flight of windows. Obediently he swung his legs over the edge of the roof.

Ganner stopped him with a hoarse shriek. "No! Stop! Do you want to break your neck? Wait!" He ran away and presently ran back with a crowd of men carrying a ladder. With them ran a group of horrified maids, and the old nurse, wringing her hands.

"My duck! Oh my duck!"

Moril sat sadly on the edge of the roof, swinging his legs and watching them all pothering with the ladder. He knew what was wrong with Ganner now. He was a fusspot.

The ladder finally thumped against the wall beside him. "You can come down now," Ganner called. "Go very carefully."

Moril sighed and got onto the ladder. He came down rather slowly out of sheer perverseness. He decided when he got near enough he would say to Ganner, "But you told me I could go anywhere I wanted." When he judged he was low enough for it to be most effective, he turned round to say it.

A man was just coming in through the door to the courtyard—a fair man with light, untrustworthy eyes, who checked for a moment when he saw Moril twenty feet up a long ladder, staring at him. Shrugging slightly, the man strolled over to Ganner and said something to him. Ganner replied. The man shrugged again, said another word or so to Ganner, and strolled out of the courtyard.

Moril forgot what he intended to say. Instead, as soon as he was down on the ground, he said, "Who was that man here just now? The fair one, who spoke to you."

Ganner looked uneasy, so uneasy that Moril's chest went tight and he felt sick. "Oh—er—just someone who's my guest here," said Ganner. "Now you are absolutely *not* to get on the roof again! It's extremely high, and the leads are quite unsafe. You might have been killed!"

"Killed, my duck!" said his nurse.

Moril bore with a long scold from both Ganner and

the nurse, without listening to a word. Both of them would have scolded anyway, but Moril was fairly sure that Ganner was scolding mostly as an excuse not to discuss the fair man. Moril did not want to discuss him. His one desire was to get away and find Lenina.

Lenina was in the great hall of the house. Presumably it was the same place where Clennen had sung and then played the trick on Ganner seventeen years before. Lenina was gaily organizing the tables for the wedding feast, and doing it as if she had done nothing else all her life. Moril had to pull her sleeve to get her to attend to him.

"Mother! One of the men who killed Father! He's staying here."

"Oh, Moril, don't interrupt me with stupid stories!" Lenina said impatiently.

"But I saw him," said Moril.

"You must have made a mistake," said Lenina. She pulled her sleeve away and went back to the tables.

Moril stood, shocked and troubled, in the middle of the hall. He saw quite clearly that his mother did not want to believe him. She had put Clennen and all that part of her life behind her and she did not want to be reminded of it. Yet if Ganner had had a hand in killing Clennen, this was the last place she ought to be—the last place any of them ought to be. Moril looked at gay, busy Lenina, shook his head desolately, and hurried away to find Brid.

Brid was hurrying through the garden in the opposite direction. "Moril—!"

"One of the men who killed Father," said Moril. "He's staying here."

"I know. I saw him," said Brid. "Did you try to tell Mother?"

"Yes. She wouldn't listen."

"She wouldn't listen to me either," said Brid. "She doesn't want to know, I think. Moril, what are we going to do? We can't stay here, can we? Do you think Ganner had Father killed?"

Moril thought about it. He remembered that though Ganner had obviously been very pleased to see Lenina, he had not perhaps been entirely surprised. And he did not like it at all. "I don't know. He *could* have done. Only he's a bit too feeble to think of it, isn't he?"

"And why not do it years ago if he felt that bad about Father stealing Mother off him?" said Brid. "But I don't care whether he did or not. I'm not staying here, and that's final!"

"Mother *is* staying," said Moril. "I'm afraid that's final, too."

"Then we'll have to do without her," said Brid. "I can cook, and we've got good clothes now. The only thing is, I'm not very good on the hand organ."

Moril did not feel as if they had come to a decision. It was as if he had known all along that they would leave. "But can we manage?" he said. "Give shows and all without even Dagner?"

"Dagner will have to come, too," stated Brid. "He'll have to. He's Father's heir, and he ought to. Besides, he shouldn't stay here even more than us. If it was old days, he'd have to avenge Father."

Moril was dubious. Wherever Brid thought Dagner's duty lay, Moril knew Dagner would want to stay with Lenina. He knew, without knowing how he knew, that Dagner had always been closer to his mother than to Clennen. And how could Dagner take up the singer's trade when he was terrified and nervous at every show? "But would Dagner do it—on his own? I mean—"

"I know just what you mean," said Brid. "But I can manage Dagner. I can always manage him when there aren't any parents around to interfere."

"Let's go and find him then," said Moril.

Neither of them had seen Dagner for a considerable while. Since they had not the least idea where to start looking, they drifted quite naturally to the stableyard first, to have a look at Olob and the cart.

Dagner was in the stableyard, polishing Olob's harness, and Kialan was helping him. Both of them looked a little blank when Moril and Brid came in.

"Do you two haunt this yard, or something?" Kialan said irritably.

Moril decided to take the bull by the horns. "We're taking the cart and leaving," he said. "Are you two coming?" Kialan was clearly astonished and stared at Moril with all the annoyance of someone who cannot believe his ears.

"I've got to go anyway," said Dagner. "Father asked

me to take Kialan to Hannart. But there's no need for you two to come."

"Oh, yes, there is!" said Brid. "One of the men who killed Father is in this house, and if that isn't a reason for going, give me a better one!"

Dagner and Kialan exchanged glances, and Kialan screwed his mouth up. "True?" Dagner said to Moril.

"I saw him," said Moril. "The fair one with queer eyes. But you didn't see them, did—"

"Yes, I did," said Dagner. "We were only in the woods. That one was the leader. Kialan, I think that settles it, don't you? We'd better leave at once, as soon as I've said good-bye to Mother."

"Don't be an idiot!" said Moril. "If you tell Mother we're going, she'll tell Ganner. And he's such a big fusspot that he's bound to say it's dangerous and stop us going."

Kialan and Dagner looked at one another again. "He's got a point there, Dagner," Kialan said. "Ganner is an awful old woman. He's bound to come after us, anyway. What do you say to waiting until the wedding feast has started and he's too busy to notice we're missing?"

Dagner pondered anxiously. He looked purple and bent with worry. "No," he said at length. "No, we daren't. Not if this other fellow's here." He jerked his head to the end of the yard. There was a big old gate in the wall there, bolted and peeling. "We've found out that leads to a back street. You two get those bolts back while I harness Olob, but don't open it till I'm ready."

Kialan helped Dagner pull out the cart and back Olob between its shafts, so they were ready almost as soon as Brid and Moril had done their part. The bolts were very stiff and rusty. Brid wanted to fetch the oil from the cart, but Moril would not let her. "No," he said. "I've an idea to fool Ganner." It took them quite a while, and cost Brid a pinched finger, to waggle the bolts back without.

"Ready," said Dagner. Olob came toward the gate, almost dancing with pleasure at being at the work he was used to. Brid and Moril swung the gate creaking open. Brid went up into the cart, with the easy spring of long practice, and sat down to get her boots off. The cart rumbled through and crunched on the gravel of the lane outside, which was so narrow that Olob for a moment seemed likely to run into the shuttered house opposite. Moril stayed inside the stableyard and carefully bolted the gate again. It looked, to his satisfaction, as if it had never been opened at all. He took a running jump at it and managed to hook his fingers in the top, where the gate did not quite meet the wall above. From there, he swarmed up onto the thick top of the wall itself. Kialan stood up in the cart to help him jump down.

"Good idea," he said. "Let's hope Ganner wastes a lot of time trying to find out which way we went."

6

In the late afternoon Markind seemed to be deserted. As they clattered northward through its shuttered, respectable streets, Moril was ready to swear that there was no one around to notice even such a noticeable cart as theirs. Nevertheless, Dagner was as tense as if he were giving a performance. He did not relax even when they were out of Markind. Instead of looking for a main road, he struck into the first small lane that went north and kept turning round uneasily as he drove to see if Ganner was following them.

Olob clattered along with a will, with his ears gaily pricked. The lane, and then the other lanes they took after it, led through apple orchards where the trees were bursting into bloom. The sun was mild and warm. Moril sat smiling sleepily and happily, listening to the familiar beat of Olob's hooves, the wine sloshing about in the great jar behind him, and the blackbirds singing in the apple trees. This was the life! He was sure they could manage, whatever Lenina thought. A cuckoo sang out, cutting across the songs of the blackbirds.

"O—oh!" said Brid. Tears began rolling down her cheeks. "Father said to me—by the lake—he hadn't heard a cuckoo yet this year. And he was sorry he was going to miss it." Her face screwed up, and her tears ran faster than ever. "He told me to listen for him, on the way North. And Mother goes and drives straight off to Markind! How could she!"

"Shut up, Brid," said Dagner uncomfortably.

"I shan't! I can't!" cried Brid. "How could she! How could she! Ganner's so stupid. How *could* she!"

"Will you be quiet!" said Dagner. "You don't understand."

"Yes, I *do*!" Brid cried. "Ganner and Mother arranged to have Father murdered—that's what happened!"

"Don't talk such blinking nonsense!" Kialan said sharply. "That had nothing to do with either of them."

"How do *you* know?" Brid wept. "Why did she go straight off to Ganner like that?"

"Because she's always wanted to, of course!" said Dagner. "Only she couldn't, because she thought it wasn't honorable. I *told* you you didn't understand," he went on, in an odd, agitated way. "You're too young to notice. But I've seen—oh, enough to know Mother hated living in a cart. She wasn't brought up to it like we are. It was all right while we were in the Earl of Hannart's household—we had a roof over our heads and that wasn't too bad for her—but—I suppose you don't remember."

"Not very well," Brid admitted, sniffing. "I was only three when we left."

"Well I do," said Dagner. "And Father *would* leave, though he knew Mother didn't want to go. And in the cart she had to bring us up and keep us clean and cook—and she'd never done anything like that in her life till then. And sometimes there was no money at all, and we were always on the move and always—well, there were other things she didn't like Father doing. But Father always got his own way over them. Mother never had a say in anything. She just did the work. Then she saw Ganner again in Derent, after all those years, and she told me it had brought her old life back to her and made her feel terrible. I just don't blame her for going back to what she was used to. You can see Ganner's not going to order her around like Father did."

"Father didn't order her around!" Brid protested. "He even offered to take her back to Ganner."

"Yes, and I thought Mother was really going to call his bluff for a moment then," said Dagner. "He knew darned well Mother wouldn't go, because it wasn't her duty, but he had an anxious moment all the same, didn't he? And then he took good care to point out how much cleverer he was than Ganner."

"That was just his way," said Brid.

"It was all just his way," said Dagner. "Look, Brid, I don't want to pull Father to pieces any more than you do, but in some ways he was—oh, maddening. And if you think about it, you'll see he and Mother weren't at all well matched."

Moril was blinking a little at all this. It was so unlike Dagner to talk so much or so clearly. He marveled at the way Dagner managed to put into words things Moril had known all his life but not truly noticed till this moment. "Don't you think Mother was fond of Father at all?" he asked dolefully.

"Not in the way we were," said Dagner.

"In that case, why did she run off with him like that?" Brid asked, triumphantly, as if that clinched the matter.

Dagner looked pensively at a new vista of apple trees coming into view beyond Olob's ears. "I'm not sure," he said, "but I *think* that cwidder had something to do with it."

Moril swiveled around and cast an apprehensive look at the gleaming belly of the old cwidder, resting in its place in the rack. "Why do you think that?" he asked nervously.

"Something Mother said once," said Dagner. "And Father told you there was power in it, didn't he?"

"There probably is, if it belonged to Osfameron," Kialan observed in a matter-of-fact way.

"Don't be silly! It can't be that old!" Moril protested.

"Osfameron lived not quite two hundred years ago,"

said Kialan, and he really seemed to know. "He was born the same year as King Labbard died, so it can't be more than that. A cwidder'd surely last as long as that if you took care of it. Why, we've—I've seen one that's four hundred years old—though, mind you, it looks ready to drop apart if you breathed on it."

Moril cast another look, even more apprehensive, at the quiet, prosperous shape of the old cwidder. "It can't be!" he said.

"Well," Dagner said diffidently, "you get used to thinking things like that were only around long ago, but—I'll tell you, Moril—didn't you get the impression you kept Father alive with it this morning?" Moril stared at Dagner with his mouth open. "I thought so," Dagner said, a trifle apologetically. "I've never heard it sound like it did then. And—and Father was dead awfully quickly after you left off, wasn't he?"

Moril was appalled. "Whatever am I going to do with a thing like that!" he almost wailed.

"I don't know. Learn to use it, perhaps," said Dagner. "I must say I was glad Father didn't give it to me."

Everyone subsided into thoughtfulness. Brid sniffed wretchedly. Olob clopped steadily on for a mile or so. Then he took a look at the sinking sun and decided to choose them a camping ground. Dagner dissuaded him. He refused to let Olob turn off the road three times, until Olob got the point and did not try again. They went on and on and on, downhill, uphill, through small valleys, pastures, and orchards. The sky died from blue to pink and from pink to purple, and Brid could bear no more.

"Oh, do let's *stop*, Dagner! Today seems to have gone on for about a hundred years!"

"I know," said Dagner. "But I want to get a really good start."

"Do you think Ganner will really follow us?" said Moril. "He ought to be glad we've gone. Then he needn't fuss about roofs and things."

"He's bound to," said Kialan. "A man with a conscience—that's Ganner. He'll probably send some of his hearthmen out tonight and set out himself first thing tomorrow. That's what—I mean, if it had been just Dagner and me, he—"

"Go on. Say it. You think Moril and I shouldn't have come," Brid said bitterly.

"I didn't *say* that!" snapped Kialan.

"Just meant it," said Brid.

"No, he didn't," said Dagner. "Stop being stupid, Brid. The thing is, I left without explaining to Mother, and even if I had explained, she wouldn't have wanted you two to go. So I know she'll ask Ganner to come after us. If he does catch us up, you and Moril will have to go back, I'm afraid."

"Oh *no*!" said Brid, and Moril felt equally mutinous.

"That's why I hope he doesn't catch us," Dagner said. "Because I don't think I could give a show on my own, and I was wondering how on earth I'd manage."

This admission mollified Brid greatly. She refrained from grumbling, although they went on until the light was all but gone. Then Dagner at last permitted Olob to select them a spot on top of a hill. This meant their camp was windy, a fact which Brid bitterly pointed out while they were fumbling around trying to put up the tent in the breezy semidark.

"Yes, but we can see people coming," said Dagner.

"And there are thistles. I've just trodden on one," Brid complained.

"Then why on earth don't you put your boots on?" demanded Kialan.

"Oh, I couldn't! I'd spoil them," Brid said, quite shocked.

Kialan roared with laughter, which seemed to restore Brid's frayed temper. She took it quite cheerfully when Moril discovered the only food they had was bread and onions.

"I *knew* we'd need those rabbits," Kialan said dejectedly.

"We all had a good lunch," said Brid.

Moril had the notion of frying the bread and onions together. Unfortunately it was then so dark that he could not see to fry. The mixture he turned out of the frying pan was extremely singed, and it was only eaten because everyone was very hungry. Then they settled down to sleep. It seemed to Moril, waking and resettling himself round the wine jar during the night, that Kialan and Dagner kept watch, turn and turn about, until dawn broke. Certainly they both looked very jaded in the morning.

Nevertheless, as soon as the sun was up and Olob fed, Dagner had the cart on the move again. They ate the last of the bread as they went. Brid moaned a little, and Dagner promised they would buy more food in the next village they came to.

"What with?" said Brid.

That was a nasty moment. There was no money in the locker where Lenina usually kept it. She must have taken it out in Markind. And none of them had any money in the pockets of their fine new clothes. For a while, it looked as if they would have to give a show before they could eat. Then Brid thought of going through the clothes locker, turning out pockets. There were a few coins in the pockets of Clennen's scarlet suit, and a further few fell out of Kialan's old good coat when Brid picked it up.

"May we use these? We'll pay you back," she said.

"Of course," said Kialan. "I'd forgotten I'd got any."

When they came to a village, Dagner drew up on the outskirts and sent Brid and Moril shopping, shouting after them at the last minute that there were no more oats for Olob. The rule was that you bought oats first—for where would you be with Olob undernourished?—and they were dear in those parts at that season. Brid and Moril came glumly back with oats, a loaf, half a can of milk, a cold black sausage, and a cabbage. Knowing that Dagner would certainly put off giving a performance if he could, Brid prepared to do battle.

"That's all we could afford. If we don't give a show

tomorrow, we'll starve," she announced, dumping the meager purchases in the cart.

"We're going to," Dagner said, to her surprise. "Father said we were to be sure to perform in Neathdale, and I think we'll be there by tomorrow. Have you found it?" he asked Kialan, who was frowning over the map. It was not a good map. Clennen knew Dalemark like the back of his hand and only kept a map for emergencies.

"If this place *is* Cindow, Neathdale's quite a way to the northwest," said Kialan. "Is it worth it? It would be almost as easy to go by the Marshes from here."

"Yes, I've got to go. And he said we'd be bound to get news there," said Dagner. "Let's get going. And," he added, "I suppose we'd better have a bit of a practice this evening."

As Olob went on, Moril, sighing rather, went and fetched the old cwidder. When he had vowed not to play it, he had been thinking of an idle life in Markind—if he had thought of the future at all—but now, whether Dagner played pipes or treble cwidder, and Brid pipes or panhorn, someone was going to have to play tenor to them. That meant Moril on the big cwidder. And he had always been in awe of it, and never more than now. By way of coming to terms with it, he laid it on his knees and polished it as Clennen had taught him. Brid gave him the note on the panhorn, and he tuned it. And tuned it again. And retuned it. As fast as he got a string to the right pitch, it went off again. All he could produce was the moaning twang of slack strings.

"I think the pegs are slipping," he said helplessly.

"Let me have a go," Brid said competently. But she could not get it tuned either.

"Let me look at the pegs," said Kialan. He looked, and seemed fairly knowledgeable, but he could not see anything wrong. He handed it on to Dagner. Dagner, who knew most of all, hitched the reins round his knees and spent half an hour trying to get the cwidder tuned. In the end he was forced to hand it back to Moril in the same state as before.

"Isn't that all we needed!" said Brid. "Perhaps it's in mourning. After all, we all should be, and look at us!"

"Try playing a lament," Kialan said thoughtfully.

"Why?" said Moril. "Anyway, I hate the old songs."

"Any lament," said Dagner. "You played your own treble over the grave, didn't you?"

Moril tried it. He began singing the "Lament for the Earl of Dropwater," and brought the cwidder in as softly as he could after the first line. The discord was horrible. Brid shuddered. But Dagner took up the song, too, and the cwidder seemed almost to follow his lead. The notes came right as Dagner sang them. To Moril's astonishment and secret terror, the cwidder was in tune by the end of the first verse. He sang the chorus, and first Brid, then Kialan, joined in.

"This was a man above all other,
Kanart the Earl, Kanart the Earl!

You'll never find his equal, brother.
He was a man above all other."

The cwidder sang on, as sweetly as it had for
Clennen. Tears poured down Brid's face. Moril felt tearful, too. They sang lustily through the whole song, and
sad though it made them, they felt heartened, too. The
oddest effect was on Olob. His pace dropped to a slow,
rhythmic walk, and he went for all the world as if the cart
was a hearse.

"Put it away," said Dagner, "or we'll never get to
Neathdale."

Moril put the alarming cwidder carefully back, and
they made better progress. As before, Dagner would not
let Olob stop at the usual time or in the usual kind of
place. A little before sunset he took Olob right off the
road into a high, lonely field full of big stones, where
they could see a good way in most directions.

"There hasn't been a sign of Ganner!" Moril
protested.

"Well, there won't be, until we see him arriving, will
there?" said Kialan.

They demolished the sausage and held their practice.
To Moril's relief, the big cwidder now behaved perfectly.
But there were other difficulties. Without Clennen or
Lenina, they found they could not do half the songs in
the way they were used to. They had to work everything
out afresh. And Dagner did not in any way take

Clennen's place. He refused to do more than a third of the singing, and that was the only thing he was firm about. Otherwise, he simply made suggestions, and he was quite ready to be overruled by Brid or Moril. The younger two felt lost. They were used to Clennen's kind but entirely firm way of telling them exactly what to do. Sometimes they were annoyed, and several times they were tempted to get very silly. It was only the grim thought that their next meal depended on this practice that kept them from breaking into loud arguments or louder laughter. Moril felt he had never truly missed Clennen till then.

Yet, in the middle of thinking that, he remembered what Dagner had said about Clennen's always having his own way. It occurred to him to wonder if Clennen had not, in fact, kept them all a little too dependent on him. Maybe this was why it seemed so hard to manage without him.

While they practiced, Kialan lay full length on a rock above them, listening and also, Moril suspected, acting as lookout. This elaborate caution began to irritate Moril. After all, it was Moril and Brid who stood to lose if Ganner found them, not Dagner and Kialan. In the morning he was exasperated to see that they had been on watch again. Both of them looked tired out.

Brid was furious. "How on earth do you think you're going to give a performance, Dagner, if you can hardly keep your eyes open? I've never known you so silly! We *depend* on you!"

"All right," Dagner said wearily. "You drive and I'll have a sleep in the cart. But wake me if—if—"

"If *what*?" snapped Brid.

"If anything happens," said Dagner, and lay down beside the wine jar with a groan. Kialan flopped down on the other side of the jar, and both of them fell asleep before Olob had the cart in motion.

It was left to Brid and Moril to find the way to Neathdale. They did it, too, half cross and half proud of themselves. The map did not help much. They were forced to follow their noses across country, turning into any road that seemed to go northwest and hoping for the best. Once they arrived in a farmyard and had to back out of it, pursued by the barking of dogs and the squalling of hens and roosters. Kialan and Dagner did not even stir. "Stupid fools," said Brid. They were still asleep when the cart came out on a rise above Neathdale.

"We did it!" said Moril.

"Unless Olob knew the way," Brid said, trying to be fair. "But I don't think even he can have come to it this way before."

Neathdale was a big cheerful-looking town lying across the main road north to Flennpass, in the last level ground before the Uplands. They could look across even its tallest buildings from where they were to where the South Dales mounted like stairs to the Mark Wood plateau.

"Say four days, and we'll be in the North," Moril said yearningly.

"Four days," said Brid promptly.

The scuffle that followed on the driving seat woke Dagner and Kialan at last. "What's the matter? What's going on?"

"Nothing. Only Neathdale," said Brid. Dagner's sleepy face at once became pinched and tense and mauvish. Brid set herself to soothe him. "We always used to get good takings here," she said. "There must be hundreds of people who remember us and know Father. I'm going to do the talking, mind, and I shall talk about Father and say who we are—though they can read that on the cart anyway."

"The cart ought to be repainted with Dagner's name," Moril observed. He did not think Brid was soothing Dagner in the slightest, but he did not mind helping.

"You'd hardly get the name on," Brid said brightly. "Dastgandlen down one side and Handagner up the other, I suppose."

"Isn't Neathdale the seat of Earl Tholian?" Kialan asked, tactlessly cutting through the soothing.

"Not really. His place is outside a bit, over to the east," Dagner said. He pointed with a hand that shook noticeably. A great white house was just visible, among trees, on the other side of Neathdale.

"Blast you, Kialan!" said Brid. Kialan looked at her in surprise. "Oh, it doesn't matter," said Brid. "Just if this show goes wrong, I'll blame you. Dagner, I think we'd better put on our glad rags now."

"No," said Dagner.

"What do you mean?" said Brid.

"Just no," said Dagner. "We'll give the show as we are. We're quite respectable."

"Yes, but we always change," Brid protested. "It gives you a feel."

"That was Father's idea," said Dagner. "And he was right in a way. It went with his style to come rolling in, singing and glittering. He could live up to it. But if I go in dressed in tinsel and singing my head off, people are just going to laugh."

"You think that because you're nervous," Brid said persuasively. "You'll feel better once you're changed."

"No, I won't," said Dagner. "I'll feel ten times worse. Brid, I just haven't got Father's personality, and I can't do the same things. I'll have to do them my way, or not at all. See?"

Brid, by this time, was near tears. "Do you mean you're not going to give a show at all then?"

"Not Father's kind," said Dagner, "because I can't. We'll give a show all right, because we'll starve if we don't, and you can introduce us and explain what's happened, and maybe it'll be all right. But if I find you boasting and ranting about us—that goes for you, too, Moril—I'll stop. We'll just have to be plain, because we're not Father."

Brid sighed heavily. "All right. But I'm going to put my boots on, anyway. I need a feel." She brightened a little. "I've always hated the color of your suit,

Moril. You look nicer like that."

"Thank you," Moril said politely. Dagner had suddenly brought it home to him that, for the first time in their lives, they were about to give a show entirely on their own. He had never, as far as he knew, been nervous before. Now he was. As Brid drove downhill toward Neathdale, Moril sat clutching the big cwidder with hands that were icy cold and sweating at once, and it would have been hard to say whether he or Dagner was the more nervous. The houses came nearer. Quite desperate, Moril laid his cheek against the smooth wood of the cwidder. "Oh, please help me!" he whispered to it. "I'll never manage. I can't!"

"Can you stop a moment?" said Kialan.

Brid drew up. Kialan immediately swung down from the cart to the road. Brid looked at him somberly. "Now you're going to give us that about not being interested in our shows, aren't you? Well don't. I won't believe you. I've seen you listening to every show we've given."

Kialan looked up at Brid's stormy face and seemed nonplussed. Then he laughed. "All right. I won't give you that. But I'm going to meet you on the other side of Neathdale all the same. See you." He set off at a good swinging pace toward the town, with his hands in his pockets, whistling "Jolly Holanders."

"I give up!" said Brid. But both her brothers were too nervous to reply.

7

The main square at Neathdale was always busy. It was not very large, but it had a handsome fountain in the middle and four inns on three of its sides. There was also a corn exchange and two guildhalls, which added to the coming and going. The fourth side was occupied by the gray frowning block of the jail. When Brid drove the cart into the square, it seemed busier even than they had remembered. It was packed with people. The reason, they saw, as Olob patiently shouldered his way toward the fountain, was that there had been a public hanging that morning. The gallows was still there, outside the jail, and so was the hanged man. A number of people outside the inns were raising tankards jeeringly in his direction.

The dangling figure made them all feel sick, although it meant a good crowd. Dagner turned green. Moril clutched his cwidder hard and swallowed. Brid could not resist leaning down and asking the nearest person who it was who had been hanged.

"Friend of the Porter's," was the cheerful reply. It was a cheerful whiskery man Brid had chosen to ask, and he looked as if he had enjoyed every second of the hanging. "Some say he *was* the Porter," he added, "but you can't tell. He wouldn't admit to anything. Taken up last week, he was, on the new Earl's orders."

"Oh, is there a new Earl?" Brid said blankly, trying to keep her eyes from the swinging criminal.

"Sure," said the man. "Old Tholian died more than a month back. The new Earl's the grandson. Got a real nose for the Porter and his like, he has. Good luck to him, too!"

"Oh yes. Very good luck," Brid said hurriedly, terrified of being arrested for disloyalty to the new Earl.

"Leave off, Brid, and let's get started," Dagner said irritably.

Brid smiled rather falsely at the whiskery man and hitched up the reins so that Olob knew to stand still. Then she blew a blast on the panhorn for attention. When sufficient people had turned their way, she stood up and spoke. Moril marveled at how cool she was. But Brid was like Clennen that way. An audience was meat and drink to her.

"Ladies and gentlemen," she called, "please come and listen. You see the cart I'm standing in? Many of you will know it quite well. If you do, you'll know it belongs to Clennen the Singer. You'll have seen it coming through

Neathdale, year after year, on its way North. Most of you will know Clennen the Singer—"

She had aroused people's interest by then. Moril heard someone say, "It's Clennen the Singer."

"No, it isn't," said someone else. "Who's the pretty little lass?"

"Where's Clennen, then? It isn't Clennen," said other people. Finally, someone was puzzled enough to call out, "Where is Clennen, lass? Isn't he with you?"

"I'll tell you," said Brid. "I'll tell you all." Then she stopped and simply stood there, upright and conspicuous in her cherry dress. Moril could see she was trying not to cry. But he could also see she was making it plain to the crowd that she was trying not to cry. He marveled at the way she could use real feelings for what was in fact a show. He knew he could not have done it.

Brid stood there silent long enough for murmurs of interest to gather and grow but not long enough for them to die away. Then she said: "I'll tell you. Clennen—my father—was killed two days ago." And she stood silent again, struggling with tears, listening attentively to murmurs of sympathy. "He was killed before our eyes," she said. At the height of a loud murmur, she came in again, loudly, but in such a calm way that Moril and most of the people present thought she was speaking quietly. They hushed to hear her. "We are the children of Clennen the Singer—Brid, Moril, and Dastgandlen Handagner—and we're doing our best to carry on without him. I hope you'll spare time to listen to us. We know our show will not be the same without Clennen, but—but we'll try to please you. We hope you'll forgive any faults in—in memory of my father."

She got a round of applause for that. "Put your hat out, then, and let's hear you!" someone shouted. Brid, with tears running down her cheeks, picked up the hat she had ready and tossed it on the ground. Several people put money into it at once, out of pure sympathy for them. Brid could not help feeling pleased with herself. She had made a considerable effect without boasting once—in fact, she had done the opposite, which, she thought, ought to please Dagner.

Though Dagner was far too nervous to show any pleasure at all, Brid knew he was not displeased because he left her to do all the announcing. That meant that Brid could more or less choose what they sang. She did her best to put together the things they had practiced in the order she thought would be most impressive. She began them with general favorites. Moril felt terrible. Without the deep rolling voice of Clennen, they sounded to him thin and strange, and they lacked the body Lenina usually gave them on the hand organ. Moril began to feel they had nothing to offer the crowd, except perhaps some well-trained playing on cwidder and panhorn.

Brid felt much the same. To encourage them, she announced that they would now play, in trio, the "Seven Marches." That was one thing she was sure they could do well. And they did. The most successful part was when Dagner, on the spur of the moment, signaled to Brid to play soft during the "Fourth March," and played his treble cwidder in double time against Moril's slow and mellow tenor. They looked at one another while they were doing it. Moril knew they were neither of them exactly enjoying it, but they were both by then desperate for some applause from the silent crowd, and they had the dour kind of satisfaction of knowing they were giving an exhibition of real skill. They were rewarded by a burst of clapping and a little shower of coins falling into the hat.

Then they did Clennen's "Cuckoo Song," which always made people laugh. After that Brid, feeling that the sooner Dagner got his part over, the better he would be for the rest of the show, announced that Dagner would now sing some of his own songs.

Brid was glad she had said "some." Dagner was so nervous that he only managed three. If she had not said "some," it was probable that he would only have sung one. Moril was disappointed and Brid exasperated, and it was altogether a pity, because the crowd liked Dagner's songs. "The Color in Your Head" went down particularly well. Brid could tell he had the crowd's sympathy. They thought of him as bravely following in Clennen's footsteps and wanted to encourage him. But Dagner was mauve and shaking, and he stopped.

Crossly Brid took the center of the cart and sang herself. Moril, without being told, came to her aid on the cwidder, while Dagner gasped to himself in the background. Brid did well. An audience always helped her.

She sang a number of ballads, though she was forced to avoid "The Hanging of Filli Ray," which she did best, because of the corpse dangling on the gallows behind the crowd. Her success was undoubtedly the patter song, "Cow-Calling," which she did instead of "Filli Ray." Brid always enjoyed it. You started with a sort of yodeling cry, to the whole herd, then you called the cows one by one, and each verse you added a new one.

"Red cow, red cow, my lord's thoroughbred cow,
Brown cow, brown cow, the woman in the
town's cow,"

Brid sang, and no one looking at her could have realized that she was frantically wondering what else she could put into their unusually short show before her voice gave out. At "Old cow, old cow," inspiration came. Brid bowed at the end of the song. Coins clattered into the hat.

"Now, ladies and gentlemen, my brother Moril will sing four songs of Osfameron."

Moril gulped and glared at Brid. He had never performed any of the old songs in public before. But Brid had gone and announced him, so he was forced to take the center of the cart, with his wet hands shaking on the cwidder. To make matters worse, he suddenly met Kialan's eye. Kialan was standing near the fountain, looking cool, attentive, and slightly critical. From where Moril stood, the hanged man on the gallows appeared to be dangling over Kialan's head. Moril took his eyes off both of them and began to play. He knew he was going to make wretched work of it.

For a short while he could attend to nothing but the queer fingering and the odd, old-fashioned rhythms. Then his tension abated a little, and he was surprised to discover that his performance was pleasing him. As Moril's voice was naturally high, he did not need to sound cracked and strained, the way Clennen did. And not being yet expert and not anyway liking the noise the old fingering made, he found he had been unconsciously modifying it, into a style which was not old, nor new, but different. Osfameron's jerky rhythms became smoother, and Moril felt that if he could have spared time to attend to them, he might almost have understood the words:

> *"The Adon's hall was open. Through it*
> *Swallows darted. The soul flies through life.*
> *Osfameron in his mind's eye knew it.*
> *The bird's life is not the man's life.*
>
> *"Osfameron walked in the eye*
> *Of his mind. The blackbird flew there.*
> *He would not let the blackbird's song go by.*
> *His mind's life can keep the bird there."*

It sounded good to Moril. And it was his own doing, he was positive, and not the cwidder's. When he had finished, however, there was silence in the square. The crowd had never heard the old songs done that way and did not know what to think. Kialan made up their minds for them by clapping loudly. Other people clapped. Then came a burst of applause which made Moril feel ashamed of himself—he was only a learner, after all—and more coins went into the hat.

The applause seemed to worry Olob. From then on he became restive. He tossed his head, he stamped, he tried to go forward, and he threatened to back. Brid pulled him up, and he backed in earnest, throwing Moril into Dagner. Brid had to take the reins up again, which put her half out of action. Seeing this, Dagner pulled himself together and led into some songs with rousing choruses, hoping the crowd would join in. He had little luck. People were in the mood for listening. But they had come to the end of all they had practiced, so Dagner was forced to go on to "Jolly Holanders" and finish.

Olob was still behaving like a colt, so Moril got down and went to his head. The crowd shifted away from the cart. Moril heard Brid say to Dagner, "Shall I go shopping? I know what to get," and the hat chinking.

"No, I'll go," said Dagner. He still seemed nervous, although the show was over. He took the hat and climbed down from the cart. Almost at once, several men that Moril recognized as friends of Clennen's came up and crowded round Dagner.

"What's this, Dagner? What's this about Clennen?"

The upshot was that Dagner went off to have a drink with them, taking the hat. Moril did not see which inn they went to because he found himself being talked to by a kindly man just then. This man first gave Moril a pie, then told him—in a fatherly way—that he had sung the old songs all wrong, and things were going to the dogs if people could take those kind of liberties.

Moril took a leaf out of Dagner's book. "Yes, but I can't do it like my father did," he said with his mouth full. He was extremely grateful for the pie, or he would have told the man his real opinion of the old songs.

When the man had gone, muttering that he didn't know what the young were coming to, Moril remembered that Brid would be a prey to murmuring gentlemen. He looked up at the cart, wondering what he would do if she was. There was—or had been—a murmuring gentleman. Brid was glaring at him like a tiger, and the gentleman was retreating, very red in the face. "I do hope Dagner remembers the shopping," Brid said to Moril, pretending the gentleman had never existed.

So did Moril. They waited, and waited, Moril at Olob's restive head and Brid in the cart, for well over an hour. Moril saw Kialan at intervals, hanging about in the square, evidently waiting, too. But Kialan made no attempt to come near them. Moril rather irritably wondered why not.

Olob tossed his head furiously. Brid said, "There's Dagner!" Moril saw Dagner hurrying back across the square with the empty hat rolled up in one hand. "Where's the shopping?" Brid wondered. Dagner waved cheerfully and came hurrying on. He had almost reached the cart when two large men advanced, quietly and purposefully, on either side of Dagner. One took Dagner's shoulder in a large hand.

"What—?" said Dagner, trying to shake free.

"You're under arrest, in the Earl's name," said the man. "Come on quietly and don't make any trouble now."

For a moment Moril had another glimpse of Kialan, looking absolutely horrified, in the crowd beyond the fountain. The people near, seeing someone being arrested, drifted quickly away from around the cart. Kialan seemed to get lost in a moving group and was gone the next second. Moril stood by Olob's head in an empty space, quite irrationally angry with Kialan. Not that anyone could do anything if the Earl took it into his head to have Dagner arrested, but even Kialan would have been better than no one. He looked despairingly at Dagner. Dagner had only time for one hopeless look back before the two men led him away across the square toward the jail. The crowd hurried away from all three— as if Dagner had a disease, Moril thought angrily. He wished Dagner would walk upright, instead of going bent and guilty-looking.

"I've never been so furious in my life!" said Brid. "Never! Of all the unjust—" She stopped, and looked uneasily round the empty space by the fountain, realizing she was on the way to getting herself arrested, too.

The two men vanished with Dagner inside the frowning jail. Moril had never felt more lonely. "I've just realized," he said. "We didn't have a license to sing, did we?"

"We're entitled to operate on Father's for six months," said Brid. "Father told me, and I *know* that's the law. I hope Dagner remembers. They can't *do* this! They're just trying—"

A man approached across the empty space, rather grudgingly, carrying what looked like a sack of oats. He stopped some way off the cart. "Your brother ordered this," he said. "Do I take it away again?"

"You'll do no such thing!" Brid said haughtily. "It's paid for—that I do know. Put it in the cart."

"Please yourself," said the man unpleasantly. He dumped the sack on the flagstones and went away.

That was nasty, somehow. Moril saw that everyone was going to avoid them now. Angrily he supposed that Kialan had deserted them in the same way. He left Olob, who seemed to be quietening down, and dragged the sack over to the cart. "What shall we *do*, Brid?"

"Do?" said Brid, more furious than ever. "I'll tell you what to do. I'll have to stay here, in case Dagner ordered anything else, but you're to go over to the jail at *once* and ask to see Dagner. Go on. Tell them he's related to the Earl. Say Mother's Tholian's niece. Make a fuss. Ask them to send for Ganner. Make it quite clear that we're well connected. And when you see Dagner, tell him to do the same. Go on. They're just trying to frighten us into paying for another license, I know they are!"

Obediently Moril scurried off across the square. He

was so shaken that he could think of nothing else to do, even though he knew in his heart that it was no good. In the South, when they arrested people, even for small offenses, it took more than a boy talking about noble relatives to get them out of prison. At the least it took a lot of money. And as they had not got a lot of money, the doors of the jail could well have closed on Dagner for good. Moril wished Ganner had found them, after all. By the time he reached the cold archway into the jail, he was heartily wishing they had never left Markind.

"Please," he said to the man on duty there, "I want to see my brother."

The man looked down at him, not unkindly. "Clennen the Singer's son?" Moril nodded. "And how old are you, lad?" asked the man.

"Eleven," said Moril.

"Eleven, are you?" said the man. "They don't hang your kind till they're fifteen, you know, so you're lucky." Moril thought this was meant to be a joke and smiled politely. "Look, lad," said the man. "Take some good advice. Get in that cart of yours and drive off. You won't do any good here."

Moril looked up at him in helpless irritation. "But—"

"Be off!" said the man, urgently. Footsteps were coming through the dark passage behind him. Moril could see the man meant kindly, but he did not move. He waited to see if the person coming would let him see Dagner.

The man who came was one of the two who had

arrested Dagner. He glanced at Moril, without seeming very interested. Then he looked again—sharply. "That's another of them, isn't it?"

"Yes, sir," said the man at the gate, and he gave Moril a reproachful look, as much as to say, "Now see what you've done."

"Come with me, lad," said the other man. Moril, with his stomach hopping as it had never done before, even before this last show, followed him into the dark passageway, through a dismal courtyard and up some stone stairs. They went into a blank room with yellow walls and a bench by one of the walls, where the man told him to sit and wait. Then he went out and locked the door.

Moril sat on the bench for some time, feeling terrible. He wondered if he was arrested, too. It looked like it. He tried to see out of the window, but it was high up and barred. He dragged the bench over to it, but he still could not see much except gray walls. There was no hope of wriggling out between the bars. He dragged the bench back to its original position and sat on it again.

Then the most dreadful part began. He could not bear being shut between walls. He was hot. He was trapped. The room seemed to get smaller every second and the ceiling seemed to be moving down on him. He thought he would have to scream. He nearly did scream, when a fortunate stain on the wall opposite caught his attention. It was almost the shape of the mountains between Dropwater and Hannart.

Moril thankfully escaped into a dream. He imagined snow-capped mountains and forgot he was too hot. He imagined wide valleys and the sky overhead, and the small room became easier to bear. He thought of the old green roads of the North and of Osfameron and the Adon walking along them. He became Osfameron himself. He and his friend the Adon made their way to imaginary Hannart. On the mountain, they were ambushed by enemies and fought their way clear. Then they went down into Hannart and strolled under the rowan trees outside the old gray castle, composing a song of victory together.

The door opened, and another man told Moril to come along now, quickly.

Moril came back to the present with a jump. He was scared and vibrating and small. He was aware of every stone and stain in that oppressive room, of the grain in the wood of the door, and the dirt in the fingernails of the man's hand holding it open. He even knew there were six hairs in the mole on the man's nose. As he got up, he suddenly remembered Clennen by the lake, saying, "You're in two halves at present." And he wondered if this was what Clennen had meant.

The man ushered him into a large, imposing room, with a heavy old table at one end. An elderly man sat behind the table, with a younger one who was taking notes. Moril could see by the gold chain round the elderly one's neck that he was a justice.

"Stand in front of the table and answer clearly," said the younger man, pausing in his writing and pointing his pen at Moril.

Moril did as he was told, still vibrating. He knew every bulge in the rather pointless carving on the wall above the justice. He could tell how many wrinkles there were in the forehead of the justice—fifteen yellowish folds.

The justice wrinkled these folds up and looked at Moril. "Full name?"

"Osfameron Tanamoril Clennensson," said Moril. "I'd like to see my brother, please."

"Quite a mouthful," remarked the Justice, while the other man wrote it down. "Osfameron?"

"He's my ancestor," said Moril. Seeing that the yellow folds of the justice were lifted toward him with slight interest, he explained, "I was called after him. And could I see Dagner, please?" The yellow folds drew closer together. "My brother," Moril said patiently.

"Your brother?" said the justice. The other man passed him a sheaf of papers, and he drew the folds of his forehead together over them until it looked like smocking. "Some other mouthful down here," he said.

Moril, with a little wobble to his stomach, realized the papers must be Dagner's answers to the questions they had asked him. He wondered what Dagner had said and wished he knew. For if he gave different answers from Dagner's, the justice might well convict Dagner of all sorts of things he had never done. "We call him Dagner for short," he explained carefully. "And I'd like to see him, please."

"You can see him presently, if you answer my questions truthfully," said the justice. "You come of a family of singers, is that true?"

"Yes," said Moril.

"And you traveled with your father, giving shows?"

"Yes," said Moril.

"How long have you been doing that?"

"All my life," said Moril.

"Which is how long?"

"Eleven years," said Moril.

The younger man leaned over. "The elder boy said ten years."

The justice smocked his forehead at Moril, calculating how old he was. He looked weary and shrewd, and Moril was just a doubtful fact to him. Moril saw that to follow Brid's advice and talk of being related to the Earl and to Ganner would do no good, simply no good at all. He knew Brid would have done it. But he was not going to try.

"I was a baby when we started," he explained.

"From Hannart?" said the justice sharply.

"Yes, but I don't remember," Moril said, knowing well enough that if he admitted to his true feelings about Hannart here, he could convict both himself and Dagner. "My father said he had a quarrel with Earl Keril."

They checked that off against Dagner's answers, and

it seemed to be right, to Moril's relief. But they seemed dissatisfied, and they became more dissatisfied as the questions went on.

"Where did you last perform before Neathdale?"

Moril thought. It seemed very long ago. Fledden? Yes, because that was the last place before they were in the Markind lordship and stopped performing. That was where Lenina had mended Kialan's coat. "Fledden," he said.

"Who did your brother talk to in Fledden?"

"Nobody," said Moril. He remembered particularly, because no girls had come up to Dagner for once, and he had talked to Dagner himself.

"But you weren't with him every moment you were in Fledden, were you?" said the younger man.

"Yes, I was," said Moril. "We were all in the cart, you see. Father always made us stay in the cart together in towns."

"Always?" said the justice, smocking his folds severely. "You don't mean to tell me your brother never went off on his own."

Moril realized he could convict Dagner of poaching rabbits unless he was careful. "No, never," he said. "Dagner's not interested in anything much except making up songs." And to divert attention from the idea of poaching, he added, "Dagner hasn't done anything you could arrest him for—and our license is in order, honestly."

The justice sighed irritably. "I'm not concerned with

your license, boy. Your brother has been arrested for passing illegal information—"

"*What!*" said Moril.

"—and I want to know where he got it," said the justice. "That surprises you?"

"I should just say it does!" said Moril. "He couldn't have done! You must have made a mistake."

"Our agents are very reliable," said the justice. "What makes you think it's a mistake?"

"Because Dagner wouldn't. He's just not interested. He's only interested in making songs. Besides, there's nowhere he *could* have got information," Moril said frantically.

"That sort of assertion is not at all helpful," said the justice. "I fancy both you brothers are concealing something. You say you last performed in Fledden. That must have been a week ago. Where have you been since?"

"Markind," said Moril, wondering why on earth Dagner had not mentioned it. "Then we came here by Cindow."

The justice and the younger man looked at one another, and seemed incredulous. It was clear that they thought Markind the last place where anyone could obtain illegal information. Moril took heart a little. "Why Markind?" snapped the younger man.

"My father was killed," Moril explained, his voice wobbling a little.

"We know. At Medmere. Why did you go to Markind?" said the younger man.

"My mother went to marry Ganner," said Moril.

"*Ganner!*" they both exclaimed, and both looked at Moril in flat disbelief. "Ganner is Lord of Markind," the justice said, as if he thought Moril did not know.

"I know," said Moril. "Mother was betrothed to him before she married Father, and she went back there."

"Very likely," the justice said cynically. "In that case, why did you and your brother leave?"

Angry tears came into Moril's eyes. "Because I saw one of the men who killed Father there, if you must know! And if you don't believe me, ask Ganner!"

"I most certainly shall," said the justice. The other man murmured something to him and they looked at one another, the wrinkles of the justice smocked into a tight yellow bunch. Moril saw Brid had been right after all to tell him to mention Ganner. But like Brid, the justice had jumped to the conclusion that Ganner had had Clennen killed, and the younger man was wagging his eyebrows at him to warn him that Ganner was far too important to be accused. The justice showed himself neither very nice nor very just by giving a cynical little laugh, smiling and shrugging. Moril supposed he should be glad, if, as Kialan had said, Ganner really had nothing to do with Clennen's death. Then the justice turned to Moril again and Moril saw, sadly and rather bitterly, that there was one law for Ganner and quite another for himself and Dagner. "Did your brother talk to any strangers in Markind?"

"No," said Moril. "Only Ganner's household."

"Then who did he talk to between Markind and here?"

"Only us," said Moril.

"Listen, my boy," said the justice, "you're not being very helpful, are you? Perhaps it will jog your memory if I remind you that your brother's crime is one for which he will be hanged in due course. Therefore, I can put you in prison for withholding information."

Moril felt sick. "I *am* being helpful," he said. "I've *told* you it's a mistake. But if you're only going to believe me if I tell you Dagner's guilty, then it's no use asking me questions. Because he didn't do it!"

The younger man half stood up, looking savage. Moril blinked and waited for them to hit him, or clap him in a cell, or both. But they did neither. The younger man, after a dreadful pause, told Moril coldly to go and sit down at the other end of the long room. Moril did so. He sat on a hard shiny stool near the door and watched the two conferring together in low voices. There were footsteps beyond the door, so that he was unable to hear anything that was said, though he thought he caught Ganner's name more than once. Then they called him back to the table.

"We're going to let you go, boy," said the younger one. "We've come to the conclusion you know nothing about this matter."

"Thank you," said Moril. "Can I see my brother now?"

The younger man glared at him and was obviously

going to refuse. But the justice said irritably, "Oh, very well, very well. I said you should if you answered my questions. I wouldn't like you to go away thinking we're unjust here."

Moril thought Brid would have made the obvious answer to this. He held his tongue, with a bit of an effort.

The man who had fetched Moril before came back. He took Moril downstairs to a great gloomy room with guards at the door. In the middle of this room were two rows of benches about three feet apart. People were sitting facing one another at intervals along these benches. Those on the farther bench were all prisoners. Moril could see they were, because they all had a dingy, sullen, dejected look and held their heads hunched forward. He had once seen a dancing bear with the same look. And the people on the nearer bench were plainly visitors, from not having that look, and being brisker and more nervous. There seemed to be guards everywhere, standing about in a bored way, and the nervous looks of the visitors were mostly directed at the guards. The room rang and whispered with shuffling feet and sad conversations.

The man told Moril to sit on the nearest bench. After a while two guards led Dagner through a door at the other end. Dagner had the same dingy, dejected look already. He looked unexpectedly small between the guards. Moril was sure he remembered him bigger.

They sat Dagner down on the bench opposite Moril. "You can have ten minutes," they told Moril. Then they left them to talk. Moril swallowed and could not think what to say.

"Just a moment," said Dagner. "Look at the room behind me, will you, and tell me if there's anyone you think can hear what we say."

Moril looked. The nearest guard was a good way off, talking to another. "No. They're two cart lengths away at least." He was about to turn round and see if there was anyone behind him.

"Don't move, you fool!" said Dagner. "I can see it's all right behind you."

"Then that's all right," said Moril. "I saw the justice and I told them it's all a mistake. They can't really think you were passing information, can they? It's just not true."

"Yes, it is," said Dagner. "I did."

Moril stared at him.

"Father asked me to," Dagner explained. "I had to give a message and some money to one of our men here. I didn't manage very well," he said sadly. "I wasn't sure—anyway, I think the one I gave it to must have been the spy. And when I think how relieved I was once I'd got rid of them, I—well, it's no use thinking of that, I suppose."

"But, Dagner!" Moril said, quite horrified. "They'll hang you for that!"

"You don't think I don't know that, do you?" Dagner said irritably. "Is there still no one near?"

"No," said Moril. "Dagner, it isn't true, is it? You're joking."

"I'm not joking," said Dagner. "If you don't believe me, take a look at that wine jar—unless they've searched the cart by now. But that's not important. What *is* important is that you've got to get Kialan into the North. You and Brid just have to go on and get him to Hannart if you can. Can you do that, Moril?"

"I suppose so," said Moril. "But I think he sloped off when they arrested you."

"No, he didn't," said Dagner. "He'll be waiting outside Neathdale, like he said."

"If you think so—Dagner, *why* is it so important?"

"Ask Kialan," said Dagner, with his eyes on someone behind Moril. "I ordered some flour and some more oats," he went on, rather artificially. "And there was a friend of Father's letting me have a side of bacon cheap. And onions. You can get bread on the way."

"And eggs," agreed Moril. "And I'll polish your cwidder for you, I promise."

"You needn't bother," said Dagner. "Right, he's gone. Now, listen. There are two things I want you to tell Kialan. One is that Henda *has* asked a ransom for him—"

"Ransom for Kialan?" said Moril. "But he's—"

"Never mind. Just tell him," said Dagner. "And the other thing is far more important. Earl Tholian is gathering an army and—"

"Tholian? He's dead," Moril objected, and he had a muddled and upsetting notion of an army of ghosts.

"This is the new Earl. He's called Tholian, too. Don't keep interrupting. There's someone on his way over behind you," said Dagner. "The point is that nobody in the North knows, and there's nobody going through but you and Kialan. Have you got those two things?"

"Ransom and Tholian," said Moril. "There's somebody coming behind *you* now."

The guards behind Dagner came right up to him. "Come on. Time's up."

"We haven't had anything like ten minutes," Moril pointed out.

"Too bad. The justice wants to see him. On your feet, fellow," said the guard.

Dagner got up and climbed back over the bench. He made Moril a face as he was marched off, which Moril thought was intended for a smile. Moril himself, feeling utterly crushed, wandered to the door and was shown briskly through to the entrance again.

"You're out again, are you?" said the man on duty. "You've been lucky."

Moril had not the heart to reply. He did not think he was lucky, particularly as the first thing that met his eyes outside was the two dangling feet of the hanged man.

Beyond the dangling feet, Brid was sitting in the cart looking haughty and impatient. The cart was still in a clear space, and the sack of oats had been joined by a number of other sacks and bundles, all of them too heavy for Brid to lift by herself.

"Where have you *been*?" she demanded, as soon as Moril was near enough. "I thought you were never coming back! What's the matter? You look like a jug of spilled milk."

Moril was feeling so lost and peculiar that all he could do was to go to Olob. He put his arms round Olob's neck and rubbed his forehead on Olob's nose.

"Well, tell me!" said Brid. "Have you seen Dagner?"

"Yes," said Moril.

"Did you tell him to say what I told you?"

"No," said Moril.

"Why *not*? Moril, I shall hit you in a moment if you don't tell me sensibly what happened!"

"I can't," said Moril. "Not here."

"Why *not*?" Brid almost shouted.

Moril realized that he must stop her attracting attention to them. "Please, Brid. Shut up," he said, looking at her as meaningly as he could from beside Olob's nose. "Let's get these sacks loaded and get on."

Brid began to see that something terrible might have happened. "Without Dagner?" she said, in a more subdued voice. Moril nodded, tore himself away from warm, soft, friendly Olob, and began to heave at the nearest sack. Brid came down and joined him. "Moril, for goodness' sake!" she whispered angrily. "It can't be that bad! You're behaving as if they're going to *hang* Dagner."

"They are," said Moril.

Brid went white, but she did not really believe him. "Oh no!" she said. "Not on top of everything! Why?"

"Get these things in, and I'll tell you when we're moving," Moril said.

They loaded the cart, and Brid drove out of the square. When they came into the cobbled streets, where the cart made sufficient clatter to cover up whispers, Moril told Brid what had happened. It turned Brid so sick and weak that had Olob been that kind of horse, he could easily have got out of control.

"I can't believe it!" she kept saying.

She was still saying it when half a mile out of Neathdale, Kialan pushed his way out of a hedge and came to join them. When he first looked at them, he was smiling, as if he were relieved. Then he saw there were only two of them, and his smile vanished. He looked along the cart to make sure Dagner was not there, and then at their faces. When he climbed up to join them, his brown face was tired and yellowish. "What happened?" he said. "Better drive on."

"Moril says they're going to hang Dagner for passing information," said Brid. "He says Father told Dagner to do it. And I can't believe it! I just can't believe it!"

"Oh," said Kialan. "They got him for that, did they? I thought that was too much of a risk on top of everything else."

"You're mighty cool, aren't you?" said Brid. "But I suppose Dagner's not your brother!"

There was a pause, in which Kialan tried to control his feelings. But his natural outspokenness won. "All right," he said. "So he's not my brother. So you think I don't know how you feel. You just thank your stars, my girl, that you don't have to stand there and watch them hang Dagner, like I had to with *my* brother!" Brid and Moril turned round in the driving seat to stare at Kialan. But they turned back, because there were large, angry tears running past Kialan's high-bridged nose, and more tears filling and reddening his light blue eyes. "I always thought the world of Dagner, anyway," he said. "I remember him quite well from when we were small."

There was silence, except for horse and cart noises. Brid encouraged Olob to make the best speed he could up the first steep hill to the Uplands. It was horrible to be urging Olob away from Dagner. There were tears in Brid's eyes, too.

"Why did they hang your brother?" Moril asked at length.

"No reason," Kialan said angrily. "It was Tholian's idea—that pale-eyed murdering swine who killed your father—but I didn't hear Hadd or Henda or any of the others making much objection. They just had us put on trial first, to make it seem respectable. And then it came out that I was only fourteen—"

"Oh! I thought you were older!" said Brid.

"People do," said Kialan. "But I was fourteen in

March. Tholian was furious, because the rest of the earls said it was against the law to hang me for another year. But they hanged poor Konian, and the ship's captain, and all the crew they could catch, and they made me watch. It was just like our luck to land when all the earls had got together to invest that brute Tholian! His grandfather died the week before."

They were now high enough above Neathdale to have, at that moment, an excellent view of the same Tholian's mansion. Moril looked down at its long white front, peaceful and pompous and bowered among trees, and felt like a mouse running over the paws of a cat. He wished the cart was not so very pink and noticeable.

"I'm beginning to think," Kialan said miserably, "that I bring bad luck on people. First Konian, then your father, now Dagner—and goodness knows what happened to the people who helped me escape from Hadd!"

"If you don't mind my asking," Brid said cautiously, "who are you exactly?"

"My father's the Earl of Hannart," said Kialan. "And if you want to dump me out and drive off, I won't blame you."

Moril looked round for Tholian's mansion again. To his relief, it was now hidden by a bend in the road. He was glad. He felt as if this piece of news had put them suddenly in great danger. He was limp with terror, although he knew that they must have been in exactly the same danger from the moment Kialan joined them. Any earl of the South—not only Tholian—would have been overjoyed to get his hands on Kialan. His father was their chief enemy. Anyone found helping Kialan was bound to be savagely punished. Moril thought back, terrified, to Kialan walking through towns so as not to seem to belong to them, sharing the cart in full view of travelers on the road, and even being introduced to Ganner as one of them. And if that was Tholian he had seen in Markind, Moril could hardly bear to think what a risk it had been. Clennen could not have known who Kialan was. He would never have done it for the son of someone he had quarreled with. But it looked as if Lenina had known.

"I should have known you were from the North," Brid said ruefully, "when you said your name was spelled with a *K*. They don't use *K*'s in the South, do they? I wondered why Mother told Ganner your name was Collen."

Kialan chuckled slightly. "Your mother's a cool one, isn't she?"

"I suppose she is. But look here—" said Brid. "What were you and your brother doing in the South? Didn't you know what would happen?"

"It was an accident," said Kialan. "Do you remember that storm at the end of April?"

"Yes. We nearly lost the big tent. Remember, Moril?" asked Brid. Moril nodded.

"Well, we nearly got drowned," said Kialan. "We'd been to our aunt on Tulfer Island, and the storm hit us on the way home. We were blown all over the place, and the boat was sitting half under water with sea pouring in, and

I don't think the captain knew where we were any more than I did. He said we'd have to get to the nearest haven before we sank. And we did. And it turned out to be Holand. And there were all the earls of the South, smacking their lips at us. To tell you the truth," Kialan said, "I didn't even feel frightened at first. I was so glad to be on land again."

"We were near Holand then," said Brid. "But we never heard—oh, yes, Father gave it out as news, didn't he? Is that how Father came into it?"

"Don't you think he was bound to be in on it?" asked Kialan. "He didn't tell me much, but I'm sure he arranged it all. I know the people who helped me escape seemed to spend all the time waiting for messages from the Porter to know what to do next."

"What? Father?" Moril said, puzzled.

"Yes. Your father," said Kialan. "You don't mean to tell me you didn't know he was the Porter?"

"He was *not*!" Brid said angrily. "The Porter's a spy with a price on his head."

"Yes, of course, in the South," said Kialan. "They were mad to catch him here, because he was the main agent for the North. You must have known! He brought all the important messages and most of the refugees. They must have come in this cart. And he organized people here against the earls—I know that, because Konian told me. Konian sent a message to your father for help, during the trial, but it didn't get to him quick enough."

There was a somber pause. Olob clopped patiently upward, zigzagging with the road across the steep hillside, while Brid and Moril tried to take in what Kialan had said. "I thought," Moril said, "that your father had quarreled with ours?"

"So did I," said Kialan. "But I think that was a pretense. I found out last year—I wish people told me things!—because my father vanished and I needed him for something. And Konian told me to shut up, because he'd gone to meet Clennen the Singer like he always did, but no one was supposed to know. I think they arranged what to do next then."

"I refuse to believe that my father was a common spy!" said Brid. "Why didn't he *tell* me? He ought to have told me! It's so sneaky, somehow!"

"Don't *shout*!" Moril said, with an anxious look round at Tholian's mansion, which had come into view again, lower down and farther off.

Kialan laughed outright. "But he wasn't sneaky! That was the splendid thing about him! I couldn't believe he really was the Porter at first. I saw this fat man with a great big voice, who spent all his time trying to impress people, and I thought there'd been an awful mistake. Then I saw him go into towns, in this shocking bright cart, in a scarlet suit just to make sure people didn't miss him, and sing his head off, and call out at the top of his voice that the price on the Porter's head was two thousand in gold. It was incredible! Then he and your mother would call out messages and hand out notes, right in front of everyone, and I knew half of them were illegal. But no one would believe it, because it was all done so openly. Nobody thought he was anything more than a very good singer. And I really think Clennen thought that was the best joke about it."

Moril blinked a little at this view of his father. But Kialan had hit Clennen off in a way. Clennen *had* treated their shows as a rather serious joke. If he was really the Porter all along, then that would be why. "I suppose that's where Dagner went wrong," he said sadly. "Trying to be secret."

"Dagner was awfully stupid to think he could carry on where Father left off, anyway," said Brid.

"He didn't," said Kialan. "Dagner wasn't trying to do that for a moment. But Clennen asked him to finish off the important things if he could. Then he was to go North and stay there. And the message to Neathdale was important because it was about a spy who'd got in among them there."

Moril sighed. He did not say that Dagner thought he had given the message to that very spy. There seemed no point. He said, "Dagner said I was to tell you Henda has asked for a ransom for you. And Tholian is gathering an army."

"Oh damn!" Kialan said wearily. "Then I'll *have* to get through somehow, won't I? You saw Dagner? Tell me."

Moril told Kialan all that happened to him in the jail. He could not help speaking low and looking nervously at Tholian's mansion each time it came into view. He was relieved when they crossed the brow of the first hill and could not see it anymore.

"You were lucky, Moril," said Brid. "If you'd known all the things Kialan's just told us, we might be in jail at this moment." Moril nodded soberly. He certainly could not have acted the surprise he felt when they told him what Dagner had been arrested for. But he knew it had been the merest good luck that he had not happened to mention Kialan.

"I couldn't think," said Kialan, "why Clennen made such a point of not telling you two anything. He wouldn't let me say who I was, and neither would Dagner. But I think it saved our skins. I wish it could have saved Dagner's."

"You don't think Dagner was really arrested because of you?" Moril asked.

"I did at first," said Kialan. "I thought we'd all had it, all the time I was sitting in the hedge. I could hardly believe it when I saw the cart coming. No. I think Dagner's trouble is separate, and thanks to you, Moril, they think he just did a bit of freedom fighting on the side. But I hope it doesn't get round to the Earl. Tholian will put two and two together all right."

"Why did Tholian kill Father?" said Moril.

"He was looking for me," said Kialan, "and he didn't want anyone to know, because I'm supposed to be Hadd's prisoner—or Henda's, only they were still arguing about that when I escaped. Dagner thought that maybe the Neathdale spy—or perhaps it was the fellow they hanged—might have given Tholian a hint about your father. But he couldn't have known much, or we'd all have been arrested. Tholian's the sort who says dead men tell no tales, so he kills Clennen and then beats the woods for me."

"If only we'd known!" said Brid. "Where were you all that time?"

"Up a tree," said Kialan, "rabbits and all. They were crashing about searching all the time you were playing that cwidder, Moril, and it worried them like anything. They kept saying that blessed boy and his music made their heads go round. Tholian suggested going back and killing you, too, but none of them could quite be bothered to. And when you left off, they'd had enough and they went."

"Could you pass it me?" said Moril. Kialan obligingly crawled back to the instrument rack and reached the big cwidder over to the driving seat. Moril took it and clutched it to him. It felt fat and hard and comforting. Apart from the fact that it seemed to have saved both his life and Kialan's, it was in its rather more awesome way as good as Olob's nose. He felt he needed it, somehow, after the events of today.

"Play something," suggested Kialan.

"No, don't," said Brid. "Not until we've decided what to do. We're slap bang in the middle of Tholian's earldom, and we've obviously got to get North, and everyone knows this cart. And we've no money. I daresay Father meant to go this way because it would have looked suspicious if he didn't, but I vote we turn east and try to get North through the Marshes."

Kialan fetched the map out and scowled at its sketchiness. "I suppose we could try the sea," said Moril. "We might find a boat that wants a singer."

Kialan glared at the map. "We'd take ages, either way. And we can't be more than four days off Flennpass here. Don't either of you understand? Tholian's getting an army together to invade the North, and Henda's sent to my father to say he'll ransom me, so my father thinks I'm a prisoner and daren't do a thing! And I suppose," he added, "Henda's message is the first news my father gets that we're not both drowned. If you don't mind, I'd like to get North as quickly as I can—but it's your cart, of course."

Moril glanced at Kialan and decided that his hectoring tone had much to do with the tears in his eyes. Brid did not notice. "Oh, *is* it our cart?" she said. The result was that Kialan managed to laugh, rather sheepishly.

"We'll go straight on," Moril said, suddenly deciding. "We'll do it Father's way and be quite open about it. It worked for him, and it worked for me in the jail."

Brid and Kialan seemed to be relieved that Moril had taken the lead. But as Olob dragged the cart into the level ground of the first Upland, they began to make nervous objections.

"Innocent little children is all very well," said Brid. "What about when the Earl hears of Dagner doing the Porter's business?"

Moril looked round on fields with green corn show-ing and sheep grazing. The hills of the North towered against the sky, so high and blue-gray with distance that, on first glance, Moril took them for a bank of cloud.

"A certain pink cart will be looked for," said Kialan. "Could you paint it?"

"Dark green would be best," said Brid. "But we've no money."

A village came in sight, looking very small against the hills of the North. Moril roused himself before Kialan and Brid could have any wilder ideas. "Tholian knows me," he said. "He recognized me up a ladder in Markind. That's the trouble with having red hair."

"Wear a hat," said Kialan.

Moril turned round to quell Kialan. "What about this village?" As he said it, he realized that Kialan was tired out. His face was as white as such a brown complexion could be, and there were dark rings under his eyes. All the watching at night and the suspense in Neathdale had been rather too much for him. "Get down in the cart," Moril said, taking pity on him. "I'll put the cover half-up."

Kialan lay thankfully down beside the wine jar, and Moril pulled the canvas forward until it hid him. They drove straight through the village, Brid holding the reins and Moril sitting beside her, gently strumming the cwid-der. On the heights above the village there was an odd little gray tower, belonging to the Lord of the Uplands. Brid looked at it and quivered with terror, knowing as she did that the Earl of Hannart's son was hidden in the cart. But Moril knew it was no different from any other risk they had run without knowing. The tower and the mountains made him think of his imaginary Hannart. He felt soothed and peaceful.

Several people looked up, or out at doors, hearing the cart and the cwidder. When they saw what it was, they smiled and waved. Brid did her best to smile and nod back. Then a woman came out of a house and walked beside them.

"Have you been through Neathdale today?"

"Yes," said Moril.

"They tell me there was to have been a man hanged."

"Yes," said Moril. "He was. We saw him."

"I knew it!" the woman said, smiling. "He was bound to come to it!" She seemed so gleeful that Moril thought she must have hated the hanged man, until he noticed the tears in her eyes. Then he saw she was just trying to hide her feelings. He wanted to say something kind to her, but she left the cart and went back into her house. Moril wondered whether Clennen had known her, and what her connection was with the hanged man.

9

A mile or so beyond the village, Olob looked at the sun moving into the blue mountains and turned toward a cart track which led away to the left. Brid tried to stop him. "No, Olob. We must get on."

"Let him find a place," said Moril. "I told you. It's no good looking guilty. Besides, we haven't eaten a thing since this morning."

"You had a pie, you lucky pig!" snapped Brid, but she gave in and let Olob pull the cart into a secluded grassy space under a cliff. A stream ran in a trickle of green mosses down the rock face. Moril came down from the cart, feeling shaky at the knees.

"If we're going to camp this near the village," said Kialan, emerging from hiding, "then we'd better set a watch tonight."

"What for?" said Moril. "Nobody's going to bother

to come at night, not after three children. And if they come while we're awake, we'll hear them."

"I'm going to watch, all the same," said Kialan.

"No you're not," said Moril. "There's no point."

"Bossy, aren't you, all of a sudden!" Brid snapped. Then she rounded on Kialan. "And if you make yourself ill staying awake every night, what are we supposed to do with you?"

Moril realized that Brid was angry because she was tired and miserable. So he said nothing and simply began to get Olob out of the shafts. Kialan must have realized it, too, because he said wearily, "Oh, all right. I give in," and started collecting firewood.

Brid investigated the provisions Dagner had bought. "What am I supposed to do with all this flour?" she demanded. "And no eggs!"

It looked as if Dagner's idea had been to stock the cart with enough food to last them until they reached the North. But as Brid said mournfully, his mind must have been on that message, for the only useful things he had bought were the bacon and a large cheese. Among the less useful things were lentils, candles, and a big bunch of rhubarb.

"Look at this!" said Brid, wagging the rhubarb about. "What was he *thinking* of?"

"Waste of money," agreed Kialan. "Did he use all you earned?"

"Yes," said Brid. "Every penny. And there's not even any bread."

They had a rather strange supper of fried bacon, cheese, and experimental pancakes made out of flour and water. Brid, after nibbling one, promptly put them in the frying pan that held the bacon, and Kialan thought of melting cheese over them to improve the taste. This left them still so empty that they finished the meal with about a quart each of stewed rhubarb; luckily, Lenina had left some sugar in the cart.

Moril felt better after that. He got up, fetched the bucket, and carefully cleaned the cart. It was looking very dusty and uncared for, and to his mind, it had a furtive, illegal look. He thought about Dagner as he worked. He wondered what he had to eat in prison and how soon he would be tried and hanged. Or did the questioning by the justice count as a trial? Moril feared that it did. He wondered again what Dagner had said when they questioned him. Then he thought of Dagner trying to carry on Clennen's work in Dagner's way. It had not seemed wise. Dagner had been nervous and secretive, and he had made a fatal mistake. But on the other hand, Dagner was so unlike Clennen that it was probably the only thing he could do. Moril thought about himself going back to Clennen's way and wondered if that was wise. He was not like Clennen either. But he did not know what he was like. He supposed that sooner or later he would have to find out, and then do things in the way best suited to what he found.

Brid and Kialan were washing the pans. Kialan was looking exhausted. Tears kept coming into Brid's eyes, and she angrily wiped them away with the back of her greasy hand. And they were both pretending they were cheerful.

"Do you think if we mixed the cheese in with the flour, they'd taste better?" Brid said.

"What about rhubarb? Sort of fritters?" said Kialan.

"Ugh!" said Brid. "When I see Dagner, I'll—" She wiped off another set of tears and said brightly, "He must have had his reasons, I suppose."

Moril tipped away the dirty water, wondering if there could be three more unhappy people in Dalemark. Kialan must know he was a danger to himself and his companions. His landfall in Holand must have been horrible. And since then, Moril realized, Kialan's life had been one long, tense escape, which was not over yet. As for himself and Brid, they had seen their family simply dwindle away, until it was down to their two selves. And Kialan had been fond of Dagner, too—fonder than he had realized.

Moril stopped himself in the midst of a snuffle of self-pity. No. Last year, as soon as they were safely in the North, Clennen had told them some of the other things that happened in the South. Whole families had been arrested. The older ones had been hanged, and children younger than Moril had been left with nothing in the world, and nobody dared help them for fear of being arrested, too. Clennen had told them how Henda had calmly doubled his taxes last year and turned those who could not pay out to starve, and how old Tholian had hunted an old man with dogs for not raising his hat to him fast enough. Moril knew there must be hundreds of people in the South even worse off than he was. They had a horse and cart, and Clennen had left them with a means of earning a living and a license to do it. If it came to the worst, they could go back to Markind. Moril did not like the idea. He tried to tell himself that they could not go back, because of Kialan. But he knew that was not it. Lenina would help Kialan. The reason for his not liking it, he was forced to admit, was that he was not at all clear whether they had deserted Lenina, or she them. And it made him uncomfortable.

"We'll give more shows," he said, putting Lenina out of his mind. He went to the cart to polish the instruments and stopped at the sight of the wine jar taking up so much room inside. "Do you know anything about this wine jar?" he called to Kialan.

"No—oh, you mean the papers?" Kialan said, coming over to the cart. "Dagner had a look in Markind, because he had to find the message for Neathdale. They're down inside its basket."

Moril scrambled up to look. Kialan took down the tailgate and told him where to put his hand down between bottle and basket. Brid hurried over and watched Moril fish about, feel paper, and pull it out. "What are these?"

"Messages that weren't so important," said Kialan. "Lucky they didn't search the cart, wasn't it?"

Brid and Moril held the papers into the sinking sun

and spelled out, in Clennen's writing: "For Mattrick. Someone in Neathdale—I think Halain—smells of lavender. Dirty washing through Pali and Fander in future."

"Lavender!" said Brid. "Really, Father!"

The other notes said the same, and were marked to be delivered to places between Markind and Neathdale.

"Go and put those all on the fire," Moril said, handing them to Kialan. "Now do you believe we can read?"

Kialan grinned and took the papers. While he was stuffing them under the embers and the air was filling with the strong smell of burning paper, Moril busily worked his hand on round the wine jar. Halfway round, he felt more papers. He pulled them out and unfolded them.

These were all in different people's writing. Some of them seemed to have come from parts of the South they had not visited in years. Others concerned the places they had passed through, and these were mostly in Lenina's writing. Moril felt oddly glad to see his mother's small, bold writing. He could see that whatever Lenina had thought, privately, of Clennen's freedom fighting, she had most scrupulously done what Clennen wanted while he was alive—even at the risk of being hanged for spying. It was queer to find her so honorable, but Moril liked it. Among other things, she had written: "Crady—169 taken north to Neathdale" and "Fledden—24 pressed yesterday, with horses." The other notes said much the same.

"What do you think this means?" said Brid.

Kialan came over to look. "Do you think," he said, after some puzzling, "those might be for my father or someone in the North? It could be about the army Tholian's gathering."

"You know, I do believe that's it!" said Brid. "They mean how many men went for soldiers from each place. Don't you agree, Moril?"

"Probably," said Moril. It seemed a bit boring to him. "We'd better take them North, then." He put them back and, just to be on the safe side, went on working his hand round the other side of the jar. There were cold, hard things. He gripped one and pulled it out. "I say!" It was a gold piece. "Whose is this?"

They were all mystified. Brid suggested that it was payment for taking Kialan North, but, as Moril and Kialan rather scornfully pointed out, if Clennen had organized that, he would have been paying himself. No other explanation seemed likely, either.

"Anyway, that means we can buy food tomorrow," Brid said. "Father couldn't mind that."

"Don't be a big idiot!" said Moril. "When did we ever have a gold piece before? Someone's going to think we stole it, and if *we* get arrested, the whole thing's going to come out." Carefully he slipped the coin back behind the basket again.

Brid sighed. "A whole bottleful of gold! Oh, all right. I suppose you're right and it would look odd. I'm going to bed. Get out of the cart."

Moril helped Kialan put up the tent. By then Kialan

was so tired that he dragged a blanket into it and fell asleep before the sun set. Moril felt too agitated to go to sleep straightaway. He sat against the cliff, with Olob companionably cropping grass nearby, and strummed on the cwidder for comfort. He did not play any particular song, just snatches of this and a bar or so of that. It seemed to express the state of his feelings. He still found it hard to believe that his father had been a notorious agent. Of all the discoveries of the last few days, that one was hardest to take. He had thought he knew Clennen. Now he saw he had not. He wondered when Dagner had found out and how he had felt. And he made an effort to think of Clennen in this new light.

But somehow, he did not want to think of his father. He wanted to forget the blood gushing into the lake, and he did not want to consider how Clennen could be so public and so private at one and the same time. Instead, by degrees, Moril took refuge in hazy memories from much earlier. He thought of the cart rolling down a green road in the North. Clennen was singing in the driving seat, Lenina doing some mending beside him, and the three children were playing happily on the lockers. The sun shone—and, somewhat to his surprise, the cwidder began to produce a muzzy sound. It was a very queer noise. Moril did not like it, and Olob looked round at it disapprovingly.

"Time for bed," Moril said to Olob. He got up and went to put the cwidder back in the cart.

Inside, the cart was hot, and Brid and the wine jar

seemed to fill it. Moril hesitated, thinking of the active elbows and knees of Kialan. But he could not bear the heat, so he took a blanket and wriggled into the tent with Kialan.

Luckily Kialan was so exhausted that he did not move in his sleep. Both he and Moril woke feeling fresher and happier. Brid was the somber one, but she improved after a breakfast of bacon steaks fried by Kialan. Then Moril fetched Olob's harness to clean. He was determined that their turnout should be as spruce and innocent as he could get it. Kialan, without being asked, went to groom Olob. And Moril realized that not only had Kialan done his full share of the chores ever since they left Markind, but nobody had either noticed or thanked him.

"You don't have to do Olob," he said. "I'll do him."

"Am I supposed to stand around and watch you wear yourself out, or something?" said Kialan. "Move, Olob, you lazy lump."

"Well, you used to," said Brid, scrubbing the frying pan. "And you're an earl's son."

"I thought I'd get that sooner or later!" Kialan said with his most fed-up look. "I didn't know what needed doing at first, and there always seemed loads of you to do it, anyway. But if you two are having to earn money now, it's only fair you don't do everything else."

"Moril," said Brid, going very somber again, "do you think we really *can* earn money? I mean, even with Dagner, we sounded so—so thin and pale, didn't we?"

"No, you didn't," said Kialan, at work on the farther

side of Olob. "You just gave a different kind of show. Only I think you made a mistake in not building it round Dagner more. You should have got him to sing again, Brid. He'd have done it in short bursts, and his songs are really good."

"They are, aren't they?" Brid said sadly. "And now—"

"Moril," said Kialan, appearing under Olob's nose, "you can't happen to remember Dagner's songs, can you? Enough to play them yourself?"

"I never thought of that!" said Moril. As soon as he had finished the harness, he fetched out the instruments. While Brid set to work polishing them, Moril took up the big cwidder and tried out the first song of Dagner's that came into his head. For some reason, it was the song Dagner had never finished, the one Clennen had forbidden him to sing until they were in the North. Moril stopped after the first few notes, to make sure nobody was about. There seemed to be no one, so he went on. He found he wanted to finish it for Dagner. It seemed the only thing he could do for him.

Dagner had only sketched out part of the tune. Since Moril had no idea what Dagner intended, he let the words take him, this way and that, through a melting blackbird phrase:

"*Come to me, come with me.*
The blackbird asks you, 'Follow me.'"

—and then to a kind of birdsong triumph in

"Wherever you go, I will go."

Kialan seemed almost awestruck. But Brid, as soon as she realized what song it was, looked up the cliff and down the slope to make sure they were not overheard. Moril knew he was breaking the law. But he wanted to finish the song, so he went, rather defiantly, on to

"The sun is up."

The cwidder produced a shrill and defiant sound. Moril, cross with himself for being scared, tried to recapture the first melting tone and only succeeded in making a scratchy, bad-tempered tinkle. Dagner would have hated it. Moril thought of Dagner and put in the first four lines again at the end, as Dagner had suggested he might. But he was not thinking very clearly of Dagner himself—more of Dagner as part of that happy family on a green road in the North that he had pictured the night before. And just as he had last night, he heard the cwidder making that odd, muzzy noise.

Moril sprang up and sprang back. He could not help it. The cwidder fell on the turf with a melodious thump.

"Moril!" said Brid. "You'll break it!"

"It was splendid!" said Kialan. "Don't stop."

"I don't care!" Moril said hysterically. "I've a good mind to jump on it! The blessed thing was playing my *thoughts*! It played the way I was thinking!"

Brid and Kialan looked at one another, then at Moril.

"Don't you think," Kialan said, "that that's the way it works? It's your thoughts that bring out the power."

"But it never did that for Father!" said Moril. "He told me! He said it only did it once."

"Well," Kialan said, rather awkwardly, "he couldn't really use it, could he? It wasn't his kind of thing."

"Except just that one time," said Brid. "Which proves it, Moril. Because it must have been when Father saw Mother in Ganner's hall. And he wanted her to love him instead of Ganner so much that he managed to make the cwidder work, and she did love him enough to come away with him."

After that Moril went and put the cwidder away. Brid got it out again and polished it for him, but he pretended not to notice. When Olob, the cart, and all the instruments were gleaming with care, they set off again through the first Upland, toward the steep hill to the second. Brid drove. Moril sat beside her, trying out another of Dagner's songs on his small treble cwidder. But it was no good. The treble cwidder just felt foolish and flimsy and shrill, and it sounded terribly ordinary. As Olob settled into a slow, heaving walk up the steep hill into the next Upland, Moril was forced to turn and ask Kialan to put the little cwidder away and pass him the big one.

The matter-of-fact way Kialan handed it to him made Moril feel much better about it. Moril took the cwidder thankfully. It felt right. He was not sure now whether it was a comfort or a burden, but if Kialan could accept so easily that it was a powerful and mysterious thing, so could he. But he knew he was going to have to learn to control the thing. You could not earn your living with a cwidder that whined if you were miserable and croaked if you were cross. "How should I start?" he asked Kialan over his shoulder.

Kialan hesitated, not because he did not understand Moril, but because he was not sure how Moril should start. "Understanding yourself, perhaps?" he asked. "I mean, I've no idea either, but try that. Er—why didn't you stay in Markind, for instance? Was it just seeing Tholian there?"

Moril, by this time, was sure that it was not. "Why didn't *you* want to stay?" he asked Brid, as a start. "Duty to Father?"

"Like Mother, you mean?" said Brid. "N-no. A bit of that. I do prefer Father's outlook to Mother's, but it was really almost more like the way Mother went back to Ganner. It's what I'm used to—this—and nothing else felt right."

Moril felt that went for him, too. But there was more to it than that. He could have persuaded Brid to go back to Markind after Dagner was arrested, but he had not thought of it, even. He had not wanted to go back when he had found out how dangerous their journey North really was. And he was still going North, as if it was a matter of course. Why?

"Why, Moril?" asked Brid.

"I was born in the North," Moril answered, rather

slowly. "When I—er—dream of things, it's always the North. And the North is right and the South is wrong."

"Bravo!" said Kialan.

Moril turned to smile at him. He found himself turning from the towering unseeable hills of the North to a low, blue vision of the South, beyond Kialan's head. "But I still don't understand," he said.

At the top of the hill there was a village, a very small place, simply ten houses and an alehouse, clinging to the steep brow of the hill.

"Don't let's perform here," said Brid. "There's a bigger place farther on, I know."

They went past the village into a wider Upland, full of grazing sheep. By the middle of the morning Moril's cwidder was sounding melancholy. "I can't see us getting much," he said. "Not just the two of us."

"Would it help at all," said Kialan, "if I were to pretend to be Dagner?"

Both their heads whipped round his way. It was almost a marvelous idea.

"Would they remember Dagner from last year?" said Kialan.

"We didn't perform in the Uplands at all last year," said Brid. "But—"

"I've been thinking," said Kialan. "No one but the earls knows I'm in the South. And it's so out of the way here that no one's going to know Dagner was arrested unless we tell them. I think it would be safe enough—and a bit in your father's style, too."

Moril made the obvious objection. "You can't sing." They looked at one another for a moment. Moril remembered Kialan listening in to his lessons with Clennen, appearing in the crowd whenever they gave a show, and seeming so knowledgeable the time the big cwidder went out of tune. "Or can you?" said Moril.

"Not as well as you," said Kialan, "but—may I borrow one of these cwidders for a moment?"

"Go ahead," said Brid.

Kialan took up Dagner's cwidder and tuned it without needing to be given a note. Moril and Brid looked at one another. Neither of them could do that. And from the moment Kialan started to play, they knew they were listening to a gifted person very much out of practice. If he did not sing as well as he played, it was merely because he was the age when his voice still moved troublesomely from low to high. Moril vividly remembered the trouble Dagner had had at the same age.

What Kialan sang was a song of the Adon's, one that Clennen never sang in the South.

"Unbounded truth is not a thing
Cramped to time and bound in place—"

"Ooh!" said Brid, looking nervously round.
"No one about. Shut up!" said Moril.
Kialan did that part meticulously in the right old

style. But then he gave Moril a bit of a wink and dropped into the same kind of different fingering Moril had used in Neathdale. The song seemed to come alive.

> *"Truth strangely changes space,*
> *By right of its reality.*
> *It moves the hills containing me*
> *Wider than the world, or small*
> *As in a nut. Truth is free*
> *And laws are stones, or not at all,*
> *And men without it nothing."*

"Oh, I liked that!" said Moril.

"I took a leaf out of your book," Kialan said, rather apologetically. "I don't like the old style either, and I don't see why old things should be sacred. Wow! I'm out of practice, though! Do you think I'll be any use to you?"

"You know you will," said Brid. "You big fraud. If you're that good, why on earth didn't you say so before? Father would have put you in the show, instead of making you walk through all the towns."

"I know he would!" Kialan said feelingly. "He'd have dressed me in scarlet and flaunted me. I didn't quite like to say anything at first—you were all so excellent—and as soon as I realized what your father was like, I'd have died rather than tell him. It was frightening enough walking."

The upshot of this was that Olob quietly pulled the

gleaming cart onto the green of the village a mile or so on, and three people stood up to sing and play. Moril and Kialan were nervous, Brid, as usual, as confident as a queen. Moril did one or two of Dagner's songs, but mostly they sang ballads, since those were Brid's specialty and Kialan's voice was not equal to anything more difficult. A scattering of people listened and clapped. Someone asked for an encore, and Brid gave them "Cow-Calling." They got a little money, enough to buy eggs, milk, and butter, and a woman gave Brid a basket of somewhat withered apples. It was not a raving success, but it was no failure either.

"We can do it!" said Brid.

Moril smiled, and strummed his cwidder as they took to the road again. Every so often he played a tune in earnest, and Kialan would come in, too, on Dagner's cwidder. Kialan was getting more in practice every moment. They experimented, and tried for effects and new settings. Moril had seldom enjoyed making music so much. He almost wished the distance to Hannart were twice as long.

10

They had a sort of cheese omelet for lunch, sitting on a point of green land between two brisk streams. Kialan would have it that what they were eating was scrambled eggs. Brid disagreed. Moril did not join in the argument because he was listening to the sound of the water. It made him think of the North. The sound of water running was never far away in the North. He was dreamily considering whether one could make a tune that captured the noise when Brid shook him sharply and told him they were moving.

"You didn't have to do that!" said Kialan.

"Why not? You know how maddening he is when he goes into a dream," Brid retorted.

"Yes, but it's just his way," said Kialan. "He's about six times as awake as most people, really. I bet he heard every word we said—didn't you, Moril?"

"I suppose I did," Moril said, in some surprise.

"Can I drive this next stretch?" Kialan asked.

Neither Brid nor Moril objected. Letting Kialan drive Olob seemed the best way to show he was a full member of the company now and not a passenger any longer. So Kialan held the reins, and Olob clopped onward through the lonely Upland. Moril sat beside him, still strumming the cwidder, looking dreamily round at the hills, the flocks of sheep, and the occasional shepherd in the distance.

They came to a steep rise to the third and last Upland. It was the highest and also the most beautiful of the three climbs, because it was clothed in trees the whole way up. The road, though it was the main road, dwindled to a rutty lane, damp and stony, boring its way upward through the woods. The sunlight fell in gay splashes through the bright leaves of springtime. All three of them looked upward and grinned at the way their faces became speckled and greenish.

But Olob, whether he objected to Kialan's holding the reins or to having to climb two steep hills in one day, became steadily more restive. At first it was simply tossing his head and stopping. Kialan persuaded him to move again, each time with more difficulty. But, as they went on upward, Olob took to trampling this way and that, so that the cart wheels caught in the hawthorns at the side of the road. Kialan grew exasperated. The fourth time Olob did it, Kialan lost his temper and swore at Olob. Olob promptly turned right across the road and seemed to be trying to climb the sheer bank into the woods. Moril thought the cart would overturn. The wine jar fell over and knocked Brid sideways, with a dreadful twanging of cwidders.

"Let me take him," said Moril.

Kialan crossly handed him the reins. Moril propped the cwidder across his knees and worked with both hands and some shouting to persuade Olob back onto the road again. Olob refused to come out of the bushes.

"What's got into him?" said Kialan.

"No idea," said Moril. As he said it, two memories came to him. One was of almost exactly the same conversation, between himself and Lenina, just before Tholian came out of the wood and killed Clennen. The other was of Olob behaving like a colt in Neathdale, just before Dagner was arrested. "Quick!" he said to Kialan. "There are enemies near, and Olob knows. Get out and go through the woods until we've passed them."

"How *can* he know?" said Kialan, with his most fed-up look.

"I don't know, but he does. Father always said he wouldn't part with Olob for an earldom, and I think that's why. Get *out*, I said!" Moril said urgently.

"Do as you're told, Kialan!" said Brid from the tilted bottom of the cart.

Kialan, entirely unconvinced, swung himself grudgingly down from the cart. As Olob was halfway through a bush, up the right bank of the road, Kialan went up beside him by the space he had cleared, and vanished among the trees higher up. Moril could hear his cross footsteps swishing along the steep hillside.

"Go quietly!" he said, but he could tell Kialan took no notice. Moril dumped the cwidder in the canted cart and went to Olob's head. Olob was most unwilling to leave the bush. "I know, old fellow, but we've got to go on and look innocent," Moril said. "*Come* on, now!"

It took some time to get Olob back on the road. When he did consent to come, Brid had to lean on the cart to keep it upright. Then she climbed in and tried to set the wine jar and the instruments to rights. Olob reluctantly climbed onward. Above them in the woods, Kialan's feet kept pace with the cart, swishing loudly and cracking twigs. Moril wished he would not make so much noise.

Olob toiled round three corners and Brid still seemed to be busy in the cart. "What are you doing?" Moril asked.

"Putting my boots on," said Brid. "If there *are* enemies near, I'm going to look respectable. And I'm putting the sharp knife down the right boot." She joined him shortly, looking flushed and determined, firmly booted. "I'll drive," she said.

Moril gave her the reins and hung the cwidder round his neck by its strap, which, he supposed, was his way of looking respectable. His boots, by this time, were nothing like as new and smart as Brid's. Brid was better at managing Olob. Olob put on a great act of this being the most difficult climb of his life and did everything in his power to suggest that they turn back, but Brid kept him going. Beyond the protesting clatter of his hooves, Moril listened for Kialan, but he could not hear him any longer. By this time they were near the top of the climb. They rounded what must have been the last corner, and Olob shied.

"Clever Olob," Brid remarked.

There was a stout wooden trestle in the road. It did not fill the road, but it was placed so that there was no room for a cart to pass on either side. There were a number of men with it, one of them sitting on the trestle. To Moril's dismay, they were all in full war gear. Each of them wore a steel cap and a steel breastplate with a pointed front—which gave them all chests like pigeons—over jackets and trousers of tough leather. They wore great black boots and long swords in black leather scabbards.

Brid drew the alarmed Olob up. "Would you mind moving the trestle? We need to get by," she said haughtily. She was frightened and daunted, but there were enough soldiers to make her feel as if she had an audience.

Three of the men strolled forward. None of them made any effort to move the trestle. "What's your business?" said one. The other two strolled on and looked over the sides of the cart to see what was in it.

"Drunkards, by the look of this wine," one said, and both of them sniggered a little.

"We're singers," said Brid. "Can't you see?"

"In that case, let's see your license," said the first man, and held out his hand for it. Brid, after a moment's hesitation, fetched the license out of the locker under the seat and handed it to him. He looked at it casually. "Which of you is Clennen?"

"That's my father," said Brid. "He was killed four days ago."

"Then you haven't got a license," said the man. "Have you?"

"Yes, we have," said Brid. "We're entitled to sing under that license for six months. That's the law, and you can't tell me it isn't."

"That may be the law in the other earldoms, but not in the South Dales," the man said, grinning. "You haven't read the small print." He unrolled the parchment and pointed vaguely to the bottom of it. When Brid leaned over to look, he took it out of reach and let it roll up again. "Too bad," he said. "You'd better come and explain yourselves."

"It doesn't say that at all!" Brid said furiously. "You're just using it as an excuse. That license is perfectly in order, and you know it!"

The man stopped grinning. "You'll do as you're told," he said. He nodded to one of the other men, who took hold of Olob's bridle. The rest moved the trestle aside. The one holding Olob hauled on him and Olob, passively resisting for all he was worth, was forced to move reluctantly on. Brid and Moril were towed after him, feeling quite helpless. It was clear that someone—

Tholian, probably—had given orders that all travelers were to be stopped. Moril looked back to see the soldiers putting the trestle across the road again and sitting on it to wait for any other comers. He wondered about jumping off the cart and running. But there was a soldier walking on either side of it and it did not seem worth trying. Their only hope seemed to be to use Clennen's method and appear as open and innocent as they knew how.

They went fifty yards or so—a difficult jerky fifty yards, because Olob was extremely frightened and did not want to move, in spite of the names the soldier called him—and came to a steep road branching to the right. The soldier dragged Olob into it. Moril had forgotten this road. It worried him that Kialan would have to cross it on his way to the last Upland.

"Where does this road go?" he asked Brid.

"To a sort of extra valley at one side," Brid said. "We camped here the year before last. Don't you remember? Moril, they will let us go, won't they?"

Moril glanced down at the soldiers. "We haven't done anything wrong," he said carefully. But the wine jar came into his mind as he said it, and he wondered why on earth he had not left it behind somewhere.

A twig snapped in the wood up to the right. Moril looked up. And looked away quickly, in case the soldiers noticed. He had a very clear sight of Kialan staring down at the cart, alarmed and rather puzzled, as if he had not gathered what was going on. Moril stared at the steep road ahead and tried to will Kialan to cross the road while he had the chance and go on North. But he was very much afraid Kialan intended to follow the cart.

The trees opened like the end of a tunnel, and they came out into the valley. Brid gave a little moan. Beyond two groups of soldiers, evidently on guard, were tents, weapons, horses, and many more soldiers, as far as they could see. It was a long, thin valley, and winding, so that half of it was out of sight. But they had no doubt that the part of it they could not see was also full of soldiers and weapons and tents.

The nearest tent was a very large one. There was a chair outside it, and in that chair sat Tholian. His head turned as the cart came out from among the trees. As far as he could tell from this distance, Moril thought Tholian smiled. And he saw that Clennen's method was not going to help them here. In fact, he doubted if any method was going to be much use.

"Get down," one of the soldiers said to Brid and Moril.

They climbed down, Brid a little awkward in her boots, Moril clutching the cwidder, and stood where they had a lower and even busier view of the teeming valley ahead. Moril dimly remembered that the year before last there had been fields and crops growing here. There was no sign of them now. As they were taken toward Tholian, he saw nothing but men drilling and training, all down the valley. It was filled with orders and curses, and the thick warm smell of many people and horses. The grass, and any crops there might have been, were trampled to earth, except for a green stretch round the large tent where Tholian sat.

Tholian signaled to the soldiers to make Brid and Moril stand to one side of the patch of grass, and turned his pale eyes from them to the soldiers. "Just these two in the cart?" he asked.

Moril seized the opportunity to look over his shoulder to see what had become of Olob and the cart. He was glad to find one of the soldiers struggling to tie the unwilling Olob to a tree beside the road.

"Could I have your attention, cousin?" he heard Tholian say, and he turned back hurriedly. Tholian sounded irritated. But when Moril looked at him, he was smiling. He could have been friendly in spite of his queer, shallow eyes. "We are related, aren't we?" he said.

Moril thought about it. "I suppose so. But it's Mother who's your cousin."

"Once removed," said Tholian. "Which makes us twice removed, I believe."

"I'm surprised you acknowledge it at all," said Brid. "Considering—"

"Why not?" said Tholian. "It doesn't hurt you. But don't deceive yourselves into thinking your mother's going to get a penny of dowry out of me. I'm content to do as my grandfather wanted. Ganner's a fool if he thinks I'm going to make him rich on Lenina's account."

This seemed a very odd thing for Tholian to start talking about. Moril wondered if he was a trifle mad. "I shouldn't think Ganner does think that," he said.

"He's fond of Mother, you see," explained Brid.

Tholian laughed. "Fool, isn't he?" He was so contemptuous that Brid all but sprang to Ganner's defense. "But I stayed for the wedding," Tholian said, before Brid could speak, "which was more than you did. You threw Ganner into a fine old fuss by leaving like that, you know. Your mother took it much more calmly. So I promised them I'd look out for you on the road and send you back to Markind when I found you."

"That was kind of you," Brid said coldly. Nevertheless, both she and Moril were beginning to feel distinctly easier. If Tholian were regarding them simply as silly young relations and himself as doing Ganner a favor, then the position was nothing like as bad as they had feared. It would be exasperating to be sent back to Markind, but at least Kialan, with luck, could get North on foot from here.

"Didn't Mother recognize you?" Moril said slowly, rather puzzled at the way Tholian was now being a friend of the family.

"Of course," Tholian said, not at all disconcerted. "But as I'm Ganner's overlord, there wasn't much she could say. Not that she would. She has a way of saying things in silence, your mother. By the way, what became of your brothers?"

They saw he had just been showing them how much he knew. It gave them both a jolt. Moril reacted best, because he was able to rely on his habitual sleepy look. He went on staring at Tholian in a vague, friendly way, though he had never felt less vague or less friendly in his life. But Brid was so shaken that she had to put on an act.

"Funny you should ask," she said, with artificial brightness. "We don't quite know—"

"Yes, we do, Brid," Moril said, fearing she was going to babble herself into trouble. "Dagner went back to Markind." It was a risky thing to say, but Moril knew that if Tholian already knew that Dagner had been arrested and why, it did not matter what he said anyway.

"Did he, indeed?" said Tholian, and there was no telling whether he had heard about Dagner or not. "And what about the other brother—er—Collen, was it?"

Moril knew Tholian had not seen Kialan in Markind. If he had, none of them would have been allowed to leave. He must have heard Ganner talk about him later. And no one would be surprised to find Ganner had got something wrong. Moril opened his mouth to say they had not got another brother, but Brid, to his annoyance, came in first, with tremendous verve: "Oh, Collen! He's so stupid you never know *what* he'll do! But we think he went with Dagner."

"Curious," said Tholian. His untrustworthy eyes slid over Brid, and over her again. "Now I thought I was reliably informed that there were three of you giving a show in Updale this morning."

That had obviously been a fatal mistake. But how could they have known Tholian was so near? The only thing to do was to say that the third one had been Dagner. Moril drew a breath to say it, but once more,

Brid rushed in. "Yes, of course. But that's what I was telling you. Collen went back after that. He said he was going to Neathdale and he—er—he got a lift in a farm wagon."

Moril sadly wished that Brid would let him do the talking. Brid was not as clever as she thought she was. No doubt she had thought she was doing very well, but she had first admitted Kialan's existence and now that he was quite near, and Moril knew there was no need to have done either. Tholian had never seen Kialan in their company. He was only going by guess. But now he was almost certain. He was looking at Brid, worrying her by just looking, and obviously enjoying the way he was worrying her.

"I don't think you quite understand the position," Tholian said when Brid, flushed and alarmed, had dropped her eyes from his pale ones to her boots. "I'm ready to send you both back to Markind safely, in exchange for Kialan Kerilsson. Not otherwise. Is that understood now?"

"I don't understand you at all," Brid said valiantly.

Tholian looked at Moril. "Do you?"

Moril tried to repair some of the damage Brid had done by saying, "Not really. Who's this person you're talking about?"

The only result of this was that Tholian turned his eyes back to Brid. "Keril," he said, "as I'm sure you know, is Earl of Hannart." Without bothering to turn round, he snapped his fingers to some of the men near.

They came hurrying up. "Listen," said Tholian. "Kialan Kerilsson is about five feet seven, solidly built, with a dark complexion and fair hair. His nose is aquiline and his eyes are much the same color as mine. Start searching the woods for a boy of that description."

The men at once turned and went hurrying farther into the thronged valley. Brid, as Moril knew she would, showed her consternation by saying, with horrible brightness, "What a queer kind of person that sounds!"

"No, no," said Tholian. "Just a typical Northerner." Beyond him, captains waved their arms and shouted orders. In a matter of seconds, quite a surprising number of soldiers left off drilling and moved at a run toward the woods behind Moril and Brid. Moril could only hope that Kialan had had the sense to cross the road and go North as fast as he could. Tholian's eyes moved sideways to make sure his orders were being carried out and then turned back to Brid. "You seem worried," he said, and laughed at her.

"Not in the least," Brid lied haughtily.

"But you don't," said Tholian, looking at Moril. "Why not?"

Moril did not see why Tholian should make a game of him. "Why did you kill my father?" he said.

Tholian was not in the least discomposed. The cool way he took the question upset Moril more than a little. It reminded him of Lenina. "Now, why was it?" Tholian said, pretending to remember. Moril thought of Lenina coolly stopping Clennen's bleeding and saw an actual family likeness to Lenina in Tholian's calm face. He wished he had not seen it. "I was having a little trouble finding Kialan," said Tholian, "as I recall. But I think the main reason I killed him was that it was probable he was the Porter."

Brid gasped, which amused Tholian. Moril felt hopeless, though he managed not to show it. "If you thought that, why didn't you have him arrested?" he said.

"Legally, instead of murdering him," said Brid, who was in such despair that she no longer cared what she said.

"But that would have been a silly thing to do," Tholian said laughingly. "A man arrested and tried for crimes like the Porter's very easily becomes a hero. You hang him, and people take his side or even rebel in his memory. Besides, I've seen Clennen give his shows in Neathdale. And I really didn't see why he should be given the chance to put on the biggest performance of his life. He'd have enjoyed it too much."

"You—" Brid hunted for the nastiest word she knew. "Fiend!" she said. Tholian, of course, laughed.

Moril said nothing. Up till then he had disliked Tholian, and he was afraid of him, because he was powerful and had such queer eyes. But after that he hated him, violently and personally. He should have hated him before, he supposed, but the fact was that in an odd way, he had thought of Clennen's death almost as if it were an accident, unfair in the way accidents were. Now he knew Tholian had intended it to be unfair, he hated Tholian for it.

"And how did you find Father?" Brid said. "Did Ganner tell you, you murdering beast!"

Tholian, luckily for Brid, still seemed to find her funny. "Ganner? Oh no," he said. "I don't have to rely on Ganner for information. Though I must say, Ganner didn't seem to be breaking his heart over Clennen when I told him he was dead." He laughed. "I suppose we put Ganner in a bit of a spot," he said, "all turning up in Markind almost together that day." He looked at Brid, to see how she took that. Brid realized Tholian was trying to torment her. She stared haughtily away at the busy soldiers in the valley. Tholian's eyes looked past her, at something behind them. "One last thing," he said. "Never try to carry on like your father. It's stupid, and it never pays. If I'd copied my father, I wouldn't be here with an army."

There was a nasty reasonableness about this that annoyed Moril. "Yes, but you see," he said, "it was something that needed doing."

Tholian was not interested any longer. He stood up. "Bring him here," he said. "Move, can't you!"

A group of soldiers hurried up, dragging Kialan. Kialan was disheveled and red in the face. Twigs were clinging to his clothes. He was resisting, rather, but he also had his head bowed in the sullen way Moril had seen among the prisoners in Neathdale. It was the way you looked, Moril realized, when you were caught. You had it whether you were guilty or innocent. It did not surprise him that Kialan was caught. He had made the mistake of staying near the cart. No doubt he had hoped to help Brid and Moril. Perhaps, since he was now the eldest, he had felt responsible for them. But Moril did not feel one twinge of gratitude. He just felt sad. Kialan had hung about, and Brid had made sure Tholian guessed he was near. That was the trouble with people who thought too well of themselves.

11

"Ah! Kialan!" said Tholian. "Nice to see you where there aren't any other earls to interfere."

Kialan looked up at Tholian from among the soldiers, with his head still a little bowed, but did not answer. Moril noticed that it was indeed true as Tholian had said, that Kialan's eyes were almost the same color as Tholian's. It made him see the difference between them. For Kialan, scared and sullen though he was, had a direct and living look, and Tholian's eyes were blank and strange. It was clear that while Tholian thought of Brid and Moril as rather funny and not at all important, he thought of Kialan as quite another matter.

"I thought you'd appear on this road sooner or later," Tholian said. "But we were watching the Marshes, too, in case. I'm hoping to let your father know you really are our prisoner. You'll have to write him a letter."

"I'm blowed if I shall!" said Kialan. "Write it your-self."

"Very well. I will," agreed Tholian. "I suppose he'll recognize one of your ears if I send it with the letter. Hold him tightly," he said to the soldiers. He took a knife from a sheath at his belt and walked toward Kialan.

Kialan tried to back away and was held in place by two soldiers. "All right," he said hurriedly. "I'll write you a letter if you want." Moril did not blame him.

But Tholian took no notice. The blank look in his eyes did not alter. The soldiers screwed up their faces. Moril, sickened and terrified, realized that Tholian just wanted an excuse to hurt Kialan. He clutched the cwidder and wondered what he could do. Kialan, even more frightened, tried to duck his head away from the knife. "Hold him, I said!" said Tholian.

One of the soldiers took a handful of Kialan's hair. Brid, without really thinking what she was doing, plunged forward and tried to catch hold of Tholian's arm. She got no farther than the nearest soldier, who pushed her sharply away. Brid staggered back and bumped into Moril, jolting his right hand on the cwidder, so that he accidentally struck a long humming note from the deepest string.

An extraordinary buzzing numbness filled the air and seemed to be eating up Moril's brain. He could do nothing, and barely think. The noise pressed into his head and forced him down on his knees. Everything out-side his head was gray and pulsating, burring and blurred, and the feeling went on and on and on. He thought he saw Tholian, looking a little bewildered, stand still and slowly sheathe his knife, while Kialan and the soldiers all shook their heads like people who have been hit. Brid pressed both hands to her eyes. Their movements made Moril feel sick. He knelt with his head bent, looking at the pulsing earth, and wondered if he was going to die.

Brid knelt down beside him. "Moril, are you all right? It was the cwidder, wasn't it?" Moril shook his humming head at her, wanting her to be quiet.

Everyone except Moril seemed to have quite recovered, except that Tholian looked puzzled, as if he had forgotten a word that was on the tip of his tongue. "Tie him up for now," he said to the soldiers, in a rather irritated way. "Get some rope, one of you."

"You made Tholian forget!" Brid whispered. "Do attend, Moril. You might be able to do it again." But Moril could not attend. His face was so white that Brid became worried, which meant that she was very cross with him in a harsh, snapping whisper which hurt Moril's numbed head. Then Brid suddenly jumped to her feet and dashed away from him. "You can't do that!" she shouted. "It's cruel!"

That jerked Moril to his senses. He looked up and saw Kialan had been tied with his hands behind him to one of the stakes that carried the tent ropes. The reason for Brid's outcry was that Tholian, not satisfied with merely tying him, had put a noose round Kialan's tied hands and was hoisting them up his back. The effect must have been like having both arms twisted at once. Moril could see Kialan was in agony.

Tholian turned to Brid as soon as he had made the rope fast. "Can't?" he said. "Go back to your brother." When Brid did not move at once, Tholian advanced on her, with his strange eyes blank. "Are you going to do as I said?"

Brid was frightened enough to turn and run back to Moril. As she came, she mouthed, *Do something!*

Tholian started off toward where several captains were hovering, wanting to speak to him. "Those two are not to move from there," he said over his shoulder to the soldiers round Kialan.

"Moril," whispered Brid. "The cwidder. Make it undo the rope."

Moril wished he could. He was sure the cwidder was quite capable of releasing Kialan, if only he knew how to work it. Osfameron had made it move mountains. But Moril had not the slightest idea how to begin and was very much afraid of making a mistake and bringing that awful humming into his own brain again. Kialan tried to give him a brave look although he was grinning with pain. Moril could see him struggling to get into a more comfortable position when there was no way of doing so. And Tholian might leave him like that for hours. It was worth a try.

Remembering the way the cwidder seemed to play his thoughts, Moril set himself to imagine Tholian's noose pulling and twisting Kialan into that unnatural position. It was horrible. His arms ached and sweat dropped out from under his hair. He thought fiercely, This must *stop*! and gently touched the slack bottom string.

It chimed like a soft, deep bell. Moril braced himself against the humming, but it did not come. Its effect, though it was not at all what he expected, was on Kialan alone. He saw Kialan's head suddenly drop and his knees give. He did not move, and it was clear that only the ropes were holding him up. Terrified, Moril clapped his hand across the string and stopped it vibrating.

Brid rounded on Moril with tears whisking down her cheeks. "You stupid idiot! You've killed him!"

"Shut up!" Moril whispered, anxiously watching both Kialan and the soldiers just beyond him. "They'll realize. Look. He's breathing. He's only passed out."

"But what about the ropes?" Brid whispered.

Moril shook his head. "I can't. I was trying to. I think I can only make it work on people."

One of the soldiers turned and saw Kialan sagging. When Tholian came back from talking to the captains, they pointed Kialan out to him. Tholian simply shrugged and passed by on his way somewhere else.

"I *hate* Tholian!" said Brid.

Moril said nothing. He knelt on the ground, nursing his cwidder, thinking as he had never thought in his life before. The soldiers, meanwhile, looked at one another, looked around to see how far away Tholian was, and undid the noose from Kialan's hands, so that Kialan slid to his knees with his head hanging almost upside down.

"Look, Moril," Brid whispered. "You did undo the ropes, sort of."

Moril had seen perfectly well, though he gave no sign of it. He was as alert as he had been in the jail in Neathdale. He could have told Brid exactly how many captains, troops, and horsemen there were in the part of the valley they could see. He was aware of every time a group of new recruits came marching in, and how many came in each group. Four groups arrived while he knelt and thought and while Kialan hung in a heap, head downward. Moril saw that they did not come by the road, but down through the woods, to keep their mustering secret. He also saw that almost every new arrival was miserable. They trailed their feet and held their heads at that sullen angle Kialan and Dagner had both held theirs when they knew they were caught. He could see that few of them had joined Tholian's army willingly. But he was thinking, thinking. For he was sure that the cwidder he was hugging on his knees was capable of saving all three of them and getting them North with news of Tholian's army. He knew how it could be done. The only thing he did not know was how to call up the power in the cwidder to do it.

Since it was his thoughts the cwidder responded to, Moril tried to understand how he might feed his entire self through it into the enormous power he knew was needed. His father had said Moril was in two halves.

"Come together," Clennen had said, "and there's no knowing what you might do." Moril supposed Clennen had meant the way Moril was incorrigibly dreamy and also unbelievably alert at times, just as he was now. But as Kialan had noticed, he was often both at the same time, unless he went vague in self-defense. Moril thought that could not quite be it.

But there was another way he was in two halves. His mother was a Southern aristocrat, and his father a freedom-fighting singer from the North. As Dagner had said, there was no doubt it was a weird mixture. It was cold and hot, strict and free, restrained and outspoken, all at once. The trouble was, this did not quite add up to Moril. He did not think he had inherited much from his Southern ancestry—certainly none of the unfeeling tyranny that made his distant cousin Tholian so detestable.

But Tholian's calm cruelty had, in a horrible way, reminded him of Lenina. Moril remembered Kialan saying, "Your mother's a cool one." And that was it, of course. Lenina never lost her head, and neither did Moril. He knew that, if Brid had only let him, he could coolly have led Tholian to believe that none of them had ever set eyes on Kialan, just as Lenina might have done. Keeping your head was part of the strict standard of the South. It was the same strict standard that had kept Lenina so loyal to Clennen, even though she hated life in the cart and disagreed with the freedom fighting. And Moril saw that it was the same kind of strict loyalty that had brought him North—only, with him, it was loyalty to the North.

After this followed something very uncomfortable, which Moril would not have faced if he had not had such a pressing need to use the cwidder. He had to admit he had deserted Lenina. He had gone off and left her when she had been trying to make them happy. He hoped he had not made her too unhappy, because he knew that seeing Tholian in Markind had only given him the excuse he had been looking for to go North. And going off like that, he had been trying to deny the Southern part of him—all the strict, honorable things which were the good aspect of the South. It did not do to deny them, even though he thought he had been doing it out of loyalty to Clennen.

Then he tried to find out what he had got from Clennen. Goodness knew what strange blood the singers came from. They could all sing and play. They saw a little more than most people, and some of them dreamed dreams. But Moril knew that all he had got from Clennen himself were ideas of freedom and his love of the North. The rest was the common stock of the singers.

The puzzling part was that these two halves added up to three quite different people: Brid, Dagner, and Moril. Brid had Lenina's sharpness and some of Lenina's efficiency, and she had Clennen's love of an audience, without Clennen's gifts—though she thought she had them. Dagner had far more of the gifts, but he had all Lenina's reserve, and more. In fact, it had been very much in

Lenina's manner that Dagner had set off North to finish Clennen's work for him, knowing he had not the personality to do it. None of them had inherited the largeness that made Clennen what he was. And why had Clennen not told Brid or Dagner they were in two halves?

Moril found himself suddenly at a dead end. He saw he would have to get at the cwidder's power some other way. He had to. The third batch of recruits had just arrived. The valley was filling with soldiers, and the North did not know. And the Earl of Hannart would not dare move because of Kialan. And Moril knew Kialan was actively in danger from Tholian. Tholian passed several times, and each time he looked at Kialan's hanging body as if he wanted it awake and writhing.

Moril thought of the cwidder itself. Though Osfameron could use it on things, it seemed that Moril was only going to make it have an effect on people. That was right for music, in a way. You performed, and people listened and were affected by it. So what did you put into a performance to bring out the power?

Moril did not know. He had only the vaguest idea what he had done to make Kialan unconscious. All right, he thought. What *didn't* my father do, that he could never use the power more than once? And he thought of Clennen, from day to day, as he had known him, huge, genial, and sociable—and boring Kialan stiff by telling the same story three times over. He thought of the way Clennen had been the Porter, quite openly, enjoying deceiving people by the simple fact that he did it all in public, as obviously as possible. Kialan had been positive that this was what Clennen enjoyed particularly. Then Moril thought of Clennen saying "Remember that" so often—almost as if he hoped one of them might write all his sayings down one day. Perhaps Brid would, Moril thought, smiling a little. Then he remembered a particular saying of Clennen's, the day they picked Kialan up. Clennen had said the cart was like life. "You may wonder what goes on inside, but what matters is the look of it and the kind of performance we give." Later on Clennen had asked Dagner about another saying, and Dagner had got this one wrong. "Something about life being only a performance," Dagner had said.

And that was it, Moril thought. Clennen was all performance. Layers of performance. He was the best singer in Dalemark and he used it to play the Porter, and he was the Porter because he was using his sincere feelings about freedom to play the singer—to and fro, over and under, Clennen had performed, even to his own family. His whole life had said, "Look at me!" He had known he was a performer, and he had used that knowledge, just as Brid had used her real sorrow to perform with in Neathdale. But he could not use the cwidder. It was not going to say, "Look at me!" It did not work like that.

If you did not say, "Look at me!" what was the right way? With a joyous feeling of being on the right track, Moril thought of Dagner next. Kialan had called what was really Dagner's performance "a different kind of show." Moril felt warmly grateful to Kialan. Kialan pointed things out. If only because of this, Kialan deserved to be rescued and taken back to the warm-hearted, cocksure, outspoken North where he belonged.

But Dagner—Dagner had been diffident. He had never said, "Look at me!" because he was shy when people did. What he did was to show people his thoughts—a little—in his songs. "Look here," he seemed to say. "Excuse me. This is what I think. I hope you like it." And people did like it—not in the way they appreciated Clennen but as if they had been told something new.

Moril knew he was unable—at least for the present—to make something new, just as he was unable to use his real feelings for show, like Brid. That left the old songs, Moril's own specialty. Did they help? Yes, they did—thanks to Kialan again. Kialan, just this morning, had sung that song of the Adon's, and it might have been made about this very cwidder! Unbounded truth! Moril thought, in rising excitement. Not a thing cramped to time and bound in place! Neither was the cwidder when its power was used.

He had it, then. You performed. But you did not say "Look at me!" Nor could you say, like Dagner, "This is what I think." If Dagner's diffident way had been right, Clennen would have given the cwidder to Dagner. No. You had to stand up and come straight out with it. "This is *true*," you had to say. "*This is the truth.* And, though I may not get it over very well, it just *is.*" And it was horribly difficult to do.

Moril blinked a little, nerving himself up. The fourth group of new recruits was shuffling its way through the valley, and Tholian was coming back again. With him were the same hearthmen who had been with him by the lake. They all had the same unpleasant look of purpose, too. When they reached Kialan, Tholian jabbed at him with the toe of his boot. Kialan flopped.

"Bring him round," he said. "He's going to write me a letter presently." Then he looked across at Brid and Moril, and his eyes were like an owl's caught in a strong light at night. They knew he had no intention of sending them back to Markind.

"Moril," Brid said humbly, "do you think you can do anything?"

Moril scrambled stiffly to his feet, carefully not bumping the cwidder. "I'm going to try," he said, and began to play.

He started with a little sequence of chords, repeated over and over, in a rocking rhythm. He had to start slowly, while he found the thought the cwidder would respond to. He was terrified that Tholian would realize what he was trying to do and stop him, but, though all the men round Kialan glanced irritably at Moril, they obviously had no idea that he was doing anything important. Moril's fear faded. "Not all of you are bad," he told them through the cwidder. "Some are just afraid, others are not good, and you are doing wrong." Over and over, he told it.

And to his relief, the cwidder began to hum under his

hands. He had got it right. Moril could feel the power gather in it and then, slowly, go humming out over Tholian and his men, right off down the valley, and turn the corner to the part out of sight. The movements of everyone he could see grew slack and a little aimless, and Tholian yawned. Moril thrummed on. He would have rejoiced, except that he knew he was going to have to bring the lowest string in soon, and he was afraid of it. If its power ate into his own head this time, that was the end of his plan. Cautiously he struck it. *Sleep*, it sang, heavily sweet, off down the valley, following the humming path of the power he had already built up. *Sleep*. Tholian's head turned slowly, and he looked at Moril, mistily puzzled. Moril himself was wide awake. He knew it was all right. He had been caught in the power before because he had simply been thinking *No, no, no!* without meaning anything else. Now he meant *Sleep, all you out there.*

Tholian seemed to understand what Moril was doing. He came slowly toward Moril, lurching as if he was very tired. "Break that blessed thing!" he said. His voice was slurred, but he was fighting the cwidder's power for all he was worth.

Quickly Moril passed into a proper tune, a lullaby.

"Go back to the time
When your feelings were blind
When they rocked you and sang
Go to sleep."

If Moril had thought about it, he would have realized he was in fact making up something new. But he did not notice, because all he wanted to do was to put Tholian to sleep. The lullaby was like a gust of power. It held Tholian to the spot. Tholian knew what was happening, but he was helpless. Moril played the tune again, louder, and took pleasure in holding Tholian in place while the tune swept beyond him, out into the valley.

Tholian rubbed his eyes and tried to take a grip on himself. Beyond him, the men round Kialan yawned and the marching and cursing in the valley faded away. The air was clear for the full force of the song, and Moril gave it to them. *Go to sleep.* It went down the valley in slow waves, washing first over Tholian, then on and out. Tholian's eyelids drooped, his knees bent, and he dropped forward onto the trampled ground with his head in his arms. There he made one final movement of resistance and fell asleep. After him, the other people dropped down, too, back and back into the valley. Horses stood still and men keeled over beside them and lay sleeping. Beside Moril, Brid fell sideways and slept curled up as if she was still kneeling. That was a pity, but Moril did not see how he could have excluded her. He played on, sending out wave after wave of sleep-song, until the valley seemed thick with it, and he could almost see it hanging in the air and pulsing gently. Under it every soul was dead to the world.

At last, a little apprehensively, Moril left the cwidder still humming, hoping like that to make the power last, and went through the heavy, silent air to Kialan. He was still tied up. Tholian's friends had not untied him, though they had been about to. Moril went back through the humming silence and fetched the knife out of Brid's boot. "Thanks," he whispered, and he thought Brid stirred a little. With the knife he hacked through rope after tough rope, until Kialan rolled loose on the grass. He was still unconscious.

Moril bent down and shook him. "Kialan!" he said.

Kialan came round as he heard his name. Moril was almost sorry, because Kialan's face was suddenly full of pain and misery.

"It's all right," Moril whispered. "Everyone's asleep. Quick. I don't know how long it'll last."

Kialan climbed to his feet. He was very stiff and winced with every movement. He stared at Tholian, lying on the earth with his head in his arms, at Brid, and out at the silent, humming valley, full of a sleeping army. "Ye gods!" he said. "Was that the cwidder?"

"Yes," said Moril. "Quick." He ran back to Brid and shook her. Brid rolled about, but she did not wake.

Kialan came limping after him. "Suppose you leave her asleep?" he suggested. "Then when she wakes up, you'll know it's worn off."

Moril saw that was an excellent idea. The thing about Kialan, he thought as he raced for the cart, was that he had brains. Olob was dozing, too, which was more serious. Moril snapped his fingers under his nose. "*Olob!* Barangarolob!" And Olob shook his head and looked at

Moril wonderingly. Moril untied Olob and brought him toward Brid at a run, much though Olob objected to going near even sleeping enemies. As he hauled on the bridle, he thought how queer the valley looked with everyone in it lying asleep except for the lonely upright figure of Kialan. He dragged Olob up to Brid and opened the tailgate of the cart to make it easier to get her in. Then he gently put the cwidder back in its rack. It was still vibrating faintly.

"Throw the wine jar out," said Kialan. "Let's make the cart as light as we can."

Moril heaved out the great jar. It landed with a sploshy thump that ought to have woken the dead, but Brid, who was nearest, did not stir.

Kialan laughed. "Present for Tholian. Information he knows and money he doesn't want. He can drink our health."

Moril gave a muffled giggle at the idea, but he did not speak. He had a feeling that the one thing most likely to wake the sleepers was his voice. He climbed into the cart and threw out most of Dagner's purchases: candles, flour, lentils, and the remains of the rhubarb.

"Oh, he'll love those!" panted Kialan. Though he was still very stiff, he managed to lift the head and shoulders of Brid and heave the upper half of her into the cart. Moril took her shoulders and dragged her right in, where she settled with a little sigh. Kialan climbed in beside her. Moril latched the tailgate and got onto the driving seat.

"Now, Olob," he whispered. "Run. Run for your life."

Olob tossed his head and set off. He did not exactly run, but he took the cart briskly across the trampled earth to the road by which they had entered the valley. Moril looked over his shoulder as they went under the trees. Tholian was lying beside their heap of provisions. Beyond him, Moril thought he could see a faint haze vibrating quietly over the whole valley. The cwidder's power still held.

"What about those soldiers by the trestle?" Kialan said, as Olob clattered down the steep road.

"I don't know," Moril said anxiously. He had no idea how far the cwidder's power spread, and the trestle had been behind him as he played. When they came to the main road, Moril held his breath and Kialan craned sideways to get a sight of the trestle.

Those soldiers were asleep, too. Most of them were sprawled in the road, pigeon breastplates upward, snoring. One was asleep with his arms on the trestle, in a most uncomfortable position. Kialan gave a wild little laugh. "He'll be stiff when he wakes up!"

12

It was a short, steep climb up the last of the hill. Then they came out onto the green spread of the last Upland. They could see Mark Wood in the distance, gay green and bronzed by the afternoon sun, and beyond it, looking deceptively near, the gray bulk of the Northern mountains.

"Now you *must* run, Olob," said Moril.

Olob ran. It could not be called a gallop—Moril had never known Olob to gallop in his life—but he ran, and ran as fast as Moril had ever seen him go. Behind him the lightened cart wove from side to side and bounded in the ruts of the road. Kialan wedged his feet against the side of the cart and tried to hold Brid in one place, but they nevertheless pitched and rolled and bounced until it was a marvel Brid did not wake up. But Brid slept on, stirring once or twice when she hit the side of the cart, but never coming out of her deep sleep. Moril began to hope that it would last until they reached Mark Wood. Once they were there, they could hide the cart among the trees, with a good chance of escaping Tholian.

"How did you work it?" Kialan called jerkily above the rilling of wheels and banging of hooves. "The sleep."

Moril could not explain, any more than Dagner could explain how he made songs. "By thinking," he said. "You said a lot of things that helped me."

They jounced and battered another half mile. "I had a weird dream," Kialan called, "while I was tied up. I dreamed—wow, what a bump!—I dreamed you took me along to your father's grave, by the lake, and opened that board I carved, just as if it was a door. Then you said, 'Do you mind getting in here for a while? I'll call you when it's safe to come out.' And—I say, what happens if we lose a wheel?—and I went in and went to sleep. What do you think of that?"

"I don't know," said Moril. "I might have done. There's no one behind, is there?"

There was no one, though they could hardly believe it. The wide Upland seemed empty. They rattled, wagging this way and that, through a village, and that seemed asleep, too. Olob pounded on, blowing now, and Brid still slept. The sun sank, and Mark Wood was nearer. Twilight seemed to come from the trees and soak into the green landscape around them. Big clouds were building up beyond the mountains. The sunset shot them with fierce pink and lakes of moist yellow.

"You know," jerked Kialan, "when I thought—in the valley—that we weren't going to get away this time, I wanted to apologize. I was pretty awful when I first came into the cart, wasn't I?"

"We were, too," Moril called over his shoulder. "We didn't know what had been happening to you. Was it horrible in Holand?"

There was a bouncing, battering pause. "Ghastly," said Kialan. "But it wasn't only that. I didn't understand. I thought you were all—beggars or something, and I thought—oh, of fleas and ignorance and so on for the whole way North. And I was fed up."

Moril laughed. "You looked it."

They reached the verge of Mark Wood almost as the sun set. Olob had not run so far for years. Moril could see steam rising off him in the thickening twilight. His sides were heaving under the scarlet harness, and there were flecks of foam along him. The road went upward into the trees, under a sloping cliff, and, though it was not a steep rise, Olob slowed down.

"I'll have to let him walk," Moril said, acutely sorry for him. "He's had enough."

So Olob fell to a weary plod, and everything suddenly seemed ten times more peaceful. They could hear birds cawing and calling in the great beech trees above.

"Good gracious!" said Brid, sitting up. "Where are we? Why do I feel so bruised?"

Moril knew it was bound to happen, but he wished it had been farther into the wood and not just when Olob was tired out. They explained to Brid. She was rather indignant.

"Using me as a kind of sleep measure! I like that!"

"It was a jolly good idea," said Kialan, "though I says it as shouldn't."

But Brid had realized that Tholian was probably after them by now and changed to being as nervous as a cat. She turned her head back over her shoulder and implored Moril to get in among the trees quickly. Moril looked over his shoulder, too. Between the tree trunks, he could see the darkening green of the Upland and a long stretch of the road. It was empty.

"I will when we get to the top of this hill. Olob's tired."

The dark gathered quickly under the trees, but it was still light enough to see. Brid squawked faintly. There were people among the trees on horses, coming slowly down the hill on the cliff side. But Olob gave no sign of alarm. Moril trusted Olob and kept on the road, in spite of Brid's imploring whispers. All the same, it was rather frightening the way that the horsemen, as soon as they saw the cart, turned toward it and increased their pace. They came fairly thudding down on them.

There were three of them. They drew up beside the cart, and Olob stopped walking. Kialan stood up and stared at the foremost rider, and the rider stared back.

"You blinking idiot! What did you have to come South for?" Kialan said, and burst into tears.

Somehow, though they would never have dreamed of

addressing Clennen as a blinking idiot, Brid and Moril had no doubt that the rider was Keril. They watched Kialan jump awkwardly down, and the man dismount and hug him, and they were sure of it.

"Konian—they *hanged* him!" Kialan said.

"I know. We heard from a fisherman," said Keril. "It was you I came for. I was hoping Clennen might know—where *is* Clennen?" he asked.

"He's dead," said Brid, and began to cry, too.

Moril sat on the driving seat and felt tears trickling down his face. As far as he knew, he was crying for the whole situation, because he was on his own now, and always would be.

"There's an army," said Kialan. "Tholian's gathered an army to attack the North. In a valley over there. They're probably after us now."

Keril exchanged glances with the two other riders. "We've a small force in the wood. How big is this army?"

"Pretty big," Moril said, sniffing. "There were five hundred men, divided into three troops, and a hundred horsemen in the part of the valley we saw. But that was probably only a quarter of it."

"How do you know?" said Kialan. "Did you count?"

"No. I just know," said Moril. "And recruits came in four batches, while we were there, twenty-three in the first, and thirty-two in—"

"Too many for us, in fact," said Keril. "Thanks, lad. Let's get back to our camp and get fortified."

The Northerners' camp was along the cliff, chosen with an eye to defense. When tired Olob dragged the cart up to it, there was already a bustle of preparation. The campfires were being put out and the two provision wagons dragged across the only place where it could be reached from the wood. These preparations should have made Moril feel alarmed, but in fact, he felt safer and happier than he had been for days. He could see by the light of the few lanterns that the mere fifty or so men bustling about had, many of them, the same dark-fair coloring as Kialan. Moril remembered now that it was something you only saw in the North. Keril was the odd man out, because he was dark, though his nose was the same shape as Kialan's.

They were taken into a tent, where they had the best meal they had had since Markind. While they were eating, Moril gathered that the Earl had been camping here for two days. The night before, he had ridden South almost to Neathdale in hopes of meeting Clennen and hearing news of Kialan, and he had been meaning to do the same that night, too. It was Henda's message offering to ransom Kialan that had brought him South. Up till then, everyone in Hannart had supposed that Kialan had been hanged, too.

In a tired and muddled way, they told their part, as far as Dagner's arrest. Keril, who had been sad rather than astonished at Clennen's death and not at all surprised to hear of Lenina returning to Markind, broke in angrily when he heard of Dagner. They felt sure he was thinking of Konian, too, when he said, "Fancy hanging a boy that age! I wish I could *do* something—er, Moril—is that your name?"

"Not really," said Kialan. "His name's Osfameron. And Brid's Manaliabrid."

Keril forgot his anger and threw back his head and laughed.

"What's so funny?" said Brid. She was sensitive about their names.

"Well, history repeating itself, I suppose," said Keril. "Kialan's the Adon, you see."

"No, he isn't," said Moril. "The Adon lived two hundred years ago. Kialan told me."

"But the heir of Hannart is always called the Adon," Keril explained, and was sad, thinking of Konian.

Moril and Kialan looked at one another by the light of the carefully shaded lantern. Moril was thoroughly put out. If Kialan was the Adon, then he had been living the life of his dearest imaginings for nearly a month without realizing it. It had not seemed like that at all. Yet, thinking of the weird dream Kialan had told him of, he suspected that it might have been history repeating itself indeed. "Why didn't you tell me?" he said.

"I didn't sort of think," said Kialan. "I was just me, trying to get home." He was thinking about his dream, too. He nodded toward his father. "Tell him about the cwidder."

Moril told Keril how he put Tholian and his army to sleep. Keril marveled a little, and he asked Kialan to confirm it, but he took it, on the whole, in the same matter-of-course way that Kialan did. "May I see the cwidder?" he said.

Moril felt his way out of the tent to the cart and came back with the cwidder. Keril took it and held it under the light of the lantern. He ran his fingers down the inlay, over the strange patterns. "Yes, this *is* the one," he said. "I used to think Clennen was boasting when he said it was Osfameron's, but I wasn't much of a hand at the old writing in those days." His square, practical-looking finger pointed to a line of swirls and dots made of slivers of mother-of-pearl. "Here it says, 'I sing for Osfameron' and there"—his finger moved to another line of signs— "it says, 'I move in more than one world.'" He smiled at Moril and handed the cwidder back. "Be careful of it."

Moril fell asleep that night hugging the cwidder, and as far removed as he could from Kialan's knees and elbows. They were a little crowded because Keril had given up his own tent to Brid. Moril had meant to do some more thinking, but he was far too tired. He awoke at dawn, because somebody came to talk to Keril, very annoyed with himself. For he was sure that, by reading the strange writing, Keril had really told him how to use the cwidder as Osfameron had used it.

There was no time for thinking for a while. The man had come to tell Keril that a troop of riders had gone by on the road during the night and that the same troop had just come galloping back, probably on their way to report to Tholian. Both times they had been going too fast to notice the camp.

It was clear the riders had been looking for the cart. Tholian must have assumed that Moril, Brid, and Kialan were driving North as fast as they could. Since the riders had not found them, Keril knew Tholian would think Kialan had already reached the North, and his news with him. "And if I were Tholian," he said, "I'd be on the march now, before the North can be ready for war. We'd better hurry."

They broke camp and went. The cart went, too, with a strange youthful horse between the shafts, for more speed. Olob looked so disconsolate that Brid said she would ride him. "He'll let me," she said, "if no one puts a saddle on him. I hate him to feel neglected." So she rode Olob bareback with her boots on—for, after all, she was in company with an earl—and Olob did not seem to object. He was just rather slow. Brid had some difficulty keeping up with the cart, where Moril sat with his cwidder, thinking. The cart was being driven by a large slow-spoken Northerner called Egil, and Kialan had borrowed Egil's horse.

"You know," Brid said to Moril, "I do wish Kialan hadn't turned out to be the Adon. I feel embarrassed about liking him."

Moril was very busy thinking, but he chuckled at this. "You'll get used to it."

"You're *hopeless*!" said Brid, not as angry as she meant to be.

Kialan's turning out to be the Adon was important to

Moril's thoughts, too. It was one of three things he kept trying to put together in his mind. The other two were what the writing said on the cwidder and his own discovery about the way you had to tell the truth with it. He thought it was odd how easily one got used to new ideas. What had seemed an entirely new thing yesterday was an old idea today, which he could use to take him on somewhere else. He went on trying to put ideas together while the band of Northerners hurried through Mark Wood.

They were not taking the road because Keril dared not risk being seen. There were clearings and villages all along the road and probably enough people in them to hold the small number of Northerners up until Tholian came to wipe them out. So they worked their way North through the trees. It was easy enough for the riders, but heavy going for the cart and the wagons. And everybody was worried about the final stretch, where they would have to come out of the trees in order to get to Flennpass. Once they were in the pass, they would be safe. It was guarded by Fort Flenn, which was the southernmost fort of the North.

Night came before they were out of the wood. Keril was anxious at their slow progress, but they had been traveling all day and they were tired. They had to risk camping for the night. After supper, round a carefully shaded campfire, they told Keril their doings in more detail. Kialan said things which confirmed Moril's feeling that his time in Holand had been more horrible than they had realized. Keril became so angry and sad that Kialan changed the subject and talked about the wine jar.

"I regret leaving Tholian all that gold," he said. "He can have the rhubarb with pleasure, and the papers, but we should have taken the money out."

"Set your mind at rest," said Brid. "I did. I put it in the money locker."

Everyone laughed. Brid wanted indignantly to know what they took her for, leaving a sum like that in a wine jar.

"But I wish I knew whose it was, and where Father got it from," she said.

"I think," said Keril, "that it was probably the remains of what I gave him for expenses. I gave him a hundred gold every year in Dropwater. No," he said when Brid offered to give it back. "Keep it. You deserve it. You can use it as pocket money when you're living in Hannart."

In this way they gathered that Keril intended them to live with him in Hannart.

"That's frightfully nice of you," Brid said awkwardly. "Because I don't know what else we'd do, do you, Moril?"

"It's the least I can do," said Keril. "I owe Clennen a great deal. If it hadn't been for him, we'd have had no news from the South worth having." Then he told them things about Clennen they had not known before. Keril had met Clennen in the South in the days when he was still only the Adon, and they had both helped in the uprising there. But Keril's father died, and he had to go North. Clennen stayed in the South, until soon after he met Lenina. Then, what with old Tholian's fury and the failure of the uprising, Clennen found the South too hot to hold him. He went to Hannart and became singer to the court. Dagner, Brid, and Moril had all been born in Hannart. It had been Clennen's idea to go South again when they heard reports of what was going on. The Porter had been his idea, too. But Keril had thought of staging the quarrel so that no one would suspect Clennen was Hannart's agent.

Moril sat staring into the fire, dreaming of Hannart.

"What is it, Moril?" Kialan said jokingly. "Dreams coming true?"

Moril looked up and grinned. He did not say anything, but he went to sleep sure that Kialan had just told him the way the cwidder really worked.

He thought it out as he rode in the cart next day. It came to him first as a memory. It had rained in Crady, so Clennen had told one of the stories of the Adon indoors, and Moril had looked up to see Kialan in the audience. He had been annoyed, because he thought of Kialan as part of dreary, everyday life, and he had felt as if he had a foot in two worlds which were spinning apart from one another. Yet Kialan was the Adon—or *an* Adon—all the time. And the cwidder itself said, "I move in more than one world."

It came on to rain just then, though not as heavily as it had rained in Crady. Moril smiled and lifted his face into the wet. They were nearly in the North, and it rained a lot there. His smile became rather rueful as he realized that in none of his dreams of Hannart or hazy imaginings of the cart on green roads had he ever thought of its raining. The cwidder had made a muzzy sound. And that was the point. That kind of dream was not true. There were true dreams, but they had to be part of life as well, just as life, to be good, had to embody dreams, or a good song had to have an idea to it. The Adon's song Kialan had sung had been saying that. But Osfameron's song had gone one farther and talked of the other worlds the cwidder moved in.

Moril thought of the way life and dreams had met for him, willy-nilly, on this journey. But he knew they met in him naturally, too, when he could be miles away, thinking, and yet count all the soldiers in that valley, or every beech tree they were passing at the moment. He saw that Clennen had not got it quite right. He had been too practical to see. The important thing was that Moril *was* in two halves. Provided he knew what was true in both, he could use the cwidder as it should be used. He could send ideas through it, into reality.

About midmorning, they came to the end of Mark Wood. Moril looked past Egil's broad back at the mountains at last, vividly close, and the deep V in them that was Flennpass. The rain had stopped, but the clouds over the mountains were heavy with more. It was a gray, threatening scene. Fort Flenn was out of sight, behind a sharp peak, since it was at the North end of the pass, but Moril could see the South's answer to it. The wood had been cleared for a mile or so in front of the pass, so that no one could go in or out of it unseen. He looked at the mountains across a desolation of tree stumps, charred from frequent burning, with new bright green bushes and saplings springing up between, because it had not yet been cleared this year.

The Northerners stopped at the edge of the trees. Moril did not at first know why.

"The Lord of Mark, I think," Keril said to his captain. "Tholian must have set him to watch for the cart."

Moril leaned round Egil, and his stomach fluttered at the number of the horsemen drawn up across the pass in the distance. They were clearly Southerners, and in war gear, and there were at least twice as many of them as there were Northerners in Keril's band.

"He can't be expecting us," said the captain. "I'll take an oath no one saw us come through. It'll give him a fair old shock when we ride out at him."

"I know," said Keril, "but I'd be more comfortable if we were twice the number."

"Oh come!" said someone else, laughing. "One Northerner's worth ten Southerners. Any day."

Moril thought for a moment. Yes. Everyone believed that. None of the band was particularly worried, and even Brid was looking confidently at Keril, sure they would get past the Lord of Mark without trouble. Northerners were famous fighters. But Keril was evidently thinking it was more important to get through to the North than to get courageously killed on the way.

"Would you like there to seem more of us?" Moril

called over to him. "I think I can do it."

Keril made a bit of a face. "I only wish you could."

"I bet he can," said Kialan.

Moril slung the cwidder round his neck and began to play the "Eighth March." It was never played in the South, for obvious reasons. But, as Clennen often said, it went to such a brisk time that only the North thought of it as a march.

> "We are the men of the North, the North,
> And I'll tell you how much we're worth, we're worth—
> One man is as good as ten Southern men
> And each of us marches as ten."

For a moment, until the cwidder began to hum, Moril was afraid he had got it wrong after all. But the hum increased and became almost like a lighthearted whistling, and the wood was suddenly full of men, horses, and wagons. Some of the Northerners cried out in alarm.

Kialan burst out laughing. "Oh, well done, Moril! Only nine more pink carts are a bit much!"

Moril glanced from side to side and could not help laughing. There were indeed nine more pink carts. One of them had a tree apparently growing through it. And a false Moril sat in each playing an illusory cwidder. What he had done was to reflect their own band nine times over, just as the song said. After all, it was an illusion that one Northman was worth ten Southerners. And the riders and wagons were exactly that, like reflections in a mirror. The Northmen realized. People began to laugh and wave at their own reflections. Consequently, the false nine-tenths waved and laughed also.

Keril laughed with the rest. "Keep playing, Moril. Off we go."

Moril played on gaily, and they moved out from among the trees, the real and the false men together. They rode among the bushes and stumps under a stormy sky, toward the road, and the real men had to go round saplings and the larger stumps, but Moril's illusions went straight through everything in their path. When they reached the road, there was a good deal of confusion and much laughter. The Northmen tried to get out of the way of their own shadows, until they grasped that there were four reflections on the left and five to the right, and that the fifth band from the left was the real one, entitled to use the road. Once they had sorted that out, they trotted on in fine style, many of them singing the "Eighth March" as Moril played. And on either side the nine repetitions went straight through the landscape, pink carts through bushes and horses through saplings.

Moril sat in the midmost pink cart beaming with elation. It was the most splendid proof that he had done his thinking right. The whistling hum of the cwidder in his hands, calling the strange army into being, took on an extra note, like a sort of purring, as it reflected Moril's pleasure and amusement. Behind him, Brid and Kialan thought it one of the funniest things they had seen. They thought it even funnier when Olob sensed enemies near and began prancing about, setting the nine other Olobs prancing, too, and the nine other Kialans grabbing at his bridle to help Brid control him.

By the pass the Lord of Mark's force drew uneasily together, seeing five hundred apparent Northmen riding merrily toward them. As Keril's band drew nearer, they could see the enemies' uneasiness mounting. Ordinary Northerners maybe they could face. But what was to be done with enemies who went straight through small trees and seemed none the worse for it? When they were near enough to distinguish faces, and only a hundred yards from the camp the Lord of Mark had set up to the right of the road, a group of the Southerners panicked and had to be brought back by some others. Moril could see a man who must be the Lord of Mark riding up and down imploring his men to keep calm. He laughed. Then two shadow wagons and a pink cart went right through the camp without disturbing so much as a guy rope. A number of the Southerners wailed with terror. Moril thought, Why not? and threw in the lowest string. *Run!* it boomed beneath the gay tune.

The Lord of Mark broke and ran, and his men with him. They galloped frantically away to right and left along the mountains and vanished in the bushes, leaving Flennpass open. A roar of laughter went up from Keril's band.

Brid's voice cut through it. "Moril! *Look!*"

Moril glanced back. Huge numbers of horsemen were on the dark edge of Mark Wood, and more were among the trees. The horses' legs were all moving steadily, but they were too far away for sound to carry, and the riders seemed to glimmer along as if they were an illusion, too. Only they were no such thing. They were the forefront of Tholian's army.

13

Moril gave the alarm with a sweep of his hand on the cwidder. Though Keril also looked over his shoulder, it was only to confirm what the cwidder said. In that same moment they were all going hell for leather for Flennpass and Fort Flenn at the other end of it. The ghostly nine-tenths had gone as if they had never been. Moril knew there was no time for illusions. As the cart bucked and wove along, he hung on to the side and looked back.

Tholian's army was coming at a steady speed across the cleared stretch. If anyone saw the cart, or the sudden decrease in the size of their band, there was no sign of it. The host of horsemen simply came onward. It might be pursuing Keril, but it looked more as if their band would be merely the first incident in the invasion. Tholian had no need to hurry, since the North was unprepared. Olob knew the army was behind and Brid could not control him. Kialan had taken the reins and was dragging him along with Egil's horse. Moril thought this might well make Olob worse. Olob had never really accepted Kialan. But there was nothing Moril could do.

They swept into the pass with a gathering thunder of hooves. It held a good road between clifflike walls, which narrowed at the Northern end. They had to string out as they went, with the cart and the wagons bouncing in the rear. Egil and the other drivers were using their whips. Brid was smacking Olob. Moril thought they would just make it to the fort, though it would be a close thing—and it seemed closer every second. The army behind had no wagons with the vanguard to slow them down. They were catching up steadily. As Keril's troop came to the narrowest part of the pass, where the fort stood chunkily above on the skyline, Moril looked round to see the first line of Tholian's cavalry coming into the wide end of the pass, and multitudes of others milling behind.

Keril had reached the fort, when Moril looked back, and was shouting to the people inside. There was a moment's delay. But the defenders must have seen all that happened. A sudden black space appeared where the great gate had been, and some of the Northmen rode into it. The space between the cliffs was filled with noise, the huge drumming of a mass of hooves, and some sharper sounds. Moril thought the fort was firing on the enemy.

Things began to fall around the cart and bounce off the wagons. They were not from the fort, but from the advancing army. Moril could do nothing but hope. It was long-range, and he thought it must be difficult to fire from a cantering horse. But to Olob, struggling against Kialan's impatient hand on his bridle, it was the last straw. In his terror, he turned clean round, dragging Kialan and Egil's horse with him. Brid lurched and hung on to his mane. A number of the Northmen saw what was happening and turned back to help. And the narrow end of the pass at once became a dangerous bottleneck, full of riders trying to go two ways at once. Egil roared out a curse and pulled the cart up. Moril jumped down, with the cwidder slung across his shoulders, and ran toward Olob.

"Let him go!" he shouted to Kialan. "Olob, stop it!"

Luckily, Kialan had the sense to let go. For, as Moril ran up, Olob reared, frightened out of his wits. There were just too many enemies for him. Moril had to dodge his lashing front hooves, and Brid slid helplessly down his back, over his tail, and onto the ground. And as Olob stood high above them, screaming and slashing, an unlucky bullet took him clean through the head. His great brown body came down between Moril and Brid with the force of a falling oak. He was dead before he hit the ground.

They stared at one another over the huge corpse.

"Olob now," said Brid.

"Right!" said Moril. "That does it!"

Keril's captain had been sorting out the bottleneck. Now he galloped up and held down his hand to Brid. "Catch hold, lass! Up you come!" Brid caught hold and scrambled up behind him.

Kialan shouted to Moril and held down a hand to him, but Moril did not attend. He raced to the cliff at the side of the pass and climbed it like a maniac with the cwidder bumping and booming on his back. He was at the top in seconds—how, he never knew. Heaving deep breaths, he went scrambling along the cliff edge until he had a view down into the pass. He saw Kialan, not very far below him, at the gate of the fort, waving and shouting something. He seemed to mean there was a door in the fort at the top of the cliff. Then he went into the fort, and the gate shut.

But Moril, now he knew the Northmen were in the fort, was not interested in the door. He looked Southward along the pass. It was packed with Tholian's horsemen more than halfway along. They were going more slowly now, because of the narrower space, and beyond the wide end of the pass, as far as he could see, there were more riders coming. It was truly an invasion.

Moril stood up and slung the cwidder in front of him. He felt a spatter of rain. There looked to be a storm coming, which was all to the good. For a second he gazed up at the heavy bruiselike clouds, feeling a little awed. He thought anyone would who was about to use the cwidder as Osfameron had used it.

Then he looked down into the pass where Olob's body lay in the middle of the road. The nearest riders were not so far from it now. He struck one sharp, rolling chord, and the power in the cwidder swelled with it.

There was no humming, but he could feel the power. "You're not coming North," he said to the jostling riders. "And this is why." He struck two more chords. The power almost choked him. The answer was a great dagger of lightning, green and perilous, lancing down over the cliffs. A peal of thunder followed, and Moril led it on, pealing the lowest note of the cwidder, so that the power in it could grow. When it stopped, he spoke, in the way the singers spoke an incantation. He said:

> *"Kialan and Konian were caught in a storm.*
> *The one you hanged in Holand had not harmed*
>   *anyone,*
> *Nor had Kialan when you caught him. This is for*
>   *Konian first."*

He struck another chord, followed by a swinging, hanging, frantic phrase, and felt the power in the cwidder grow again. Then he said:

> *"Unlucky Clennen lies by a lake in Markind,*
> *The singer you stabbed on suspicion only*
> *And prevented him performing. This is for the Porter*
>   *Clennen."*

He struck a sharp chord and a rolling one. The first horsemen were now right beneath him. They did not pause when they came to Olob but trampled over him and on. Moril saw, but he looked beyond them, to the center of the pass. Tholian was there, jostled on either side by his favorite friends. Moril waited, quite confident and implacable, and let them come on while the power in the cwidder grew yet again. Then he spoke his last stave:

"There was no mercy shown by the magistrate in Neathdale
To Dastgandlen Handagner. There was death in the South
And weeping in the Uplands. Now war comes North,
And all through Tholian. This is for Tholian."

He struck the cwidder again, and again, and yet a third time, vengefully. The power grew enormous, until it possessed Moril, the sky, the clouds, and the entire pass. Then, as Moril had known they would, the hills began to walk.

They started mildly and slowly, as if the mountains on either side of the pass were shrugging their shoulders. But in a second or so, the shrugging was a deep rhythmic jigging. The tops of the cliffs bent and marched, regularly inward and downward, walking, piling, inescapably trudging together to fill the pass. The thunder pealed and was drowned in the grinding of ton after ton of rock, moving and jogging inward. Almost lost in the greater din was the lesser screaming of men and horses. At the far end of the pass Moril could see riders swirling and struggling to get back or get out. But leisurely, sleepily, rhythmically, the mountains were filling the center. The cliff Moril was on marched with the rest, downward and forward. Moril leaned backward to keep his balance and let it take him, until he was standing at the head of a heap of jumbled rocks, almost over the place where Olob had been shot. The rocks were piled into the rift, choking it so that it was no longer a pass.

Moril did not spend long looking, because the rain came down, and the torn surfaces of the rocks were black with it. But he knew, as he turned round to keep the cwidder from the worst of the wet and stripped off his coat to cover it, that Tholian was underneath somewhere and Barangarolob had plenty of company. He looked across to see that the fort was safe, as he had intended. It was there, standing on a steep-sided block of steady rock, and Keril was picking his way over the ruin of the cliff toward him.

"I've just done something really horrible," Moril said to him. "Haven't I?"

Keril jumped from one rock to another and then onto the one where Moril stood. "I don't think we had much chance of holding the pass otherwise," he said.

"You don't understand," said Moril. "I did it because of Olob." He leaned against Keril and burst into tears. Keril took off his own coat, wrapped it round Moril, and led him quietly back over the rocks to the fort.

They left the fort the following day, after a big force of men from the North Dales arrived there to make sure the Southerners did not attempt to attack over the fallen rocks. Moril did not see as much of the journey to Hannart as he would have liked. He was exhausted and spent most of the time asleep in one of the wagons. Every so often he woke to find they were on a green road, or in a wood where the trees were still only budding in the later spring of the North, and went to sleep happy. He was awake to see the Falls at Dropwater, which he would not have missed for worlds. And by the time they reached Hannart he had come to himself again.

He was disappointed, but not really surprised, to find Hannart a city far larger than Neathdale, in the center of a big valley. Flags were flying in honor of their arrival. There were crowds of people carrying flags or flowers. Hannart was full of flowers in fields, in gardens, on trees, and growing wild, thick as the grass, on the steep sides of the mountains. Moril could smell them as soon as they entered the valley. At the end of the valley was a great tall thing, like a castle four times life-size, picked out in gold and blue and green.

Moril stared at it. "Whatever is that?"

"That's the steam organ," said Kialan. "Haven't you heard about it? They'll probably play it tonight. It makes the most splendid noise."

"I wish someone had told me," said Moril.

There was a feast that night, in their honor, and as Kialan had thought, the steam organ played. In a strong steamy smell of coal and oil, it thundered out well-known tunes, like a mountain singing, or the grandfather of all music, and made Brid and Moril laugh. It seemed most fitting that Hannart should own such a thing, because the place was full of music, not only then, but at all times. Cowbells clinked in the steep meadows. Women called the cows home in a kind of song, not unlike Brid's "Cow-Calling" song. In the city there were tunes for crying everything that was on sale and for telling the hours of the watch. There was singing and dancing somewhere almost every night. The saying was that you could tell someone came from Hannart because whatever they did, they sang, and if they did not sing, they whistled.

Keril lived right in the center of the city, in a house twice the size of Ganner's. Unlike Ganner's house, it was always open. The cheerful people of Hannart seemed to use its front courtyard as another part of the main square. There was always someone there, gossiping or selling something, and, if anything unusual happened, they came on into the rest of the house to tell Keril about it. Since there were also large numbers of people who actually lived in the house, Moril found it almost impossible to sort out who came from where.

Brid loved it. She had never been happier in her life. "I often remembered it, but I didn't think it was real!" she was fond of saying.

Moril enjoyed it, too. He liked the liveliness, the carelessness, and the way people rushed up to Keril and said what they pleased. He could not imagine anyone doing that in the South. Moril liked Keril. He liked Halida, Kialan's mother. He enjoyed being with Kialan, and he loved the perpetual music. But he was too hot in the city and far too hot in the house. He kept having to go out on the hillsides. At night it was worse, and he slept in one of the gardens when he could. When Halida realized this, she gave him a room on the ground floor, opening on one of the gardens. Moril was grateful, but he hardly went into the room, and he only slept there if it was raining.

Brid and Kialan consulted about it and went to see what Keril thought.

"Yes," said Keril. "I'm afraid he'll be off again, one of these days. I hope not yet, though. I owe it to Clennen to see he has an education."

After that Brid watched Moril like a hawk. Moril showed no sign of wanting to leave. He seemed perfectly happy getting the education Keril thought he should have. He spent long hours playing his cwidder with Kialan, arranging songs and trying to make new ones. He rode with Kialan and Brid and walked on the hills with them. It was just that he was too hot indoors, and there was something at the back of his mind he did not want to think about yet.

Now Flennpass was blocked, there was very little news from the South. It was nearly a month before some fishermen brought news that Tholian had indeed been killed by the fall of rocks, and his army, most of it having been unwilling, anyway, had packed up and gone home. Some time after that, a trader arrived to say that things had gone very quiet in the South. Yes, he said, when Keril questioned him, the lords and earls were very shaken. But the cause of the quiet was the ordinary people. They did nothing, but they seemed powerful. The earls were afraid of them. They dared not even try for peace with the North, in case that stirred up a revolution.

A month later still a cart drove into Hannart. By the black mud on its axles, it had clearly come north through the Marshes. Apart from the mud, it was gaily painted in green and gold, and trim enough. It was driven by a very pretty girl. Beside her on the driving seat sat a dreamy-looking man with a thin face and a thin, graying beard, who smiled round at the gaiety of Hannart with a look of mild pleasure. The small gold lettering on the side of the cart said he was HESTEFAN THE SINGER.

The people of Hannart realized that here would be both music and more news of the South. Numbers followed the cart as it jogged through the streets and drove into the front court of the Earl's house.

"Oh look! A singer!" Brid said to Kialan.

"Do you know him?" Kialan asked Moril.

"I've heard of him," said Moril. He looked at Hestefan's mild face and dreamy eyes, and it came to him that he would probably look like that when he was older.

The cart stopped. The mottled gray horse blew, as much as to say, "Good—that's enough for today, thank you." The canvas cover came back a little, and a third traveler rather hesitantly stood up in the cart.

"*Dagner!*" shrieked Brid, Moril, and Kialan.

They rushed up and hurled themselves on him.

Dagner, grinning and blushing mauve with pleasure, climbed out of the cart and was thrown against it by their onrush.

"What happened?" said Brid.

"How did you get out of prison?" said Moril.

"Ganner got me out," Dagner said when he had got his breath back. "Ganner's a good fellow. I got to like him a lot. He did follow us, you know, but he went back to Markind when he didn't find us. Then—I don't know what you said to that old snob of a justice, Moril, but when they had me up in front of them again, they didn't seem at all sure I was guilty and kept asking me about Ganner. So I told them he was marrying Mother, and they sent all the way to Markind to ask if it was true. It was marvelous. As soon as Ganner heard I was in prison, he came to Neathdale and raised a real stink. And while he was doing it, news came that Tholian was dead. Ganner upped and sacked the justice, and said he was in charge now. It was marvelous! He let half the other prisoners go, too. But seeing that I really had been passing information, Mother thought I'd better go North for a while and got Hestefan to take me."

"How is Mother?" asked Moril.

"Terribly happy," said Dagner. "Runs about all the time laughing. I don't know why—she laughed when she heard Flennpass was blocked and said you and Brid must have made it to the North. She sent me with a letter for you both."

Brid and Moril snatched the letter and bent over it

eagerly. It was a good long letter, all about Lenina's doings in Markind. Lenina wrote of everything from the speckled cows to the roof where Moril had walked, and reminded Brid of this and Moril of that, and sent Ganner's love—and to Moril, it was like a letter from a distant acquaintance. He felt it might just as well have been written to the baker's boy round the corner. He was sad that he should feel like that, but he could not help it.

"What a lovely letter!" said Brid. "I shall keep it."

While they were reading it, Hestefan's pretty daughter had driven the cart away to the stables. Moril was annoyed, because he had wanted to talk to Hestefan. He dashed away to the stables, but the green cart was already standing empty in the coach house beside their battered and faded pink one. Moril went back to the courtyard, where Dagner, delighted to see them all again, was being uncharacteristically chatty.

"Shall I tell you something really silly?" he said to Kialan as Moril came up. "You won't believe this!"

"Try me," said Kialan.

"Well," said Dagner, "I'm the Earl of the South Dales. They won't have me," he said hastily, as Kialan burst out laughing. "Nothing will possess them to invest me. But it's true. Tholian wasn't married, and all his cousins were killed, too, when Flennpass collapsed—you *must* tell me about that, by the way—and the only living heir left was me. And Moril after that. Honestly."

Moril stood silent in the crowded courtyard and left Brid and Kialan to do the exclaiming. Now he knew what it was that he had not wanted to think about. He had done that. He had worked a huge destruction and killed so many people that Dagner was now an earl. Everyone no doubt thought he had done right. He had saved the North, prevented a war, and avenged Clennen and Konian. But Moril knew he had not done right. He had done it all because Olob was killed. With the cwidder in his hands, he had behaved as if it was for Konian, for Clennen, for Dagner, and for the North, but it had all been for Olob, really. He was ashamed. What he had done was to cheat the cwidder. That was the worst thing. If you stood up and told the truth in the wrong way, it was not true any longer, though it might be as powerful as ever. Moril saw that he was neither old enough nor wise enough to have charge of such a potent thing as that cwidder.

That night, there was a feast in honor of Dagner, Hestefan, and Fenna, Hestefan's daughter. Keril asked Hestefan to sing. Hestefan sang, old songs, new songs, and many that Moril had never heard. When he sang, you forgot it was Hestefan singing and thought only of the song. Moril was impressed. Then Hestefan told a story. It was one Moril did not know. And while Hestefan was telling it, he found he forgot who was telling it and simply lived in the story. Moril realized he still had a lot to learn.

After that they wanted Dagner to sing. Dagner was nervous, but surprisingly ready to perform.

"Huh!" said Brid. "He just wants to impress Fenna, that's what."

Whatever the reason, Dagner took his own cwidder, fetched for him by Kialan, tuned it, and sang the song Moril had tried to finish for him. He did it nothing like the way Moril had made it go. The new parts of the tune were quite different from Moril's, and he had changed the beginning. It now went:

"Follow me, follow me.
The blackbird sings to follow me.
No one will know where we go—
All that matters is we go."

Kialan looked at Moril and made a face to show that he liked Moril's version better. Moril smiled. Everyone had to do things their own way. While Dagner went on to sing his "Color" song, Moril slipped quietly away, fetched the old cwidder, slung it on his shoulders, and went to where Hestefan was refreshing himself with beer beside an open window. Hestefan looked as if he was too hot, just like Moril.

"Please," Moril said to him, "will you take me with you when you go?"

"Well," Hestefan said dubiously, "I was thinking of slipping off now, while nobody's noticing."

"I know you were," said Moril. "Take me, too. Please."

Hestefan looked at him, a vague, dreamy look, which Moril was positive saw twice as much as most people's. "You're Clennen's other son, aren't you?" he said. "What's your name?"

"Tanamoril," said Moril. "I'm called Osfameron, too," he added, as an inducement.

Hestefan smiled. "Very well then," he said. "Come along."

· DROWNED AMMET ·

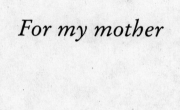

For my mother

PART ONE

· FREE HOLANDERS ·

1

People may wonder how Mitt came to join in the Holand Sea Festival, carrying a bomb, and what he thought he was doing. Mitt wondered himself by the end.

Mitt was born the day of the Holand Sea Festival, and he was called Alhammitt after his father. Perhaps the first sound Mitt heard as he burst bawling into the world was his parents laughing about both these things.

"Well, he took his time," said Mitt's father, "and chose his day all right. What does this make him? A man of straw, born to be drowned?"

Milda, Mitt's mother, laughed heartily at this, because the Sea Festival was something of a joke. On that day, every autumn, Hadd, the Earl of Holand, was required by tradition to dress up in outlandish clothes and walk in a procession down to the harbor carrying a life-size dummy made of plaited wheat. The dummy was known as Poor Old Ammet. One of Hadd's sons walked after him carrying Poor Old Ammet's wife, who was made entirely of fruit, and her name was Libby Beer. The procession that went with them was both noisy and peculiar. When they reached the harbor, they said traditional words and then threw both dummies into the sea. Nobody knew why this was done. To most people in Holand the ceremony was just an excuse to have a holiday, eat sweets, and get drunk. On the other hand, everyone would have thought it horribly unlucky not to have held the Sea Festival.

So Milda, even though she was laughing until her dimple was creased out of existence, bent over the new baby and said, "Well, I think it's a lucky birthday to have had. He'll grow up a real free soul, just like you—you wait! That's why I'm calling him after you."

"Then he'll be common as dirt," said Mitt's father. "Just like me. You go into town and shout 'Alhammitt' in the street, and half Holand will come to you." And they both laughed at the thought of the common name they were giving their baby.

Mitt's early memories were full of his parents' laughter. They were very happy. They had the good luck to rent a smallholding on the Earl's land in what was known as the New Flate, only ten miles from the port of Holand. It had been reclaimed from sea marsh by Earl Hadd's grandfather and grew lush emerald grass, big vegetables, and corn in narrow yellow stripes between the dikes. Dike End holding was so fertile and the market of

Holand so near that Mitt's parents had plenty to live on. Though Earl Hadd was said to be the hardest man in Dalemark, and other farmers in the Flate were always being turned out of doors for not paying their rent, Mitt's parents always had just enough money to go round. They laughed. Mitt grew up running carelessly along the paths between the crops and the dikes. It never occurred to anyone that he could drown. When he was two, he taught himself to swim by falling into a dike when his parents were busy. Since no one was there to help him, he had to help himself. He struggled to the bank and got out, and his clothes dried in the stiff breeze as he ran on.

The sound of that breeze was as much part of his early memories as his parents' laughter. Apart from the hill where Holand stood, the Flate was flat as a floor. The wind blew straight across from the sea. Sometimes it came storming in, laying the grass over, chopping the sky reflected in the dikes into gray Vs, and hurling the trees sideways so that their leaves showed white. But most days it simply blew, steadily and constantly, so that the dikes never stopped rippling and the leaves of the poplars and alders went *rattle-rattle* up and down the banks. If the wheat was ripe, it rustled in the wind, stiffly, like straw in a mattress. The constant wind sighed in the grass and hummed in the chimney, and kept the sails of the big windmills always turning, *creak-thump, creak-thump*, to pump the water to the dikes or grind the flour. Mitt used to laugh at those windmills. It was the way their arms pawed the air.

Then one day, shortly after Mitt had taught himself how to swim, the wind suddenly dropped. It did that sometimes in early summer, but it was the first time in Mitt's life that he had known the Flate without wind. The sails of the windmills creaked and stood. The trees stopped moving. There was blue sky in the dikes, and trees upside down. Everything went quiet and unexpectedly warm. Above all, there was suddenly an extraordinary smell. Mitt could not think what was happening. He stood on the bank of the dike nearest the house with his ears tipped to the silence and his nose lifted to the smell. The smell was cow dung and peat and trampled grass, mixed with smoke from the chimney. But that was only in the foreground. Beyond that was the smell of fresh things growing—cow parsley, buttercups, a hint of may, and strongest of all, the heavenlike scent of willows budding. While, at the back of it, there and not there, so that Mitt almost missed it, was the faint boisterous bite of the distant sea.

Mitt was too young to think of it as smells, or to realize that the wind had simply stopped. He thought it was a place. It seemed to him that he had got an inkling of somewhere unspeakably beautiful, warm, and peaceful, and he wanted to go there. Yes, it was a land. It was not far off, just beyond somewhere, and it was Mitt's very own. He set off at once to find it while he still remembered the way.

He trotted to the end of the dike, crossed the footbridge, and continued trotting, northward and inland. He passed all the places he knew, impatiently—they were obviously not his land—and trotted on until his legs ached. Even then he was still in the New Flate, lush and green, with its dikes, poplars, and windmills. Mitt knew his land was different from the Flate, so he was forced to toil on. And after a mile or so, he came out into the Old Flate. Here it was different, all right. The ground was wide and treeless and covered with pinkish marsh plants. In some places, long lines of rushes and green scum showed where there had once been dikes and farms, but now it was all flat and blank. Nothing seemed to be alive there but mosquitoes and plaintive marsh birds. In the wide distance, it was true, there were one or two islands of higher ground with trees and houses on them. The roads to them crossed the pink waste on causeways, raised up like the veins on an old man's hand. Otherwise there was nothing until, away on the edge of the distance, there was what Mitt took for a line of clouds but was in fact the beginning of the land above sea level, where Holand joined Waywold.

Mitt was a trifle daunted. This was not the kind of land he had in mind. His vision of his perfect place faded a little, and he was no longer sure this was quite the way to it. Nevertheless, he set forward bravely into the dismal landscape. He felt he had come too far to turn back now. After a while he thought he saw something moving, out in the marsh. He set his eyes on the movement and waded toward it. It was extremely dangerous. There were snakes in the Old Flate. And if Mitt had walked into one of the scummy pools, he could have been sucked down into it and drowned. Fortunately he had no idea. And even more fortunately the moving things he could see were a troop of the Earl's soldiers combing the Flate for a runaway revolutionary.

Mitt could see they were soldiers before long. He stood on a clump of rubbery plants, with the marsh sucking and gobbling around him, and wondered whether he ought to go near them. When people in the New Flate talked about soldiers, they talked as if soldiers were something to be afraid of. There was a causeway quite near Mitt. He wondered if he ought to climb up on it, out of the soldiers' way. While he was wondering, a muddy horse heaved itself onto the causeway from the marsh behind it. The young officer on its back reined in and stared at the sight of such a very small boy standing all alone in the middle of the Flate.

"What on earth do you think you're doing?" he called to Mitt.

Mitt was rather pleased to have company. "I'm looking for my home," he told the officer chattily. "I come a long way, too."

"I can see you have," said the officer. "Where is your home?"

"There." Mitt pointed vaguely northward. He was busy examining his new acquaintance. The gold on the officer's coat took his fancy. So did the officer's face, which was very smooth and pale and narrow, with a nose that went out much more sharply than any noses Mitt had known before and a mouth which Mitt somehow thought of as clean. Altogether Mitt felt he was a person worthy of knowing about the perfect place. "It's all quiet, with water," he explained, "and it's my place where I'm going to, but I can't find it yet."

The officer frowned. His own small daughter had been found marching out into the Flate only yesterday, saying she had a house on a hill that was hers and she had to find it. He thought he knew the signs. "Yes, but where do you live?" he said.

"Dike End," Mitt said impatiently. It was unworthy of the officer to ask such things. "Of course. That's where I come from, and I'm going to my home."

"I see," said the officer. He waved at the distant soldiers. "Come here, one of you!"

The several troopers who came running at his shout were somewhat astonished to find not a full-grown revolutionary but an extremely small boy. "He shrunk with the wet," one suggested.

"He says he lives in Dike End," said the officer. "One of you take him home and tell his parents to take more care of him in future."

"Dike End's not my home. It's where I *live*!" Mitt protested.

Nevertheless, he was taken back to the New Flate almost dangling from the hand of a huge trooper in the Earl's green uniform. Mitt was sullen at first, disappointed and vaguely humiliated. And he was deeply disillusioned about the officer. Mitt had told him a valuable secret, and the officer had barely even listened. But the trooper was a cheerful man. He had children of his own, and it had been hot, wet work, hunting the revolutionary in the windless Flate. The trooper was pleased to have a rest. He was very jolly to Mitt, and before long Mitt cheered up and chatted happily about how far he had walked and how he thought he would like to be a soldier, too, when he grew up, and a sea captain as well and sail the Earl's ships for him.

When they came to the New Flate, people came to doors and gates to stare at Mitt trotting along with his hand stretched above his head in order to reach the great warm hand of the trooper. The stares were unloving. Earl Hadd was a hard man and a vindictive one. The soldiers were the ones who carried out the Earl's harsh orders. And lately the Earl's second son, Harchad, had taken command of the soldiers, and he was even harder than his father, and a good deal more cruel. But since, all over Dalemark, an earl in his earldom had more power than a king, in the times when there were kings, Harchad and his soldiers did exactly as they pleased. Therefore, soldiers were hated heartily.

Mitt understood none of this, but he saw the looks. "Don't you look like that!" he kept crying out. "This is my *friend*, this is!"

The trooper became steadily more uncomfortable. "Take it easy, sonny," he said every time Mitt cried out. And after a while he seemed to feel the need to justify himself. "A man's got to live," he told Mitt. "It's not work I enjoy, but what can a poor boy off the harbor edge do? When I get my bounty, I aim to take up farming, like your dad does."

"Did you fall in the harbor?" Mitt asked, fixing on the only part of this he understood.

They came to Dike End. Mitt's parents had missed Mitt about half an hour before, and they were by then in a panic. Mitt's father received him with a great thump, and his mother hugged him frantically. Mitt did not understand the reason for either. The vision of his perfect land had faded by then. He was not sure what he had gone away to do.

The trooper stood by, very stiff and correct. "Boy was found out in the Old Flate," he said. "Said he was looking for his home, or some such story."

"Oh, Mitt!" Milda cried joyously. "What a free soul you are!" And she hugged him again.

"And," said the trooper, "Navis Haddsson's compliments and would you keep more of an eye on him in future."

"Navis Haddsson!" exclaimed both Mitt's parents, Milda in considerable awe, and Mitt's father with surprise and resentment. Navis was Earl Hadd's third and youngest son.

"Big of Navis Haddsson," Mitt's father said sarcastically. "Knows all about bringing up boys, I suppose?"

"Can't say, I'm sure," said the trooper, and he made off, having no wish to get into an argument with such a thickset and aggressive person as the elder Alhammitt.

"Well, I think it was very kind of Navis to send us our Mitt back like that!" Milda said when he had gone.

Mitt's father spit in the dike.

All the same, Milda remained extremely impressed by the kindness of Navis. She told people about it whenever her husband was not by to resent it, and most people she told were impressed, too. Earl Hadd and his family were not, as a rule, kind to anyone. After that Milda took a great interest in Navis for a while and found out everything about him that she could. There was not very much known. The Earl's eldest son, Harl, and his second son, Harchad, were the Earl's favorites and the ones people heard most about. But about the time Navis sent Mitt home, Navis was enjoying a little more of the Earl's favor. The reason was that three years or so before, the Earl had chosen Navis a wife, as he had chosen wives for his other two sons. Milda heard that Navis and his wife adored each other and went everywhere together. Then Navis's wife gave birth to a daughter. That was the reason the Earl was pleased with Navis.

The Earl valued granddaughters. He did not like girls in the least, but he needed granddaughters because he was an extremely quarrelsome man. Granddaughters could be married off to other earls and lords, who would then become Hadd's allies in his quarrels. But so far only Harl's wife had had a daughter. So when Navis's wife, too, had a daughter, Hadd was delighted with them. Milda learned that Navis's wife was expecting a second child shortly, and Hadd was gleefully expecting another marriageable granddaughter.

The baby was born the following month. He was a boy, and Navis's wife died having him. It was said that Navis was so stricken with grief that he could not be bothered to find a name for his son. The nurses were forced to ask Earl Hadd to think of a name, and Hadd was so annoyed at not having a granddaughter that he called the boy Ynen, which was the name of a lord he particularly disliked. Hadd was consoled later on that year when Harl's wife and Harchad's both had girl babies. As for Navis, he gave up his commission in the Earl's army and fell into total obscurity. It was soon quite impossible to learn anything about him or about his children, Hildrida and Ynen.

Mitt did not quite forget his perfect land. He remembered it, though a little fuzzily, next time the wind dropped, but he did not set off to look for it again. It was plain to him that soldiers only brought you back again if you went. It made him sad. When an inkling of it came to him in silence, or in scents, or, later, if the wind hummed a certain note, or a storm came shouting in from the sea and he caught the same note in the midst of its noise, he thought of his lost perfect place and felt for a moment as if his heart would break. But then he would shake off the feeling and laugh with his parents.

It seemed to Mitt that the three of them could laugh at anything. He remembered laughing with Milda one evening during a rainstorm. Mitt was trying to learn his letters. He found them so difficult that he had to laugh. Then the door came clapping open in a gust of rain, blowing everything in the house to the end of the room, and there stood Mitt's father, soaking wet and laughing, shouting above the gale that the cow had calved. At that the door came off its hinges and fell on Mitt's father. And they all laughed till they ached.

The very funniest thing happened when the calf had grown into a young and gamesome bull. Mitt and his parents were all in the pasture, trying to mend a place where the dike bank was giving. The bull stood watching them, rather interested. Life was a little dull in the pasture. Then Hadd's rent collector climbed over the fence and stalked irritably over to the dike.

"I've been all the way to the house," he said. "Why couldn't you—?"

The bull, with a look of pure mischief in his merry red eye, lowered his horns and charged. He would not have dreamed of harming any of the family, but the rent collector was another matter. And in a misty, bullish way, he may have noticed that the family was not altogether pleased to see the rent collector. Anyway, up went the rent collector in a graceful arc, moneybag and all, and down he went again, moneybag and all, into the dike, where he gave out a truly tremendous splash. He came up. He swore horribly. He floundered to the bank and tried to get out. The bull was there to meet him and simply prodded him back in again. It was the funniest thing Mitt had ever seen. It never occurred to the rent collector to cross the dike and get out on the opposite bank where the bull could not reach him. He kept floundering up, clutching his moneybag. And prod, prod went the bull, and the rent collector was sitting in the dike again. Over and over again, with the rent collector, floundering, reeling, sitting down *splash*, and squawking "Can't one of you control this beast!" and Mitt's parents leaning head to head, too helpless with laughter to do a thing about it. It was Mitt, laughing as hard as anyone, who at last hooked his finger in the ring on the bull's nose and let the raging rent collector scramble out. And the rent collector was not pleased.

"I'll teach you to laugh, boy!" he snarled.

He did. Next time he came for the rent, he asked double. When Mitt's father protested, he said, "Nothing to do with me. Earl Hadd needs the money."

Probably Hadd was short of money. The rents were put up all over the Flate. Rumor said that there were riots in the town of Holand, and the Earl needed to pay more soldiers to deal with the rioting. But only at Dike End was the rent doubled. That was the rent collector's private revenge. And there was nothing Mitt's parents could do about it. Theoretically they could have gone to law and accused the rent collector of extortion. But the rent collector was the Earl's official, and judges always upheld the Earl's employees against ordinary people—unless, of course, you gave the judge a big enough bribe. Mitt's parents had no money for bribes. They needed more than they had to pay the rent collector. They had to sell the bull.

Next quarter they sold the mule. Then some furniture. And by that time they were in a vicious circle: The more things they sold from the farm to pay the rent, the less they had to make money with to pay the next quarter's rent, and the more things they had to sell. Mitt's parents stopped laughing. That winter Mitt's father took to spending most of the week away in the port of Holand, earning what money he could there, while Milda tried to run the farm with what help Mitt could give. It was desperately hard work. Milda's pretty face acquired a seam of worry down one side—a sort of pucker where her dimple had been. Mitt hated that pucker. He did not remember how his father looked at that time. He remembered a curt, bitter voice and his father's square back plodding away from them down the causeway to Holand to find work.

He could not have found much work. He spent longer and longer away in Holand, and brought very little money back, but what he did bring enabled them to drag on at Dike End for the following summer. But Milda on her own was a poor, forgetful manager. Mitt did all he could to help, but they lost money steadily. There were still a few times when Mitt was able to lie on his back by the dike, looking up at the rattling leaves, and think yearningly about his perfect land. As times grew harder, he seemed to want it more and more. He longed to set off again to find it, but of course he was older now and he knew he had to stay and help his mother.

Then quarter day came round again, and there was no money at all. It did no good for Milda to beg the rent collector to wait a day or so. He came back the next day with the bailiff and three of the Earl's soldiers, and Mitt and Milda were turned out of Dike End. A short while before Mitt's sixth birthday, he helped his mother pack their few belongings into a handcart and push it into Holand to join his father.

2

Mitt always hated to remember that first winter in Holand. His father was living in one room in a big tenement block down by the harbor. Mitt and Milda joined him there. The tenement had perhaps once been the house of a wealthy man. Outside, on its greenish, peeling walls, there were the remains of pictures—once fine paintings of garlands of flowers and people out of stories, sheaves of wheat, and bunches of fruit. But they were so old that Mitt could not quite tell what they were, and anyway, the inside of the building was what he saw most. The large rooms had been chopped into as many small ones as possible, so the house was crowded as full as it would hold of people. It was filthy. The buckets on the dark stairs stank. Bedbugs lived in all the walls. They came out at night and bit, viciously. What with that, and the strangeness, and the noise of all the people, Mitt could not sleep very well. He lay awake and listened to his parents quarreling as they had never quarreled before.

Mitt could not understand what the quarrels were about. It seemed as if his father was not pleased to have them with him in Holand. "Hanging round my neck!" he put it. He wanted them to go back to Dike End. When Milda shrieked at him that there was no rent, he cursed her for laziness.

"Why should I work my fingers to the bone to keep you in idleness?" Milda screamed at him. But after a week of quarreling, she found a job in a workroom which made fine embroidered hangings, and she was there, sewing, from early morning until light failed in the evening.

After this the quarrels Mitt's parents had became even harder for Mitt to understand. His mother kept saying to his father, "You and your Free Holanders! *Free* Holanders! There's no such *thing* as freedom in this place!" Mitt had no idea what that meant.

Mitt was shocked and shattered by the town of Holand itself. He hated the dirt and the noise and all the people. His job for the day was to carry their bucket to the waterfront and tip it in the harbor. As Milda said, the one advantage of living in that tenement was that you did not have to go far to get rid of your rubbish. Mitt hated the smell on the greasy waterfront, where fish scales glimmered on the flagstones like sequins on a dirty dress. The crowded harbor appalled him. There were tall ships with many masts and pennants flying, merchant ships,

ships of the Earl's fleet, loading and unloading going on most of the time. In between were small boats, packed and bustling, rowing boats, cutters, jollyboats, and a good hundred fishing boats. Mitt was always glad when the fishing fleet sailed out, because the crowded water seemed a little emptier then.

After Mitt had brought the bucket back to the door of their room, he was all on his own once Milda had found work. He had nothing to do but keep out of the way of the other children. He hated them most of all. They were town children, shrewd, nimble, and knowing. They made rings around Mitt. They jeered at him for not understanding town ways. They made him look a fool, then ran away laughing.

Mitt hid from them, usually, in the dark holes and corners of the house or the waterfront. But one day he felt he had had enough of that and ran away instead, up the hill from the harbor, into the better part of the town. Here, to his surprise, the streets were cleaner, and became wider and cleaner still as he went upward. The air smelled almost fresh. There was a tang in it of the sea, and an autumn smell from the Flate. Better still, most of the houses were painted, and unlike the tenement, the paint was fresh and bright, and Mitt could see what the pictures were about. He walked slowly, looking at trees and fruit, red swirls and blue flowers, until he came to a particularly fine tall house, where the painting was in gold as well as other colors. On one gable, a stiff sort of lady in a green dress held out a very purple bunch of grapes to a stiff man on the other gable, whose hair seemed to be solid gold. Mitt much admired them. They reminded him a little of the figureheads on the fronts of the big ships. And perhaps because of the fresh air smell, they made him think of his perfect land.

He was standing lost in admiration and daydream when a servant of the merchant who owned the house came out with a stick and told him to be off. He called Mitt a guttersnipe and said he had no business to be there. Mitt ran away, terrified. As he went, he looked back and upward. And there, on the very top of the hill, was the Earl's palace, larger, whiter, brighter, and with more gold paint than any other house in Holand. Mitt felt it was squashing him. He felt like a pip in a cider press.

That was the last time for many years that Mitt remembered his perfect land. Holand quashed it out of his mind entirely and left him simply bewildered.

When Mitt's birthday came, a few days later, and with it the Sea Festival, that was bewildering, too. Everyone had a holiday, so there were more people about than ever. Mitt watched the Festival procession, hoisted onto the shoulders of a kindly man called Canden, who seemed to be a friend of his father's. Down the street came a boiling and a bubbling of brightly clothed people. There was terrific shouting and yelling, and ribbons, fruit, and flowers on everyone. Some had silly hats. Images went by on sticks—heads of cows and horses, with hats and ribbons on, too. Big boys went tearing in and out of the procession, shouting and swirling wooden rattles. It was noise, noise, noise. Every so often came a group of people playing the traditional tune on traditional instruments. There were pipes called scarnels, which sounded just like their name, and triangular stringed things you played with a horsehair bow. They were cruddles, and they sounded just like their name, too. And the groups of musicians were so far apart from one another that it was only by accident that they played the same part of the tune as the rest. Then, *drub, drub, drub*, came people banging at horsehair drums and drowning out even the scarnels. In the midst of it, Mitt glimpsed a straw dummy, fantastically looped with cherry-colored ribbons, riding along in somebody's arms.

"Look," said the kindly Canden. "There's Poor Old Ammet. That's Earl Hadd carrying him."

"What's he going to do with him?" Mitt asked anxiously. He had never heard of Earl Hadd doing anything good with anything.

"Throw him in the harbor, of course. For luck," explained Canden.

Mitt was horrified. Earl Hadd must be quite heartless. He thought of Poor Old Ammet being tipped into the harbor just like the bucket of muck Mitt tipped in daily, and Poor Old Ammet sinking, soaking, drowning, his ribbons getting spoiled. "Doesn't he float?" he asked tensely.

"Not too often," Canden said, quite unaware of

Mitt's state of mind. "Mostly he falls to pieces and sinks in the harbor or just outside it."

"He doesn't!" Mitt said frantically.

There was another friend of Mitt's father's standing beside Canden. He was called Dideo, and his face was a mass of tiny lines. Mitt thought Dideo's eyes looked like two shiny fish caught in the net of his skin. Dideo said, "He doesn't always fall to bits—Old Ammet. If the tide's right, he goes out on the tide in one piece. Or they say he does. Floats for miles. And those in a boat that can find him and pick him out have a lucky boat ever after, they say."

If anything, Mitt found it even more distressing to think of Poor Old Ammet floating, floating, all on his own out to sea. He tried to change the subject. "Who are those boys with rattles?"

Canden glanced at the procession, where boys in red and yellow trousers were having great fun whirling their rattles under the noses of cruddle players. "Boys from the Palace. All them in the procession come from the Palace," he told Mitt, and turned to Dideo again. "I've never seen Old Ammet float. He goes down almost as quick as Libby Beer."

"Would they let me run about with a rattle?" Mitt interrupted desperately.

"No. You're born a nobody," said Dideo. "He does float," he said to Canden. "You've not been in Holand long enough to know, but he was picked up once, a good ten miles out, by the old *Sevenfold,* and I heard every man on that ship made a fortune afterward. That was the only time I ever knew it happen, though," he added regretfully. "I was about Mitt's age at the time." Here he looked up at Mitt and, finding him inexplicably white and tearful, nudged Canden.

Canden took Mitt down and peered at his face. "What's the matter? Would you like an Ammet of your own?"

"*No!*" said Mitt.

Nevertheless, he arrived in front of a stall where dozens of tiny straw Ammets were for sale. With them came another friend of Mitt's father's, a man with a dour, blank face, called Siriol, who stood by without saying anything while Canden and Dideo bent over Mitt, doing their best to please him. Would Mitt have this Ammet here? Or how about this one with blue ribbons? And when Mitt firmly refused to have anything to do with Poor Old Ammet in any color ribbons, Canden and Dideo tried to buy him a wax model of Libby Beer instead. But real and enticing though the wax fruit looked, Mitt did not want Libby either. She was thrown into the sea just like Poor Old Ammet. He burst into tears and pushed her away.

"But they're lucky!" Canden said, quite mystified.

Dour-faced Siriol picked up one of the toffee apples from the other end of the stall and stuffed it into Mitt's damp fist. "There," he said. "That'll please you best, you see." He was quite right. Mitt forgot his distress, somewhat, in the difficulty of getting his teeth through the toffee into the apple underneath.

There was some mystery about these friends of Mitt's father's. Mitt knew his mother did not care for them. He heard her objecting to them every night when his parents quarreled. Her objections seemed to mount steadily through that winter, until around the new year, when Mitt heard her say, "Oh, I give in! Only don't blame me when the soldiers come for you!"

It must have been about a week after Milda said this, in the very heart of winter, when Mitt woke up suddenly in the middle of the night. A red light was flickering on the ceiling. He could hear crackling and distant shouting, and smell smoke. One of the big warehouses on the waterfront was clearly on fire. Mitt could see it, when he raised himself on one elbow, blazing into the sky and down into the dark water of the harbor. But what had woken Mitt was not that. It was the slow shuffling outside the door of the room. The sound made Mitt's back prickle. He could hear Milda trying to light the lamp, whimpering with haste and annoyance because she could not get the wick to burn. Then the light came at last, and Mitt saw his father was not in the room. Milda ran through the room with the lamp, making lurching shadows as she ran, and tore open the door.

Canden was on the other side of it. He was clinging to the door frame to hold himself up. Mitt could not see him well because Milda was holding the lamp all wrong, but he knew that Canden was either hurt or very ill, or both. He could see it in Canden's face. He had a feeling that the part of Canden which was behind Milda and the doorpost was the wrong shape. It did not surprise him that Milda gave a dreadful strangled scream.

"Eeeeh! What—? I knew it would go wrong!"

"Harchad's men," said Canden. He sounded disgusted. "They were there waiting for us. Informers—that's what they were. Dideo, Siriol, and Ham. They informed on us."

After that Canden gave a quiver of indignation and slid down the doorpost to the floor. Milda knelt down to him, hugging the lamp and whimpering. "O ye gods! What do I *do*? What can I do? Why doesn't somebody help?"

After that doors began cautiously opening and shutting up and down the stairway. Ladies came in nightgowns and old coats, with more lamps or candles. There were troubled whispers and soothing words, while Milda rocked about on her knees, moaning. Mitt was too appalled to move. He did not want to look at Canden or his mother, so he lay and looked at the ceiling instead. The bustling ladies thought he was asleep, and after a while he must really have gone to sleep. Canden was not there in the morning. But he had been there. He had left a stain on the floor. And Mitt's father was still not there either.

Mitt knew both of them were dead. Nobody told him, but he knew. What he did not know and wanted to be told was what had happened. He wanted to know why ladies in the tenement came and told Milda, "I should lie low, if I was you. You don't want to get your-self arrested, too." Milda stayed away from work for a while, sitting very still by the window. Her face was so drawn in by worry that the seam where her dimple used to be looked more like a puckered scar than a line. Mitt hated her face like that. He crouched beside her feet and asked to be told what had caused it.

"You're too young to understand," said Milda.

"But I want to know," said Mitt. "What's happened to Dad?" He asked at least forty times before he got an answer.

"Dead," said Milda. "At least, I hope that's what he is, because they all say it's better to be dead than have Harchad after you. And I shall never forgive them that did it to him—never, never, never!"

"What did Siriol and Dideo and Ham do?" Mitt prompted her.

"Leave me be, if you know so much!" Milda said irri-tably. But Mitt went on asking, and in the end Milda told him as much as she knew.

It seemed that when Mitt's father had found it so hard to get work in Holand, he had felt so bitter against the Earl that he had joined a secret revolutionary society. There were a lot of them in Holand. The Earl's son Harchad had spies and soldiers hunting out these soci-eties night and day, at all times. But when he found one and marched the members off to be hanged, there was always another to take its place.

The one Mitt's father joined was called the Free

Holanders. It was composed mostly of fishermen who felt there should be more justice and better living for the ordinary people of Holand. Their ambition was to have the whole city rise against the Earl, and, as far as Milda knew, they had never done much except talk about it. But when Milda and Mitt had been turned out of Dike End, Mitt's father was so angry that he had tried to stir the Free Holanders to action of some kind. Why not set fire to one of the Earl's warehouses, he said, to show the Earl they meant business?

Canden and the other younger Free Holanders were delighted by the idea. It would hit Hadd where it hurt, they said—right in the moneybags. But the older members, particularly Siriol, Dideo, and Ham, were clean against it. If they fired a warehouse, they said, the Free Holanders would be hunted down by Harchad's men, and how would that help the city to rise and overthrow the Earl? The society split in half over it. The younger members went with Mitt's father to fire the warehouse. The older members stayed at home. And when the younger ones reached the warehouse, Harchad's men were waiting for them. All that Milda knew beyond that was that someone had managed to start a fire even so and that no one had come back from it except Canden to say that Siriol, Dideo, and Ham had informed on them. And Canden was dead, too.

Mitt considered all this. "Why did Siriol and them inform, though?"

The crease of worry down Milda's face drew into a

tighter seam. "Because they were frightened, Mitt, like I am now."

"Frightened what of?" Mitt asked.

"Harchad's soldiers," Milda said, shivering. "They might come banging at this door any moment now."

Mitt considered what he knew of soldiers. They were not so frightening. They brought you home when you were found wandering in the Flate. "How many soldiers are there? More than everyone else in Holand?"

In spite of her misery, Milda smiled. To Mitt's relief, the crease on her face turned into a dimple again for a moment. "Oh no. The Earl couldn't afford that number. And I don't suppose he'd bother to send more than six or so to come and take *us* away."

"Then," said Mitt, "if all the people in this house, or all the people in Holand, all got together, they ought to be able to stop the soldiers, oughtn't they?"

Milda was forced to laugh. It was quite beyond her to explain why everyone in Holand lived in dread of soldiers, and even greater dread of Harchad's spies, so she said, "Oh, Mitt, you're a real free soul, you are! You don't know what fear means. It seems such a waste when Hadd and the Free Holanders have done for us between them, it does really!"

Mitt realized that by talking in this sturdy way, he had managed to comfort his mother. He had sent the hateful crease of worry out of her face twice. Better still, he had made Milda comfort him by calling him a free soul. Mitt was not sure he knew what a free soul was—it never occurred to him that his mother had no idea either—but he thought it was a splendid thing to be. By way of earning it, he said stoutly, "Well, you're not to worry anymore. I'll make it all right for you."

Milda laughed and hugged him. "There's my Mitt!"

3

Miraculously, no soldiers came for Milda and Mitt. It seemed as if Dideo, Siriol, and Ham had contented themselves with getting rid of the younger half of the Free Holanders and had not bothered to include wives and families. All the same, Milda and Mitt had a hard time of it for a while. When, after a week or so, Milda dared to go back to work, she found her place had been taken. Mitt was furious.

"It's the way things are in this town," Milda explained. "There's hundreds of poor women willing to work their fingers into blisters. And the rich people have to have their curtains ready on time."

"Why?" said Mitt. "Can't the poor people get together and tell the rich ones where they get off?"

That was the kind of question which made Milda call him a free soul. Mitt knew it was, so he made a point of asking such things. It was a great comfort to know he was a free soul who did not know what fear was, while Milda was out trudging from workshop to workshop. Mitt himself, hungry and miserable, spent the days hanging round the back doors of counting houses, or on the edges of boatbuilders' yards, hoping to be sent on an errand. Few errands came Mitt's way. He was too small, and there was always the crowd of bigger, quick-spoken city boys to jostle Mitt aside and run the errand instead. And of course they jeered at Mitt, too. But Mitt would tell himself that *he* was a free soul, he was, and wait patiently on. It helped him greatly.

At night Mitt had horrible dreams. He dreamed repeatedly that Canden was coming shuffling to the door again. Then the door would open, and there would be Canden, hanging on to the doorpost and slowly falling to pieces like Poor Old Ammet in the harbor. "All dead," Canden would say, as pieces dropped off him, and Mitt would wake up trying to scream. Then Mitt would lie and tell himself sternly that he did not know what fear was. In the middle of the night that was not always so easy to believe. But sometimes Milda woke up when Mitt yelled. She would tell Mitt stories she had learned as a girl until he went back to sleep again.

Milda's stories made good listening. There was magic and adventure and fighting in them, and they all seemed to happen in North Dalemark in the time when there were kings—though there were earls in the stories, too, and ordinary people. Mitt puzzled about the stories. He knew Holand was in South Dalemark, but this North Milda talked about seemed so different that he wondered for a while if it was real.

"Do they have kings still in the North?" he asked, to see what Milda would say.

But Milda knew disappointingly little about the North. "No, there's no kings anymore," she said. "I've heard they have earls in the North just like we do, only the earls there are all freedom fighters like your dad was."

Mitt could not understand how an earl could be anything of the sort. Nor could Milda explain.

"All I can say is I wish there *were* kings again," she told Mitt. "Earls are no good. Look at Hadd—us poor people are just rent on two legs to him, and if we do anything he doesn't care for, he claps us in prison, or worse."

"But he can't put everyone in prison," Mitt objected. "There wouldn't be anyone to catch his fish for him or sew his clothes."

"Oh, you are a free soul, Mitt!" Milda exclaimed.

Mitt was not sure when or how it happened, but in the course of these talks he had with Milda in the night, it began to be understood between them that Mitt was one day going to avenge his father and put right all the wrongs in Holand. It was an accepted thing, even before Milda found work. She found work fairly soon, in another sewing house, because the one thing she could really do well was fine embroidery. They managed to pay the rent on their room in time to prevent the landlord turning them out. But they were still short of food. Milda spent the rest of her week's earnings on a new pair of shoes.

"To celebrate," she said. "I just happened to see them. Aren't they pretty?"

Mitt would have been very hungry indeed had not Siriol, the dour-faced informer, sent round his daughter, Lydda, with a basket of sea fry. Lydda was a fat, meek girl of twelve. She showed Milda how to cook the fry, and she much admired Milda's pretty new shoes. Perhaps she described them to her father. At any rate, Mitt and Milda had a square meal, and there were still enough fish for breakfast. Milda put them out on the windowsill of their room to keep fresh. The ants came out of the wall in the night and ate them up. When Mitt opened the window to fetch in breakfast, all he found was some tiny scraps of bone. He was looking miserably at them when Siriol came clumping up the dark stairs in his clogs and came into the room without being invited.

"Lost your breakfast, I see," he said. "You'd better come round to mine and have some. And best thing I can see, Milda, is for him to sail with me in future. I was thinking of taking an apprentice."

"Well—" said Milda.

"Free Holanders look after their own," said Siriol.

Knowing what he knew about Siriol, Mitt was speechless. He had to stand there and let Milda do the refusing for him. But to his astonishment, Milda smiled gratefully at Siriol, thanked him over and over again, and agreed that Mitt should sail with Siriol.

"I don't need breakfast," was all Mitt could think of saying.

"Be round at my place in half an hour," Siriol said, and clumped away again.

Mitt rounded on Milda. "But he informed!" he said passionately. "What did you want to go and agree for?"

Milda shrugged, with the crease in her face very deep and bitter. "I know. But we have to live. And maybe you'll see your way to getting even with him if you keep close to him."

Mitt was mollified by that. And it made a great deal of difference that he had a job, too. Siriol was very scrupulous. Mitt had an apprentice's share of the takings, so that when the catch was good, he earned nearly as much as Milda. That almost made up to him for the kind of job it was. He did not like fishing. He did not like Siriol. He hardly knew which he disliked most.

Fishing was a mixture of boredom, hardship, and frantic bursts of work. Siriol was sour and surly and insisted that everything should be done exactly right. Mitt very soon learned that he was not allowed to make a mistake. The first day he forgot to coil a rope as Ham had shown him. Siriol picked up the end of the offending rope—which had a knot in it—and hit Mitt across the back with it. Mitt glared at him.

"Do it," said Siriol. "Do it right. Or else. You'll be glad to know how one of these days."

Small as Mitt was, he shared watches with big, slow

Ham, who was Siriol's partner. He learned to patch the much-patched sail, to mend nets, and to gut fish. Siriol and Ham taught him to steer, at first by day, which was simple, then to find his way by night, by the stars, or in pitch dark, by the feel of the wind and the water, and the pull of the sails. They taught him to smell bad weather before it was near enough to hurt. Mitt also learned what chilblains were and how it felt to be too wet and too cold for too long. And he learned all these things, loathing them, until they were second nature, and learned them so young that they were with him all his life.

One thing that surprised Mitt was that he was never in the least afraid at sea. He expected to be. When he first climbed gingerly down into the *Flower of Holand,* and she rocked, and he knew there were only salt-swollen old boards between him and sinking into the sea like Old Ammet, he had to tell himself very hard that he was a free soul who did not know what fear was. Then *Flower of Holand* went dipping out to sea with all the rest of the fishing fleet, and he forgot all about it. Sailing was just a job, like Milda's sewing. And it was good to have a job and earn money when the host of bigger boys hanging round the waterfront had no such thing.

Sometimes, on a fine day, when Siriol's boat went bluntly out of the harbor on the tide, rich people's pleasure boats would be putting out, too, from the West Pool. The West Pool was a shallower mooring just beyond Holand, where the dues were so high that only wealthy people could keep boats there. Mitt enjoyed watching them. But Siriol and Ham had nothing but contempt for them. They spit in the water when they saw them.

"Rich men's toys," said Siriol. "Half out of the water in this little breeze! Put one of those in a gale, and she's under in five minutes." Siriol's respect was reserved for the stately merchant ships. Let the *Proud Ammet* or the graceful *Lovely Libby* come nodding out of Holand, crowding up sail as she came, then Siriol's face would light up, and Ham's also. "Ah!" Siriol would say. "That's a ship for you!" And he would look round his thick and fishy *Flower of Holand* as if she disappointed him.

After a year of fishing, Mitt felt himself the equal of any boy in Holand. He did not grow much—probably because he had to work so hard—but he was as tough and quick-witted as any lad on the waterfront, and much quicker-tongued. He knew every bad word there was. He had a retort for everyone. Boys and girls alike treated him with respect now. Indeed, many of them would have liked to make friends with Mitt. But Mitt kept himself to himself. These children, or children like them, had made his life a misery when he first came to Holand, and he found he could not forget it. He preferred grown-ups. He cracked jokes onshore and on board that made big slow Ham guffaw and even Siriol smile. That pleased Mitt. It made him feel grown-up and independent—a proper free soul.

It was just as well Mitt was independent. Milda had simply no sense of economy. It became a habit with her to "just happen to see" something whenever she came home with her wages. One week it would be a huge iced cake, the next, a pair of pretty earrings.

"You have to keep up your self-respect," she told Mitt when he protested. "I'm being ground underfoot, I am, and if I don't keep my spirits up somehow, I shall just go under, I know I will!"

This was all very well, but if Mitt was out and the thing Milda "just happened to see" cost more money than Milda had, she did not scruple to take Mitt's hard-earned money, too. Mitt had to hide his money, or they would have starved. He felt terribly put upon and responsible. One evening, when he crawled home, tired out, to find Milda had bought a whole tub of oysters, it seemed like the last straw. She had opened the tub, too, and left it in the sun under the window. It was already smelling rather queer, and the ants were swarming up the sides of the tub to investigate.

"What did you want to buy that for!" Mitt yelled.

Milda was injured. "Oh, Mitt! I thought they'd be such a treat for you."

"But there's thousands of them!" Mitt bawled. "How are we going to eat all that lot? If you wanted oysters, I could have *got* you oysters—for nothing, from Dideo. Honest, you need more looking after than a kid! How am I going to pay Siriol out for informing, or do anything else, if you're going to carry on like this?"

"You sound just like your dad," Milda said coldly. "Let me tell you, those oysters were a bargain at two silver, and you ought to be grateful."

"Two *silver*!" Mitt raised both his chilblained hands to the blotchy ceiling. "That's no bargain. That's daylight robbery, that is!"

Mitt and Milda—and the ants—had oysters for supper and for breakfast, and after that they both felt unwell, although the ants seemed as lively as ever. Ham kindly helped Mitt throw the rest of the tub into the harbor.

"And she went and paid two silver for them!" Mitt groaned.

"Don't be too hard on her. She's used to better things," Ham said. "She's a lovely good woman, she is."

Mitt stared at him. "If I didn't feel sick as a dog already," he said, "I would after I heard you say that!" And he went back upstairs, muttering, "Lovely good woman!" to himself in the greatest disgust. Of course he knew his mother was still young and pretty, in spite of that hateful crease on her face where her dimple should have been, and he knew she was not like those other ladies in the tenement who were always down on the waterfront, making up to the sailors whenever a ship came in, but for Ham to say *that*! Mitt had never noticed that Ham deeply admired Milda. Ham was too slow and shy to let Milda know it. And Mitt's feeling was that all women were born stupid and grew worse.

Alda, Siriol's wife, was the worst of the lot. Mitt supposed he should be thankful that his mother did not spend all her money on arris, the way Alda did. Alda was usually too drunk to sell the fish Siriol, Ham, and Mitt had caught. She sat on a barrel at the corner of the stall, while Lydda stood dumbly behind the heaps of fish, letting people have them too cheap. It pained Mitt to his soul. After all their trouble, out half the night pulling in fish in the drizzling rain, a rich merchant's housekeeper or a mincing man from the Palace had only to appear and point to a pile of sweet whitebait, and Lydda would humbly halve the price. It was not fair. The ones who could afford to pay the full price always got it cheap. But that was Holand all over.

At length, Lydda's spineless meekness was more than Mitt could bear. If the fish was to go cheap, he felt it should go cheap to the right people. He elbowed Lydda aside and tried selling the fish himself.

"Hadd, Hadd, haddock!" he shouted. "Fit for an earl, and dirt cheap, too!" When people stopped and stared, Mitt took up a haddock and waved it about. "Hadd," he said, "ock. Come on. He won't eat you. You eat *him*." He picked up an eel in the other hand. "And here's an earl—I mean a Harl—I mean an eel—for sale. Who wants a nice fresh Harl for supper?" It was great fun, and it sold a lot of fish.

After that Mitt always sold the fish. Lydda weighed and wrapped it, while her mother sat on her tub chuckling at Mitt and breathing arris fumes over the customers. Mitt was often very tired. His hands were chapped and covered with little cuts from the fish scales, winter and summer, but it was worth it, just to be able to shout rude things about Hadd.

"You want to watch it, Mitt," Siriol said whenever he heard Mitt's sales talk. But he let Mitt go on. After all, there was always a laughing crowd round the stall, buying fish. Even the Palace lackeys sniggered as they bought.

Then one day, as soon as *Flower of Holand* was out of the harbor and no one could overhear, Siriol amazed Mitt by asking him if he wanted to join the Free Holanders.

"I'll have to think," Mitt said. And he missed selling the fish that next morning, in order to hurry home and ask Milda what he ought to do, before she went to work. "I can't join, can I?" he said. "Not after what they did to Dad?"

But Milda went dancing round the room, her skirts held out and her earrings swinging, and her dimple deep and clear. "This is your chance!" she said. "Don't you see, Mitt? This is your chance to get back at them at last!"

"Oh yes," said Mitt. "I suppose it is and all."

So Mitt became a Free Holander, and great fun it was, too. At first it was simply the great fun of being in the secret, with, behind that, the further secret that he was only in it to get revenge for his father. Mitt grinned to himself at both secrets all through long, boring watches when he was alone at *Flower of Holand*'s tiller, and the stars wheeling overhead seemed to glimmer with sheer glee.

"Ah, shut up, he's useful!" Siriol said to Ham when

Ham protested. "Who's going to bother with a lad who looks just like all the other kids? People think boys don't count. Look at the way he gets away with selling fish. He's safer than what we are."

Taking messages for the Free Holanders was pure bliss to Mitt. He reveled in going unnoticed through the crowded streets. It was good to be small and ordinary-looking, so that he could get the better of Harchad's soldiers and spies. He would memorize the message carefully and slip off after selling the fish, mingle with the crowd in this street, watch a fight in that alley, loiter round the barracks, joking with the soldiers, and still go unsuspected. He was Mitt of the free soul, who did not know the meaning of fear. And the greatest fun of all was when he chanced to be in a street while soldiers stopped off both ends of it and questioned everyone in it about their business.

Harchad ordered this done quite often, as much to keep people properly subdued as to catch revolutionaries. In a tense silence, broken only by the clopping of soldiers' boots, his men would go from person to person, searching bags and pockets and asking each one what he was doing in this street. Mitt delighted in inventing business. He loved giving his name. It was marvelous to have the commonest name in Holand. Mitt, with perfect truth, could call himself Alham Alhamsson, Ham Hamsson, Hammitt Hammittsson, and Mitt Mittsson, or any combination of those that he fancied. He enlivened boring hours of fishing by thinking up new ways to fool Harchad's men.

The only trouble about being a Free Holander was that Mitt did not understand what the meetings were about. Once the novelty wore off, they bored him to tears. They would sit in someone's shed or attic, often without a candle even, and Siriol would start by talking of tyranny and oppression. Then Dideo would say that the leaders of the future were coming from below. Below what? Mitt wondered. Someone would tell a long tale of Hadd's injustice, and someone else would whisper things about Harchad. And sooner or later Ham would be thumping the table and saying, "We look to the North, we do. Let the North show its hand!"

The first time Ham said this, Mitt felt a shiver of excitement. He knew Ham could be arrested for saying it. But Ham said it so often that Mitt lost interest. He found he was using the meetings to make up sleep in. He never got enough sleep in those days.

Mitt felt this would not do. If he was to get his revenge on the Free Holanders, he needed to know what they were up to. "What do they think they're doing?" he asked Milda. "It's all looking to the North, or whisper, whisper, about Harchad, or tyranny and that. What's it *about*?"

Milda looked nervously round the room. "Hush. They're getting at rebellion and uprising—I hope."

"They don't get at it very fast," Mitt said discontentedly. "There's no plans at all. I wish you could come to meetings and see if you could make some sense of them."

Milda laughed. "I might—I bet they wouldn't have me, though."

When Milda laughed, the crease on her face gave way to a dimple again. It was a thing Mitt always tried to encourage if he could. So he said, "I bet they would have you. You could stir them up a bit and get them to come out with something. I'm sick of old tyranny and the rest!" And since this made Milda smile broadly, Mitt did his best to keep her smiling. "Tell you what," he said. "While I'm getting back at them for informing, I'd like to get back at old Hadd, too. I'd like to give him what for, because of him trampling you underfoot all these years."

"What a boy you are!" said Milda. "You don't know what fear is, do you?"

After that, it was understood between Mitt and Milda that the mission of Mitt's life was a double one. He was to break the Free Holanders and rid the world of Earl Hadd. Mitt was sure he could do it. So was Milda.

Milda joined the Free Holanders, too. Mitt was delighted. He had high hopes of it. Milda came to meetings, and she talked as eloquently as anyone there. She loved to talk. She loved leaning forward over the secretive night-light and seeing everyone's listening face shadowy and attentive. But the sole result was that Milda became as ardent a freedom fighter as anyone there. She talked revolution to Mitt whenever he was at home.

"Flaming Ammet!" Mitt said disgustedly. "It's like being at a meeting all the time now!"

All the same, Milda's talk did make things clearer to Mitt. He was soon able to talk of oppression and uprising, tyranny and leadership from below, and feel he knew what it meant. And when he had leisure to think — which he sometimes did while *Flower of Holand* ploshed her sturdy way to the fishing grounds — he decided that what it amounted to was that there were two parts to Dalemark: the North, where people were mysteriously free and happy, and the South, where the earls and the rich people were free and happy enough, but where they made darned sure that ordinary people like Mitt and Milda were as unhappy as possible.

Right, Mitt said to himself. I reckon that sums it up. Now let's get busy and *do* something about it.

But the Free Holanders seemed simply content to talk, and Mitt became increasingly annoyed by them. He was very pleased when another secret society actually killed four of Harchad's spies. Siriol was not. He told Mitt, with a glum sort of gladness, that things would be very much worse now. And they were.

Harchad imposed a curfew. Anyone found in the streets after dark was marched away and never seen again. Siriol forbade Mitt to carry messages during that time. Mitt did not quite understand why he should not.

Then a thief on the waterfront tried to rob a man. He knocked the man down and was taking his money when he found a gold button with the wheatsheaf crest of Holand on it, hidden in the man's coat. The thief knew it was the badge Harchad gave all his spies, and he was so frightened that he jumped into the harbor and was drowned. Mitt did not understand this story at all.

"Well, if you don't, I'm not telling you," was all Siriol would say.

Then Earl Hadd quarreled with four other earls at once. Everyone in Holand groaned. Much as they detested Hadd, they almost admired him for being so very quarrelsome. "Fallen out with Earl Henda again, has he?" the women in Milda's sewing shop would say. "Honestly, I never knew anyone like him!" This time, however, Hadd fell out not only with Henda, but with the earls of Canderack, Waywold, and Dermath, too. And so powerful were these earls, and owned so much of South Dalemark between them, that there was some doubt in Holand whether Hadd could hold his own against them all.

"Bitten off more than he can chew this time for sure, the old sinner," Dideo said to Mitt. "Maybe this is where the Free Holanders get their chance."

Mitt hoped so. But Harl, Hadd's eldest son, managed to put himself into Hadd's good books by suggesting a way to deal with the four earls. Harl, fat and indolent though he was, could sometimes be seen with his brother Navis and a crowd of beaters, servants, and dogs, walking over the Flate and shooting birds with a long silver-inlaid fowling piece. Harl was allowed to use a gun, being an earl's son. No one else was, apart from lords and hearthmen, because there had been so many uprisings in the South. Big ships carried cannon, as a protection against the ships of the North, but guns were otherwise banned. But, said Harl, why not give all the soldiers guns as well? That would make the four earls think twice before attacking Holand.

Hadd agreed that it would. And that put paid to the hopes of Mitt and the Free Holanders. Up went rents and taxes and harbor dues. The people of Holand admitted grudgingly that Hadd was up to everything, even while they groaned.

"It's not right," said Ham. "Give Harchad's men guns and they'll be ten times worse than they are now. But you have to admire Hadd. Fair play."

But Hadd took other precautions, too. The Earl of Canderack, since most of the coast north of Holand was his, owned a fair-size fleet he could send against Holand if necessary. Holand also had its fleet. But to be on the safe side, Hadd betrothed his granddaughter Hildrida to the Lord of the Holy Islands, north of Canderack. The ships of the Holy Islands were famous. As Siriol remarked to Ham, the Holy Islands fleet was probably the main reason why the North had not long since conquered the South and brought freedom to everyone. Milda, as she sewed with three other women at a great bedspread to be covered with blue and gold roses, thought of it from another point of view. One of the women said that Lithar, Lord of the Holy Islands, was twenty years old. And, another added, Hildrida Navisdaughter could only be about nine.

Milda remembered she had once been interested in Navis and his family. "Then in that case I don't think it's fair at all!" she said warmly.

4

It did not seem fair to Hildrida Navisdaughter either. She thought at first she was in trouble. She and her brother, Ynen, had gone sailing. They had been tired of being told they were too young to go out in a boat alone and of being taken tamely up and down the coast by the sailors the Earl employed to sail his family. Ynen had wanted to sail a boat himself. So they slipped away and borrowed their cousins' yacht. It had been splendid fun, and very frightening, too. Ynen had nearly laid the boat on her side, just outside the West Pool, before he got used to the wind. And they had twice found themselves nearly aground in the shoals beyond. But they had managed. They had brought the yacht back and not even bumped the jetty.

Then, as soon as she reached the Palace, Hildy was told her father wanted to see her. Naturally she thought he had found out about the sailing.

Too bad for him! Hildrida thought, while she was having a good dress put on and her windblown black hair brushed. I shall be very angry. I shall say we're never allowed to do *anything*. I shall say it's *my* fault, and I shan't let him send for Ynen. And I'll tell him that it doesn't matter whether we drown or not. It's not as if we were important.

The lady-in-waiting who led Hildrida by her hand through the lofty corridors to Navis's rooms rather thought Hildrida must have found out what was in store for her. She had never seen her so white and stormy. The lady-in-waiting was glad she was not in Navis's shoes.

Navis was well aware that his daughter had an awkward personality. He had taken refuge in a book. When Hildy was shown in, she found him sitting on the window seat, with his calm profile outlined against the Flate beyond the window, and his eyes on a song by the Adon. She was exasperated. The ladies-in-waiting told her that Navis was still grieving for her dead mother, but Hildy found that hard to believe. To her mind, Navis was the coldest and laziest person she knew.

"I'm here," she said piercingly, to stir him up a bit. "And I'm not sorry."

Navis winced a little and kept his eyes studiously on his book. But like the lady-in-waiting, he assumed that Hildrida had already heard about her betrothal, and he was heartily relieved. "Then, if you're not sorry, I suppose you're glad," he said. "Whoever told you has saved me a great deal of trouble. You may run away and boast now if you wish."

Hildy was taken aback at not being scolded. But it seemed to her that her father was washing his hands of her, just as he always did, and she wanted to do battle with him instead. "I never boast," she said. "But I could. We didn't sink her."

Navis was puzzled enough to take his eyes off his book and look at Hildy. "What are you talking about?"

"What did you send for me for?" Hildrida countered.

"Why, to tell you that you've just been betrothed to the Lord of the Holy Islands," said her father. "What did you think it was for?"

"Betrothed?" said Hildy. "Without asking *me*!" It was such a bombshell that, for the moment, she clean forgot she had been sailing. "Why wasn't I *told*?"

Navis found himself facing a blazing white daughter, out in the open, as it were, without a book to hide behind. "I am telling you," he said, and hastily picked up his book again.

"When it's too late!" Hildrida said, before he could find his place again. "When it's done. You might have asked me if I minded, even if I'm not important. I'm a person, too."

"Most people are," Navis said, rather desperately scanning his page. He wished he had not chosen to read the Adon. The Adon said things like "Truth is the fire that fetches thunder," which sounded unpleasantly like a description of Hildrida. "And you are very important now," he added. "You're forming an alliance with Lithar for us."

"What's Lithar like? How old is he?" Hildrida demanded.

Navis found his place and put his finger on it. "I've only met him once." It was hard to know what else to say. "He's only a young man—twenty or so."

"Only—!" Words nearly failed Hildy. "I'm not going to be betrothed to an old man like that! I'm too young. *And* I've never met him!"

Navis hastily got his book in front of his face again. "Time will cure both those objections."

"No, it won't!" stormed Hildrida. "And if you go on reading, I'll—I'll hit you and then tear that book up!"

Realizing that strong measures were necessary, Navis laid his book down. "Now listen, Hildy. This is something that happens to all our family. Your cousin Harilla is being betrothed to the Lord of Mark, and what's her name—Harchad's daughter—to one of the—"

Hildy interrupted with a screech. Her father could call her Hildy all he liked—usually only Ynen did—but the thought of being lumped in with the dreadful girl cousins was too much for her. "Just you unbetroth me!" she said. "And do it at once, or you'll be sorry!"

"You know I can't," said her father. "It's your grandfather's doing, not mine."

"Then he'll be sorry, too!" Hildy proclaimed, and swept to the door.

Navis called after her. It was easier talking to her back. "Hildrida! Don't make an undignified scene, there's a good girl. It won't do any good. I advise you to go to the library instead and read about the Holy Islands. You'll find they're rather interesting."

Hildy paused, with her hand on the doorknob. Islands were places surrounded by water, weren't they? Perhaps she could turn this bombshell to some advantage at least. "I ought to learn to sail, oughtn't I, if I'm going to the Holy Islands?" she said.

"Yes, I suppose so," Navis said. Rather relieved to find her no longer raging, he added consolingly, "But you won't be going for some years yet."

"Then I've got time to learn," said Hildy. "If I promise not to make a fuss, will you get me a boat of my own?"

"Er—if you like," said Navis.

"I do like. But you must give the boat to Ynen, too, because he never gets anything," said Hildy. "Or I shall make a fuss to Grandfather and all over the Palace."

By this time Navis's one desire was to be left in peace with his book again. "Yes, yes," he said. "If you run away like a good girl and don't make a scene, you and Ynen shall have the best boat money can buy. Will that do for you?"

"Yes, thank you, Father," Hildy said, primly and bitterly, and swept out.

The Palace people kept out of her way. Even her cousins, when they saw Hildrida marching, white, upright, and staring like a mask out of the Sea Festival, knew better than to cross her path. They all knew Hildrida had inherited her temper from Grandfather Hadd himself. Only Ynen dared go near her, and he dared not say a word. Hildy swept to her own room. There she collected all the ornaments, from the gilded clock to the gold-painted chamber pot, put them in a heap on the floor, and broke them with the poker. Ynen crouched on the window seat, wincing at the carnage. He still dared not say a word when Hildy flung aside the poker, somewhat bent, and went to sit by her dressing table, where she stared long and earnestly at the thin white face in the mirror. She had left the mirror unsmashed on purpose.

"I am a person," she said at last. "Aren't I?"

"Yes," said Ynen. "What happened, Hildy?"

"And not a Thing," said Hildy. "What's happened is I'm betrothed. And nobody told me, just like a Thing. Do you think I should sit quiet and not mind and *be* a Thing? The girl cousins are betrothed, too."

"They'll make a fuss," Ynen predicted. "Have you been forbidden to go sailing?"

"No," said Hildy. "We're getting a boat out of it. You have to get between the islands somehow. I think I shall go to the library now." And she got up and went. Ynen went with her. He was still mystified, but he was used to that. He knew he would have to be very patient and tactful if he was to hear more about this promised boat.

The library was very tall and built of speckled

marble, with a domed window in its high ceiling. Hildrida, looking very small, followed by the even smaller Ynen, marched across to the librarian. "Give me all the books you have on the Holy Islands," she said.

Rather astonished, the librarian went away obediently. He returned shortly with one big old volume and one small newish one. "Here we are. Not too much, I'm afraid. I advise you to take the little book. It's easy, and it has pictures."

Hildrida gave him a scathing look and took the big book. She marched to the nearest table and opened it. Rather helplessly, the librarian gave Ynen the small book and left them to it.

"This book is all pictures," Ynen said dolefully. "Read me yours."

"Quiet," Hildy said severely. "I'm concentrating." But she did not like to think of Ynen sitting humbly there with nothing to do, and, besides, the book was the difficult, old kind that is easier to read aloud. So she read, "'Indeed men say that the Holy Isles been of all places in the South marks the sole place where enchantment abides.'"

"I like that," said Ynen. "What are marks?"

"The old name for earldoms. Quiet. 'Of legends that do there pertain, there is said by some to be a certain enchanted Bull which appears, no man can say how, now on one isle, now upon another. By some it is said that this Beast may grant wishes, and certainly to see it is deemed by all a great good fortune. Further, there may be heard in clear weather a strange piping among the islands, most piercing and pleasant to hear, though no piper can be seen, and which goeth like the Bull from island to island. This has been heard by many, and many good ships been foundered following the sound. Withal come the horses of the sea, and, it is said, at times the Sea himself in the likeness of an old fellow of the Islands, who will oft speak fair with those that meet him, but oftentimes be rough and violent. For this reason, the men of the Islands count themselves holy and favored above others. And certainly the Holy Islands are a fair place, mild, fruitful, and full of fair havens.'"

"They sound wonderful," said Ynen. "I'd like to go there."

Hildy shut the book. "You shall," she said. "You can come with me when I go. I think I shan't make an undignified scene after all. I'm important. There's no magic Bulls in Mark, are there?"

"I didn't know there were any anywhere," said Ynen. "When are we getting our boat?"

"I don't know. But Father promised," said Hildy.

Later that day their cousin Harilla learned that she was betrothed to the Lord of Mark and lay on the stairs, drumming her heels and screaming, while everyone near ran for smelling salts and made a great to-do. Hildy managed to smile a little. It was a dry, stretched smile, but very dignified. And as, one by one, her four other girl cousins learned of their betrothals and promptly followed Harilla's example, Hildy's smile grew more and more dignified. She was still not exactly glad to be betrothed, but she did almost feel it was worth it when the yacht *Wind's Road* was towed into the West Pool.

Navis kept his promise lavishly. He had heard of the smashed ornaments, of course, but knowing Hildrida's temper, he felt she had shown great self-control. *Wind's Road* was twice the size of the cousins' boat—Navis did not think his children were old enough to sail alone, so he provided space for a crew, as befitted the grandchildren of an earl—and she was sheer beauty, from the golden ears of wheat carved on her prow to the rosy apples decorating her stern. Her hull was blue, her cabin white and gold, and her canvas snowy. She carried two foresails, too, to Ynen's joy. In fact, Hildy felt that the look of pure bliss on Ynen's face almost made up for any number of betrothals.

5

That autumn, when the Festival procession poured, scraping and banging and colorful, down to the harbor to drown Poor Old Ammet, it was guarded by soldiers with the new guns. Mitt did not like watching it. Each Festival brought back his nightmares about Canden falling to pieces in the doorway. But the tenement was so near the harbor that it was hard to avoid watching. This year Dideo came to lean out of the window between Mitt and Milda, with his netted eyes wistfully on those new guns.

"The stuff they use in those," he explained, "can blow a man up, used right. Years back I used to sail with a man who could get the stuff, and we went after fish with it. You might call it unfair to the fish, but I know to this day how to make a bomb. And I was thinking that a bomb in the midst of Old Ammet could rid the world of Hadd and give us uprising all over Holand in one moment."

Mitt and his mother exchanged a long, startled look over Dideo's gnarled hat. That was it! What an idea! They discussed it excitedly as soon as the procession was over and Dideo gone.

"If you were to get a bomb and throw it at old Haddock—you *do* throw bombs, do you?" said Milda. "You could shout out that Dideo and Siriol set you on."

"But I might not be heard," said Mitt. "No—I'd have to get myself taken. Then when Harchad comes to ask questions, I tell him the Free Holanders set me on to do it. But how can we get hold of some of that gun stuff?"

"We'll get some," said Milda. "We'll think of a way. But you'll have to do it before you're old enough to hang. I couldn't bear to think of you taken and hanged!" She was so excited that she went out and spent the rest of her wages on fruit and sweets to celebrate.

Mitt looked at the bundles of toffee apples as dourly as Siriol. He sighed. He saw he would have to put off throwing any kind of bomb until he had earned enough money to rent another farm for Milda. She would certainly starve if he was arrested and she left to manage all by herself. He thought he might have to wait until he was at least as old as Dideo.

It did not happen that way. A week later Mitt came home from selling fish, smelly, slimy, and pinched with cold. He wanted only to go to bed. But to his annoyance, his mother was entertaining a visitor. The visitor was a square, sober-looking man, with an air that reminded Mitt vaguely of something—or someone—else. He was wearing much more respectable clothes than most people wore on the waterfront, and to Mitt's further annoyance, Milda had squandered her money this week on a bottle of Canderack wine for this visitor. Mitt stood in the doorway glowering at him.

"Oh, Mitt!" Milda said happily. She was looking very pretty, and the dimple was back in her face. "You remember Canden?" Mitt did remember Canden—too well. He was still having nightmares about him after the Festival. He had to hold hard to the doorpost when he heard the name. Milda, quite unaware how Mitt was feeling, said, "Well, this is Canden's brother, Hobin, all the way from Waywold. My son, Mitt, Hobin."

The visitor smiled and came forward, holding out a square, useful-looking hand. Mitt shuddered, clenched his teeth, and put out his own fishy hand. "I'm all covered with fish," he said, hoping the visitor would not like to touch him.

But the warm, square hand seized his and shook it. "Oh, I know what it's like to come in dirty from work," Hobin said. "I'm a gunsmith myself, and sometimes I think I'll never get the black off. You go and wash and don't mind me."

Mitt smiled shakenly. He realized Canden's brother was a very nice man. But that did not alter the fact that he had a nightmare for a brother. Mitt went over to the bucket in the corner to wash, hoping that Hobin would go back to Waywold at once and never be seen in Holand again.

That hope went almost immediately. "Yes, I've got a tidy little house, up in Flate Street," he heard Hobin telling Milda. "Workshop below, plenty of room to live upstairs. Earl Hadd's done me proud."

Mitt realized that Hobin had come to live in Holand. He was so dismayed that he called out, "And who did Earl Hadd turn out of there, in order to do you proud?"

"Oh, Mitt!" said Milda. "You mustn't mind him," she told Hobin. "He's a real free soul, Mitt is."

Mitt was furious. She had no right to tell a stranger private things like that. "Yes," he said. "Bit poor and common for you here, aren't we?" And, to make sure that Hobin would not want to visit them again, he wandered round the room swearing as hard as he could. He could tell that worried Hobin. He kept giving Mitt sober, concerned looks. It worried Milda, too. She apologized for Mitt repeatedly, which made Mitt angrier than ever. When Hobin at last put out his hand to say good-bye, Mitt turned his back and pretended not to see it.

"You didn't have to be like that, Mitt!" Milda said reproachfully when Hobin had gone. "Didn't you understand? He's a gunsmith! And you can see he was fond of Canden. If I can only get him to join the Free Holanders, then we can have that bomb—or a gun would be better. You could shoot Hadd from this very window, then!"

Mitt only grunted. He knew he would rather take a gun off a soldier in the open street than get one from Canden's brother.

To Mitt's acute misery, Hobin called again, repeatedly. It took months of visits before Mitt could forget Hobin had a brother who fell to pieces in his nightmares. When he did, he found he quite liked Hobin. Meanwhile, Hobin was firmly but kindly resisting all Milda's persuasions to become a freedom fighter. He agreed that the earls made life needlessly hard. He agreed that things were bad in Holand. He grumbled at taxes like everyone else. But he did not hold with freedom fighting, he said. He called Canden—sadly and a little severely—a boy who played with fire, and when Milda talked eagerly of injustices, he smiled and said it depended on her circumstances. After a while he took to scolding her kindly for buying him wine she could not afford.

Ham grew increasingly gloomy over that winter. Mitt could not understand why, until the spring, when *Flower of Holand* was gliding out on the tide one morning.

Siriol said, "Your ma going to marry that Hobin?"

"*No!*" Mitt said indignantly.

"Good for the cause when she does," Siriol said.

Ham sighed. "Good for her, too," he said nobly. "Hobin's a good man."

Mitt was furious. And when Siriol and Ham proved right, it made another grudge he bore them. Milda did marry Hobin. And all through the wedding Mitt was muttering to himself that he would get Siriol and Ham for this if it was the last thing he did. Probably will be, too, he thought. Since last Festival, he had been living as if there was nothing to look forward to, beyond the moment he somehow planted a bomb under Earl Hadd.

The only good thing he could see in this wedding was that he would be living in reach of a store of gunpowder.

Milda and Mitt moved into the upper part of the house in Flate Street, some way west of the waterfront. It was a good house, though small and peeling. It even had a yard with a mangle in it, and a target on its dingy brick wall where, to Mitt's interest, Hobin tested the guns he made. Mitt had his own room for the first time for years, and though he was far too proud to admit it, very lonely he was in it, too. Milda gave up her sewing and bustled round their four upstairs rooms, singing and laughing, and the crease of worry seemed to have left her face for good. It saddened Mitt. He had only been able to send that crease away from time to time, yet Hobin had banished it forever. Hobin offered to send Mitt to school, but Mitt preferred to go on working. The Free Holanders would not find much use for a boy who was tied up at lessons all day. And besides, Mitt felt that freedom fighting was almost the only tie left between himself and Milda.

It was then that Hobin showed a surprising strictness. "You're a fool, Mitt," he said. "You've got a brain and you ought to learn to use it, not waste your time talking freedom with a bunch of boatmen who don't know what the word means. You'll wish you'd done otherwise when you grow to be a man."

This kind of argument is always irritating. Mitt twisted about and did not answer. He wanted to say he was not going to grow up—he was going to kill Hadd instead—but with Hobin's sober blue eyes fixed on him, he did not like to.

"Well, if you *must* work," said Hobin, "you can do one job and one only. You can learn my trade from me, or Siriol's from him, or you can sell fish if you want. But you do no more than one."

Mitt passionately wanted to go on selling fish. He enjoyed shouting out rude things about Hadd even more than he loved fooling Harchad's soldiers. Fishing—well, he was glad of any excuse to stop doing that. On the other hand, he knew that he would have far more chance of getting his hands on some gunpowder if he was Hobin's apprentice. He shifted about, kept his eyes on the floor, and finally swallowed his annoyance enough to say grudgingly, "I'll learn your trade, then."

"You did quite right, Mitt," Milda said, and hugged him delightedly. That consoled Mitt somewhat.

But it was unexpectedly awkward when Hobin went with Mitt to Siriol's house to explain to Siriol and buy out the remainder of Mitt's apprenticeship. Alda threw both arms round Mitt and gave him an arris-scented kiss on both cheeks. Slow tears trickled down Lydda's face. "I shall miss you on the stall, Mitt," she said. Mitt was prepared for this. But what he had not been prepared for was the look of disappointment and resignation on Siriol's face.

"I should have thought of this," Siriol said, and he got out the arris bottle and poured everyone a glass, by which Mitt knew that this was a special occasion. "Yes, I should have thought," Siriol said when they were all sitting stiffly round the table. "You got right on your side, Hobin, and Mitt's worth a better trade than fishing. But it's not easy for me—having no son of my own."

Hobin looked uncomfortable. Lydda and Alda cried. Mitt sat squirming on his stool. "It made me feel all slimy, sort of," he told Milda afterward. "As if I was covered in fish juice. *And* I can't abide the taste of arris."

Siriol fetched the crumpled paper that Milda had signed on Mitt's behalf nearly two years back. At first he refused to take any money for it. Hobin insisted. Everything got more and more awkward, until Ham was called in to witness the bargain. Ham clapped Hobin on the shoulder, and wrung Mitt's hand until Mitt wondered if he would have the use of it again, and was generally so cheerful and so pleased for Mitt that all the awkwardness vanished. Everyone had another glass of arris—Mitt poured his secretly into Alda's glass—and then he and Hobin came away.

"But I feel bad, I do, really," Mitt told Milda. "As if I owe it them to tell them we need the gunpowder."

"Well, why don't you tell them?" Milda said. "Dideo knows how to make a bomb. It wouldn't do any harm to get them to help."

"You mean, bring the Free Holanders into it, really?" Mitt said. It seemed a very good idea.

Unfortunately Hobin came in at that moment and caught the words *Free Holanders*. Again he showed surprising strictness. "I'm not having freedom fighting talk in this house," he said. "Silly cloak-and-dagger stuff! And don't get the idea I'm scared of Harchad either. He knows I can go back to Waywold if I want. What gets me is the way those boatmen don't grow up. It's like a game to them, just like it was to Canden. Nobody's playing that silly game in my house!"

Mitt and Milda could only continue their talk in utmost secrecy, either in snatched moments or when Hobin was out at the Gunsmiths' Guild. The upshot of their planning was that Mitt lied himself blue in the face to Hobin and managed to attend the next meeting of the Free Holanders. There he laid before them his suggestion: that he steal enough gunpowder for a bomb and plant it under Hadd when he next carried Old Ammet down to the harbor to drown.

The suggestion made a startled hush. Ham broke it by saying reproachfully, "It wasn't because of the gunpowder I was glad for you, Mitt. I hope you don't think that."

"Funny. I made sure you was expecting it," said Mitt, who could seldom resist teasing Ham.

"Now, Mitt—" Ham began.

"Hush," said Siriol. "Learn to take a joke, Ham. Mitt, that's a risk. Horrible risk. You'd get taken."

This was fighting talk from Siriol. He was really considering the idea. Highly delighted, Mitt made haste to assure Siriol that he had no intention of being taken.

"Suppose I was dressed up in red and yellow, like the Palace boys. They'd not know who I was until it was too late. I can run."

"I know you can run," said Siriol. "Your ma never agrees, does she?"

"Ask her," said Mitt. "Only not when Hobin's there. She can sew the clothes if we can get her the stuff."

Siriol pondered, long and deep.

"Mitt looks just like any other lad I ever saw," Dideo said persuasively. "Half the time I don't recognize him myself. And I would love to get making a bomb." Indeed, all the other Free Holanders were loving the thought, too. They leaned forward, murmuring eagerly across the night-light.

"Boom!" said someone. "Up goes Hadd. Lovely!"

"And all Holand rises to us!" said someone else. "He can do it, Siriol."

"Quiet!" said Siriol. "I know he can do it. But he has to get away after. This is going to take careful planning."

Mitt scampered home to Flate Street, wholly delighted. "We did it!" he whispered to Milda when she met him anxiously on the stairs. "We're on!"

"And you're not afraid at all?" Milda whispered, wonderingly.

"Not a bit," said Mitt. And it was true. He was looking forward to it. He felt dedicated.

The Free Holanders began to lay their plans, carefully and thoroughly as Siriol did everything. Mitt and Milda laid theirs. And all of them very soon realized that it would not be next Festival that Mitt planted his bomb. As Siriol said, they would need to study the road the procession took, and the way the soldiers were placed, to find out where and when would be the safest time for Mitt. And he had to look into escape routes and possible hiding places for Mitt afterward.

As Mitt had no intention of escaping, he never attended when Siriol talked of things like this. But after the first week he spent as Hobin's apprentice, he knew that it would take him years, literally, to steal enough gunpowder to make Dideo a bomb. Hobin was only allowed enough gunpowder to test the guns he made. Harchad's arms inspectors called once a week to make sure there was no more. Sometimes they made surprise visits, to make doubly sure. They would weigh the powders and count the guns, and, unless their seal was on everything, Hobin was not allowed to work. They were a great annoyance to Mitt, though Hobin did not seem bothered by them. He would joke with them, almost as if they were friends.

Gunpowder, Mitt discovered, was made of three things, which Hobin mixed, very carefully, himself. One was charcoal, which Mitt never bothered with. Dideo could get that easily. But the sulfur and the saltpeter were, as far as Mitt knew, impossible to get any other way than by stealing them. Mitt supposed they must be made somehow, but he never found out how. They were delivered in sealed bags by the inspectors and locked away by Hobin. It was months before Mitt was allowed even to touch any. He had to spend his time instead melting lead and casting boring little bullets in a string of small sausage-shaped molds. And watching, watching.

Hobin himself was the other great drawback to Mitt's plans. He was such a careful man, and so patient. Mitt suspected that even without inspectors, Hobin would have kept all his things under lock and key anyway. And he was much in demand. There was scarcely an hour when there was not someone else in the workshop besides Mitt and Hobin. Troopers and captains came, bringing guns which had problems. Other gunsmiths came, to consult Hobin on difficult technical matters. Mitt discovered that Hobin had invented a way of making a gun shoot true, by putting a spiral groove up the inside of the barrel. That was why the bullets Mitt so boringly cast were pointed, and not round like the shot Harl used when he shot birds on the Flate. Twice Hobin was actually summoned to Harchad to be consulted. By the time Mitt had graduated to carving butts and even weighing a little powder, he had grasped that Hobin was the best gunsmith in South Dalemark. Mitt was quite proud, and glad on his mother's behalf. But it did mean he had chosen the very worst man to filch from. Hobin had a name for honesty. He was respected in the Guild. And for a long time Mitt dared not do anything but pretend he was honest, too.

Hobin was truly anxious for Mitt to learn, and to become what he called "a decent citizen." Mitt had to wear better clothes—which were certainly warmer in winter, but which he despised on principle. He had to wash when they came up from work. Once a week he was forced to wash all over in front of the fire, in spite of his conviction that washing took the strength out of you. And every evening Hobin produced a book. It was called *A Reader for the Poor*, and it bored Mitt to tears. "If you won't go to school, you must learn at home," Hobin said, and he made Mitt read a page aloud every night after supper.

Mitt's only wonder was that he did not die of boredom in the first year. It seemed to him that he only came alive when he began to be able, at last, to take Dideo tiny packets of sulfur and saltpeter. Then it was even better than running errands for the Free Holanders. Mitt would lie to Hobin, as he told Milda, like a fishmonger's scales, and slip off into the streets with his packet, knowing that if he was caught with it on him, there would be trouble indeed. It was a marvelous feeling of danger, and marvelous to know he was getting somewhere at last.

He did not get on very fast, either as a gunsmith or a thief. Hobin was a patient man, but he sometimes grew irritated with Mitt. Mitt's mind was wholly on filching powders. He did not intend to be a gunsmith, so he attended to Hobin as little as he attended to the plans Siriol insisted on making about a hiding place for him after his bomb was thrown. Meanwhile, Milda had a baby, and another the year after. Mitt was rather astonished to find himself with two sisters long before he had a bomb. They were rather a nuisance. They would cry, and they would cut teeth, and they would take up Milda's time when Mitt needed her. But they would not believe they were nuisances. Whenever Milda dumped a sister in Mitt's arms, the baby would start to laugh and gurgle, as if Mitt liked her.

Mitt started to grow then. That astonished him, too. He was used to being the smallest boy in the street. Now he was one of the bigger ones, with long, long, thin legs. The woman who had stolen the red and yellow cloth to make Mitt's bomb-throwing clothes from had to steal more, and Milda put off making them until she was sure Mitt would not grow out of them.

"All to the good," Siriol remarked. "If you keep on this way, you'll have changed so after a year's hiding that even Harchad's spies won't know you."

The trouble was that Mitt needed a lot to eat, and Hobin became increasingly hard up. Hadd put the rents up again all over Holand. His guns had done very little good. Every other earl in South Dalemark had hastened to get guns, too. Hadd was forced to bargain for peace, and bargains cost money. Hobin, Mitt was glad to see, grumbled just like everyone else. He led a petition from the Guild of Gunsmiths, asking to be allowed to raise the price of guns. Hadd refused.

"Now don't you think there's some use to freedom fighting?" Mitt asked him.

"It only makes things worse," said Hobin.

"No, see," Mitt said persuasively, "you could set all the earls fighting one another, then have an uprising, and the North would come and help us. They'd have to!"

"If the North did any such thing," said Hobin, "you'd find the earls would stop fighting one another and start on the North. And you'd find yourself on their side, Mitt. You couldn't help yourself. You're born a Southerner. The North knows that better than you do. It's history. It'll take more than an uprising to make things better in Holand."

"The trouble with you is you're so patient!" Mitt said.

In spite of his patience, Hobin began to look a little worn by springtime. There were the babies and Mitt to feed. And Milda was still rushing out and "just happening to see" expensive things, though these days it was mostly furniture. Hobin began to talk seriously of moving back to Waywold.

"We can't do that!" Mitt told Milda in a panic.

"I know. Not after I've trained you all these years," said Milda. "But he'd stay if only Hadd was gone. Run and catch Siriol." And she broke a whole bowl of eggs to give Mitt an excuse to go out.

Mitt was lucky enough to catch Siriol just as he was boarding *Flower of Holand*. Siriol stood on the quayside and thought so long that Mitt wondered whether to suggest he would miss the tide. "Ah," said Siriol. "Well. You better do it this autumn then."

"This autumn it is!" Mitt agreed, and the muscles at the back of his legs jumped with excitement. "And thank goodness! After three flaming years, I can't wait much longer!"

PART TWO

· THE SEA FESTIVAL ·

6

There were great gales that spring. The sea broke the dikes in two places, and even in the harbor, boats blew this way and that and masts snapped. Siriol could not put to sea for a fortnight, and few people in Holand went out much because the wind in the street filled your face with sand and salt until you could barely see. Mitt was kept very busy. The old Earl of the South Dales died, and all the earls of the South began to gather in Holand to invest the new Earl, as the custom was. People asked one another whether Hadd would manage to quarrel with them all or only half of them. Mitt thought Hadd must be determined to. Hobin was busy making and mending guns day and night. The Palace must have bristled with them. Mitt got little chance to look at any earls. He saw one windswept fine person, who looked as if he would very much rather have been indoors, but no one could tell Mitt if he was an earl or not.

"Down with him, anyway!" Mitt muttered, and hurried back indoors.

Then a strange boat was sighted, beyond the shoals, beating her way to the harbor. There was intense excitement. The boat was said to be a Northerner. Mitt could think of nothing else.

"We'd best settle this for you before you ruin any more bullets," Hobin said. He and Mitt put on pea jackets against the gale and went out to look, along with most of the rest of Holand.

The ship was wallowing in the great waves outside the harbor wall, black in the yellow stormy light. Though all her canvas was in and she was riding only on the rags of a storm sail, Mitt saw at once that she was indeed a Northerner. She had the square rigging which few ships in the South used these days. People round Mitt shook their heads and said it was daft to go out in this gale with a little square-rigger like that, but then Northmen were all daft. And it was clear the ship was in bad trouble. For some minutes Mitt doubted that she would make the harbor at all. Then she rounded the wall, and it was clear she would be safe.

The harbor was lined with soldiers to meet her. Behind them, a lot of ordinary people had come out with knives and stones. And Mitt watched with the most extraordinary mixed feelings. He was glad the ship was safe. But how *dared* they! How dared they put into Holand harbor like this! The ship wallowed her waterlogged way to the quayside. When some of the sailors on board saw the soldiers waiting, they dived into the harbor rather than be caught.

"What cowards!" he said to Hobin.

"They haven't a chance, anyway," said Hobin. "Poor devils."

The Northmen who stayed on board were taken prisoner as soon as soldiers could jump onto the ship. The crowd hid most of it from Mitt. But he had a glimpse of them being taken uphill to the Palace, a bunch of soaking, draggled fellows with fair hair and brown faces, who all had a thicker, healthier look than anyone in Holand, even though they were plainly almost too exhausted to realize what had happened to them. Mitt's shaken thought was that they looked like people. He had expected them to look mysteriously free. But they held their heads low and shuffled along, just like anyone else taken by Harchad's men.

Their arrival caused quite as much excitement up at the Palace. Everyone had been in a ferment there, anyway, because of the investment of the new Earl. Feasts and fuss and arrangements had gone on for a week now. All the children were bundled out of the way and ordered to be seen and not heard—and not seen unless asked for. There was much excited peeping and giggling. To Hildy's scorn, all the girl cousins decided that the new Earl of the South Dales was *terribly handsome* and spied on him whenever they could. They all wished they had been betrothed to him and not to whomever they *were* betrothed to. Hildy herself thought Tholian looked rather unkind. She made the mistake of telling Harilla so.

"All right, Lady Be Different!" said Harilla. "I'm not telling you my spyhole for that. Go and find your own."

Hildy did not mind. Ynen and she were better than any of them at finding places where they could see what was going on. They watched a great deal of the feasting and music, until it was obvious that the Lord of the Holy Islands was not going to arrive.

"Why not?" Hildy wondered.

"I don't think he's anyone's hearthman," said Ynen. "His job is to keep the North's fleet out."

Then it was learned that one Northern ship at least had slipped through. Half the earls were convinced that it was the first of an invasion. The messages, the orders, and the bustling about made Hildy think of an ants' nest stirred with a stick, and there were more still when the soaking prisoners were marched in. The prisoners were questioned. It came out that two of them were nobly born—and not only that, they were the sons of the Earl of Hannart himself. The excitement was feverish. The Earl of Hannart was a wanted man in the South. Ynen reported to Hildy that when he was a young man, the Earl of Hannart had come South and taken part in the great rebellion, just as if he were a common revolutionary.

The fate of the Northmen was no longer in doubt. They were all put on trial for their lives.

Now it is a fact that if you are brought up to expect

something, you expect it. Hildy and Ynen were used to people being tried and hanged almost daily. It did not worry them particularly that the Northmen were going to be hanged. Most of the Palace people said they had asked for it by putting into Holand anyway. But Hildy and Ynen were very anxious to catch a glimpse of the Earl of Hannart's sons while they were still alive to be seen. It was not easy to do. Hadd was afraid that some of the freedom fighters in Holand might attempt to set the Northerners free, and nobody was allowed near them who had no business to be. But on the last day of the trial Hildy and Ynen managed to stand in an archway near where the younger son was being kept prisoner.

They saw soldiers come out. They saw their uncle Harchad in the midst of them, and with him the Earl's son. When they came level with the archway, Hildy was astonished to see that the Earl's son was quite young—no older than Harchad's own son—just a big boy, really. And when they were beside the archway, Harchad suddenly turned and kicked the Earl's son. Instead of glaring or swearing at Harchad, as Hildy herself or any of the cousins would have done, the boy cringed away and put one arm over his head. "Don't!" he said. "Not anymore!"

Hildy stared after the soldiers as they marched the prisoner away to the courtroom. She had sometimes seen revolutionaries cringe like that. She had thought that was the way common people behaved. But that an Earl's son should be brought to behave like that shook her to the core.

"I wonder," she said. "Is Uncle Harchad very cruel, do you think?"

"Of course he is," said Ynen. "Didn't you know?" And he began telling her some of the things he had heard from the boy cousins.

Hildy stared at him. Even though she realized Ynen was quite as shaken as she was, some of the things he said made her feel so sick and cold that she had to run at him with both arms stretched out and bang him against the side of the archway to shut him up. "Oh be quiet! Don't you *mind*!"

"Of course I mind," said Ynen. "But what can I do?"

The prisoners were hanged the following day. Hadd gave permission for the Palace children to watch if they wanted. Ynen said he did not want to. Hildy was trying to decide whether, after what she had seen, she wanted to or not when a message came from Navis. He forbade Hildy and Ynen to watch. Hildy found she was relieved.

But in some ways a dreadful thing you do not see is more dreadful. Hildy tried not to watch the clock, but she knew the exact moment when the executions started. When a groaning sort of cheer came up out of the courtyard, Ynen covered his ears. What made it seem all the more dreadful was that their cousin Irana was carried out screaming, their cousin Harilla actually fainted, and all the rest, boys and girls alike, were sick as dogs.

"It *must* have been horrible!" Hildy said, quite awed.

After that neither she nor Ynen went near their uncle Harchad if they could help it.

The gales dropped, and the earls all went home. Hildy's cousin Irana Harchadsdaughter ran feverishly from window to window trying to get a last glimpse of the Earl of the South Dales.

This sentimental behavior so disgusted Hildy that she said, "I don't know why you carry on like that. He hasn't even looked at you. And I bet he's twice as cruel as your father is. His eyes are even meaner."

Irana burst into tears. Hildy laughed and went out for the first sail of the year in the yacht *Wind's Road*. But Irana went weeping to her cousin Harilla and told her how beastly Hildy had been.

"She said that, did she?" said Harilla. "Right. It's time someone taught Lady Superior a lesson. Come with me to Grandfather. I bet he doesn't know she's gone out sailing."

Hadd did not. He was in a very bad temper, anyhow, having quarreled furiously with Earl Henda. And the coming of the ship from the North had brought home to him just how important it was to have an alliance with the Lord of the Holy Islands. The thought that this alliance was at that very moment in danger of drowning in a squall was almost too much for him. He was so angry that Harilla was almost sorry she had gone to him. She got her face slapped, as if it was her fault. Then Navis was summoned. Hadd raged at him for half an hour. And when Hildy came in, she found herself in the worst trouble of her life. She was utterly forbidden ever to go sailing again, in any kind of boat whatsoever.

For three days after that, even Ynen hardly dared go

near Hildy. She stole a fur rug from her aunt and sat wrapped in it, up on the leads of the roof, looking out over the lovely whelming sea, streaked gray, green-blue, and yellow where the sandbanks were, too angry even to cry. It's just the alliance. He doesn't care about *me*, she thought. Then, after two days, she remembered she would be able to sail once she got to the Holy Islands. I wish I could go now, she thought. Away from this horrible cruel place. She spent the rest of the day making a loving drawing of *Wind's Road*. When it was finished, she cut it carefully in half and labeled one half "Ynen" and the other "Hildrida." Then she crossed out "Hildrida" and wrote "Ynen" on that half, too. After that, she came down from the leads and handed both halves to Ynen.

"There you are. She's all yours now."

Ynen sat holding both halves of the drawing. He was glad, but it seemed a shame. It was the high price Hildy had to pay for being important. Ynen reflected that this autumn he would at last be old enough to take part in the Sea Festival. He swore to himself that if he died in the attempt, he would catch his grandfather one on the nose with a rattle. Hadd deserved it if ever anyone did. Then he thought about the Earl of Hannart's sons and hoped Uncle Harchad would be in the procession, too. He would catch a whopper.

Down in Holand, they were still talking about the Northmen. As Milda said, it seemed hard to hang them when they had only come in for shelter. Hobin said it was only to be expected. Mitt gradually forgot his mixed feelings. As time went on, he remembered more and more his glimpse of the Northerners shuffling like all prisoners. It came to something, he thought, when the tyranny of Holand could make free men of the North look so abject. In fact, as a free soul himself, he despised the Northmen a little for it. Come autumn, and I'll show them! he thought.

Most people were sorry for the Northmen. Feeling ran high against Hadd all that summer. Then rumors were heard that the North had defeated the South in a great battle and blocked the last of the passes in the mountains between them. After that even people who were in favor of Hadd began saying it was Hadd's fault. He had let them in for a shameful defeat by hanging twenty innocent men.

"Good," said Siriol. "Things are going our way nicely."

The Free Holanders were planning long and carefully all through that summer. Among other things it suddenly dawned on Mitt and Milda that no one must connect Hobin with Mitt when Mitt threw his bomb. Give Harchad's spies half a clue, as Mitt said, and Hobin would be hanged. Mitt was confident that he could lie well enough to keep Hobin out of it. "I've had years of practice," he said. "The wonder is that I know how to tell the truth these days. But will Hobin keep himself out of it?" That was the trouble. Hobin seldom bothered to watch the Festival. But he might take it into his head to do so, and if he saw Mitt being arrested, he was quite capable of going with Mitt and spoiling everything. "That's the worst of him being so honest," Mitt said.

Mitt took this problem to the Free Holanders. They put their heads together. The result was that Ham, who had always liked Hobin, struck up a proper friendship with him. The two of them went for walks together, out in the Flate, all that summer. Ham managed surprisingly cunningly. He got Hobin used to longer and longer walks. By the end of the summer they were spending all day in the Flate, having supper at an inn, and not getting back to Holand until after nightfall.

"See?" Ham said, with his big, slow grin. "Then on the day of the Festival, we go out to High Mill, twenty-odd mile, and we'll be seen. I'll make sure the innkeeper swears to us."

Then, to Mitt's exasperation, another society of freedom fighters put its oar in. It was called Hands to the North. It tacked notices to the gates of the Palace and the barracks which promised, in crude writing and even cruder language, to kill Hadd during the Sea Festival. "AND AS MANY ER THE REST ER YU AS WE CAN GIT."

"That's torn it!" Mitt said as soon as he heard the news. Milda broke the eggs again, and a jug of milk for good measure, and she and Mitt both seized a baby apiece and hurried round to see Siriol. "What shall we do?" said Mitt. "There'll be spies and soldiers all over now. Who are these Hands to the North anyway?"

"Not any lot I know," said Siriol. "This is bad. It could have the Earl stopping the Festival."

"He'd better not!" said Milda. "I've trained Mitt for this for years. And the clothes won't fit him if we have to wait another year."

Siriol thought, in his customary unhurried way. "If the Palace thinks of staying at home," he said, "we'll hear it soon enough on the grapevine. Meanwhile, it wouldn't do no harm to see if we couldn't start a bit of a panic. Go round letting on that it'll be terrible bad luck for Holand to stop the Festival, and that kind of thing."

So the Free Holanders dropped a word here and another there. Most of them were content simply to hint at dire bad luck. But Mitt felt he could not leave things so much to chance. Whenever Hobin was not by to listen, Mitt would whisper passionately to anyone who happened to be in the workshop, of floods, fires, famines, and plagues. "And that's just the least of what'll happen if old Hadd's too scared to hold the Festival," he would conclude, and pull a dreadful face to suggest all the other unspeakable kinds of bad luck. When Milda was out shopping, she said things even more highly colored.

Four days later the rumor came back to Mitt when the arms inspectors called on their weekly visit. "Hear what they're saying?" said one. "They say if Hadd stops the Festival, the sea rises up and spews out monsters over Holand, and all manner of ignorant nonsense."

"Yes," said the other. "Monsters with heads like

horses and horns like bulls. I mean, I know it makes you laugh, Hobin, but you must admit it shows how much happier everyone would be to know there *is* going to be a Festival this year."

Hobin was still laughing after they had gone. "Monsters!" he said. "Don't let me catch you listening to that sort of nonsense, Mitt."

"No fear!" said Mitt. Secretly he was awed by the way the rumor had grown.

Next day Hadd announced that the Festival would be held as usual. Hadd was no coward, and no fool either. The news Harchad's spies brought him showed him well enough how much he was hated in Holand. He knew that to cancel the Festival might be the thing that could spark off a real revolution. So he did not cancel it. But he forbade any of his grandsons to take part in the procession. The procession, this year, was to consist of servants and merchants and their sons—all people who did not count.

The news was a great blow to Ynen. He had looked forward to the Festival for months. He had *counted* on hitting Hadd with a rattle. He had dreamed of himself whirling the rattle round and round under Hadd's great pointed beak, closer and closer, and at last, *bash*. But now . . . It did not console Ynen in the least that he was allowed to come to the feast afterward. And it was the last straw to learn that his father was to be in the procession. Harl was quite content to stay in the safety of the Palace. Harchad, of course, would be busy supervising the soldiers and spies posted to keep Hadd safe. But someone in Hadd's family had to carry Libby Beer, and Hadd chose Navis. Navis was his most expendable son. Besides, Hadd did not like Navis much.

"It's not fair!" Ynen said to Hildy out of his disappointment. "Why is Father allowed in the procession, and not me?"

"Now you know how I feel," Hildy said unsympathetically. Girls were never allowed in the procession at all.

When this news filtered down through devious ways to the Free Holanders, Siriol was rather pleased than otherwise. "Less chance of our Mitt being recognized," he said.

The other safety measures were much more disturbing. In the week before the Festival, all boats were ordered to the far side of the harbor. Siriol had to move *Flower of Holand* to a distant mooring, where she was bumped and rubbed by six other boats crammed in round her. He grumbled furiously. He grumbled even more when, for two days before the Festival, no boats were allowed in or out of the harbor, and all were searched by soldiers every few hours. At the same time Harchad had all the tenements on the waterfront knocked down, and a large rubbly space cleared in front of the harbor. This was more serious. The street where Mitt was supposed to join the procession vanished. They had hastily to choose the next inland. Milda and Mitt were furious. They had lived in one of those tenements.

"The whole lot down, just to keep his nasty old pa safe!" said Mitt. "Talk about callous tyranny!"

"They should have come down years back," said Hobin. "They were nothing but rats and bedbugs. And 'callous tyranny' is the kind of talk I'm not having."

"But those poor people are turned out in the street!" Milda protested.

"Well, it's cleaner there," said Hobin. He was combing his hair and getting ready for a Guild meeting. "Anyway, to my certain knowledge, three trades have offered them room in their guildhalls, Gunsmiths included. But there's new houses being built for them, back in the Flate."

"The Earl's building them houses?" Mitt asked incredulously.

"No," said Hobin. "Would the Earl do a thing like that? No. It's one of the sons—Navis, I think." He put on his good jacket and went away downstairs, as far as Mitt could see, rather annoyed with Navis for stealing the Gunsmiths' thunder.

"He'll come back talking of Waywold," Mitt said as the door slammed. "You see. Still, it won't matter you going back there after tomorrow."

"Mitt, I'm nervous!" said Milda. "All our planning!"

Mitt felt pleasantly excited, no more. "Don't you trust me or something?" he said. "Come on. Let's have a look at those clothes."

Milda laughed excitedly as she fetched the red and yellow costume from its hiding place under her newest carpet. "I don't think you know the meaning of fear, Mitt! Honest, I don't! Here, now. See if they fit."

It was a strange and rather ridiculous costume. The breeches, which came halfway down Mitt's thin calves, had one yellow leg and the other red. The jacket was red and yellow in the opposite halves. Mitt was a bit thin for the jacket. But he buttoned it up and added the jaunty cap, which had a double crown like a cock's crest. "How do I look?"

Milda was delighted. "Oh, you do look handsome! You look just like a merchant's son!"

Mitt looked in the little mirror, all prepared to agree. He felt very fine. And he had rather a shock. He looked good, it was true. But there were things in his face one never saw in the smooth faces of wealthy boys—lines which made it look old and shrewd. It was the knowing face of the poor city boys who ran about in the streets, fending for themselves. And yet—this was the thing which shocked Mitt most—it was a babyish face, too. Under the lines there were empty curves, emptier than in any boy's face he had ever seen, and his eyes stared as round and wide as his baby sisters'. Mitt made haste to alter it by putting on his most jokey smile. The empty cheeks puckered, and the eyes leered long and sly. Mitt flipped the crest of his cap. "Cock-a-doodle-do!" he said. "Roll on, Festival!" Then he turned away from the mirror and did not look in it again.

7

On the day of the Festival, Ham called for Hobin soon after dawn. That's got rid of him! Mitt thought, hearing them clattering away downstairs. To tell the truth, he had not slept as well as usual. But since this was a holiday, he stayed in bed another good hour. I reckon they'll be questioning me all tonight, he thought. I better get all the rest I can. But when Milda called him, he was very glad to jump up and put his own holiday clothes on, on top of the Festival costume. They were supposed to be spending the day at Siriol's house. So they went there first, Milda, the two babies, and Mitt, very bulky and warm in his double set of clothes. They were not to go to the side street until word came that the procession had already left the Palace.

The procession left the Palace a little before midday. Ynen watched it from the upstairs window of a merchant's painted house. He was crowded round with hearthmen and hearthmen's sons, all of whom had strict instructions to keep Ynen safe. Ynen could hardly see for them. His was the first and worst position anyway. The other boy cousins were all in houses from which they could see the cleared space by the harbor. Ynen could see it only if he craned, and if he craned, someone was sure to take hold of the back of his jacket and pull him respectfully back inside.

Ynen could hardly bear it, even before the first of the procession came past. When at last he heard the *thump, thump, thump* of the horsehair drums, followed by the squealing of scarnels and joined finally by the groaning of cruddles, his frustration was almost boundless. Perhaps he was not very musical. It struck him as the most exciting sound in the world. Then he heard shouting. Then the lovely, lovely din of the rattles. And at last came the first of the procession, ribbons fluttering from silly hats, banging and blowing and scraping as they marched, with a beribboned bull's head bobbing among them, and the lucky boys with rattles tearing in and out between their legs. Lucky red and yellow boys.

"Oh, why can't all the revolutionaries drop dead!" wailed one of the hearthmen's sons.

Ynen wished they would, too. But for Hands to the North, he would be down there in the stirring din and the bright colors. And here came Grandfather, looking strange and rather silly. Ynen had an excellent view of Hadd's cantankerous old face under a hat loaded with fruit and flowers. On Hadd's shoulders, and trailing behind him, was a magnificent creamy mantle, embroidered with scarlet and cherry red and gold. Over that was draped a garland of wheat-ears and grapes. Not much of the rest of Hadd was visible, because Old Ammet was in the way. Ynen had very little attention to spare for Old Ammet. All he saw was ears of wheat bristling at head, hands and feet, cherry ribbons, and a girdle of apples. Ynen was chiefly impressed with Hadd's skinny legs, cased in scarlet stockings, strutting underneath Old Ammet. Ynen giggled at the important way those legs walked. He had not realized before how vain his grandfather was and how much he enjoyed being an earl. At the sight of those red, strutting legs, Ynen longed to seize a rattle and whirl it in his grandfather's face. To his annoyance, the red and yellow boys were on their best behavior. None of them dared wave a rattle at Hadd. If only they would! Ynen thought, craning, and being pulled back.

Navis came next. Ynen giggled again. His father's feet were in buckled boots, so his legs did not look as ridiculous as Hadd's. But he had ribbons at his knees and fruit in his hat. And juice was coming out of Libby Beer and running into Navis's ribboned sleeves. Flies were following her. Navis was looking hot and bothered—most unusual for him—and obviously wondering if he could get Libby Beer to the harbor still in one piece.

Behind Navis were two merchants who had been pressed into the procession. One wore a hat with ears, the other a hat with horns. They looked right idiots, and they knew they did. All the boys at the window shrieked with laughter. Ynen leaned out again and yelled insults, which were drowned by the next batch of cruddle players. After that the procession was all music, things on sticks, boys with rattles, until it got smaller and smaller and wound downhill out of sight. Ynen sat back with a sigh. He desperately envied Hildy. She and the girl cousins, as the most important of Hadd's grandchildren, had seats at the window of a house on the very edge of the cleared space.

Mitt was by now in the side street, with Milda, Siriol, and Dideo, hastily climbing out of his own clothes. In front of them were the backs of the crowd lining the main street. They were solidly Free Holanders and their families. Most of them had been there since dawn to make sure of the position. Mitt could already hear the thumping and skrawking of the procession, very near. As he passed his jacket to Siriol and put the crested cap on his head, a bull's head on a stick went by above people's heads. The noise was deafening.

"Be careful, Mitt," said Siriol. "And remember you say, 'I've come to meet Flind's niece,' to the one that meets the cart at Hoe. If he says, 'She's expecting another little one,' then it's all right to go with him. Got that?"

"Yes, all in my head," Mitt said, attending to this no more than he usually did when Siriol talked of such arrangements. The din of the scarnels was making the back of his legs jump.

"Old Ammet's coming!" said someone in the crowd. "Pass it back."

"Old Ammet in sight."

Siriol handed Dideo the lighted taper. Dideo bent over the bundle he was carrying.

"Oh, Mitt, be careful!" Milda said. She was smiling and looking sad, both at once. Mitt looked from her to the sister in her arms, and then down at the other sister, unsteadily standing and holding Milda's hand. They upset him. He could not think of anything to say to them.

He was glad when Dideo passed him a bundle on a strap. It was scarlet to match Mitt's left side, and it had a stiff twist of paper coming out of it, which sent off little puffs of smoke. "There," said Dideo, and his face was netted in smiles. "That's long enough to last to the cleared space." He patted Mitt's shoulder as he hung the bag on it.

Siriol passed Mitt a rattle and banged his other shoulder. "Off you go. Good luck."

Mitt slipped in among the crowd, and they parted to let him through. He was on, after years of waiting, and he could hardly believe it. He came to the soldiers, who stood in a line in front of the crowd. They ought to stop him.

A soldier glanced down and saw the red and yellow suit. "Sorry, sonny," he said, and moved to let Mitt by.

Mitt was in the roaring, skirling, streaming procession. For just one second, he was small and sort of blunt and did not believe he was really there. But he was. And there was Hadd. Mitt had not seen Hadd close to before, but he knew him by Old Ammet in his arms. The bad-tempered old face was exactly what he expected. That face, Mitt told himself, is asking to have a rattle under its nose before it gets blown up. And he was off to do it, whirling from one side of the procession to the other, rattle spinning, crested cap flopping, and keeping a wary eye on the puffing bundle under his arm as he went.

He caught up with Hadd just on the edge of the cleared space. Hildy saw him clearly, from where she sat at the window jammed in among her five cousins. They had soldiers in the room with them, soldiers downstairs, and soldiers lining the new open space by the harbor. They were safe. Nevertheless, the cousins were very nervous and disposed to scream at things. They screamed when the first musicians came between the soldiers and straggled across the open. They screamed at the bull's head.

"Oh, look!" screamed Irana, as Mitt ran in front of Hadd, whirling his rattle neatly under Hadd's irascible nose as he went.

Mitt checked after he had done that. Holand looked so strange with no waterfront buildings and all the shipping cleared to one side of the harbor, that he had another moment when he could hardly believe it was real. But the bundle under his arm fizzed. Sparks puffed out with the smoke. Mitt knew the time had come to get rid of it. He turned and plumped it down at Hadd's scarlet feet. Then he did not know quite what to do next.

Hadd's legs stopped walking. His bad-tempered look did not alter. He simply stopped and stood like a statue, with Old Ammet beneath his chin. Both of them stared at Mitt, and Mitt stared back. And the cousins round Hildy screamed in earnest at the sight of the smoking bundle on the ground. Behind Navis, everyone in the procession began to run into the backs of the people in front, and still Hadd stood, and so did Mitt. Hildy could not think what the boy thought he was doing. It seemed stupid behavior, even for a revolutionary. Old Ammet seemed to be staring at him, unblinking as a cow over a gate, from under raised wheat-ear eyebrows, as if he shared Hildy's wonder.

Sparks poured out of the bundle. Navis saw that nobody else was going to do anything. He hoisted Libby Beer to his shoulder and dashed forward. This was more what Mitt had expected. He got ready to pretend to run. But to his astonishment, Navis took no notice of Mitt. Instead he aimed a great kick at the fizzing bundle. Mitt saw the ribboned leg go out, the buckled boot connect, and the bundle, in an arch of smoke, sail away behind into the open space.

And the fellow hasn't a hair out of place! Mitt thought, rather astonished. He wanted to shout to Navis, "Hey! I dedicated a lifetime to this lot! And you just wasted it!"

By this time the merchant with ears on his hat had pulled himself together, too. He made a rather dubious grab for Mitt. Mitt dodged him easily.

This made Mitt think: Might as well give them a run for their money.

He turned to run. As he did so, the explosion came and sent him reeling. The force of it rattled all the windows and sent a gust into Hildy's face. The cousins screamed again. The rest of the procession came jostling out from behind Navis, some of them demanding to know what had happened, some of them after Mitt. Hadd turned and made a sign to one of the captains that Mitt should be taken alive. Since Hildy now knew that this was the worst way to be taken, she shivered a little as she watched the boy running. He ran like a deer, ribbons fluttering, dropping his rattle as he ran, straight toward the soldiers coming out from the edge of the crowd to meet him. Hildy thought that if it had been her, she would have run to the edge of the harbor and jumped in.

So would Mitt have done if he had meant to escape. But he was supposed to be caught. His ears hurt from the explosion. They seemed to be plugged with wool. He saw the soldiers mouthing as they came but could not hear a word. Mitt dodged and swerved as only someone brought up in the poorer parts of Holand could. Looks more natural, he thought. A huge hand snatched at his face. Mitt ducked under it and twisted sideways. A blurry face mouthed curses. A bevy of big boots clod-hoppered at him from all directions. This way and that went Mitt, that way and this. He leaped a boot, dodged another, missed an enormous stretching arm, and tripped over another great boot. A jerk and a sudden coldness on his back told him—where his furred-up ears could not—that his jacket had been grabbed and torn. He was flat on his face and up again in one moment. But he was still not caught. He felt his jacket leave him, jerk, jerk, and he was still sprinting forward. Too good to last, Mitt thought, and he dived, pushing and shoving, among the big bodies of the ordinary people crowded behind the soldiers.

Come on, some of you! Stop me! he thought. But no one succeeded, though Mitt thought some of them tried. Just barely, he could hear their voices now: "Stop him! Don't let him get away!"

Ah. Ears come to their senses again, Mitt thought. Good. Couldn't see myself lip-reading all the questions I'm going to be asked.

He pushed on, very glad he was not deaf. And shortly, the voices round him were saying, quite loudly, "What's happened then?" and, "Who are you shoving?"

Mitt, to his extreme astonishment, plunged out from the back of the crowd into a narrow street. Hey! he thought. This won't do. He stopped. He turned round and saw the backs of the people filling the street heaving and bumping about as the soldiers tried to force their way through after him. He cast a longing look up the narrow street. He could really almost get away. They would not run fast in those boots.

Better make it easier for them, Mitt thought, sighing. And he went back into the crowd.

Out in the open space, the procession had re-formed

and was straggling toward the water's edge. Hadd behaved as if nothing had happened at all. As soon as Mitt vanished among the soldiers, he went on walking as if the whole thing were not worth thinking about. Hildy could not help admiring him. That was how an earl should behave! Hadd's behavior was so dominating that Hildy and everybody else were soon watching the procession going up and down the quays, drumming and droning and skirling, as if Mitt had never existed.

Mitt was in the crowd just beneath Hildy's window. He found he was still wearing one red and one yellow sleeve. They were a nuisance, so he took them off and threw them on the ground. He seemed to have lost his cap. He stood there in his threadbare undershirt, hoping the soldiers would recognize him by his two-colored breeches. But he was surrounded by tall citizens and nobody saw him. Above the noise of the procession he could hear the boots of the soldiers hammering away up the narrow street.

Right fools, some people are! Mitt thought. Better make myself obvious.

He squirmed his way along the painted wall of the house until he came to its front door. It had six steps up to it, for fear of flooding, as did most houses in Holand. People were crowded on the steps, staring out toward the harbor. Mitt climbed up and squeezed in among them. He was easy enough to see, had anybody been looking his way. But everyone was watching the Festival.

The procession had formed into a line along the jetty,

with Hadd and Navis in the center. The heads on poles were lowered. Garlands were taken off. Everyone waved these downward, pretending to beat the water. In fact, the water was too far below to reach, but the Festival went back to the days when Holand harbor was just a low ring of rocks and none of it had been altered since. The same old words were said:

"To tide swimming and water welling, go now and come back sevenfold. Over the sea they went, on the wind's road. Go now and come back sevenfold. For harbor's hold and land's growing, go now and come back sevenfold."

This was repeated three times by everyone in the procession. It was a growling, ragged chorus. Yet, by the third repetition, Hildy's arms were up in goose pimples from sheer awe—she did not know why. Mitt's eyes pricked, as they always did, and he was annoyed at himself for being so impressed by a load of out-of-date nonsense. Then the musicians gave vent to a long groaning chord. Hadd raised Poor Old Ammet above his head, ready to throw him in the harbor.

A little star sparkle of flame blossomed for a second on one of the ships tied up at the side of the harbor. Hadd jerked, half turned, and slid quietly to the ground. It looked at first as if he had suddenly decided to lay Poor Old Ammet carefully at Navis's feet. Then came a tiny, distant *crack*.

Nobody understood for a moment. One of Hildy's cousins laughed.

After that there was a long, groaning uproar. Mitt's voice was in it. "Flaming Ammet! I been *diddled*!" The fat woman beside him was saying, over and over again, "Oh, what bad luck! What terrible bad luck!" Mitt had no idea whether she meant bad luck to Hadd or to Holand. The ladylike girls overhead somewhere were screaming. Mitt leaned his head against their painted front door and cursed. All he could think of was that the unknown marksman had cheated him. "Half my life, and now it's wasted!" he said. "Wasted. Gone!"

Overhead the cousins hung on to Hildy and to one another, whimpering and crying. Hildy found herself saying, "Ye gods, ye gods, ye gods!"

A soldier in the room behind shouted, "He's in that boat—*Proud Ammet!* Run, you, and we'll get him!"

"They mustn't leave! We're not safe!" screamed Harilla.

They had already left. The door behind Mitt burst open, and soldiers pelted out of it. Mitt leaped clear. But he had no chance to make himself obvious. Everyone on the steps was pushed off and toppled in all directions. The fat woman landed almost on top of Mitt and knocked him sprawling. By the time he had picked himself up, and then her, the soldiers had pelted off.

"Shut *up*!" Hildy snapped at Harilla. She was trying to see what was happening on the waterfront. Navis was bending over Hadd, and the rest of the procession was crowding round. Soldiers were running. People from the crowd were surging forward to see. Uncle Harchad, keeping prudently among a crowd, was running, too. Hildy saw her father stand up and point to the boat where the shot had been fired, wave to the soldiers, and wave the crowd back. Then he stooped again, and stood up holding Poor Old Ammet. He turned this way and that with him, showing people what he was doing, and then threw him into the harbor with the traditional shout. Then he picked up Libby Beer and slung her after.

Hildy felt a mixture of pride and horrible embarrassment. She could see her father was trying to assure the citizens of Holand that this did not mean unmitigated bad luck. But it was doubtful if anybody noticed. People were surging about. Numbers were leaving. Soldiers were running out to *Proud Ammet* along the curving harbor wall. There were screams and shouts which drowned Navis's voice. Nevertheless, the rest of the procession followed his lead. In a ragged, unconvinced way, garlands began to loop out from the quay and fall on the water. By this time Uncle Harchad had reached the waterfront. Hildy watched him and Navis kneel down beside her grandfather, with red and yellow garlands sailing around them, until the harbor seemed full of bobbing fruit and wet flowers, and wondered what they were feeling. She could see Hadd was dead, but she seemed to have no feelings about that at all.

The fat woman was very grateful to Mitt. She clung to him, and he had to help her to the street beyond the house. "You're a sweet boy," she kept saying. "Come on up to the stalls, and I'll buy you something."

Mitt refused. He had to be where the soldiers were. It was the only thing left for him to do. Half his life's work had fallen to someone else's bullet. Hands to the North, curse them! he thought. He knew he would never get a chance to be revenged on Hadd now. But the other half remained. He had to get caught and get questioned and, with the utmost reluctance, let out that it was Siriol, Ham, and Dideo who set him on to plant the bomb. So, as soon as he had shaken off the fat woman, he went back to the waterfront.

By the time he got there, the other murderer had very thoroughly stolen his thunder. Soldiers were shouting to people to get back and get home, while other soldiers tried to open a path for what was left of the procession, carrying Hadd's body. More soldiers were in and out of the house where the screaming girls were. The place was full of groups of people hurrying purposefully this way and that, in uniform, in Festival dress, or in holiday best. The result was utter confusion. The only thing which did not seem to be happening, Mitt thought bitterly, was the revolution the Free Holanders had confidently expected once Hadd was dead.

Mitt shrugged. For lack of any better plan, he did as he used to do three years back and joined a hurrying group of total strangers. With them, he was swept right across the waterfront to the other side of the harbor. And when we're there, I bet we hurry all the way back again, he thought.

He was right. An officer stopped them near the harbor wall. "Only authorized persons past this spot."

Mitt's group obediently turned away. "Alham must have gone up Fishmarket then," someone said, in a worried, busy voice, and they all set off again in the opposite direction.

Mitt lagged and let them hurry away. He could see the masts of the smaller boats from here, sawing the sky as heavy soldiers jumped from one to another, hunting the murderer. Even the masts of the big ships were swaying sedately, so many were the soldiers searching them. A group of seamen who had been on the ships were being herded and prodded roughly along the harbor wall.

They'll catch *him* all right, Mitt thought resentfully.

A new group of people surged up beside him. These were clearly important. They were officers in braid, well-nourished men in good cloth, with, in their midst, a tall, thin man with a pale jagged profile. The man's clothes had a wonderful sober richness. Mitt saw the sleek glint of velvet, and fur, and the flicker of jewels, worn where they did not show, because the man was too used to having them to bother with their value. Mitt knew that pale, jutting face, though he had never, to his knowledge, seen the fellow before. It had the same bad-tempered lines as Hadd's. The nose was the one he had whirled his rattle under. The rest of the features were like the ones he had seen advancing on him behind Libby Beer to kick the bomb away. This could only be Harchad.

Proper flinty flake off the old block, he is, Mitt thought, looking up at him with interest. Wearing six farms and ten years' fishing on his back, and *he* don't care!

"Oh, stop bleating, man!" Harchad snapped at the man with the most braid. "Those seamen are to be questioned till we get something. I don't care if you kill them all. And I want the brat who threw the bomb, too. He was obviously an accomplice. I want him brought to *me* when you find him."

Mitt's stomach, for the first time in his life, gave a cold little jolt. He lowered his eyes from Harchad's face and gently backed away. Wonder how he'd look if he knew I was right beside him, he thought. Accomplice, was I? O flaming Ammet! I think everything's gone wrong. He tiptoed hurriedly sideways to join the nearest group of hurrying citizens.

The man in braid shouted. "There he is now! That's him!"

"Who?"

"The brat who threw that bomb."

Mitt had the merest glimpse of them all staring at him. Harchad's face jutted out of the rest in a way that dried Mitt's mouth, tongue and all, and almost wrung a scream out of him. It was as horrible as his nightmares about Canden. He turned and ran, mindlessly. His only idea was to make his legs go faster than their fastest. He had to get away from the gathering shouts behind him. He had to escape from that face. He shot across the waterfront, not knowing whether he hit people or avoided them as he ran. He dived into the nearest road and ran there for all he was worth. It filled with banging feet behind him. Mitt ran harder still, turned a corner and ran, and ran again, and went on running. The only thing in his mind was the shouting and ringing feet behind him, and he did not stop running until they had grown faint and died away.

When his breath came back, he wandered wearily round a corner into the next street. He was deeply ashamed of himself. What had got into him? What had made him, the free soul, fearless Mitt, who had never turned a hair during all the errands he had run for the Free Holanders—what had possessed him—to panic at the mere sight of Harchad and run away? Mitt could not understand it. What had made everything go so wrong?

"Here, love. Have hold of this and cheer up."

Mitt looked up to find himself in an airy, respectable street, quite some way above the waterfront. It was full of handsomely painted houses. Mitt dimly remembered the one just up the hill from him, with the double gable and the two stiff figures painted on it. The street was full of quiet, cheerful people in respectable holiday clothes, who were buying things at the stalls which lined the street. It did not seem as if a whisper of the events at the harbor had reached this far. All was peace and sober enjoyment.

The person who had spoken to Mitt was a woman behind one of the stalls. She was leaning forward across rows of little Ammets and Libbys, holding a toffee apple out toward Mitt. She smiled when he looked, and waggled the apple invitingly on its stick. "Here. Take this for luck. Your face is as long as Flate Dike, my love."

Mitt did his best to grin. Running had filled his mouth with thick, bitter juice. He did not want a toffee apple. But he could see the woman meant to be kind. "Oh, no, thanks, lady. I just lost a lifetime's work, see, and I'm off my food a bit."

"Well, then, you need an appetizer," said the woman, and she tried to push the toffee apple into Mitt's hand.

Mitt found he really could not bear the thought of sticky toffee and sour apple, and he backed away. "No, thanks, lady. Honest. Much obliged."

"Please yourself," she said. "But I've got to give you *something* now I've started, or it's bad luck for both of us. Here." She picked up one of the little images of Libby Beer from the line on the front of the stall and held her out to Mitt. "You can have her then. I'm just clearing up to go, anyway." Mitt did not know if the woman really wanted luck or if she was simply trying to cheer him up, but he took the little image and tried to grin again. "And don't try eating her. She's made of wax," said the woman. "The year's luck to you."

"Luck to you, ship and shore," Mitt said politely, just as he should. He wandered on down the street, clutching the knobby little figure and wondering what to do with it. Perhaps I could make Harchad a present of her, he thought.

He was three stalls lower down when boots hammered on the flagway behind him. Six soldiers with an officer at their head swung round the corner the way Mitt had come and halted by the woman's stall. "Hey, you. Anyone. Seen a boy in Festival breeches, no jacket, very skinny?"

The sober respectable hum in the street died away completely. Nobody moved. Mitt froze, bending over the stall beside him, pretending to look at little Ammets. He tried to will himself to make a dash down the street and bring the soldiers after him. But there was no question of that, somehow. He could only wait for the woman who had given him Libby Beer to give him away.

"Yes, indeed, I have seen him, sir," she said. "Just this minute. I offered him a toffee apple, and he went away down the street."

The soldiers nodded and came on down the street.

Mitt stood with a bright imitation Libby Beer in one hand and the other stretched out to touch the plaited corn of an Ammet and still could not move. He did not blame the woman. Other people had seen her talking to Mitt, and she dared not deny it. In the old days it used to make him amused and rather scornful, the way even respectable people like these went in dread of Harchad's soldiers. It made him think he must be the only free soul in Holand. But now he did not seem to be a free soul any longer. He dared not move. He had to stand there till the soldiers saw him.

The boots clomped by. Mitt could see and feel everyone's eyes moving between him and the green uniforms. But nobody said a word. The boots clomped on to the end of the street and faded out of hearing. There was sighing and shifting all round. Someone behind Mitt, who must have blocked the soldiers' view of him, said, "Go on, lad. Run while the going's good." Mitt did not see who said it, but he ran.

Isn't that Holand people all over! he thought as he ran back round the corner and plunged downhill toward the harbor again. Where they could be, they were kind. But you could never count on it. Yesterday this kindness had amused him. Now there did not seem to be anything left to laugh at. Tears trickled across Mitt's cheeks as he ran, as he thought of all those years of planning gone to waste.

I wonder if there's something wrong deep inside of me, he thought. It don't surprise me. He tried to wipe the tears off his face and found he was brushing it with something knobbly. He looked, and there was the little Libby Beer, made of wax cherries and rose hips and miniature apples, glistening with his tears. "Goh!" said Mitt, and stuffed her angrily in his scarlet pocket. Crying did no good. Next time he met any soldiers, there would be no mistake. He was going to get caught.

He came down into the old town, through a street of peeling houses breathing the smell of the poor quarters out through their open front doors—the smell of too many people, dirt, damp plaster, and cheap food. All the children from the houses were playing in the road. There was hopscotch nearest, marbles a little way on, and then two of the running, shouting kind of games. And through the shrill yells, Mitt sensed more soldiers coming. The rhythm of their boots was in the very air.

Mitt did not decide what to do. He moved without thinking, round the hopscotch to the game of marbles, and dropped down to squat in the ring of smaller boys. It was a trick he had often played three years back. Unless the boys were doing something very secret, they usually did not mind. But as he hurriedly wiped the tears off his face with his wrist, Mitt was amazed at himself. Here, he thought. What am I doing?

The rhythm of boots beat in the dirty pavement under him and a green block of soldiers swept round the corner. When they saw the children, the *clump-clump* of their boots slackened and became a slow puttering. They had broken step and were coming slowly down the street, looking very carefully indeed.

The yelling and the games stopped. The children stood in awkward rows, staring. The small boys round Mitt were not really playing marbles anymore. They were waiting for the soldiers to pass. And Mitt crouched with them, in such terror that he could hardly see or feel. He had not known it was possible to be so frightened. He knew he stuck out like a sore thumb among these children. He was half as big again as any of them. His red leg blazed and his yellow leg shone. And he could not trust little kids like these not to give him away, either by accident or on purpose, for spoiling their games. At any moment a shrill voice might say, "That's the one you want, mister."

As the soldiers puttered toward him, Mitt no longer had any doubt what he was doing. He was trying not to be caught. And as wave after wave of pure fear swept over him, he knew he was going to go on trying. By the time the soldiers were level with him, his terror was worse than the worst pain he had ever known. Mitt crouched down over his blazing legs, squeezing himself into himself to look as small as possible, and forced himself to put out a hand, take a marble, and roll it casually into the middle of the ring. He had to fight his terror every inch in order to move at all. He thought he could have rolled Siriol's boat across the pavement more easily. The effort made him weak.

As soon as the marble left his hand, he was sure he had done the wrong thing. The boy next to him shot him a nasty look. The puttering boots went slower, as if the movement had attracted their attention. Mitt almost lost his senses, he was so terrified. Time swam forward, sickeningly slow and blurred.

The boots puttered down past the hopscotch, stopped, and started again, in step this time. *Clump-clump-clump*, they went, away into faintness.

"Buzz off," said the boy. "You spoiled my go."

Mitt stumbled to his feet. He felt dizzy, and as cramped as if he had spent a winter night fishing. He had to limp down the street. None of the games started again. The children watched Mitt as they had watched the soldiers. Bad, that was bad. They would tell of him to someone. Mitt hoped they would not tell too soon because he felt far too tired to run. He felt like curling up in the nearest doorway and crying himself to sleep.

Get a hold of yourself! he thought angrily. You're on the run, that's all. People go on the run all the time in this place. I don't know how it keeps happening, but it's like I can't help myself from running. What's gone wrong with me? This was a question Mitt simply could not answer. He only knew that he had got up this morning, intending, as he had intended for the last four years, to finish Hadd and the Free Holanders at one stroke. And now he had failed to finish Hadd, his one idea seemed not to be caught.

Oh, now, wait a minute! Mitt stopped and pretended to loiter in a yard doorway. There were still the Free Holanders. If he was too scared to get himself caught, he could easily just go to Siriol's house, or Dideo's. Where Mitt went now, Harchad's spies would swiftly follow. It was just as good a way of getting the Free Holanders caught. But the reason Mitt stopped, leaning on the doorpost and gaping at nothing, was that he was not even tempted. "Not even tempted!" he repeated to himself. And it was true. It was nothing dramatic. Mitt could not tell himself he would rather die than go to Siriol's house—he knew he would do anything rather than die—but he was still not going there. Or to Dideo. "What do you think they are then? Friends?" Mitt asked himself derisively.

It seemed as if they were. He remembered the smile on Dideo's netted face when Mitt brought him the first little packet of saltpeter, and Siriol glowering at him over a rope's end but never hitting him more than just that once. And I reckon he ought to have done, Mitt thought. He ought to have knocked me through a Mitt-shaped hole in the side of *Flower of Holand*, over and over. He found himself smiling a little. Siriol always understood his jokes, and Ham scarcely ever did. Then there was Alda, puffing arris at everyone, and Lydda going to marry that sailor off *Lovely Libby*. I got to know them too well, Mitt thought.

It did no good to stand there, smiling and staring. Mitt walked on. He supposed his best plan was to use the escape arrangements Siriol had so carefully made for him.

"No!" Mitt exclaimed. It was not that he did not want to use them. He did. He would have given his ears to. But he could not remember a thing about them. Thinking he would not need to escape, he had attended to Siriol's plans probably even less than he had listened to Hobin telling him about guns. He had a vague idea there was a cart somewhere and a password. But that was absolutely all he knew. Of all the fools!

But what was he to *do*? He could not spend the rest of his life sneaking round the streets of Holand. If he looked for all the carts he could find, he would certainly be caught. The soldiers would think of that. He dared not go home. That would get Hobin and Milda arrested, too. The only thing he dared do was take to the Flate, like so many freedom fighters before him. But he knew a bit about that. You got hunted down there. And it was a miserable life unless you were lucky enough to have a gun and could shoot marsh birds for food. Mitt had no gun. He knew where guns were, though: locked up in Hobin's workshop. And he dared not go near there. Oh, it went round in circles. *Why* hadn't he attended to Siriol? Mitt knew why, really. He had simply not thought of anything beyond the moment when he was to plant that bomb. I must be flaming insane! Mitt said to himself. *Do* something, can't you!

He wanted to go home, that was what he wanted to do. And he dared not.

Or dared he? Hobin was out for the day. Milda was at Siriol's with the babies. If Mitt went there, spies would follow. But spies would probably go there, anyway, because Hobin had gunpowder. Suppose Mitt were to go there, take gun and ammunition, and make it look like a burglary? It would have to look like a burglary, anyway, because he would have to break locks and the seals of the inspectors to get anything. Hobin could not be blamed for being burgled. It would be a way of keeping suspicion from him. In fact, the more Mitt thought about it, the more it seemed his duty to go and burgle Hobin. Then do what? Go out in the Flate and try to get North, Mitt supposed.

It made a considerable difference to have a purpose again. Mitt felt far less tired. Flate Street was quite near. Mitt purposely doubled the distance to it. He wanted to be seen in as many places as possible, to confuse the spies. When he finally arrived behind the high greasy wall which cut the light off the back of the workshop, Mitt was fairly confident that any spy trying to trace him would not arrive until tomorrow. He thought two days was more likely. But he said tomorrow, because it never paid to underestimate Harchad's spies.

The wall made one side of an alley, with another sightless wall opposite. Mitt stood facing it, breathing deeply. He had to reckon on being seen going over the top of the wall. If he allowed time for whoever saw him to fetch help and break down the front door of the workshop—or fetch soldiers to do it—there should just be time to take what he wanted and then break the place up a bit. But it was only a very short time. Mitt knew it might be a close thing. He wished his knees would not tremble and his heart knock so. He was not *used* to being frightened like this.

9

"And I missed everything!" was Ynen's disgusted comment when at last Hildy arrived back at the Palace and he managed to find her.

The Palace was all doubts and hushed voices and indecision. Only one thing was certain: Hadd was dead, and Harl was now Earl of Holand. But when you had said that, you had said everything. Nobody knew if there was an uprising, or whether to take off the Festival clothes, or what would happen about the feast which had been prepared. Harl did nothing but sit in his room. He had not given one order. Harchad came and went and gave orders perpetually, but nothing seemed to come of them.

"Well, in that case there can't be an uprising," Hildy said rather snappishly when Ynen told her what it had been like. "We didn't see anyone but soldiers all the way back." She felt as if she wanted to be alone, but Ynen looked so lost that she stayed with him. They wandered stairs and corridors together, among people who had as little idea as they had what to do.

Ynen told Hildy some of the rumors about the murderer. He had been caught; he had not been found. He was a discontented seaman; he was a dangerous revolutionary and an agent for the North. He was a superb marksman; he was a fool who had fired a lucky shot; he had used a new secret weapon from the North. He had poisoned himself; he had jumped into the harbor and escaped. No one knew what the truth was. "Now tell me what it was *like,* by the harbor," Ynen said.

"I don't know," Hildy said, quite honestly. "Anyway, you know what it's like when Harilla has hysterics." But she did try to describe what had happened. It was not Ynen's fault he had missed it.

"Did Father really do all that?" Ynen asked. "I didn't know he could move fast enough." He added wistfully, "I *wish* I could have seen that boy twirl a rattle under Grandfather's nose."

"It wasn't as funny as you think," said Hildy. "It—it was queer. He didn't run away. I suppose he's caught by now." Then she found she really did need to be alone and went to her room. But Ynen came with her, and she had not the heart to tell him to go away. He sat curled up on the window seat, while Hildy sat cross-legged in the middle of her big square bed.

Here Hildy tried for the hundredth time to sort out

how she felt. It was a very shocking thing that her grand-father had been murdered. That she knew. And it was a shocking time to kill him. Everybody said it meant terrible bad luck. Hildy found she was still far more embarrassed than proud at the way her father had tried to save the day. It was the way nobody had noticed that made her so uncomfortable. But about the actual murder, she simply felt awed and respectful—and subdued all over, so that she moved gently and quietly and wanted to be alone. She could not manage to feel strongly about it. And this was odd, because she knew that somewhere, about something, she felt very strongly indeed. She was raging with feelings, but she did not know what *about*. It reminded her of the way she had felt when her father had told her she was engaged to Lithar.

Here Hildy sprang up. "Wait," she said to Ynen when he sprang up, too. Ynen sat down with a sigh, and Hildy sped to her father's rooms.

She knocked at the heavy door. There was no answer. Hildy, a little hesitantly, turned the handle and went in. There was no one in the first room. She went on to the second.

Navis was sitting by the window, still in his Festival clothes. Perhaps he was trying to sort out how he felt, too. At any rate he was not reading the book he had in his hand. He was staring out into the Flate.

Hildy saw at a glance that he had gone back to being cold, idle, and proud. There was little chance of anybody making him do anything which was not absolutely necessary. Hildy ground her teeth with fury. How could he rise to the occasion at the waterfront and then sink from it like this? And if he was still mourning about her mother, Hildy had no sympathy for him whatsoever. He had been like this far too *long*!

"Father," she said.

Navis jumped slightly. "Did I forget to lock my door?"

"I'll go away in a minute," said Hildy. "Are you sorry Grandfather's dead?"

"Er," said her father. "He was an old man."

Hildy thought angrily that *that* was no way to speak. She wondered whether to flatter him by saying she thought he had behaved extremely well by the harbor. But it was beside the subject, it was not true, and she did not think it would rouse Navis, anyway. "I came to ask you," she said, champing at the words because she was so angry, "if I need to marry Lithar now."

"What's that got to do with the situation?" Navis asked.

"Grandfather arranged it," Hildy said, trying to be patient. "But I don't want to marry him. So will you cancel it, please?"

Navis looked at his book as if he would rather attend to that than Hildy. "I think you'll find the alliance is prized quite as much now."

"What does that mean? *Can't* you cancel it?" Hildy demanded.

"I doubt it," said her father.

"Don't you *care*?" said Hildy.

"I fancy I do," Navis admitted. "But with things in this state of upheaval—"

Hildy lost her grip on her temper. "Ye gods! Nobody cares in this place! You're the worst of the lot! You just sit there, after all that happens, and you don't even care that nobody even knows if there's going to be a feast or not!"

"Don't they?" Navis asked, rather surprised. "Really, Hildy, there *is* nothing to do at the moment but sit. I'm very sorry—"

"You're *not* sorry!" raved Hildy. "But I'll make you sorry! You just wait!" She turned to storm out of the rooms.

Navis called after her. "Hildy!" She turned round to find him looking oddly anxious. "Hildy, will you make sure you and Ynen stay where I can find you?"

"Why?" Hildy said haughtily.

"I may need you in a hurry."

This was such an unlikely thing that Hildy simply made a scornful noise and crashed out of her father's rooms, slamming each door behind her as hard as she could. She was so angry, and so determined to make Navis sorry, that she reached the gallery outside her uncle Harl's rooms on a surge of blind fury and had almost no idea how she got there. She was fetched back to her senses by running into her cousins Harilla and Irana. They were hurrying the other way. Harilla's face was still streaked with red from her recent hysterics.

Irana's was red all over.

"It's no good," Irana said. "If you're going where I think you're going. They're both pigs."

Harilla gasped, "I wish I was dead!" and burst into tears. Irana led her away.

Hildy wondered what was the matter with them this time. When she saw that there were guards outside her uncle's rooms, she supposed that meant Harl had refused to see them. She marched up to the guards, prepared for battle. But they stood aside, most respectfully, and one opened the door for her. Hildy marched on into the antechamber, rather puzzled. The servants there bowed. She heard her uncle Harl's voice from the room beyond.

"I tell you I owe the fellow a favor! He killed old Haddock, didn't he? Let him get away."

"Don't be an ass, Harl!" snapped Uncle Harchad's voice.

"With my blessing," added Harl.

"Look, Harl, if we don't catch him—" Harchad broke off irritably as Hildy came in.

Harl looked at her and let out a great guffaw. He was sitting in great comfort, with his shoes off and his feet on a chair. A table under his beefy elbow was crowded with wine bottles. He seemed very happy. He was grinning and sweating with happiness all over his big, bluff face. Harchad, on the other hand, was sitting tensely on the edge of his chair, nervily twiddling a full glass of wine. His face was paler than usual.

"Ha! Ha!" bellowed Harl. "Now it's Hildrida. That

makes the full set of them. We haven't any more, have we, Harchad? Daughters and nieces and things?"

"No," said Harchad. He did not seem to find it funny. "If you please, Hildrida. We are trying to talk business. Say what you have to say quickly, and then go."

Hildy stared at them. She had never paid much attention to her uncle Harl before. He had always been a lazy, sober, silent man—and so ordinary. Nothing he said or did was ever remarkable. But now Uncle Harl was drunk, drunker even than the soldiers got on their nights off. And he was not drowning his sorrow either. He was celebrating. And Uncle Harchad was no more sorry about Grandfather than Harl was. But he was frightened: scared stiff in case he got shot next.

Harl pointed a drunken finger at Hildy. "Don't say it. We know. All the rest said it." He put on a high, squeaky voice. "'Please, Uncle, will you break off my betrothal, please?' Who's she betrothed to?" he asked Harchad.

"Lithar," said Harchad. "Holy Islands. And the answer's no, Hildrida. We need all the allies we can get."

"So it's no good asking," said Harl. He wriggled his stockinged toes at Hildy and produced strange cracking sounds.

At this Hildy's anger blazed up again. "You're quite wrong," she said haughtily. "I wasn't going to ask. I was going to tell you. I am *not* marrying Lithar or anyone else you try to choose for me. I'm quite determined about it, and you can't make me."

Her two uncles looked at one another. "She's quite determined, and we can't make her," said Harl. "This one had to be different. Her father's Navis."

"I'm afraid you'll find you're mistaken, Hildrida," said Harchad. "We *can* make you. And we will."

"I shall refuse," said Hildy. "Utterly. There's nothing you can do."

"She'll refuse utterly," said Harl.

"She will not," said Harchad.

"She can if she wants," said Harl. "She'll be married by proxy, anyway. Can't expect Lithar to come all this way. You refuse, my dear girl," he said to Hildy. "Refuse all you want if it makes you happy. It won't bother us." He wriggled his toes at Hildy again, and once more they cracked. Harl was impressed. "Hear that, Harchad? That noise was my toes. Wonder why they do that."

Hildy clenched her teeth in order not to scream at him. "Lithar might bother if I refuse."

Harl bawled with laughter. A small smile flitted on Harchad's face. "Well, it'll be you he takes it out on, won't it?" said Harl. "That doesn't worry me!" He lay back in his chair and grinned at the idea.

"All right," said Hildy. "Don't say I didn't warn you." She swung round and swept out, with her back very straight and her chin up, willing herself not to let the tears in her eyes fall until she was past the attendants, and then the soldiers. Then she ran. She ran to find Ynen. He was the only person in the Palace who was kind.

She could not find him. She dried her tears on her

sleeve and searched grimly, high and low, right down to the kitchens. The cooks there were cursing. Hildy discovered that Navis had bestirred himself sufficiently to cancel the feast. She was angrier than ever. To think that out of what she had said to him, this was the one thing he had attended to! She wanted to bite something and tear things up. She stormed to her own room, wondering if a sheet or a curtain would be best to tear.

Ynen was there, still curled up on her window seat. By this time he was feeling very doleful. Hildy was a little ashamed to think she had clean forgotten telling him to wait.

"Hildy," he said plaintively before he noticed her state of mind. "Why is it all so miserable?"

"Can't you *think* why?" Hildy snapped. She seized the coverlet on her bed, a good handful in each hand, and wrenched. It gave way with the most satisfactory ripping noise.

Ynen's eyes widened. He wished he had not spoken. Now he knew he would have to say something else, or Hildy would turn on him for sitting there like a dumb idiot. "Yes," he said. "It's because nobody's even pretending to be sorry Grandfather's dead."

"How right you are!" Hildy snarled. Carefully, almost with enjoyment, she tore a long strip off the coverlet.

Ynen watched her anxiously and kept talking. "People are more sorry about the Festival being messed up. They go on about bad luck. And the awful thing," he said hurriedly as Hildy began on another strip, "is that I don't care about Grandfather either. I just feel sort of shocked. It makes me think I'm wicked."

Hildy finished the second strip. Then, fists up and elbows out, she began on a third. "Wicked! What a stupid way to talk! Grandfather was a horrible old man, and you *know* he was! If people didn't do exactly what he wanted, he had them killed, or tried them for treason if they were lords." She dragged the third strip down to the selvage and wrenched to tear that. She began on a fourth. "The only people who dared argue with him were other earls, and he quarreled with them all the time. Why should you be sorry? Even so," she said, rending the fourth strip loose, "I felt sick when I heard Uncle Harl calling him old Haddock."

Ynen judged that Hildy's temper was cooling. He risked laughing. "Everyone called him that!"

"I wish I'd known," said Hildy. "I'd have said it, too."

This encouraged Ynen to believe she was almost calm again. "Hildy," he said, "that was rather a good coverlet."

It had been a good one. It was blue and gold, and worked in a pattern of roses. The sewing women down in Holand had taken a good month to embroider it. Hildy's four furious strips had left it a square of ragged, puckered cloth about four feet long. "I don't care," said Hildy. Her rage flared up again. She seized the puckered square and tore it and tore it. "I hate good things!" she raged. "They give us good coverlets, and golden clocks, and beautiful boats, and they don't do it because they like us or care about us. All they think of is whether we'll come in useful for their plans!"

"Nobody thinks I'm useful at all," Ynen said. That was the reason for his misery, but he had been ashamed to say it before.

Hildy glared round at him, and he shrank. "I could murder them for thinking that!" she raved. "Why do you *have* to be useful? You're nice. You're the only nice person in this whole horrible Palace!" Ynen went pink. He was very flattered, but he would like to have been told he was useful, too. And he wished Hildy would realize that she was quite as alarming raging *for* him as she was raging *at* him. "I intend to teach them a lesson," Hildy proclaimed.

"They probably won't notice," Ynen said. "I wish we could go and live somewhere else. Somebody told me Father preferred living in the country. Do you think if I asked him—?"

Hildy interrupted him with a squawk of angry laughter. "Go and ask one of the statues in the throne room! They'll pay more attention."

Ynen knew she was right. But now he had talked about going away from the Palace, he knew it was the one thing he really wanted to do. "Hildy, couldn't we go out for the rest of the day? I hate the Palace like this. Couldn't we go sailing—oh, I forgot. You're not allowed to anymore, are you?"

"Don't be a fool! The place is full of revolutionaries.

They won't let us go out," said Hildy. But she could see from the window behind Ynen that it was perfect weather for sailing. "Won't all the sailors have a holiday today?"

Ynen sighed. "Yes. I wouldn't have a crew." Still, it had been a good idea. "Suppose we rode out to High Mill then?"

But Hildy stood looking from the window to the ruins of her coverlet. There was going to be trouble about that. It was a silly thing to get into trouble about on its own. She ought to do something worse. She was aching to do something really terrible and show everybody. She remembered Navis had asked them to stay where he could find them. That decided her. "Let's go sailing, Ynen," she said. "And let's give them a fright. Let's knot the coverlet and hang it out of the window, and make them think we've run away." Ynen looked at her dubiously. "I can crew," said Hildy. "You can be captain because it's your boat."

"You don't mind getting into awful trouble?" said Ynen.

"I do not," said Hildy.

Ynen jumped up, so full of pleasure and mischief that he looked like a different boy. "Come on then! We'll need warm clothes, and we'd better pinch some food, too. We'll have to sneak out past the kitchens, anyway."

Hildy laughed at the change in him as she snatched up two strips of coverlet and knotted them together. She pulled the knot tight. There was an ominous ripping noise. "It wouldn't bear a sparrow, this stuff," she said.

"It's only got to look used," Ynen pointed out. "Pull it as tight as you can without tearing it." He helped her make the knots and then to tie the fraying strip to the window frame and let it down outside. It did not reach very far. "It'll do," Ynen said hopefully. "We could have jumped down onto the library roof."

Hildy leaned out beside him. Their rope dangled a pitiful sixteen feet. The library dome was twenty feet or more below that. "They'll wonder how we didn't break our necks," she said. "Go and get warm clothes. I'll come to your room when I've changed."

Ynen raced off, hardly the same boy who had sat miserably on Hildy's window seat half the afternoon. Hildy, as she changed into a short woolen dress, sea boots, socks, and a pea jacket, told herself she was doing right. Ynen was so happy. She still felt wonderfully rebellious, but she was also just a little scared. There were people in Holand with bombs and guns. She had seen them.

"They won't know who we are," she told her reflection in the mirror. "And I'm sick of being important." She took her hair down and did it in pigtails, to look as ordinary as possible, and collected dust from all the corners where she could find it and rubbed it on her face. Then she threw her good clothes to the back of a closet and set off for Ynen's room.

Her cousins Harilla and Irana were coming along the passage. Hildy dodged behind a grand china vase. She heard them go into her room. Harilla was saying: "Well, Hildy, did they let you break off your betrothal? You needn't think—Oh!"

Hildy dodged out from the vase and ran, as quietly as she could in sea boots. "Quick!" she told Ynen. "Harilla found the coverlet."

"It would be her, wouldn't it?" said Ynen.

They could tell the alarm was up as they crept down toward the kitchens. There was a great deal of noise and running about. But everyone seemed to believe that Hildy and Ynen would be found in the direction of the library. It was easy to avoid the people running there from the kitchens, and once they reached the kitchens, there were very few people left there. They heard someone whistling and dishes clattering, but the sounds echoed with emptiness. Ynen risked opening the door of a pantry.

"Look at that!" he said. The pantry was full, from floor to ceiling, with pies—glazed pies, golden pies, puffy pies, tarts, flans, pasties, and pies with flowers and birds on them. "Pass us a couple of those sacks," said Ynen. "Let's make it look as if we took enough for a week."

They pulled the pantry door to behind them and, in the half-dark, seized what pies came first to hand and stuffed the sacks with them. While they were doing it, footsteps hurried outside, backward and forward. They waited for whoever it was to go away, and took the opportunity to eat a pasty each.

"Seems quiet now," Hildy whispered.

They wiped gravy and crumbs off their mouths and tiptoed out. The kitchen gate was just beyond. The footsteps had been Uncle Harchad's. He had done them a favor. The soldiers who should have been on guard at the gate were standing stiffly just inside the kitchen door up the passage, listening to Harchad, along with the scullions left in the kitchen.

"And you're absolutely sure neither of them has gone past?" they heard Harchad saying.

"Quite sure, sir."

"If you see them, I want them brought to me, understand? Not to Earl Harl," said Uncle Harchad.

Nobody saw or heard Ynen and Hildy tiptoe to the gate, open the small postern carved in the big door, and slip out of it with their sacks.

⚜10⚜

Mitt took a last deep breath, hurled himself across the alley, and ran up the wall. If you are light and strong and determined, you can get a long way up a wall like this. Mitt's feet scrambled, his breath sawed, and his fingers caught and slipped in the greasy bricks overhead. His right hand managed to clench in a crumbly crack. He threw the other arm over the top of the wall. Then, with a rasping slide and a slither, he was over and down, in his own backyard, terrified at the noise he had made.

It was queer. It looked like a strange backyard already. Mitt had not remembered it so small and grimy, or the target on the wall so pitted, or the mangle so rusty. As he stole over the slippery earth, he could hardly believe that just as usual, he would be able to slide up the workshop window and unlatch the back door. Yet just as usual, he put his arm in and the cold latch clicked upward under his fingers. He pulled open the door, *creeeak,* and slipped round it into the grimy, gloomy workshop.

Remember to break that window, Mitt thought. Noisy. Pity. Do it last. He crept across the room and picked up a crowbar. He looked at the rack of finished guns—locked, with the seal of Holand dangling from the lock—and the chests of powder—each kind separate, and locked, with the seal of Holand dangling there, too. He wished Hobin was not so careful. He was going to have to break everything, mix his own powder, make his own cartridges.

There was a soft, purposeful movement behind him. Mitt's heart hammered, and his tongue suddenly grew too fat for his mouth. He whirled round, with his hand wet on the crowbar. Hobin was just latching the door which led upstairs to the house.

"That you, Hobin?" Mitt said weakly. Cold despair set in. Everything was going wrong. Hobin should have been out at High Mill, but he was here instead, and wearing his good clothes, as if he had never been out for a walk at all.

Hobin nodded. "I was hoping you'd be along. You've got some sense left, I see." He walked deliberately across the workshop, even more solid and grave than usual. Mitt could not help backing away, even though he knew he would be cut off from the back door. And he was. Hobin stationed himself by the back window, and Mitt knew he was doing it on purpose.

"But you went out," said Mitt. "With Ham."

"And I came back," said Hobin. "Without him."

"And—" Mitt pointed jerkily upward with the crowbar. "My mother. She in?"

Hobin shook his head. "At Siriol's, isn't she? We'd best keep her out of this. Mitt, what kind of fool do you think I am to get taken in by someone like Ham? And what did you think you were aiming to do?"

Mitt swallowed. "I—I came for a gun. I was going to make it like robbers broke in. Honest, Hobin, I wasn't meaning to get you into trouble."

"No, I mean out there on the waterfront," said Hobin.

"Oh," said Mitt.

"You do take me for a fool, don't you?" said Hobin. "I can tell my gunpowder to a grain. I knew it was you taking it, but I never thought it was you who was going to use it. Who was the one that shot the Earl? Another of your precious fishermen?"

"I don't know. Hands to the North, I suppose. Hobin," said Mitt, "let me have a gun. Then I'll go away and never bother you again. Please. Everything went wrong."

"I saw it go wrong," said Hobin. "I was right by you when you chucked your fizz-bang. And it was lucky for them, after that Navis kicked it away, that none of them caught you. Then there was nothing I could do but hope you'd have the sense not to trust those fishermen to get you away. Because you're in really bad trouble, Mitt. And it's not funny. Not this time."

"I know!" said Mitt. "I know! There'll be spies here

by tomorrow asking for me."

"Tomorrow!" said Hobin. "You must be joking! They'll be here by sundown. I give them till then to notice it was one of my guns shot the Earl."

"One of yours? How can you tell?" Mitt wished Hobin would come away from the back door. He felt trapped.

"It had to be one of mine to throw straight over that distance," said Hobin. "And it fired first time. Now do you see why I keep well in with the arms inspectors? Or was that what you were counting on?"

"No, I was not," Mitt said wretchedly. "Why do you think I set Ham on you? What did you do with Ham, anyway?"

"Nothing, only gave him the slip," said Hobin. "Being the fool he is, he's still walking round in the Flate looking for me. No, I didn't see you thinking that way, but I couldn't help being riled over Ham. I could see through Ham easier than through that window." Hobin pointed to the grimy glass and came away from the back door at last. Mitt eyed the distance and was wondering whether to dash for it when Hobin said, "What did you aim to do when you'd pinched a gun?"

Mitt heard keys jingle. He looked round to see Hobin unlocking the rack of guns. He could hardly believe it. He knew the risk Hobin was running. "Go out on the Flate," he said. "See here, I don't want you in trouble. Make it look as if I stole it."

Hobin looked at him over his shoulder, almost as if he

was amused. "You keep taking me for a fool, Mitt. I'm not giving you one of these. If a man can make one gun, he can make two, can't he?" The whole rack of guns swung out from the wall. Hobin took two loose bricks out of the wall where it had been and reached into the space they left. While he was fumbling inside it, he said, "I wish you'd tell me what made you start on this freedom fighting nonsense, Mitt. Was it your father, or what?"

"I suppose it was," Mitt admitted. It seemed like confessing to one spot when you had measles, but it was the best he could do. Like an admission of failure, he laid the crowbar gently down.

"I thought that was it." Hobin wriggled the bricks back into place and swung the rack back to its usual position. He turned round carefully, carrying a strange, fat little gun. "And I hoped you'd grow up, Mitt," he said. "You've got your own life to live." Gently he spun the strange fat barrel of the gun round. Mitt had never seen a gun like it before. "Have you ever thought," Hobin asked, "what kind of man leaves you and Milda on your own like that?"

This was such an untoward question that Mitt was quite unable to answer it. "What kind of gun is that?" he said.

"The one I had in my pocket while you were planting your banger," said Hobin. "In case of trouble. I kept it loaded for you. But I can only let you have the six shots in it, so go easy on them. I can't cheat the inspectors much more than you can."

"*Six* shots?" said Mitt. "How do you do for priming?"

"You don't. Ever thought what I did with those percussion caps I set you making?" Hobin said. "They're in here, see, on the end of the cartridges, and the hammer fires them off. There's a barrel for each shot. You spin the next one up after you've fired. It doesn't throw far, or I wouldn't let you have it. This is to get you out of trouble, not get you in it, see. If it wasn't for Milda and the girls, I'd have kept you with me and sworn myself blue in the face you were with me all along, like I used to for Canden. But there's them to consider, too. There you are."

He put the gun in Mitt's hands. Like all Hobin's guns, it was beautifully balanced. Mitt hardly felt the weight of the chubby six-holed barrel at all. "What did you make this for?"

"Experiment," said Hobin. "And because one of these days there's going to be a real uprising here in the South. The earls can't hold people down forever. So I've made ready. I hoped you'd be patient and be ready, too. But there. You'll find your pea jacket on the stairs, and my belt to carry the gun in."

Mitt went to the stair door. There, sure enough, were his old pea jacket and the belt. "You—you had this all ready," he said awkwardly.

"What did you expect?" said Hobin. "Sometimes I think I'd make a better freedom fighter than any of you. I put a bit of thought into it. And I'll give you some advice, too. Don't go out in the Flate."

Mitt stopped in the middle of fastening Hobin's belt round himself. "Eh?"

"Eh?" said Hobin. "You're all the same. Do what the other man did. You've got a brain, Mitt. Use it. They'll expect you out in the Flate. You'll be caught by tomorrow lunchtime if you go that way. What you want to do is go up along the coast and see if you can't get a boat at Hoe or Little Flate. Or it's worth looking at the West Pool."

"Over those mucky dikes?" said Mitt.

"That won't kill you, and it's nearest. But I don't know what guard they set over their boats there. See how you go. And if you get anywhere in Canderack or Waywold where there's a gunsmith, go to him and tell him I sent you. They'll all know me. Come on," said Hobin. "I'll give you a lift up over the wall."

Mitt pushed the gun into the belt and put on his jacket. "But what are you going to tell them when they come—these spies?"

"Nail up this window for a start," said Hobin. "Then you may have tried to break in, but you didn't manage it. I'll be very grieved and disappointed in you, Mitt. You'll never darken my door again."

Though Hobin smiled slightly as he said that, Mitt knew that he was not likely to see Hobin again. As he went across the yard with him, Mitt felt unexpectedly wretched about it. He had never treated Hobin right, never even thought of him in the right way. He wanted to apologize to Hobin. But there seemed no time to say anything. Hobin had his hands joined ready for Mitt to tread in. Mitt sighed and put his foot on them.

"Happy birthday," Hobin whispered. "Luck ship and shore."

There had been so much else on Mitt's mind that he had clean forgotten it was his birthday. He wanted to thank Hobin for remembering. But Hobin heaved. Mitt went upward. He had only time for a hasty grin down at Hobin, before he was on top of the wall and slithering over the other side.

No one seemed to have seen him. Mitt set out into the depressed corner of Holand between the causeway to the West Pool and the dunes. It was not far. Flate Street was some way west to start with. And Mitt saw Hobin had been right to tell him to go this way. He only saw one party of soldiers, and these he hid from in a doorway, fingering the fat little gun as they passed and thinking: Better not come too near. Hobin gave me a birthday present you won't like.

The soldiers passed without seeing him. Mitt went on. The town petered out into marsh and shacks made of pieces of boat. There was no one about at all. Mitt, the seagulls, and the rubbish thrown into the pink marsh plants had it all to themselves. Mitt was glad of his coat. There was a fresh wind ripping over the dunes on his left, from the sea, which brimmed to the horizon above the dunes and looked higher than the land. Ahead was a bright green stretch where a network of brackish dikes broke through the dunes. Mitt would have to cross those in order to get to the seawall of the West Pool. He was still not too keen on the idea. But beyond that black line of wall there were masts—several hundred pleasure boats, large and small, awaiting Mitt's pleasure.

Good old Hobin! Mitt thought, making squelching strides through the pink marsh.

Then he came to the dikes. They were gray-green muddy ditches, just too wide to jump, threading the squashy green turf in front of the wall as intricately as the patterns Milda used to embroider on hangings for the Palace. Once they had been simply sea marsh. Now they were where the Palace sewers came out. As the tide was going out, they were running sluggishly, with scummy bubblings and a foot of gray mud above the waterline.

"Yuk!" said Mitt, and looked rather desperately toward the causeway, wondering whether he dared go that way instead. There were people on it. He could see them moving between the trees. Once again that awful, unusual fear seized him. He was afraid to move at all. I better wait for dark, he thought.

But the people, whoever they were, continued flickering slowly to and fro between the trees. Mitt, with his hands shaking, tore up an old stake and prodded the nearest ditch with it. The nasty water was only knee-deep.

I'll have a go, thought Mitt. He slithered down into the sour, salty mud. "Oh yuk! Shershplottle-shloosh! What filthy filth!" said Mitt. He waded through and climbed out. "Careful of that gun, now," he warned himself. A couple of yards on was another ditch. "Second sewer," said Mitt, sliding in with a shudder. "And now"—as he climbed out—"here comes another."

He was struggling out of that ditch when there were shouts from the causeway. Figures ran between the trees and leaped gingerly down on the green morass—green figures, darker than the marsh. Harchad had thought of the West Pool, too. Mitt went down, through and up out of that next dike quicker than the rats through the garbage on the waterfront. He was through the next two before the running soldiers reached their first. As he plunged down yet another slimy bank, he saw them stop there, about a hundred yards away.

Take them a while to bring themselves to go in, he thought. The wall of the Pool was about a hundred yards away, too. Mitt knew he would never get there. It was hopeless. He doubled over and ran along the ditch, splashing and squelching, keeping one hand over his coat and the gun. "Keep it dry. You might get one or two with it," he said to himself. The ditch bent and joined another one. When Mitt looked up, the wall of the Pool was quite a bit nearer. There was a buttress he might climb up. But he would have to come out of this ditch to get to it. Mitt rolled out and dived across the moist green turf.

Something went *pheeew* past his head and thudded *smick* into the bank of the dike beyond.

Mitt found himself up and running. He was so frightened that he felt as if he had got some dreadful disease. His legs hurt, his breathing hurt, and he felt giddy.

Bullets were going *pheeew-smick* all round him now. He thought he was like a chicken, running about with its neck wrung. He was sure he was dead.

Hey! thought Mitt. He was on the edge of another dike. *Pheeew-smick*. He threw up both arms, spun round, and fell. While he was falling, he had time to hoik Hobin's belt round him, so the gun was at his back, out of harm's way. He fell on his face on the cold, salty turf and let himself slide over sideways into the bubbling slime in the dike. He hardly noticed the smell.

There was one more shout from the distance, then businesslike silence.

Good, thought Mitt, and began to claw his way along below the bank on hands and knees.

"There are a lot of people," Ynen said uneasily when he and Hildy were halfway along the causeway. "Soldiers, I think. By the Pool gate."

They stopped, confounded, and humped their sacks of pies to the side of the road, where the trees hid them.

"It must be the uprising," said Hildy. "Do you think they'd let us past if I offered them a gold piece? I've got one."

"I don't know. There are an awful lot of them."

They loitered forward, under the trees. It was hard to know what to do. The soldiers might not stop them. On the other hand, Uncle Harchad had told the guards by the kitchen to bring them to him. He could have sent the same message to these soldiers.

"And it would be the most terrible waste if they sent us back *now*," said Hildy.

Before they were near enough to see or be seen clearly, they saw the figures at the end of the road flicker to the side of it, one after another, and disappear through the trees. It looked as if they had jumped off the causeway.

"Don't they want us to see them?" Hildy said, and stopped, thinking of bombs and revolutionaries.

"Oh come on!" said Ynen, and began to run. "Quick! While they're away."

Hildy caught him up, and they ran hard, with the pies butting at their shoulders and the trees flicking past on either side. There was a salvo of little blunt bangs down below the road. Between the flicking trees they saw puffs of smoke and a flash or so. It sent both Hildy and Ynen over to the other side of the road, where they ran still, but more slowly. Neither of them wanted to run straight into a battle.

But the firing stopped after a round or so. Ynen panted to Hildy to hurry, to get to the gate before the soldiers came back. But no soldiers appeared. They reached the big pitch-painted gates before they saw them. There were about twenty soldiers, all down in the marsh to the left, jumping and slithering among the smelly dikes there. They were peering into each one they came to, and shouting to one another to cover the next one. Some had poles and were prodding the mud.

"They're looking for someone," Ynen said, greatly relieved. "I bet it's the murderer."

"I suppose they shot him," Hildy agreed. "Ynen, how lucky! They've left the gates open. They must have been searching the Pool." It did not really occur to them that someone's misfortune had caused their good luck.

Mitt slithered up that buttress. Like a horrible great slug, I am, he thought. He rolled onto the top of the wall. Left a slimy trail like one, too, he thought, looking at the wide smear of gray-green mud behind him. Below, the soldiers were prodding at ditches, convinced he was dead. Mitt rolled off the wall and thumped onto the jetty beyond before any of them chanced to look up and find reason to revise their opinion. He lay propped on his elbows, panting, clammy and almost tired out, and wondered which of these many little boats he had better get into. He knew it would have to be one he could manage easily alone. For that reason he rejected the beauty moored about ten yards down. "Too big, my lovely," he told her. "One of them Siriol used to spit at, too."

He looked round the rest. Some were big, some tubby, some the merest cockleshells. They all gleamed with splendid paint. Mitt thought he was weighing each one up as he looked at it, but in fact, all he was doing was comparing them with that blue beauty ten yards away and finding them trash in comparison. He did not have time to make himself decide reasonably. A soldier down in the marsh yelled. Mitt bolted on hands and knees like a monkey. He was rolling across the blue beauty's cabin roof before he had time to think. She had a steering well—purest pleasure boat stuff, Mitt thought, dropping down into it. At least it hid him from the soldiers.

But not for long. Before Mitt had believed it possible, footsteps were pattering on the jetty outside. He tore open the double cabin doors and dived inside. If he had not been in such a hurry, he would have stopped then and stared. He never could have imagined a ship's inside could be so beautiful—blue blankets and blue plush, a charcoal cooking stove, white paint and gold, and everything carved and ornamented and cleaned until it was more like a floating palace than a boat.

Ah, I always said the best wasn't good enough for me! Mitt thought, tiptoeing in a trail of green slime to the far end of the cabin. The boat's name was embroidered on all the blankets. Mitt could not resist pausing to spell out the name all this luxury went under. *Wind's Road,* he read. Very suitable. Suits me fine.

The next second *Wind's Road* dipped and swung under people's feet. "Isn't she beautiful!" Ynen said, dumping his sack on a locker. Mitt fumbled open a gilded cupboard, sweating with panic, and found himself confronting a bucket with a gilded seat. The bucket seemed to have roses painted all over it.

Flaming Ammet! thought Mitt. There really *is* nothing but the best on this ship! He shot the polished brass bolt to the cupboard with slimy, shaking fingers, and leaned against the gilded wall, listening to feet scampering and shrill, haughty voices calling overhead.

PART THREE

· WIND'S ROAD ·

11

"Help me get the mainsail up, and then stand by to untie her," Ynen said. "Oh, look at this! She's all over mud! I knew those blessed sailors used her for lobsters when my back was turned!"

"I'll wash it down when we're sailing," Hildy said. "But do let's get going before those soldiers come. Most of the mud's only on the sail cover." She jumped on the cabin roof and helped Ynen unlace the cover.

Ynen unlaced busily beside her. He was not often angry, but he was now. Someone had been on *Wind's Road*, the apple of his eye, the one lovely thing that was truly his own, and made a mess of her in his absence. He could not forgive them. "Honestly!" he said. "Green, smelly mud! You trust people, and they go and take advantage of you."

"Father said you can't blame people for that," said

Hildy. "I'll fold from my end, and be *quick*! He said the poor see the rich as their natural prey."

"Just the kind of thing he would say!" Ynen said irritably. "Fold it, don't just scrunch it! Mind you, he was probably right. I'll ask for a guard in future."

"Some soldiers have just come through the gates," said Hildy, causing Mitt to stand stiffly in his cupboard with his hands clenched. He had no idea who these arrogant fugitives could be or why they were in such a hurry, but he knew they could not be in too much of a hurry for him.

"Cast off the moorings and push her off, then," Ynen called, "while I get the sail up. Make sure you don't push us out of the deep channel, though."

Yes, and hurry up about it, for Old Ammet's sake! Mitt thought.

In a flurry of thumping, Hildy untied the mooring ropes and threw them on the planking, ready to be coiled later. Then she heaved on the jetty with all her might. Mitt gathered from the shifting and dipping what was happening. He heard the rhythmic *rattle, rattle* as Ynen sent the mainsail up, hand over hand, and then a further pounding of feet combined with a stiff tilting, as Ynen bounded to the bows to get the foresails up, and Hildy plunged to the tiller and turned *Wind's Road* to catch the wind. After that came a slow *ripple, ripple. Wind's Road* got gently under way and slid along the channel toward the open sea.

They won't find us so easy to stop now, Mitt thought. Whoever these rich youngsters were, they could handle a boat all right. He supposed it was lucky they could. But he was still scared stiff. He could not see them getting away with it.

Hildy and Ynen anxiously watched the harbor wall glide by and wished it would glide faster. Four or five soldiers were now running along the jetty behind, stumbling among ropes and shouting.

"What are they saying?" Ynen wondered.

Hildy gave a nervous giggle. "*Stop*, I think."

"What am I supposed to do? Pull on the reins?" Ynen said, and laughed, too.

Soldiers appeared on the harbor wall, struggling up from the marsh behind, most of them muddy and all in a great hurry. No sooner did they see *Wind's Road* sliding proudly past and beginning to lean a little in the sea wind than they became quite frantic. They shouted to one another and yelled at Hildy and Ynen to come back. One or two raised their guns.

"They're awfully close," Hildy said.

"I know, but I daren't leave the channel," said Ynen. The soldiers seemed so angry that he thought he had better pacify them. He jumped up onto the seat of the steering well, with his foot on the tiller, and waved. "It's all right," he shouted cheerfully. "We're only going out for a sail."

A soldier sighted along a gun at him. Ynen overbalanced out of sheer astonishment and pitched down into the well, kicking the tiller as he went. As *Wind's Road* veered, the shot fizzed slantwise across where Ynen's head had been, only just missing the lovely whiteness of her mainsail.

"Ye gods!" said Hildy, and plunged for the tiller. Wind was hard in the sail, and she could feel the deep keel dragging in the mud of the Pool. Another shot zinged across behind Hildy's head.

Ynen rolled over as if he had been stung and stared anxiously up at the sail. "Filthy swine! If he's holed my canvas, I'll have his guts for garters!"

Hildy dragged the tiller across. *Wind's Road,* her sail now properly filled, gathered majestic speed and foamed past the end of the wall. If the soldiers fired any more shots, they were lost in the sudden buffet of waves and the singing of the fresh wind. "They can't possibly stop us now," said Hildy. "But, Ynen, they fired at us! What *did* they think they were doing?"

"They must all be filthy revolutionaries," Ynen said. He was still very shaken. "I'll make sure they're all hanged when we get back."

"I think it must have been a mistake," Hildy said, almost equally shaken.

Mistake all right, Mitt thought, shaking all over. They thought one of you was me. Now you had a taste of the way the rest of us feel. Don't like it, do you? What did I have to go and choose this boat for? I can't do a thing right today, can I? If only I'd got on any of the other ones, I could have sat tight and let the soldiers think these two was me.

"It must have been a mistake," Ynen agreed, recovering. "I was just furious in case they'd spoiled the boat. We can sort it out when we get back."

"We might not be able to," said Hildy. "Don't forget we'll be in awful trouble when we get back."

"Oh, don't let's think of that now," said Ynen. "Hand over the tiller. I want to stand well out to miss the shoals."

It was beyond Mitt to imagine what these two thought they were doing. First they ran from the soldiers as fast as he had. Now they talked about going back. The one thing Mitt was certain of was that he was going to change that idea for them. He wriggled the bolt quietly back and came out of his gilded cupboard. There he suddenly felt tired out. He stood listening to the sea frilling briskly past the hull and the creak and rattle of ropes. Feet batted the roof as Hildy began coiling ropes and resetting the foresails. Then came the clank and slosh of a bucket being dipped overboard. Rubbing and trickling sounds told Mitt that someone was washing off the mud he had brought aboard.

That's right, he thought. Bustle about. Siriol taught me to keep my boats particular. Ah, I feel like a wet wash leather! And since it was obvious that neither of his companions was intending to come into the cabin, Mitt flopped onto the port bunk for a rest. He could wait a bit to change their plans. The cabin, as small places do, quickly got up a fug. The mud on Mitt, the blankets and the floor dried in big green flakes. Mitt drowsed.

When Hildy had washed the deck, she joined Ynen

in the well. "I love the way the wind blows in your face and makes your eyes all cool," she said.

"It's my favorite feeling," Ynen said.

Mitt hoped they would not go on like this. He did not want to hear their silly private thoughts. He was glad when Hildy said, "The land's a long way off already."

"The tide's running out," Ynen explained. "We'll be past the shoals in a minute. Then we'll turn north."

"I like the south best," Hildy objected.

"So do I. But the wind's wrong. We'd be close-hauled, and I wouldn't dare tie the mainsheet when we had supper."

"But there's a current to the north, isn't there? If we get into that, we'll never get back before dark, not close-hauled," Hildy pointed out.

"I wasn't going that far," said Ynen. "I want to be back in daylight because of the shoals. I thought we'd go north till slack water, and then have supper, and then come back when the tide turned."

"Supper at slack water sounds a nice idea," Hildy admitted. "And you are captain."

Mitt thought supper at any time was a nice idea. And you'll share it three ways, he thought. Two for me and one for you. Then we'll see about who's captain, and carry on up North. He bestirred himself enough to fetch out Hobin's gun and see how it had fared in the dikes. To his relief, it was dry. He laid it by his head, within easy reach, and dozed again. *Wind's Road* rose and fell. The wind creaked in her sails. The water splatted past. Ynen and Hildy did not talk much. They were too happy. Time and the land slid away.

The next thing Mitt knew, *Wind's Road*'s motion was a more sluggish one. Hildy was saying angrily, "Why did you tell me you knew if you didn't?"

Ynen answered patiently, in the overfirm way people use when they are trying to convince themselves as much as the other person, "I do know. That must be Hoe Point over there, and I'm sure Little Flate is in the dip beyond it. All I said was that we'd come a bit farther than I expected."

Mitt blinked at the gilt and white portholes and was surprised to see it was still daylight, if they had come that far. *Wind's Road*, even allowing for the tide which helped her, was a fine, fast boat. Unless it was tomorrow, of course. So much had happened to Mitt today that he felt as if it had gone on for a fortnight, even before he boarded this boat.

"Are you saying you think we've got into that current?" Hildy asked sharply. "Because, if so, we'd better turn straight round now."

"No, no. It's only slack water," Ynen assured her anxiously. "I can tell it's slack water by the way she's sailing."

Mitt thought about the new motion of *Wind's Road*. It felt much more as if she were in a current to him, which suited him perfectly. In which case they were not where that flaming amateur at the tiller thought they were.

"Where does the current begin?" Hildy demanded.

"That's the trouble," Ynen admitted. "It may be Hoe Point, or it may not be till Little Flate. I'm not sure."

Mitt cast his eyes to the elegant ceiling. The current began off Hoe Point, and Hoe Point came after Little Flate. I thought everyone knew that, he thought. Anyway, what's the fuss about? You can go right out to sea and get out of it again.

But *Wind's Road* was simply a pleasure boat. Ynen had never been out of sight of land in her. And he had always had sailors with him before who knew the coast. "I think perhaps you'd better fetch me the chart," he said to Hildy. "It's in the rack over the port bunk."

"I think I'd better, too," said Hildy, and she set off.

Whoops! thought Mitt, as he heard her coming. The time had come for him to act. He snatched up Hobin's gun and cocked it as he scrambled off the bunk. Then he grabbed open the door and whirled through it, just as Hildy was trying to come in.

They collided heavily. Hildy was slightly taller than Mitt and weighed a great deal more. But Mitt was moving twice as fast. Hildy crashed over backward with a shriek. Mitt was thrown against the cabin. The gun went off with a bark and a jerk and all but kicked itself out of Mitt's hand. It was like being hit over the wrist with a hammer. The shot, in a spatter of splinters, plowed across the deck and into the sea. The well filled with sharp-smelling smoke.

"Ye gods!" wailed Hildy. She thought her back was broken.

Mitt choked for breath against the cabin door and peered resentfully through the smoke at the gun. He thought Hobin might have warned him that it kicked like that. Then, as the smoke cleared, he saw Ynen in front of him, hanging on to the tiller and the rope from the mainsail, very white in the face, and staring at the long splintered groove in *Wind's Road*'s beautiful planking. A right ninny, Mitt thought. Cares more about his boat being damaged than he does about his brother—sister, I mean. Hildy was painfully up on one elbow, glaring at Mitt. Mitt looked at both of them with the utmost contempt. They both had such a smooth look, with their skin well filled and their hair thick and dark and healthy. He could see neither had gone hungry in their lives. What aroused his dislike most—though he did not realize it—was that Hildy and Ynen both inherited their looks from their father. Mitt looked at Ynen and saw a gentle version of Hadd's nose and at Hildy and saw the narrow, pale face of both Navis and Harchad, and though he did not recognize either, he detested them both on sight. And since his opinion of females was low, anyway, he encountered Hildy's glare and thought: She makes me sick—worse than her brother!

It was not surprising that they felt much the same about Mitt. They stared at Mitt's young-old face and his lank, dull-colored hair. They saw his bony hand was gripping a gun that looked like a collector's piece, that his pea jacket was ragged, and that green mud was peeling from his long, skinny legs. They knew he must be riffraff from the waterfront. They suspected he was a thief, too. They thought he was disgusting.

"Well, we know what the soldiers were after. And where all the mud came from," said Hildy.

"Are you badly hurt?" Ynen asked her. He felt very helpless. He dared not let go of the tiller to help Hildy, nor did he dare turn straight round and head back to Holand, much as he wanted to, for fear this disgusting stowaway loosed off with his gun again.

"No. I'm all right," said Hildy, and struggled to her feet. "He missed me, of course."

"I was not aiming to hit you," Mitt said with great scorn. "You ran into me like a whole herd of cows. You want to look out. This is a hasty kind of gun."

"I like that!" said Hildy.

"If it's that hasty, why don't you put it away?" Ynen suggested.

Mitt ignored him. He looked up at the sail and the streaming flag at the masthead. It was a fair wind for the North, all right. The land was low blue hummocks to his right. It took Mitt only one glance to spot Hoe Point nearly a mile astern. The hump Ynen had taken for Hoe Point was Canderack Head. Mitt was impressed. It was still an hour off sundown, too. He could not help grinning.

"Well, well," he said. "A good fast boat you got here. All set for the North, aren't we?"

Ynen's face went rather whiter as he grasped what the stowaway might be planning. "We're not going to take you North," he said. "If that's what's in your mind."

"Not got much choice, have you?" said Mitt. He pretended to rub the gun on his sleeve. He did not really rub it, because he was very much afraid it would go off again. "I've got this gun, haven't I?"

"You can shoot me if you want," said Ynen. "But I'm not taking you North." He wondered if it would hurt very much and thought that it probably would. He could only hope he would die quickly.

"Ynen, don't be an idiot!" said Hildy.

"He thinks I wouldn't dare," said Mitt. "Well, I would. Because I happen to be a desperate man." That sounded good. And it had the advantage of being true. Mitt began to enjoy himself. "If you won't take me North," he said, "I wouldn't kill you. I'd just put a bullet in your leg. Maybe both legs." He was pleased to see Hildy glaring at him. "Then in her," he said. "And then it would be rather a pleasure to knock this boat about a bit—scrape off the pretty paint, carve silly pictures in the decking, and so on."

As Mitt had hoped it would, this threat truly upset Ynen. "You dare touch my boat, you guttersnipe!"

"He doesn't know any better," said Hildy.

"I thought that would worry you," Mitt said in high glee. "All you've got to do to stop me is carry on as you are. Just keep sailing North."

Ynen and Hildy exchanged a miserable look. They seemed to have gone from perfect happiness to a nightmare in a matter of seconds. Hildy wondered what had possessed her to lead Ynen into this. She had known there were revolutionaries at large. They should have stayed in the Palace. Ynen was thinking mostly of that current and how he could persuade the boy that *Wind's Road* simply could not take him all the way North.

"Look here," Ynen said, trying to sound fair and reasonable. "We can't go North. We have to be back in Holand tonight or people will worry. What do you say to our landing you somewhere on the way back? How about—" Ynen looked over at the land and could not help feeling extremely uneasy about the shape of it. "Hoe Point?" he said doubtfully.

Mitt gave what he hoped was an evil laugh. "Go on! You couldn't get back to Holand tonight even if you went this second! You're in a nice fast northerly current, and in this wind you'll be lucky if you make it back by morning. Hoe Point is where that current starts, and that's Hoe Point back there, you flaming amateur! Look at your chart if you don't believe me." He saw he had demoralized them. Ynen's face was warm pink, and he was staring at Hildy as if the end of the world had come. Mitt was so pleased that he added, "I was sailing out of Holand before you were born." That was a mistake. Hildy gave him a jeering look. Mitt scowled at her. "Just sail North and don't give me any trouble," he said. "And you won't have any trouble from me. I can't say fairer than that, can I?"

Hildy sighed to cover up her thoughts. Unpleasant as this boy was, he did bluster rather. To judge by Ynen's face, he was right about the current, but that did not mean he had thought of everything. "I suppose we'd better humor him, Ynen," she said. She stared hard at Ynen, slowly shutting her eyes and opening them, to show him that the boy would have to sleep sometime.

Mitt knew that, too. Even a sweet boat like *Wind's Road* would take three or four days to reach North Dalemark waters. No one could stay awake that long. Mitt was tired to death already. He felt his only course was to keep these children thoroughly intimidated by being as rough and dangerous and brutal as he could. He seemed to have made a fairly good start. So, while Ynen was nodding gravely at Hildy to show her he understood, Mitt roared out, "Right, then. Now that's settled, go and get out your eatables. I'm starving. Hurry up!"

Hildy gave him a poisonous look. But it was fully suppertime, and she was hungry herself. She got up and dragged one of the sacks of pies out of the locker. Ynen took a careful breath, hoping it was not his last, and said, "I'd rather you didn't speak to my sister like that."

"What's she done to deserve any better?" Mitt said nastily. "You watch it." He was annoyed to see the two of them exchanging a look which was anything but intimidated. "Come on. What's in that sack?"

He was relieved to see it was pies. He had been wondering how he could eat and still keep hold of Hobin's gun. He was afraid that if he let go of it for a moment, he would find himself being pushed overboard. But he could eat a pie with one hand.

The pies were scarcely as tempting as they had been. Gravy had run and juice had leaked, and then mingled and soaked back into other pastry. But Mitt was not in a state to care. He had not properly eaten anything since breakfast. He intended to go on with the intimidation by eating with great gobbling noises and huge slurpings, but as soon as he had a pie in his hand, he forgot everything but how hungry he was. He only thought of eating. He was hardly able to attend to the splendid, unusual tastes, he was so frantic for food. He ate five steak pies, a pheasant patty, six oyster puffs, a chicken flan, four cheesecakes, and nine fruit tarts. He thought, as he drew at last to a gentle halt, that his gluttony had served to intimidate the children almost as well as making noises. They were staring, looking thoroughly chastened. Mitt managed, with no effort at all, to produce a monstrous belch, to make sure they knew exactly how rough and foul he was.

In fact, Ynen and Hildy were simply awed. They had not known it was possible to be so hungry.

That explains those thin legs, Hildy thought, looking at them. The sun was melting down into the sea, in a buttery haze. By its strong yellow light, Hildy saw that most of the mud had flaked off the boy's legs, showing him to be wearing odd old-fashioned breeches, with one leg red and the other yellow. The sight gave Hildy such a jolt that she burst out, "I know who you are! You threw that bomb Father kicked away!"

12

Mitt looked from Hildy to Ynen. He saw the likeness now. His huge meal had left him slow and almost unbearably sleepy. His first thought was that it was funny. Hadd ruined him. Navis spoiled all his plans. And now these were Navis's children who were willy-nilly rescuing him. He chuckled. "Now that's what I call justice," he said. "Navis is your pa then?"

Hildy stuck her chin up and did her best to overawe Mitt. "Yes," she said haughtily. "And I'll have you know that I am betrothed to Lithar, Lord of the Holy Islands."

"Oh, shut up," Ynen said uncomfortably. "You sound just like the cousins."

Hildy had been imitating her cousin Irana boasting of her betrothal. She was annoyed with Ynen for noticing. She turned her back on him and looked hopefully at Mitt, hoping she had upset him by it at least.

Mitt laughed. "Betrothed!" People got betrothed at Lydda's age, when they were eighteen and grown-up. Hildy was only a little girl in pigtails. "Bit young for that, aren't you?" Then the implications struck him. He was quite as alarmed as Hildy could have hoped, but he kept on laughing. He dared not let them see he was upset. This girl was important, all right. He remembered Milda telling him about Lithar. That made certain that ships would pursue them from Holand, and more ships would be out to meet them from the Holy Islands. Mitt knew he was going to have to make them take this boat right out into the ocean. It was going to take days, and even then he might be caught. Just to think of it made him feel tired. "Well, it's your business," he said. "Doesn't worry me." He stood up. "I'm off for a visit to that silly bucket in the cupboard. The one with roses on. No tricks while I'm gone now."

Ynen's face was pink in the yellow light. "They aren't roses. They're poppies," he said.

"Roses," said Mitt. "And with a golden rim, too. Amazing the way your kind has to have things pretty!" He went into the cabin.

Ynen shouted after him, "Your kind built this boat!" Then, as soon as Mitt was at the end of the cabin, he whispered to Hildy, "What are we going to *do*?"

Now that Mitt had laughed at Hildy for being betrothed, she was determined to get the better of him. "I've got an idea," she whispered, "to make him go to sleep."

"Then we'll turn round," Ynen agreed. "What idea?"

"What are you whispering about?" Mitt yelled.

They dared not whisper anymore. Ynen looked at the long splintered groove in *Wind's Road*'s planking and shivered. It was getting hard to see now. The sun had swum down below the horizon, leaving a yellow sky spread with straight black clouds. The sea was a melting, lighter yellow, as if the light had soaked into it. Hildy's face was dark. "We're saying we ought to have a light at the masthead," he called. "It's the law."

"Haven't you noticed?" Mitt bawled. "I got nothing to do with the law."

"Unlike you, we were brought up to be lawful," Hildy called. "Can I light the lamp in the cabin at least?"

Mitt came out of the cupboard and fumbled his way through the cabin. It was certainly getting dark. He felt sour and grim, and he ached all over. The red and yellow breeches would not do up properly after his great meal. He came out of the cabin and flopped down on the lockers. "Please yourself," he said. He was horribly weary.

Hildy smiled slightly and went into the cabin, where she was some time fiddling about before the lamp came on, as yellow as the sky outside. Then she moved on to the fat little water barrel, which was clamped to a special shelf above the stove. She undid the clamps and shook it. The barrel was completely full, so full that it did not even slosh. It took all Hildy's strength to shake it convincingly, but she had been prepared for that, because it was always kept full. No one dared let Hadd's family go thirsty.

"Oh dear!" Hildy said. She was surprised how convincing she sounded. "There's no water in this at all! I'm horribly thirsty, too." This was true, but she thought she could bear it in a good cause.

As soon as she said this, Mitt realized that one of the many things wrong with him was an appalling thirst. It was all those highly spiced pies he had eaten. The thought of going without water for all the time it took to get North nearly made him burst into tears. Ynen was almost equally dismayed. His mouth suddenly seemed quite dry, and he had a moment when he would have liked to report those negligent sailors to Uncle Harchad. He licked his sandpapery lips and said, "They sometimes keep wine in the lockers over the starboard bunk. Have a look, Hildy, for Old Ammet's sake!"

Hildy turned round to hide a triumphant smile and fetched the two bottles she had already found there. One was a half-full bottle of wine. The other was a square bottle of arris. It had been full before Hildy had poured a generous dollop of it into the wine. One way or another, she thought she had done for this wretched boy.

"Which will you have?" she said, showing Mitt the bottles in the twilight.

Mitt knew the rough, foul drink was arris. But he hated it too much. "I'll have the wine," he said, and he snatched the bottle from Hildy, feeling he could make up on roughness and foulness that way, and took a long, guggling swig from it before Hildy could get him a cup from the cabin. He intended to drink the lot. But it tasted rather unpleasant. He passed Hildy back the bottle, a good deal less than a quarter full.

Hildy distastefully wiped the neck of the bottle and shared the rest into two cups for herself and Ynen. They sipped it and settled down to wait, while twilight grew into night.

Shortly, Ynen began to feel cheerful and Hildy slightly dizzy. As for Mitt, the wine, on top of his weariness, on top of his huge meal, had the inevitable effect. The low black humps of land kept spreading under his eyes like inkblots. The stars came out and looked fuzzy. His head kept dropping forward. At length he stood up unsteadily.

"Going to have a lie-down," he said. "No stunny fuff, now. Got ears in the back of my head." He staggered off into the cabin, while Hildy and Ynen each stuffed a fist into their mouths in order not to scream with laughter, and flopped heavily down on the port bunk.

Hildy nudged Ynen meaningly and sat down with her back against the lockers, where she could see into the cabin. They waited for Mitt to fall asleep. But, with the best will in the world to do so, Mitt could not go to sleep. The movements of *Wind's Road* and the movements the wine had set up in his head seemed to be in direct conflict. Sometimes he was convinced the boat had got into a whirlpool. Sometimes he was sure his legs were high above his head. He sat up several times to see what was going on. And each time the elegant gilded cabin was exactly as it should be, gently rising and falling, and the lamp swinging. At length he realized the queer things only happened when he had his eyes shut. So he kept them open.

The result was a set of horrible, half-waking dreams. Mitt stared at Harchad's face in a gilded porthole, paralyzed with terror. He ran endlessly from soldiers. He struggled through innumerable dikes. Several times he was shot in the stomach. Once he threw his bomb in front of Hadd, and Poor Old Ammet bent down, put out his straw arms, and threw the bomb in Mitt's face. "You're in really bad trouble," he said, and he sounded just like Hobin. Then he fell to pieces like Canden. Mitt sat up with a yell of horror. After this, when he lay down again, things got a little quieter, until it was Libby Beer's turn. She ran at Mitt, with her fruity eyes wobbling on stalks, and kicked the bomb at him. "I brought you up to do this, Mitt," she said reproachfully. Then the bomb exploded, and Mitt started up with a scream.

Hildy and Ynen wished he would stop yelling and go to sleep. They wanted to turn round and sail home. The yells perturbed them. The boy must be disgustingly sinful. And the sounds made them think of the things they had heard about Uncle Harchad, and that terrible day the Northmen had been hanged. Meanwhile, true night came on, and Ynen became frankly terrified. By this time he had been at the tiller longer than he had ever been in his life. He had never sailed at night before. He was cold and cramped and tired, and scared of shoals he could not see. What he could see scared him even more.

It was not dark the way it was in a closed room. The sea was there, faintly, all round, heaving and swelling limitlessly. The sky was a huge empty bowl, dark blue, covered with a littering of stars, and the land was only a feeling, far away to the right. The sail noises, and the swish and fizz of waves passing, only seemed to show how small and lonely *Wind's Road* was. Ynen suddenly became aware of fathoms and fathoms of empty water underneath them, too. He was hanging all alone in the middle of nowhere. Ynen clenched his teeth and kept the Northern Cross grimly over *Wind's Road*'s bowsprit, and it was all he could do not to yell out the way the boy in the cabin kept doing.

It was midnight before Hildy dared signal that Mitt was asleep. In fact, he had been asleep all along, but so restlessly that Hildy had not realized. She pulled the cabin door quietly shut and shot the elegant little bolt home.

"Thank goodness! You go to the foresails," Ynen whispered.

Hildy crept forward, round the starboard side, to avoid any noise near Mitt. Ynen could see her clearly against the pallor of the sails. As soon as she was ready, he put the tiller over hard. *Wind's Road* surged round. Her sails ran out to the end of their ropes and swung back. The wind seemed suddenly twice as strong. Ynen kept his foot against the tiller and hauled in the mainsail frantically. Hildy collected the clapping foresails and dragged them the other way. *Wind's Road* stood still, head on to the wind, and seemed to flap and tremble in every part. Then she was round, tipped over much farther, and apparently rushing through the water, but actually making very little way against the current. Ynen hauled in the mainsail as close as he could, in order not to waste time tacking, and they were now headed back to Holand. Hildy came back to the well, and they both sagged with relief.

Holand meant safety and bed and warm rooms. They had got the better of that dreadful boy. That was their first thought. Then they both remembered the trouble they would be in once they were back. That could not be helped, but they did wish the thought of the trouble did not go along with an empty, forsaken feeling. It was no good pretending Navis would defend them from the uncles. On the other hand, Uncle Harchad might forgive them a great deal if they brought him the boy who had thrown the bomb.

Hildy and Ynen peered at one another's faces, trying to see what the other thought about that. The boy was a criminal. He had tried to murder their grandfather. Perhaps he was a friend of the man who had actually done so. But all the same, he was a human being, much the same age as they were, and having bad dreams in the cabin. They both thought of Uncle Harchad kicking the Earl of Hannart's son, and the Earl's son cringing. It was easy enough to replace the Earl's son with a picture of that skinny, cocksure boy, and quite as unpleasant.

"We could put him off at Hoe Point, couldn't we?"

Ynen whispered, and relieved Hildy's mind considerably.

Mitt, as he slept, was encountering Poor Old Ammet and Libby Beer at once. They rushed at him, one from either side. The world spun about and went wrong somehow. When Mitt opened his eyes, he knew the world was still wrong. It was going with a blunt, blundering, bucking motion, and tipping the wrong way. Those early years with Siriol had put some things deep in Mitt's brain. Funny, he thought. Close-hauled against a current. *Flaming Ammet!* He snatched up Hobin's gun and burst out of the cabin. He did not even notice the door had been bolted.

Outside, he had only to feel the wind on his face to know he was right. The children's smitten faces in the lamplight confirmed it. So did the Northern Cross low down behind them.

"Turn her back round!" he yelled. "You sneaking idle rich, you! You think you can do just as you like, don't you! Go on, turn her back round!"

At this, despite the waving gun, Hildy lost her temper. He spoiled her entire scheme, and then he shouted insults. "Don't you talk to me about doing just as we want!" She was so angry that she stood up and yelled in Mitt's face. "You sneak aboard our ship, and order us about like dirt, and eat our food, and make us go where *you* want to go, and then you have the nerve to say *we* always do what we want! You're worse than—than Grandfather! He was honest about it at least!"

"*Honest!*" bawled Mitt. "Haddock honest! Don't

make me laugh. He was robbing all Holand for years!"

"So you try to murder him, and order us about like dirt on top of that!" Hildy screamed.

"You *are* dirt, that's why!" Mitt thundered, waving the gun. "Turn this boat back round!" Ynen clutched the tiller and feared for Hildy's life. In fact, neither he nor Mitt noticed that Mitt had not even remembered to cock the gun. He had not spun the empty barrel on either.

Hildy did not know and did not care. "If we're dirt, I shudder to think what your family is!" she roared.

"Oh shut up!" Mitt pointed the gun at Ynen. "Turn this boat round, I said!"

For the second time that night Ynen thought he was about to be shot. It gave him a cool kind of resignation. "You did try to murder our grandfather," he said. "Give me one good reason why we should do anything to help you."

Mitt noticed he was pointing the gun at Ynen and realized that Ynen did not regard the gun as a good reason. It sobered him rather. He felt considerable respect for this smooth-faced, hawk-nosed little boy, though, as for his sister—! "Well then," he said, "your precious grandfather bust up my family. Is that a reason?"

"How did he do that?" Ynen asked, shivering with cold and weariness.

Hildy added angrily, "Whatever he did, *we* didn't do anything to you!"

"I'll tell you," said Mitt. He rested his arm on the

cabin roof and began to talk, jerkily and angrily at first, and then more reasonably, as he realized neither of them was trying to interrupt. He told them how he had been born at Dike End, and how the rent had been doubled, and how this had forced his father to work in Holand and then forced them out of the farm. He told them how his father had never found proper work and so joined the Free Holanders, and how he had been betrayed over the warehouse—though he did not mention names—and disappeared, leaving Milda and himself to manage alone. He described how they had lived after that, and he could not help thinking, as he talked, that this was a funny kind of way to tell your life story, with *Wind's Road* bucking through the water in the dark, and the half-lit faces of Hadd's grandchildren staring up at him as he talked. He told them about Hobin. "And if it hadn't been for him," he said, "we'd have been turned out into the street when they knocked the houses down to make the Festival safe."

"They didn't just turn them out, did they?" Hildy said. "I thought—"

"Father had houses built for them," said Ynen. "But I don't think anyone else was going to bother. All the same," he said to Mitt, "you and your mother weren't there then. You were all right. You still haven't given me a reason."

"Isn't that a reason?" Mitt demanded. "There was Hobin never daring to put a foot wrong for fear of the arms inspectors, and us near on as hard up as ever because Hadd would put the rents up all the time. But never the price of guns—not he! We had to pay through the nose to support those soldiers, so that they could make us scared to stir hand or foot. You don't understand—can't you think how it feels when everyone you know is scared sick all the time? You couldn't trust people. They'd turn round and tell on you, anytime, even if it weren't you done it, because they didn't want to get marched off in the night themselves. That's not how people should be."

"It isn't," Hildy agreed.

"I grant you that," said Ynen. "But you're talking about everything. You haven't told me one thing Grandfather did to *you*. I still don't see why we should help you. But I've heard things about Uncle Harchad. I don't mind landing you at Hoe Point, so you'll have a chance to get away."

Yes, Mitt thought, in full view of all the ships coming out to look for them. Very safe. Talking to this boy was like bashing down a weak little plant that kept springing up again in your face. "You might as well take me back to Holand and be done," he said. "If I'm not caught landing, I'll be caught in the Flate straight after."

"Well, you did throw a bomb," said Ynen. "And I can't see why you did. There must have been lots of people in Holand far worse off than you. Why did *you* do it?"

That was a home question. Twenty-four hours earlier Mitt could have given all sorts of answers. He could have told them at least that it was to be revenged on Siriol, Dideo, and Ham. But he had gone out of his way *not* to be revenged. And he had run and run and run. He did not know what he thought he had been doing. He was reduced to answering with another question. "Could *you* have seen things so wrong and not think you ought to do something about it?"

This in its turn was a home question to Ynen and Hildy. They had indeed seen things wrong. All Ynen had done was wish he could whirl a rattle in Hadd's face. All Hildy had done was tear a bedspread and make empty threats. Then they had gone out sailing—a piece of defiance which had thrown them in the way of this boy. And he had not only told them more things that were wrong but had demanded that they help him. With the result that they were now sailing back to Holand to deliver him to Uncle Harchad.

"Ynen—" said Hildy.

"I know," said Ynen. "All right. We'd better take you North. Hildy, could you go to the foresails again?"

Mitt was rather taken aback. He knew he had not given Ynen a reason. He felt dishonest, and shamed. What would happen to these two in the North? He thought of the Northmen shuffling through Holand to be tried and hanged. "See here," he said. "All you got to do is land me near Kinghaven or whatsits—Aberath—and I'll do nicely. Or you might try Tulfa. Then you go back to the Holy Islands. You'd be all right there if she's betrothed to Lithar—What's your name, by the way?"

"Hildrida," said Hildy. "Hildy for short. And this is Ynen. What's yours?"

"Mitt," said Mitt.

"Oh, not another Alhammitt!" said Hildy. "That must make at least twenty I know!"

"Common as dirt," agreed Mitt.

Ynen had been thinking over what Mitt had suggested. Tired as he was, he began smiling. "Let's go to the Holy Islands, Hildy. I'd love to see them."

Hildy just could not see herself sailing up to the Holy Islands and announcing she was Lithar's future wife. The idea made her stomach squirm. But she looked at Ynen and decided he was too tired to be argued with.

Mitt could see how tired Ynen was, too. He remembered how he used to feel on a long stint aboard *Flower of Holand*. "How about you getting some rest, now we seem to know where we're going?" he said. "I can sail her for you. Can she?"

"Naturally I can," Hildy said haughtily.

So it was settled that they divide the rest of the night into three watches. Ynen reluctantly took his numb hand off the tiller and watched Mitt settle into his place. He felt very dubious as he stumbled off to the cabin. But he supposed that if Mitt could tell in his sleep when they turned the other way, he must be able to handle *Wind's Road*. As Ynen lay down, he heard Hildy walking uncertainly forward over the roof, half blind from the light of the cabin. He saw Mitt's bony hand pushing the tiller firmly over. Once more *Wind's Road* surged round. Her sails ran out, clapped, and filled. Ropes rattled as Mitt and Hildy reset them. And shortly Ynen felt the tug and surge of *Wind's Road* riding properly northward, and he knew Mitt could indeed manage her. He fell asleep, to the creak of ropes and the hurrying of dark water.

13

The night seemed extraordinarily long. Mitt stayed at the tiller for as much of it as he could. He wanted to get a good start Northward. It felt good to be handling a boat again, particularly a responsive racing boat like *Wind's Road.* But with the good feeling went long, mindless boredom. There was nothing to do but watch the slowly wheeling stars and listen to the whelming of the huge sea. Mitt did make several honest efforts to decide just what he thought he had been doing back in Holand. But every time he started to think, he came to, some time later, to find he had been thinking of nothing at all. At length the stars began taking little jumps through the sky. Mitt did not know if he had been asleep while they moved or not, but he saw he had had enough. He hitched up the tiller and woke Hildy.

Hildy was so sleepy that she took her watch almost

unconscious. It seemed a very long time. Then Hildy found herself doubled painfully over the tiller in a paler world. The sea was dark and glossy. A white wave fizzing past had woken her. Hildy hobbled off like an old woman and woke Ynen.

Ynen, much more refreshed by six hours' sleep than Hildy felt he had any right to be, went gaily out into whitening dawn. The bank of mist where the land was seemed too near. Ynen corrected their course and tightened ropes, and sang while the sun came melting red and yellow out of the mist. Now it was settled, and they were going North, it felt like the best holiday Ynen had ever had. When Mitt came out a while after, *Wind's Road* was sailing briskly in a brisk wind, under a streaky gray sky. The land was a chalky smudge, and the vigorous gray waves were galloping North, too, dividing into two lines of white round *Wind's Road*'s eager bows. Hildy crawled out later still, groaning. It was so early.

They got the pies out. They were staler, soggier, and much less appetizing. "I reckon," Mitt said, "that they'll be old enemies by the time we make Kinghaven—if they last till then."

"They ought to. We've got two sacksful," said Ynen, and could not help laughing at the look on Mitt's face.

"Then it's only water that's the worry," said Mitt.

"Well, actually, the water barrel's full up," Hildy confessed.

For a moment Mitt could hardly credit that he had been so taken in. Then, to Hildy's relief, he shouted with laughter. "I bet you were mad when I didn't have the arris!" he said. "Us rough fellows are supposed to love that, aren't we?"

Hildy bent her head, embarrassed. She was even more embarrassed when Mitt tasted the water and remarked that it was some of the sweetest-tasting water he had ever drunk. She and Ynen were both shuddering at its musty wooden taste.

Ye gods! What must the water be like down in Holand! Hildy thought. She was so uncomfortable that she jumped up and fled across the cabin roof, babbling that she thought the foresails needed looking at.

"Want a hand?" Mitt called.

Hildy did not know what to say and did not answer. Mitt was just getting up to help her when Ynen said, in great surprise, "I say! What on earth are those doing here?"

Mitt looked. To his astonishment, a number of half-submerged apples were bobbing in the waves beside the boat. He watched them apparently climb a wave, then get left behind by it, the way floating things do. There were dozens of them—bright red and yellow water-sodden apples, all round *Wind's Road*. And there were what looked like wisps of grass as well, and some almost waterlogged flowers.

"Oh, I know!" said Ynen. "Those must be the garlands from the Festival. I suppose the tide brought them out into the current."

"No good to eat, are they?" Mitt wondered.

There was a scream of excitement from Hildy. She was pointing, jabbing her finger seaward, at something floating ahead. For a nasty second Mitt and Ynen both thought it was a drowned person. There was sodden flaxen hair and an outflung hand. Then it rolled and seemed simply a mat of white reeds.

"Can't you see!" screamed Hildy. "It's Poor Old Ammet!"

Wind's Road veered and shivered in the excitement of that moment. Ynen almost let go of the tiller. Mitt ran from side to side. Whatever the differences between them, they were all three Holanders, and they knew this was the lucky chance of a lifetime.

"We'll miss him, we'll miss him! Hurry up, Mitt!" Hildy screamed. "Bring me the boathook!"

Mitt plunged round on Ynen and seized the tiller from him. "You go. I'll bring her round for you."

Ynen knew the maneuver was probably beyond him. He let go of the tiller almost before Mitt had it and shot up along the deck, snatching up the mop and the boathook as he went. He thrust the mop at Hildy, and the two of them, waving their implements, balanced jubilantly on the pointed prow. As Mitt took *Wind's Road* racing past Old Ammet and then round again toward the wind, he was very much afraid either or both of them would join Old Ammet in the water. But they clung on. Mitt let the mainsail out with a long rattle, to take the speed off *Wind's Road*, and she plowed on, *bash-bash-bash*, with waves smacking at her bows and spraying

Hildy and Ynen thoroughly. When they were a few yards off the floating straw figure, Mitt turned *Wind's Road* right into the wind, and she stood almost still, shaking and flapping. Hildy and Ynen both threw themselves on their faces and lunged at Poor Old Ammet.

Their efforts were agony to Mitt. They knew nothing about how to get things out of the sea, those two. Hildy prodded. Ynen was hanging right under the bowsprit like a monkey, wasting Mitt's accurate work by pushing Old Ammet farther and farther away. It was so clear that they were going to lose him that Mitt hitched the tiller up and set off to help. *Wind's Road* promptly jigged round sideways to the waves, where the strong wind threatened to fill her sails again. Mitt saw that she could capsize that way and hurried back to the tiller.

"Flaming mind of your own, you have!" he told *Wind's Road*. "Sail me or I'll drown the lot of you—that's you!"

That jigging gave Ynen the extra foot he needed. He managed to get a grip on Old Ammet with the boathook. Hildy planted the mop on him to steady him, and together they tossed Poor Old Ammet aboard like the stook of corn he was.

Mitt marveled that he could have taken that intricate mass of plaited corn for a drowned man. Old Ammet still had arms, legs, and a tufted head, but he was now more the shape of a starfish than a person. Most of his fine red ribbons were gone, and his face was cockeyed and blurred. He was a Poor Old Ammet indeed. All the same, they were delighted to see him. They all shouted, "Welcome aboard, Old Ammet, sir!" which they all knew was what you said. Mitt turned *Wind's Road* joyfully back on her way again, while Hildy and Ynen first did an unsteady dance of triumph on the cabin roof and then set about fixing Old Ammet to the prow like a figurehead—which was the other thing you were supposed to do.

Poor Old Ammet was limp and waterlogged. It was no easy matter to make him into a figurehead. Ynen fetched rolls of twine and rope. Mitt called advice. Hildy ransacked the cabin for things which might support that weight of wet wheat. Mitt called so much advice that Hildy snapped, "Oh shut up! We all know you get Old Ammet out of the sea every year!"

There was really no answer to that. Mitt shut up, bitterly annoyed, and soothed himself by muttering, "Flaming females! They're all the same. It goes right through." He watched, haughtily, Old Ammet being threaded on a besom, a gilded picture rail, and two wooden spoons and then being lashed to half the door of the gilded cupboard that concealed the rose-covered bucket. Then he was tied very firmly across the bowsprit, where he lifted and fell proudly to the movements of the boat. Mitt knew he could not have done it better himself. So he said knowledgeably, "He'll stiffen up. He's full of salt. Mind you, he may niff a bit." Then he gave way to honest pride. "Looks good, doesn't he?"

Ynen and Hildy thoroughly agreed. "But," Hildy

said, "why doesn't anyone ever find Libby Beer?" She lay down to peer under the mainsail, as if she expected to find Libby Beer just in the offing, in the other half of the gray, leaping sea.

"She's all grapes and squashy berries," said Ynen. "She must get waterlogged in no time. It would be a miracle if we had her, too."

Mitt laughed and slapped the knobby pocket of his red and yellow breeches. "I clean forgot to this moment! Miracle it is. Here. Look." He dragged the little wax model of Libby Beer out of his pocket. Like Poor Old Ammet, she was rather the worse for wear. The wax berries were flattened, with cloth marks imprinted on them, and the ribbons were muddy strings. But she could hardly have delighted Ynen and Hildy more had she been new and gay and gleaming.

"Oh, beautiful!" said Ynen. "We must be the luckiest boat in the world. May I lash her to the stern?"

"Carry on," said Mitt.

"She's lovely!" said Hildy, fingering Libby Beer while Ynen unrolled more twine. "I've always wanted one of these, but they won't let us buy things at the stalls. Those little tiny rose hips. How did you get her?"

"While I was on the run," said Mitt. "Lady at a stall gave her me for luck."

"You mean she knew you were running away?" Hildy asked, reluctantly giving Libby Beer to Ynen to be tied behind the tiller.

"No," said Mitt. He fixed his eyes on the gently

heaving horizon and wished this silly female would understand what Holand was like for the likes of him. "She found out I was on the run just after, when the soldiers came asking. She gave me Libby Beer to cheer me up—I had a face as long as Flate Dike, see, not knowing where to go or what I dared do. Then, when the soldiers asked, she had to say she seen me. She didn't dare not tell. That's how people are. It's different for you."

Ynen considered this while he tied careful knots round the wax figure. "We're on the run, too, now—in a way. Why is it different? If a fisherman sees *Wind's Road*, he'll tell. And I don't feel miserable about it."

Mitt knew Ynen had missed the point. He thought of Milda, Hobin, and the babies, of all the waterfront people who used to laugh at him selling fish, all the dozens of people he would never see again, and he was almost exasperated enough with Ynen to push him from the stern, where he was crouching, into the sea. "But you've not put yourself outside the law, have you?"

"Yes, we have, in another way," Hildy said. She thought Ynen had missed the point, too, and the only way to cover it up seemed to be to let Mitt know that they had their difficulties as well. She told him about their pretended escape with the bedspread and their real escape with the pies. Mitt tried not to grin. It was all a game to them.

It did not seem to Ynen that he had missed any point. He looked admiringly at the little Libby Beer, already shiny with spray, and proudly over at Old Ammet, lifting and falling at the bowsprit, while he thought over all he now knew about Mitt. It did not add up properly. He wanted to know why. "Look here," he said. "You must have known you'd be on the run, and what it would be like, once you'd thrown the bomb. Didn't you make *any* plans to get away?"

"Were you standing there waiting to be blown up?" Hildy asked, thinking this would explain Mitt's odd behavior on the waterfront.

Mitt eyed the heaving horizon. He supposed he might as well tell them, if they could tell him about their silly escape with their pies. There was something odd about Hildy's story, though—something not quite right. Mitt felt that as strongly as Ynen evidently felt it about his. "They made plans—the Free Holanders," he explained, "but it wasn't in me to listen, because I was planning to get myself taken. I was aiming to kill Hadd, and when they caught me, I was going to tell them the Free Holanders set me on, to pay them out for informing on my father. It was them that informed on him. I've been planning that half my life. You might say my mother brought me up to do it. And your pa goes and spoils it in half a second. That's what had me standing there—the waste!"

There was silence from Ynen and Hildy. Mitt did not wonder he had shocked them. He took his eyes off the horizon and caught them exchanging a look that was not shocked but deeply puzzled.

"And so it *was* a waste!" he told them aggressively.

"Three years I saved gunpowder. Five years me and my mother planned it. And your pa kicks the bomb instead of grabbing me. Then I run straight at those fool soldiers, and they lose me. What was I supposed to do after that? Walk in the Palace gates and say, 'Here I am'?"

"It's not that," said Ynen. "You keep saying everyone informs because they're frightened—and I believe you— but why do you blame the Free Holanders for informing and not the woman who gave you Libby Beer?"

"She wasn't a friend of mine, was she?" Mitt said gruffly.

There was a further silence, puzzled and uncomfortable, filled only with the sound of *Wind's Road*'s ropes pulling in a wind that seemed to be slackening. Hildy and Ynen looked at one another. They were both thinking of the Earl of Hannart's son and wondering how to say what they thought.

"I don't understand about mothers," Hildy said cautiously. "Not having one myself. But—" She stopped and looked helplessly at Ynen.

"You do know," Ynen blurted out, "your mother does know, does she, the kind of things that happen when people get arrested for your kind of thing? Do you know about my uncle Harchad?"

Harchad's face, and the terrible fear that had gripped Mitt when he saw it, seemed to have mixed in Mitt's mind now with his nightmare of Canden shuffling to the door. Under his thick jacket, his skin rose in gooseflesh. But he was not going to let Hildy and Ynen know how he felt.

"I've heard things about Harchad," he conceded.

Hildy shivered openly. "I saw. One thing."

"That's why we said we'd take you North," said Ynen.

"Thanks," said Mitt, and he stared woodenly at the horizon. He was not sure quite what was the matter with him. He felt sick and cold. He shook Canden and Harchad out of his mind, but he still felt as if a load of worry had fallen on him, making his head ache and drawing his face into a strange shape. Ynen and Hildy stared, because Mitt's face seemed all old, with scarcely any young left in it. "See here," Mitt said, after a minute, "I feel wore out again. Mind if I go for a lie-down?"

Hildy took the tiller without a word. Mitt plunged into the cabin, onto his favorite port bunk, and fell heavily asleep.

"Ynen, what did you have to go and say all that for?" Hildy whispered, wholly unfairly.

"Because I didn't understand," said Ynen. "I still don't. Why has he gone to sleep like that?"

"I think it's because you—we—upset him more than he wanted to think about," Hildy answered. "He's in an awful muddle. It must be lack of education."

"He's muddled me, too," Ynen said crossly. "I don't know whether to be sorry for him or not."

The slackening wind brought a drizzle of rain. Ynen and Hildy found a tarpaulin and wrapped it round their heads and shoulders. The rain increased, and the wind strengthened slowly, until the sea was so choppy that

Hildy found it hard to steer and hold the sail rope, too. The sail was yellow-gray and heavy with rain.

"Miserable!" she said. Water dripped off the end of her nose and chin.

"I wonder if we ought to take in a reef," Ynen said.

Just before midday, the choppiness woke Mitt. Wind's changed, he thought. Coming more off the land.

He stumbled muzzily out into the well to find a real downpour. Rain was battering down into the well and swirling along the planking, going *putter, putter* on the tarpaulin over Hildy and Ynen's heads, and making myriad pockmarks in the yellow-gray waves alongside. Mitt was not sure he liked the angry tooth shape of all those pockmarked waves.

"I've been wondering if I ought to reef—just in case," Ynen said to him.

Mitt looked at him, frowning sleepily against the cold water in his face. Beyond Ynen, the little figure of Libby Beer was shiny as new with rainwater. Beyond her, dim behind veil upon veil of silver rain, was what looked like a mountain walking up the sky from the land, monstrous, black and impending.

"What do you think about reefing?" Ynen asked.

Mitt stared at that mountain of black weather, aghast. Last time he had seen anything like it, Siriol had made for Little Flate as fast as *Flower of Holand* could move, and they had hardly got there in time. This was twice as near. There was no chance of making land. Those two had been sitting with their backs to it, but all the same! "Flaming Ammet!" said Mitt.

"Well, I thought I'd reef," Ynen said uncertainly.

"What am I doing standing here letting you ask?" Mitt said frantically. "You should have woke me an hour ago. Three reefs we'll need, and let's be quick, for Old Ammet's sake! I bet this boat handles real rough."

Ynen was astounded. *"Three?"* Hildy was so surprised that she lost her hold on the wet tiller. *Wind's Road* tipped about, and the boom swung over their heads. Mitt caught it, braced himself against the weight of wind and sopping sail, and tied it down with such haste that Ynen began to see he was in earnest. He slipped out from under the tarpaulin and scrambled onto the cabin roof in the hammering rain, to the ropes that lowered the mainsail. When he saw the weather the tarpaulin had been hiding from him, he did not feel quite so surprised at Mitt's command. Ynen had never been out in any weather so black himself, but he knew when the sky looked like that, you saw all the shipping making for Holand as fast as it could sail. He let the huge triangle of the sail down a foot or so. Mitt began tying the resulting fold down against the boom by the little strings that dangled from the canvas, and tying as if for dear life. "We have got a storm sail," Ynen called.

Mitt shook his head, knowing how long it would take two boys to get in this mass of great wet sail and bend on another. "We'd be caught with our pants down. Maybe we are, anyway. She rides awful high. Get tying. Quick!"

They tied cold, wet reef knots until their fingers ached. Hildy stood on the seat, with her foot on the tiller, and laced away at the sail over her head. Mitt and Ynen crawled up and down the cabin roof, tying knots there. They did it again with a second fold, and then all over again with a third. By this time, *Wind's Road*'s sail was an absurd little triangle, with the long bare mast towering above it. The rain was coming in gusting clouds now. They could see nothing much beyond a gray circle about thirty feet across. But, inside that circle, the waves were yellow-green, heaving high and pointed. The bare mast swept back and forth. The deck was up and down, sickeningly steep both ways.

"Don't untie that boom till we got the foresails in," Mitt shouted at Hildy. Somehow the weather was much louder, though it was hard to tell what was making the noise. Mitt and Ynen hauled and grappled at the clapping sails in the bows, slithering on the wet planks round Old Ammet. One moment they were skyward, soaring into lashing rain. The next Old Ammet was plunging, like a man on a toboggan, down and down a freckled tawny gray wave side.

Ynen swallowed giddily. "Is it going to be bad?" he yelled.

Mitt did not try to deceive him. "Real shocker!" he bawled back. But he thought it was just as well that he did not have breath to spare to explain to Ynen that these autumn storms sometimes went on for days. Mitt knew they would be drowned long before the day was out.

Now he was fully awake, he knew, with nasty vividness, that *Wind's Road* would capsize. He could feel it in the movement of her. She was only a rich man's pleasure boat, after all. And as Old Ammet launched himself furiously down another freckled hill of water, Mitt was as terrified as he had been when he crouched among the marble-playing boys in Holand. He was blind with panic. It was as if he had run away from himself and left the inside of his head empty. Mitt knew this would not do. It was no use thinking Ynen could manage by himself. He had to run after himself, inside his head, and bring himself back with one arm twisted up his back before he was able to pick up an armful of soaking sail and stagger with it to the hatch. He thought, as he pushed and kicked it down and clapped the cover on and banged the bolt home, that there really was nothing left of the old fearless Mitt anymore. He had never been in charge of a boat before. He wanted to whimper because Siriol was not there.

He and Ynen crawled back across the seesawing cabin roof. Hildy, seeing them coming, obeyed instructions and started to untie the lashings round the boom. She knew they had been idiots, she and Ynen, sitting under that tarpaulin and letting the storm creep up on them. She had been trying to behave with smart efficiency ever since. She did not want people like Mitt thinking her a fool. But she had no notion how fierce the wind was now. She loosened the main knot.

The wind tore it all out of her hands. The sail

slammed round sideways, jerking *Wind's Road* broadside on to the next huge wave. The boom mowed across the cabin roof and caught the side of Ynen's head with a *thuck*. It knocked him clean out. He was carried helplessly with it toward the side.

14

Hildy screamed. Mitt flung himself after Ynen and just managed to catch him round the ankle with both hands. Water thundered down over them, hard and heavy, and fell away, sucking and rilling, pulling Ynen against Mitt's straining arms and dragging both of them down the tilted cabin roof. Mitt had no idea how they survived, any more than Hildy. Hildy knew *Wind's Road* had gone like a bullet, slantwise through the top of that wave. But how she came to have the fighting tiller in one hand and the sail rope in the other she did not know.

"Ye gods! I'm sorry!" she screamed at Mitt when she saw him, drenched and horrified, sliding down from the cabin roof and heaving Ynen after him.

"Don't dare do that again!" Mitt screamed back. *Wind's Road* was plunging downhill now, and he made use of it to slide Ynen into the cabin. Ynen was alive, to his great relief, stirring and muttering miserably. Mitt did not dare linger with him. He wedged him hurriedly in place with blankets. "Don't move!" he bawled, though the cabin was almost quiet. "You took a knock there." *Wind's Road,* trembling sickeningly, mounted upward again. Mitt threw himself downhill into the well and wrestled the tiller out of Hildy's weak hand. The storm was too loud even for screaming now.

Mitt found he had arrived just in time. The huge autumn storm roared and howled and bashed around them. *Wind's Road* was half sideways in the trough between two heaving walls of water, caught in the backwash of the last wave. Worse still, while she wallowed there, half the thundering gale was blocked by the water. The sail was coming smashing across and threatening to capsize her. Mitt, as he worked at the sluggish tiller, shrieked and made gestures at Hildy to pull the rope in and hold the sail. It seemed a lifetime before she understood and the rope came yelling over its blocks into her hands. She still had a silly, puzzled look on her face, but Mitt had no time to attend. He could only thank Old Ammet he was stronger since he was last in a boat. *Wind's Road* was the hardest thing he had ever had to handle. She would *not* come about. They were creeping crabwise up a great slope of water, up and up, until they were hanging, almost over on one side, just beneath the raving crest of the wave. *Wind's Road* had suicidal urges. Mitt felt her going over, and heaved on the flaccid tiller.

The full force of the storm hit them as he did so. Mitt

and Hildy both screamed. Their voices burst out of their throats without their being able to help it. The wind hit with a roar and a crash. The sail rope yelled out from between Hildy's fingers, nearly dislocating both her shoulders. Great lumps of water loomed and fell, smashing across the bows, banging down on the cabin, thundering over Hildy and Mitt, until they were as bruised as they were wet, and went fizzing and boiling away behind.

The man in the bows with the flying fair hair understood their danger and leaned into the wave, dragging at *Wind's Road*'s forward rigging. *Wind's Road* did not want to come, but Mitt thought the man dragged her round by main force. He saw him clearly for a moment, with his hair as white as the snarling spray, gesturing aside the horses that were trying to overwhelm *Wind's Road*. Then *Wind's Road* lashed herself over the edge and down another watery hillside, and Mitt had all his work cut out to hold her straight. Beside him, Hildy, to his relief, was trying to help the sail rope as it came rattling in again when *Wind's Road* plunged.

Mitt could not hold her straight. *Wind's Road* went down into that valley of water and wallowed sideways, with every intention of never coming up. But the man was there against the foam-laced surface of sliding black water, wrenching *Wind's Road* straight for him. Mitt wanted to thank him, but by that time *Wind's Road* was on her sickening way upward again to lay herself sideways to the next wave top.

And so it went on. Mitt thought they went from sudden death to sudden death so often that they lost count of how long. The world was a lathering uproar, and *Wind's Road* hit and buffeted until she jerked all over. Mitt and Hildy were bashed by water until they hardly felt it. Water fizzed into the cabin and swirled round Ynen. The tarpaulin floated round the well, mashed up and neglected, and got in the way, but neither Hildy nor Mitt had time to get rid of it. Hildy's attention was all for the rope, either yelling out or rattling in, and Mitt's for battle with the tiller, *Wind's Road*'s yawing death urges, and the gestures of the fair-haired man when the wind hit with a clap and a shout.

He and Hildy got quite used to seeing him, up there in the bows, either gray with storming rain or whiter against the black side of a wave. They were glad to see him there. But the horses bothered them both. They were beautiful gray horses galloping, arching their necks under flying manes, dashing up the slopes of waves, frolicking and rearing on the crests. Mitt and Hildy never had time to look at them properly, but they saw them all the time out of the corners of their eyes. They knew they were imagining things. Sailors told stories of horses playing round doomed ships, frolicking at the death of mortals. Mitt and Hildy would much rather not have seen them. They kept their eyes ahead on the next danger coming. But there were still horses galloping on both sides of the boat, though ahead there was nothing but fizzing foam and shuddering waves and occasionally the man with the flying light hair.

He's doing us no harm, that's for sure! Mitt thought.

In the cabin Ynen got to his elbows and put a hand to the big tender lump on the side of his face. He could have sworn somebody had shaken him and told him to get up. But he was all alone, lying among sopping blankets. "Ugh!" he said. He could feel *Wind's Road* yawing and staggering, and he wondered what was causing this awful sluggish movement.

The cabin door slammed open against the stove, and a wave of dirty water rushed down on Ynen, soaking him to the bone. He stared uphill at two pairs of slithering feet and more water bashing across them. Ye gods! he thought. The water we must be shipping! He scrambled up while he was thinking it and climbed uphill into the well.

The first thing that met his eyes was the lovely head of a thoroughbred gray horse, flying past among the rain and spray. It was gone at once, as if it was galloping faster than *Wind's Road* could sail. Ynen was hit by the rain and gasped. It was lashing down. He could hardly see the withered and wind-whipped figures of Mitt and Hildy, let alone the woman kneeling on the stern behind them. It was as much as Ynen could do to make out that this woman had long red-gold hair, flapping and swirling in the wind. He saw she was giving Hildy a hand with the rope—or he thought she was, until he realized she was pushing at the tiller as Mitt braced his feet and shoved it. The rain made Ynen very confused. But he realized the woman was pointing at the locker where the pump was.

"Yes, of course," Ynen said to her. He was still dazed, but he clipped the lid of the locker up, moved the tarpaulin off the scuppers and began to pump.

The storm raved on for another hour or more. Ynen pumped away, without a hope of emptying the boat, but perhaps doing just enough to prevent *Wind's Road*'s swamping. Sometimes he wished, in the fretful way one does in dreams, that the lady in the stern would help him, too, though he knew she had enough to do with Mitt and Hildy. Sometimes he thought the man up in front might come back and give him a hand. He knew this was an ungrateful thought. The man had stopped *Wind's Road* from turning over several times, and he was keeping off the horses, too. But Ynen's arms ached so.

At length the roaring and thundering grew less. *Wind's Road,* from sliding up and down, went to heaving and lurching, and from that to a staggering *slap-slap-slap,* with only the odd spout of water coming aboard. They sailed through a brown light. The rain hissed down and seemed to flatten the tossing sea further. Then the rain stopped. Ynen, pumping and pumping, felt far too hot.

"We did it!" Hildy said. "It's over." As she said it, Ynen heard the squelching that meant the bilge was nearly dry. He straightened his back thankfully.

There was a blinding sun right in front of the bows, low on the edge of the sea. The storm clouds were above the sun in a heavy black line, getting smaller and smaller. It was hot. *Wind's Road* had steam rising from her decking and salt crystals forming like frost on her. The small triangle of sail sagged. There was a mess of tangled ropes everywhere, and *Wind's Road* was riding with a surge and swing unlike any Ynen or Hildy had ever experienced. Mitt knew it for the surge and swing of deep ocean. He looked back, across the little salt-coated figure of Libby Beer, away and away over empty sea. There was no land.

Weak and trembly though they all were, they burst out talking and laughing, in overloud hoarse voices, telling one another what each had thought the worst bit was. Ynen said it was when he saw the boom on its way to hit him. Hildy said it was the horses.

"No," said Mitt. "It was that first time she tried to capsize, just before we saw the man."

"I thought that, until the horses kept being there," said Hildy. "And I tried to tell myself I was just imagining them because I was so scared and tired. But I knew they were there."

"I saw one quite close to, just before Libby Beer told me to pump," Ynen said. "Didn't they go fast!"

"Hey, look," said Mitt. "We haven't all run mad, have we?"

"Of course not," said Ynen. "Libby Beer was sitting behind you, helping you sail her, and Old Ammet was standing in the bows stopping her sinking and keeping the horses off. I saw both of them."

Hildy looked anxiously at the big purple bruise on the side of Ynen's face and then at the tiny, salt-coated figure of Libby Beer on the stern. "I didn't get a chance to turn round, but isn't she rather small?"

"Old Ammet got carried away in that first big wave, for sure," Mitt said, and hoisted himself weakly on the cabin roof to see.

He could see a bundle of whitish straw, gently rising and falling in the bows. He crawled forward, hardly able to believe it. Old Ammet was still there, contrary to all reason, every plaited wheat stalk of him, miraculously in one piece. There were strips of seaweed wrapped about him and tangled in his wheaten hair, as if he had got his lost ribbons back, changed by the sea to green and brown. But round his neck, broken and sodden, was draped a garland made of wheat, burst grapes, and drooping flowers.

"Come and look at this!" Mitt yelled.

They left *Wind's Road* to sail herself and stood in a row with their clothes steaming, looking down at Old Ammet and his garland from the Festival. "I think we ought to thank him, and Libby Beer," said Hildy.

Mitt was very self-conscious at the idea, but he made himself growl, "Thank you, sir," with Hildy and Ynen, and then turn round and say, "Thank you, lady," to Libby Beer. After all, he had seen Old Ammet with his own eyes.

Then Hildy started to shiver violently. Mitt knew what was needed. He waded through the soaked blankets on the cabin floor and fetched the bottle of arris. He made Hildy and Ynen have a good swig and then took one himself. They stood about in the well going *"Um-pwaugh!"* and making awful faces.

"Shocking taste, isn't it?" said Mitt. "Wait a moment, though. There comes a sort of *boing* inside, and then it warms the insides of your ears."

The *boing* came. It made them feel so much better that they got out the pies and fell on them ravenously. Their hands shook as they ate, and their fingers were white, wrinkly, and blistered, even Mitt's, which had got a little soft-skinned in Hobin's workshop.

"I can't sail all through the night," Hildy said wearily.

"We've got a sea anchor," said Ynen, and looked at Mitt to see what he thought.

Mitt was dog-tired, too. But he knew autumn storms could come one on top of the other. He did not know what to do.

"I know," said Hildy, and she crawled forward to the mast. Mitt, with Ynen nodding and yawning beside him, stared at the soles of her feet and heard her say, "Please, Old Ammet, can you look after the boat tonight? But if there's another storm, could you wake Mitt up and tell him, please?"

"That's right! Pick on me!" Mitt called. "Tireless Mitt they call me. Think I don't wear out or something?" He turned to the figure of Libby Beer. "Excuse me, lady. She wants you to wake me if there's trouble. She thinks I'm made of the same stuff as what you are. So, if I'm needed, and you have to give me a nudge, do you mind waking her up, too? She can sit and feed me nips of arris."

The cabin was crowded and close that night. Nobody needed blankets, so they hung them in the well to dry. They all slept like logs, even Hildy, who had the small forward bunk which had been designed for her when she was nine. If Old Ammet or Libby Beer had tried to call Mitt in the night, he did not hear them. But all seemed well in the morning. The sea was flat, and the sun made a liquid yellow path to the gently drifting *Wind's Road*.

"I think I hate pies," said Hildy.

"You want to try mixing about a bit," Mitt told her. "You know—cherry flan and steak. Makes a change."

"You're cheating," said Ynen. "Those were squashed together, anyway. Try oyster and apple, Hildy. It's—well, it's different."

After this decidedly strange breakfast, they cleaned up *Wind's Road* and got very hot doing it. The heat told them all that they could not yet be very far North. None of them had the slightest idea where they were. As there was no land in sight, no chart Ynen could produce was any use to them. The only thing they were sure of was that they had been blown out into deep ocean, probably more west than north.

"I'll steer north and east," Ynen said. "When we sight land, I'll keep it just on the horizon, until we see somewhere we can recognize. Tulfa Island should be easy to find. And we know that belongs to the North. Let's get the sails up."

Shortly, with sails set again, in a light wind, *Wind's Road* was sailing on. Mitt sat lazily just above Old Ammet, listening to the water running past her sides and admiring the way her bows cut the sea sweetly asunder. In fair conditions *Wind's Road* was a beauty, he thought. He could hardly believe she had been doing her damnedest to drown them all yesterday.

"There's something to port over there," Ynen called. "Can you see what it is?"

Mitt looked too far, then too near, and finally saw a small dark thing lolloping on the swell, about a quarter of a mile away. "Could be a boat," he called.

"That's what I thought," Ynen called back, and pushed the tiller over, with a fine *ruckle-ruckle* of water from *Wind's Road's* elegant bows.

"Hey! What are you doing?" Mitt called, jumping up.

"Going to look. If it's a boat, it will have been in the storm," Ynen said and, for the first time for over a day, he gave Mitt a frankly unfriendly look. Hildy, beside him, gave Mitt the same look.

Mitt felt hurt, and irritated. "You don't have to look at me like that! I don't want to get seen and caught, do I?"

"If there's anybody in it, they can't possibly hurt you," said Ynen. "But I have to make sure. It's the law of the sea."

"Or weren't you brought up to keep to any law?" said Hildy.

Mitt felt Hildy need not have said that. He knew the rule as well as she did. "Don't talk so stupid!" he said. "Can't neither of you get it in your heads this isn't a pleasure trip?" Then, as Hildy went white and drew in her breath to make a powerful answer, Mitt added, "But please yourself—please yourselves. Don't mind me. I'm only the passenger." He could see the thing was a boat now, but only a small one. It looked to be just a ship's cockboat, torn loose in the storm. No danger there, Mitt thought.

But when *Wind's Road* had leaned nearer, in a pleasant riffling of water, they saw the boat was larger than that, about a third the size of *Wind's Road* herself. There was a mast in it, still flying tag ends of rope and some fluttering pieces of sail. There was no sign of life in it.

"It *was* in the storm," Hildy said, rather hushed.

"I'll go alongside," said Ynen.

Mitt stood up to offer to do that for him. Ynen pretended not to see. *Wind's Road* was his. Mitt sat down dourly by the mast. So Ynen did not trust him not to sail straight past then? Very well. Mitt grinned as Ynen went about too soon and hit the smaller boat a fair old wallop. Ynen winced at the damage to *Wind's Road*'s paint. The smaller boat simply bobbed about. It was salty, battered, and draped with seaweed. It had to be hard to sink, Mitt thought, to have survived the storm. It was empty, except for a tangle of tarpaulin in the bottom. Ynen had scraped *Wind's Road* for nothing, by the look of it.

Hildy read the name painted on the stern of the derelict. "*Sevenfold II.*"

"Funny!" said Mitt, coming to look. "That's a big merchant ship out of Holand. She was tied up in harbor there the day of the Festival. What's her boat doing here with a sail in it?"

"She must have sailed out later and got caught in the storm," Ynen suggested. "I suppose her crew took to the—Oh, dear!"

The tangle of tarpaulin heaved and humped. A wet and unkempt head was thrust out, as if its owner was shakily on his hands and knees. A hoarse and wretched voice said, "Take us aboard, for pity's sake!"

No one had expected this. Hildy and Ynen were quite as dismayed as Mitt. In fact, it was Mitt who first pulled himself together and said, "Up you come, then. How many are you?"

"Just me, guvnor," said the man, and seemed to fall flat on his face again.

Mitt exchanged a resigned and dubious look with Ynen and swung himself down into the bobbing derelict. The worst of it was it could be someone who knew him. He heaved back the tarry canvas. Underneath were several inches of water and, lying sprawled in it, a soaking, unshaven man in sailor's clothes. He was a square, powerful sort of fellow—the kind of man you could trust to survive a storm, Mitt thought, taking the man under the arms and trying to heave him upward. He was no one Mitt knew. But when Mitt had wrestled the fellow to his knees, he thought the man had a faintly familiar look. He must have seen him around on the waterfront. One thing was certain about him. The man was a good deal better nourished than most people in Holand. Mitt simply could not lift him.

They only got him aboard *Wind's Road* because the man seemed to come to his senses enough to help a little. Mitt boosted. Hildy leaned over and dragged. The man, groaning and feebly scrambling, pulled himself over the side into the well and collapsed again. It took them some time to pull and push him into the cabin and get him onto a bunk. Meanwhile, Ynen left *Sevenfold II*'s boat to bob by itself and sailed on.

"Would you like a drink of water?" Hildy asked, thinking the man must be parched with thirst.

The answer was a growl, in which the only words they caught were "little lady" and "arris."

"Give him a nip of it," Mitt said. "Bring him around."

Hildy fetched the bottle and put it to the man's pale, waterlogged lips. He took such a long drink that she was alarmed. When at length she managed to drag the bottle away, the man made a feeble pounce after it. "Arragh!" Hildy backed away quickly. He seemed like an angry wild beast. But he became calmer almost at once and mumbled something else with "little lady" in it. "S'some sleep," they heard him say.

"That's right. You drop off. Do you good," Mitt said heartily. He took Hobin's gun off the rack above the bunk, where he had left it, and put it in his belt, just to be on the safe side.

Hildy, in much the same spirit, put the arris bottle in a locker and shot the bolt. She looked back as they left the cabin and saw that the man's eyes were wide open. He could have been watching. But he could also have been half unconscious. "Do you think he's all right?" she whispered.

"You do get rough types," Ynen said, very much wishing he had left *Sevenfold II* to drift.

"He'll survive," said Mitt, "if that's what you were asking. Must be made of iron to be still alive. Let's hope he'll be more agreeable when he's had some sleep."

"So do I," said Hildy. The man's eyes were still wide open, staring from a broad pale face covered with long black stubble.

15

For the rest of that day, the new passenger slept, with his face turned to the wall. Everyone felt this was the best thing he could do. They left him alone and almost forgot he was there.

Ynen stayed at the tiller. It was his way of claiming *Wind's Road* back after the storm. He did not exactly resent Mitt's taking charge then, but *Wind's Road* was *his.* She was the loveliest and the luckiest boat out of Holand, and Ynen loved her passionately. This left Hildy and Mitt nothing much to do but lounge on the cabin roof. Hildy understood Ynen perfectly. Mitt was amused, though he had to admit that if he had had the luck to own *Wind's Road,* he might well have been just the same. And a bit more careful of my paint, he thought.

Wind's Road clipped her way elegantly northeast. No land came in sight. While they watched for land, they fell to talking, mostly about Holand. Mitt irritated Hildy because he would seem to think that life in the Palace was one of perfect bliss. So she told him what it was really like. It was beyond her to describe properly the emptiness and the lonely, neglected feeling she and Ynen had lived with, but she could tell Mitt how Hadd was as much of a tyrant in his own home as he was in his earldom.

"Everybody was so—so obedient that they'd no characters," she said. "The aunts were just fine ladies. And those cousins! All 'Yes, Grandfather,' and 'No, Grandfather,' and pretty dresses and despising people who didn't feel like being obedient."

"The boys were worse," Ynen said feelingly. "They had such a good opinion of themselves under the obedience."

"Like the uncles," said Hildy. "I don't think Uncle Harl ever did anything but crawl to Grandfather while he was alive and go around looking smug and being boring. But when Grandfather got shot, Uncle Harl got drunk to celebrate. It made me feel awful. And I will say this for Father—he wasn't like that."

"Then what was—*is* he like?" Ynen asked resentfully. "You got more sense out of a fish on a slab!"

"Except fish don't make jokes at your expense," Hildy added.

"Ah, now I've had quite a bit of dealings with fish, on slabs and off," Mitt said. "Sad look, they often have. And speaking as an authority, as you might say, I get to feel quite sorry for your pa, hearing you talk. Happy family, weren't you?"

"*Sorry* for him!" said Hildy.

"I know. That's a fine thing, coming from me, isn't it?" said Mitt. "But as far as I can see, he's not let do anything, except maybe play soldiers or go out for a shoot now and again. All he's let do is sit about in the happy family and take orders, and since he's not booked to be Earl or anything, he'll be doing that till he dies. Not much of a life, is it? On a slab, you might say, until he's under one."

Hildy and Ynen sat digesting this unusual view of their father for some time. Even then, all Ynen could think of to say was, "Well, I don't know," which he said very dubiously indeed. They seemed so perplexed that Mitt tried to cheer them up by telling them stories from the time he used to fish with Siriol and how he used to sell the fish. He amused Hildy and Ynen mightily. Hildy nearly rolled overboard laughing, and Ynen doubled up over the tiller. But this led to another difficult moment.

Ynen straightened up, tenderly shifted *Wind's Road* a point or so, and asked: "Is Siriol a Free Holander? He seems to have been very kind to you."

"Yes." Mitt went to pick at a blister the storm had raised on the cabin paint. He caught Ynen's eye and stopped, trying to grin. The puzzled, serious look he was growing to dread was settling on Ynen's face. "All right. He was one of them that informed," Mitt said. "Only don't start asking things again! I tell you straight I don't know *how* I feel about him. So he was good to me. So I didn't want to go near him after the bomb, for fear I brought the soldiers on him. That's all I know."

Ynen's mouth opened to ask another question. Hildy saw Mitt's face had gone elderly. She nudged Ynen and hastily got out the pies. The survivor from *Sevenfold II* was still asleep, so Hildy left a rather withered steak pie between his face and the cabin wall. When she came out into the well again, Mitt was still elderly, and she could tell from Ynen's face that he was going to ask more questions any minute.

Hildy began to talk brightly about the Holy Islands. She was not sure why she did, except that it was clear to her that Mitt's feelings were in a most painful muddle, and she knew a little how that felt. Perhaps the Holy Islands was not a good choice of subject. Hildy's feelings about them and about Lithar were in as bad a muddle as Mitt's about the Free Holanders. Because of this, and because she was so anxious to keep off Mitt's feelings, Hildy began to boast. All through the long afternoon, while *Wind's Road* ruckled her way gently through small blue waves, Hildy sat on the cabin roof and boasted about Lithar's famous fleet and the beauty and the strangeness of the Holy Islands. She told Mitt about the magic Bull, the mysterious piping, and the old man of the sea and his horses. She told him the Holy Islands were the most favored place in Dalemark. Before long, she began to feel that she was indeed extremely lucky to be going there, and she told Mitt all over again about the fame and beauty of the Holy Islands, in even more glowing terms.

On the third repetition Mitt felt he had had enough. "All right," he said. "You were so lucky to be betrothed, you ran away the first opportunity. So stop swanking."

"Yes, do stop, Hildy," said Ynen, who was as bored as Mitt.

Hildy was furious. "Why should I?"

Ynen looked at her whitening face and did not answer. Mitt could see Hildy was angry, too, but he did not see that was any reason for holding his tongue. "Because you said three times," he said, "that you're going to be Holy Hildrida. You're going to ride about on a bull, blowing a little whistle and hopping from island to island, granting everyone wishes. Now tell us how poor old Lithar feels about it. Pretty sick, I shouldn't wonder."

Hildy stood up on the cabin, so blazing white that Ynen winced. How dared Mitt make fun of her! She had only been trying to help him, too! And he repaid her like the street boy he was. She was so angry that she wondered whether to jump down on him where he sat in the well and hurt him as much as she could. Mitt grinned up at her, not in the least dismayed. Hildy realized he was probably stronger than she was. "You," she said, "are just a horrible little murderer, and don't you forget it!" She turned on her seaboot and stalked to the bows of the boat.

Mitt saw he had gone too far. He was sorry at first. Then, as Hildy continued to sit, white and blazing, looking out over Old Ammet, he became resentful. "Give me the tiller," he said to Ynen. "You need a rest, anyway. And go and tell that sister of yours to jump in."

Ynen took Hildy a pie instead. She refused to speak to him. He took a pie to the man from *Sevenfold II*. The man had not eaten the first pie. Ynen was just going away when the man roused a little. When Ynen asked if he wanted a pie, he growled. The only word Ynen heard was "guvnor." He leaned over, rather nervously, and asked the man his name. The man growled to call him Al, guvnor. Then he reached out and snatched the pie Ynen was just taking away again. Ynen retreated to the well, feeling he was the only good-tempered person aboard.

"He's horribly hard to get on with," he said to Mitt.

"He's a right brute," Mitt agreed. "Mind you, he may be better tomorrow."

They settled the watches for the night, with Ynen having to run back and forward between Mitt and Hildy because Hildy would not speak to Mitt. Mitt took the dawn watch. He wanted to be on hand in case they reached land then.

But by morning there was still no sign of land. The wind was brisker, and the day promised to be clear. Mitt leaned against the side of the well, with his foot up on the seat, humming a tune and feeling fresher and calmer than he had felt for years. He wondered what he would do when he reached the North. Go back to fishing, he supposed, or get work on a farm. But he was sure there were a hundred other things, as yet unthought of, which he could do quite as well.

He was so cheerful and confident that he was really hurt when Hildy came out of the cabin and pushed past him without a word. "What am I supposed to have done—bar teased you a bit?" he demanded.

"And why should I put up with that?" asked Hildy. "It's not your place to criticize me."

"Oh, go and get a nice long drink of arris!" Mitt said disgustedly.

Hildy was looking at him, uncertain whether to laugh or fly at his throat, when *Wind's Road* vibrated to a string of swearwords. Hildy had never heard the like. Even Mitt had seldom heard so many at once. Al stuck his head out of the cabin and gave Mitt a bloodshot look.

"Isn't there a razor in this godforsaken tub?"

"There may be," said Hildy. "The sailors often leave things. I'll look."

"I didn't mean you, little lady. I meant him," said Al. "Let him look."

"I'm steering," said Mitt. "And I don't know where to look."

Al gave him another bloodshot look. "Then she'd better do it," he said, and went inside again. Hildy followed him, and found a razor. Mitt stood outside, scowling, hearing things like, "It'll be none the worse for a bit of sharpening, little lady," and the sound of Hildy stropping the razor. "This is all the soap you have, is it? Thank you, little lady, much obliged, but a man needs a bit of hot water to shave with." That meant Hildy had to get the charcoal stove alight, draw water, set it to boil, and work away at the stove bellows. Mitt watched her working away with a set, cross look on her face, while Al sat at his ease on the bunk, and wished they had left that boat to rot.

When Ynen came out, he was wishing the same, though all he said was "No land yet?"

All Mitt said was "No. I reckon that storm blew us a good long way out." But he could see Ynen knew how he felt.

Al emerged from the cabin at last, rubbing his smooth chin and looking satisfied. He climbed on the cabin roof and stretched. He was square and stocky. His face, now they could see it properly, was square, too, and unremarkable except for some bitter creases round the mouth and a general look of being well pleased with itself. His clothes, in spite of being faded and creased by the sea, were better than Mitt had realized, and he had a well-nourished look that made Mitt think he must have been mate or perhaps bosun on *Sevenfold II*.

"What are you staring at?" Al demanded. Hildy was looking at him resentfully. Ynen was puzzled because he had a feeling he had seen Al before somewhere. Al laughed and looked round *Wind's Road.* "Lucky ship, eh?" he said, nodding from Old Ammet to the little Libby Beer. Then he nodded at Mitt. "Hand that tiller over, and let's have something to eat."

"I'll do it," Ynen said, opening the locker where the

second sack of pies still lay untouched.

"Don't you, guvnor," said Al. "Let him."

"It's still Mitt's watch," said Ynen.

"Yes, but it's his station," said Al. "It's not your place to cook."

"Nobody's cooking," said Mitt. "And what do you take me for?"

Al shrugged his wide shoulders. "Servant. Body-guard, by the look of that gun you got there."

Mitt looked down in annoyance, wishing he had buttoned his coat over Hobin's gun. "I'm no servant," he said.

"Don't tell me!" Al said, laughing loudly. "I suppose you come aboard and held the guvnor and the little lady up at gunpoint!"

Mitt could not look at anyone. Hildy seized the sack out of Ynen's hands and dumped it on the cabin roof. "Help yourself," she said. "That's what everybody else is doing on this boat."

"Thank you kindly, little lady," said Al. "After you. After the guvnor." He would not touch a pie until Hildy and Ynen had each taken one. Then he took one himself, remarking that Mitt could eat when he came off duty. Ynen promptly passed Mitt his own pie and took another. But Al was clearly not a man to pick up hints. He waved a piece of oyster patty at Ynen and asked with his mouth full, "And where, may one ask, is this boat bound, guvnor?"

They munched in uneasy silence. They all realized

that they had forgotten to invent a story to tell him. "Kinghaven," Ynen said at last, in a haughty way he hoped would shut Al up.

Al ducked his head respectfully. "Sorry I spoke. Sorry I spoke, guvnor. Never wish to offend the gently born. Friends in the North, have you? Not many Holanders could say the same. I mean, I know you'll pardon me for mentioning it, but I can see this boat's from Holand by the images back and front. Not a deep-water boat, either, is she? Pleasure vessel, more like."

Hildy drew herself up, as her aunts did when they were displeased. "Yours was hardly even that, was it?"

Al shut his eyes and muttered things. "Oh, it was horrible! Filthy little tub. Never been so seasick in my life!" That surprised them, in a sailor, but Al's other remarks had so alarmed them that they all tried to look sympathetic. Al grinned. "I lay down in the bottom and let it all happen. Only thing I knew how to do. That was after I lost my gun. Damned wave took it off me. I regret that gun. It was as good as the one you got there." Mitt found Al's eyes open again, staring at Hobin's gun in his belt. "Mind if I have a look?" said Al.

"Sorry," said Mitt. "It's got sentimental value. I never let anyone else touch it."

"Fair enough," said Al, to Mitt's considerable relief.

Mitt finished his pie, handed the tiller to Hildy, and retired to the cabin, sick of Al already and hoping heartily that it would not prove far now to Kinghaven. They must all make sure to give Al the slip there. Mitt did not trust Al. He disliked his elaborate deference to Hildy and Ynen, his plain intention of not doing a hand's turn, and, above all, his smug and prying manner.

Above him, Mitt could hear Al asking if they had anything to eat but pies. He added discontentedly that it seemed rather a rich diet. Yes, let's have you seasick again, Mitt thought, and went up the cabin to the rosy bucket.

When he came out, Al's voice was in the well, saying, "Oh, no offense, little lady. It's not my place to question the provisions. I just thought you could get that lazy boy to catch a few fish now and then. His kind get above themselves if they're let stay idle."

"You can fish if you want," Ynen said. "We don't want you idle either."

"That's right, guvnor," Al agreed heartily. "I'll go and set him to it, shall I?"

There was a frustrated silence in the well. Al bent down and entered the cabin. Mitt braced himself against the remaining half of the cupboard door, ready to whisk past Al and out on deck. Al would soon find Mitt was nobody's servant. Al advanced. Mitt waited his moment and shot forward. But instead of sliding by under Al's elbow, Mitt found himself hurtling into Al's solid body and grunting with the impact. He was seized in a punishingly strong grip. Al laughed in his ear. "No, you don't!"

Nothing like this had happened to Mitt for years. He was as humiliated as he was angry. He struggled hard. They bashed against the cupboard, a bunk, and the cupboard again. "Let go of me!" panted Mitt as they bounced against the gilded door.

Al, by this time, had both Mitt's hands helpless under one brawny arm. "Right you are," he said. He plucked the gun out of Mitt's belt and let go of Mitt the same instant. Mitt was flung against the bunk again.

"How dare you!" said Hildy.

"Give that back, please," said Ynen.

Both of them had come into the cabin, too, which explained why *Wind's Road* was tipping about so, Mitt realized, as he was rolled onto the floor.

Al raised the gun. "You see to the boat, guvnor," he said, and walked toward the cabin door. Ynen, Hildy, and Mitt, too, backed out in front of him in a dismayed cluster, treading on one another along the tipping floor. Ynen seized the tiller and set *Wind's Road* to rights again, while the other two crammed themselves beside him, as far as they could get from Al in the cabin doorway.

"That's right," said Al. "Now this is much more comfortable. I didn't feel safe with this gun where it was. Went off once already, didn't it?" he said, pointing to the splintered groove beside the well. He turned the gun over admiringly. "Where did you pinch this?" he asked Mitt. "This is one of Hobin's—one of his specials."

Mitt set his face sullenly. He was not going to discuss Hobin with Al.

"Well, it's in good hands now," Al remarked. "Five shots in it. Got any more?"

"No," said Mitt.

In rippling, rope-creaking silence, Al swung himself up to sit facing them on the cabin roof, with his legs dangling and the gun laid across one knee. Mitt watched his square, smug face and was almost shamed enough to cry. He knew he was having a very vivid experience of exactly how Ynen and Hildy felt when he first came out of the cabin himself, and it made him feel sick. It seemed hard on Ynen and Hildy to be having it again.

"Now let's make sure we understand one another," Al said comfortably. "I've been having a good deal of trouble lately, and it's made me nervous. I don't want any more, understand—guvnor? Little lady? You?"

"The name's Mitt," said Mitt. "What trouble?"

"I'll tell you," said Al, "so you won't get any wrong ideas about me. I'm a marksman. Best shot in the South—so do remember I don't want more trouble, won't you? That's why I'd rather be on the right end of this gun—nothing personal. As for the trouble, I had the good fortune to be employed by a noble gentleman in Holand—well, let's call him Harl, shall we?—to take one of my best shots at a certain Earl—let's call him Hadd, not to beat around the bush—"

Hildy's eyes and Ynen's slid sideways to each other. *Wind's Road* veered. Mitt had to nudge Ynen before he realized. Mitt felt nearly as bad himself, and the nature of the badness dragged his face elderly again.

"And I did," Al said earnestly. "It was as sweet a shot as you ever saw and dropped Hadd like a stone. But then the trouble started because I had to get away, hadn't I?

Naturally, Harl had promised me I'd be safe, but I knew better than to trust that kind of promise. Noble gentlemen who make these arrangements always prefer you to be dead, too. You can't blame Harl. I'd have done the same myself. So I made a little outlay of my own, on some soldiers, not to search a certain ship's boat where I was. But there were so many soldiers, and they got so eager, that I had to knock a couple into the water and then cast that filthy tub loose. And I got shot at, and rowed after, and if I hadn't happened to catch the tide, I wouldn't be here now. So I don't want more trouble this time. You don't blame me, do you, little lady?"

"I can't honestly say," said Hildy, "that I don't."

Al blinked a little at this, and scratched his tousled head. He smiled incredulously at Ynen. "She's a sharp one, your sister. She is your sister, isn't she? Lucky I never mind what people say." He moved Hobin's gun round on his knee until it pointed to Mitt. "You. Find some tackle and catch us a fish for lunch."

"If you don't mind what people say—no," said Mitt.

Al snapped back the trigger so that Hobin's gun was ready to fire. "You can say what you like as long as you do it," he said, and the look he gave Mitt made it quite clear he intended to shoot him.

"There may be some tackle in one of those lockers," Ynen told Mitt, in the slow, serious way people only use when they are truly frightened.

‖16‖

For the rest of the day Mitt sat fishing. Not venison, oyster, or pheasant tempted any fish to bite. Mitt sullenly watched the line trailing a little pucker in the sea and hated Al more every hour. It was no comfort to see Ynen and Hildy hated him, too, for Al had divided them from Mitt in every possible way.

Al liked talking. He lounged on the cabin roof, between Mitt and the well where Ynen and Hildy were, laying down the law about this, telling them the truth about that, and always treating Hildy and Ynen with great deference and Mitt with none at all. He told them the North was nothing like as free as it was cracked up to be, that a diet of pies would give them scurvy, and that Waywold was a better place to live than Holand. Then he came round to Poor Old Ammet and Libby Beer.

"Funny superstition, having a couple of dummies in

your boat," he said, waving from the straw figure to the wax one. "It's not as if you Holanders believed in them. When I was in Waywold, they had a saying there that Holanders kept gods they didn't own to. And that's true. I bet you didn't know they were gods one time."

"They're all right now," Mitt said.

"And we know they're something special," said Ynen.

"Surely you do, guvnor. No offense. But I've been in the Holy Islands all this year past, and I know a bit more than you do. They call those two things gods there. That's how the islands got their name, see. But—this is a funny thing—they don't call them anything there. You ask what are the names of these two dummies, and people just look at you. Oh, they're funny people—half crazed with god fearing, if you ask me—and all the gods are is two dummies."

"I think you might let Mitt stop fishing now," said Hildy.

"Little lady," said Al, "you've a kind heart, and he can stop when he's caught a fish. You hear that?" he said to Mitt. "She's a nice girl—considerate. All her kind are like that. They can afford to be nice, and frank, open, and generous, too. They've got the means behind them, see, where your kind and mine can't afford it. It's a high-priced luxury, being nice is."

Mitt humped his shoulders bitterly. He was sure Al was right. Al could not have chosen any better way of describing the way Ynen and Hildy had treated him all along. It hit the nail on the head.

Ynen said to Hildy as Al talked on, "Who *is* he? I've seen him before somewhere."

Hildy knew Ynen had a far better memory for faces than she had. "I don't care who he is," she said. "I'm going to push him in the sea." She meant it.

But Al was too old a hand to let any of them have a chance to harm him. Having divided them from one another, he talked until he had bored them into numbness. Then he demanded food. Then he talked until nightfall, and still no land was in sight. By now they all thought of land as the thing which would rescue them from Al.

"Well," said Al, as soon as supper was over, "I think I'll be turning in."

They made an effort to suggest he took a watch during the night.

"Who, me?" said Al. "I don't know the first thing about this game. I'm a landsman."

"You had a sail up in that boat," Ynen said. "And you're a Holander. I've seen you. Holanders aren't landsmen."

"I never denied it, guvnor. But that was all years back, before your time. Good night, then." And, since none of them could stop him, Al went into the cabin and fell asleep with the gun hidden under his body where nobody could get it.

While Mitt was dourly stowing the fishing tackle back in the locker, Hildy looked vengefully into the cabin. "He's just like the cousins, Ynen, only I hate him more."

"I hate him harder every time he calls me guvnor," said Ynen.

"He's bound to," Mitt said, kicking the locker to vent some of his feelings. "He's respectful of you." It was on the tip of his tongue to ask them if he had been as bad as Al, but he had not the heart to. He knew he had been. Instead he found himself arranging the night's watches, in a constrained and businesslike way, and taking the dawn watch himself again. Mitt felt in his bones it would be dawn when they sighted land.

In fact, the numb hatred they all felt for Al was very different from the way Ynen and Hildy had felt about Mitt. Ynen pondered about this while he steered *Wind's Road* into darkness. Mitt had scared them horribly at first. But Ynen had never felt unequal to him, the way he felt with Al. As soon as Mitt had started to argue, Ynen had stopped being scared. There were things they had in common with Mitt, but with Al there was nothing. You could not trust him or argue with him. Ynen hoped the wind would be fresh tomorrow, because if it was and if Al stayed on the cabin roof, he was fairly sure he could bring himself to give the tiller a quick shove and sweep Al off the roof with *Wind's Road*'s boom.

Hildy spent her watch thinking wretchedly of Uncle Harl. Ye gods! It was as if she, or Ynen, had paid Al to shoot Navis. Hildy felt so sickened that she was truly thankful Mitt had forced them to sail North, out of that horrible situation. Only now they had Al on board. Hildy knew they were going to need all their cunning, and Mitt's, too, to escape from Al once they did reach land. And she had quarreled with Mitt. Of all the stupid things to lose her temper over! After what Al had said, Mitt was not going to believe in anything friendly Hildy said. Hildy hated Al for the way he had treated Mitt. It was like Uncle Harchad and the Earl of Hannart's son, except that Al had used words instead of kicks.

She tried to show Mitt she was friendly by being very pleasant when she woke him up for his watch. Mitt hardly spoke to her. He pretended to be very sleepy and stumbled past her into the well, mumbling. When he took the tiller and set *Wind's Road* heeling away into the faintly silvering sea, he was too perplexed and miserable to notice what he was doing. The awful similarity between himself and Al was all he could think of. "He did it for money, and I did it for a cause—that's all the difference I can see," he said to himself. "But what cause?"

He felt a sharp nudge on his back. He looked up to find *Wind's Road* yawing about in a white sea, against a white sky. The wind had dropped and changed. It was quite a bit colder. Mitt set *Wind's Road* to rights, buttoned his coat, and turned to have a good look at Libby Beer. She was a tiny, dark figure, too far away to have nudged him. Yet she had.

"See here, lady," Mitt said to her, in his misery, "can I talk to you? Will you answer?" The little dark knobby shape did not move or make any sign. "What I want to know," said Mitt, "is: Am I going to end up worse than Al if I started so young?" Libby Beer gave no sign of having heard. "All right," said Mitt. "I promise to leave murdering alone in future. Will you help me now?" There was silence, except for the fitful rilling of water. "I can't seem to think things in my head without talking them," Mitt explained. "I went through life thinking I was on the right side—one of the good ones, you know—and now I can see I'm as bad as Al. So I got it all to think about again. I want to know what I thought I was doing there in Holand." There was still no sign from Libby Beer. She sat at the end of the tiller among her twine lashing, and the faded colors began to come back to her because the sun was rising. Mitt did not dare talk anymore, in case someone in the cabin heard him. He stared round the welling yellow waves. There was still no land in sight.

No land came in sight all that day. The wind sank to a light, fitful breeze, in which they all buttoned their coats and shivered. It was so much colder that they were sure they must be in Northern waters. That was their one comfort. The pies were smelling strange, the water was low, and got lower still when Al refused to shave in sea-water—and there was Al.

Al announced he was bored. "You must have brought a pack of cards or some dice with you," he told Mitt, evidently thinking he was the most likely one.

Since Libby Beer had nudged him in the dawn, Mitt felt just a little more equal to Al. "Me?" he said. "People in my station can't afford games."

Al roamed about grumbling for a while. Then he suddenly went below and came up with the bottle of arris. "This'll have to do then," he said. "Should just be enough. Mind you, little lady, I'm not grumbling, but you should be sure your bottles are full before you sail."

He settled himself on the cabin roof and got drunk. They could all see Hobin's gun stuck in his belt, but Al's hand was never far off it, and he patted it lovingly from time to time. Al sang a little. Ynen looked yearningly at the sail. But the wind was so light that he knew the boom would only give Al a gentle bump if he did swing it over. He sighed and handed the tiller over to Hildy, hoping she would have better luck.

When Al had drunk half the arris, he began to talk again. They all closed their ears. It was easy to do. They were all half asleep after their night watches. For an hour not one of them heard a word Al said. Then he began to laugh uproariously and shout at them.

"I tell you, I've been around all right! And my advice to you is *two games at once*! Rich against rich—they pay better—but rich against poor, if you can't have that. I'll tell you—I'll tell you—*Come here and look, the lot of you!*"

Hildy was steering, but Ynen and Mitt did not dare disobey. Reluctantly they went toward the cabin roof, where Al was fumbling and pawing at his jacket and staring at them with angry, unfocused eyes. As they reached him, he managed to turn the top of his jacket inside out, to show the drab strip of tape in the lining. Fixed to the tape was a tiny round piece of gold with a wheatsheaf crest on it.

"There. Know what that is?"

"Yes," said Ynen. "You're one of Harchad's spies."

Al slapped himself with triumph. "Right!" he said. "Right, right, right! Been Harchad's man for seven years now. So you see what I done?" he asked shrewdly, and became earnest and confiding before either of them could answer. "Rich against rich is the best way. Harl pays me to shoot old Haddock. Harchad gives me a bounty to shoot old Haddock. Offers of safety from both. Al's all right whatever happens, see."

"Just what we'd have expected of you, Al," said Mitt.

Ynen was quite unable to stay near Al any longer. He backed away beside Hildy and was glad when she took a chilly hand off the tiller and squeezed his arm so hard that it hurt.

Al seemed quite content to concentrate on Mitt. He laughed and waved one finger under Mitt's nose. "You take my advice and go in for the double game. Do what I done. You can't beat the earls, so you join them. Find freedom fighters, join them with the Earl's blessing. Then bust them up. I done that all over South Dalemark. Harchad pays—wants information. Earls pay. Lovely life."

Mitt felt his face being pulled elderly as he listened.

There seemed no end to the similarities between Al and himself. He turned away from Al's wagging finger and saw that Hildy and Ynen were as hard hit as he was. Their heads were hanging at wretched doll-like angles, and their faces were blurry. Mitt would have liked to say something—something rude to Al, at least—to cheer them up. But he was in such a blazing misery himself that he thought: Being nice is a high-price luxury. Why should *I* bother? He jumped up onto the decking and scrambled toward *Wind's Road*'s bows.

"Hardest bunch of freedom fighters are in Waywold," said Al. "Where are you going?"

"To talk to Poor Old Ammet," said Mitt. "He's better listening. He keeps quiet."

"But the cushiest job," said Al, as if Mitt had not spoken, "was in the Holy Islands. They don't know the meaning of freedom fighting there—only I'm not telling Harchad that. I'm on to a real good thing there." He laughed. "They think the world of me. And all because of my name. Did you know my name was Alhammitt? But I'm not telling that in Holand. I'd have half Holand coming and trying to set themselves up in style there."

"Oh shut up!" Hildy whispered.

But Al talked on, until there was very little arris left in the bottle. Then he sang the "Ballad of Fili Ray." It was about a man who was hanged.

"At least he knows what he deserves!" Ynen said. "Hildy, I know where I saw him before. He was in the Palace last week. The first time I saw him, he was with

Uncle Harchad. The other time was out at the back, where Father was having those new houses built. Al came out and talked to Father there, I'm afraid."

Hildy knew, by the dead, sick feeling inside her, that she had feared this all along. "You—you think Father paid him to shoot Grandfather, too?" If Navis had been expecting someone to shoot Hadd, it would explain his unusual presence of mind.

"I don't know," Ynen whispered wretchedly. "He kicked Mitt's bomb away."

"But that could have been because it wasn't part of the plan," said Hildy, and they both looked over to Mitt's hunched shape beyond the mast. They were both quite sure Mitt would want nothing more to do with them now.

The song stopped. Al drank the last of the arris. Then he stood up and staggered toward the well. Hildy and Ynen, both thoroughly frightened, pressed back against the stern and stared up at his swaying, grinning face. There was simply no knowing what Al would choose to do next.

"Funny thing, guvnor and little lady," Al said slurrily. "You look as though you seen a ghost. Another funny thing—I don't feel quite myself. Think I'll go and lie down." He came off the edge of the roof and collapsed on his knees in the well. Neither Hildy nor Ynen could bear to touch him. They turned their feet sideways out of his way, as he floundered round and crawled into the cabin. After two attempts he got onto a bunk and was shortly snoring.

"The gun's underneath him again," Hildy said hopelessly.

They waited for Mitt to come back to the well. It seemed the most important thing in the world that Mitt should come and be friendly with them. It had nothing to do with the fact that they were both sure Mitt was the only one who might get the better of Al. It was that if Mitt disowned them, then they were disowned indeed. But Al snored for two hours before Mitt moved. Old Ammet was as little help to Mitt's misery as Libby Beer had been, although Mitt reached out several times and pleadingly touched the stiff, salty straw of him. Mitt knew he would have to talk to someone. The only way he could think was aloud.

Wind's Road's movement altered. The dip and swing of her became shorter and stronger, though the wind was still the merest chilly breeze. Mitt knew they must be in coastal waters again. He jumped up, but there was still no sign of land. He hurried across the cabin roof to tell Hildy and Ynen what he thought, but when he looked at them, below him in the well, he wondered if he was going to be able to speak to them at all. Their searching expressions, and their very faces, put him off. Ynen's nose had blistered in the weather, but it was still Hadd's nose. Hildy's two pigtails were loose and puffy, and wisps of black hair blew across her narrow cheeks, but the sharp, tanned face was like Harchad's even so.

Hildy made an effort to talk about Navis. "I know what you're thinking—" she said to Mitt.

"I'm no good at thinking," Mitt said sadly. "Not like you." It sounded much nastier than he intended. Hildy took it for a snub and did not go on.

After that none of them tried to talk about anything important, much as they all wanted to. The things Al had said were like a sore place none of them wanted to touch. This had a very odd effect. They found themselves chattering, and even laughing, about things that were not important, so that someone who did not know might have thought they were three great friends. They got the pies out again and picked out the parts that were still good. The rest—more than half—they had to throw in the sea.

They had just finished eating when Hildy exclaimed, "Seagulls!" White birds were bobbing on the water behind, riding high and light like *Wind's Road* herself. Others wheeled above the well on big bent wings, each with a bead of an eye watching for more pie. Ynen looked at Mitt.

"Land," said Mitt. "Can't be too far off."

They exchanged excited looks. Not only was the long voyage nearly over, but if they could reach land while Al was still asleep, they had a real chance of getting away from him. Ynen tiptoed into the cabin and rustled all the charts there were off the rack above Al's bunk. Al did not move. He tiptoed back to the well with them. Most of the charts, naturally enough, were detailed maps of the water round Holand, but there was one which showed the whole curved coastline from Aberath in the far North to the sands round Termath in the South. Just above the middle of the curve, there was the large diamond-shaped block of Tulfa Island, about thirty miles out from Kinghaven. Below Kinghaven was the wicked spike of the Point of Hark, dividing North from South Dalemark waters. Below that again, much closer inshore, was a scatter of small and large blobs that were the Holy Islands.

"We should recognize that," Ynen whispered, pointing to Tulfa Island, "and I think we'd know the Point of Hark, too. It looks like sheer cliff. I wish we knew how far North we'd come."

"There'll be light on Tulfa, if—" Mitt began.

Al surged out of the cabin like a bloodshot bear. "What's all this whisper, whisper, guvnor? Can't a man sleep?"

The three of them exchanged baffled looks. "Seagulls wake you?" asked Mitt.

"You don't get charts out for seagulls," said Al. He gave the horizon the benefit of his bloodshot look, and seemed as annoyed as they were at finding no land there. "Fuss about nothing. Where's the food?"

They took pleasure in assuring him that all the pies were gone. There was, in fact, a hunk of cheesecake left, but none of them saw any reason to waste it on Al. Al annoyed them by taking the news philosophically. He said his stomach was not too good, anyway, and turned to go back to his bunk.

It occurred to Ynen that if Al was this alert, the thing

to do was to make use of him. "How well do you know the coast?" he asked him.

"Like the back of my hand," Al said over his shoulder. "Told you I'd been around, guvnor."

"Then could you stay on deck?" said Ynen.

Al said nothing. He simply went into the cabin and back to sleep again.

But as things turned out, they had no need of Al, nor of the charts, that day. The wind continued light. No land appeared. It was clear that they were in for another night of standing watches.

"We'd best turn due North," Mitt said. "We could run aground in the night on this course." And again he settled to take the dawn watch.

Ynen called Mitt earlier than usual. The sky was hardly beginning to pale. But Ynen was horribly sleepy. He kept nodding off and kept feeling that gentle nudge in his back from Libby Beer. The last nudge was not quite so gentle. Ynen jumped awake, into air that was chilly and muggy at once, and knew something was different. *Wind's Road* was riding in a high, jerky way. Ynen had not felt the like since the day they picked up Poor Old Ammet, and, for a moment, he was as terrified as he had been that first night, when there was space all round him and Mitt crying out in the cabin. He put his hand on Libby Beer to steady himself and realized that the only thing to do was to wake Mitt.

"I think we must be in coastal waters," he said to Mitt as he fell onto the warm bunk Mitt had just left.

Mitt knew they had been in coastal waters since yesterday. He got to the tiller before he was really awake. While he was furiously jerking the rope from the mainsail, which Ynen had tied in a manner Siriol would have given him the rope's end for, Mitt could tell *Wind's Road* was in alarmingly shallow water. He searched that paler side of the sky, but there was only misty darkness. Yet while he searched, he could hear the roar and rumble of waves breaking.

"Flaming Ammet! That's a reef somewhere," Mitt said. He wiped a sudden sweat out of his eyes and stared forward into the paling dark. He thought his eyes were going to burst out of his head with the strain. He could hear the waves clearly, but he could not see a thing.

The figure with flying light hair, half hidden by the foresail, was pointing right and slightly forward. Yes, but which? Rocks there, or go there? Mitt wondered frantically. The tiller swung firmly left under his hand. *Wind's Road* leaned right, in the crisp wash and guggle of a current. Waves crashed over to Mitt's left, and he saw the dim white lather above the rocks she had only just missed.

"Phew!" said Mitt. "Thanks, Old Ammet. Thanks, Libby. Though I don't know what call you have to keep on helping, with me and Al on board. I suppose you got Ynen and Hildy to consider. Thanks all the same."

He heard the waves round more rocks ahead as he said it. This time he did not hesitate to turn *Wind's Road* as soon as he saw the light-haired figure pointing. He was pointing the other way almost at once. Waves crashed on both sides of *Wind's Road,* and the white spray showed whitish yellow in the growing light. Mitt found he was following Old Ammet's pointing arm through a maze of rocks it made him sweat just to think about. Once or twice, in spite of Old Ammet's care, *Wind's Road'*s deep keel grated, and she was snatched sideways in an undertow. Then Mitt would feel Libby Beer's strength on the tiller, pulling them to rights. Frightened as he was, Mitt smiled. The light was growing all the time. If this kept on, he was going to see them as they really were. Old Ammet looked more of a man every second. If Mitt pushed his eyes sideways, he had glimpses of a long white hand behind his on the tiller. It was worth the danger.

The last reef he saw clearly for himself. It was a welling and a milling of yellow water. It was nearly light. Then it was full day. The sun was up, making the sea look as if it was scattered with broken glass. The mainsail was cloth of gold; the island ahead was half golden, and the birds circling it were stabs of dazzling white; and the mist over to the right was a molten bank. The only sign of Old Ammet was a tuft of sunlit straw beyond the mast. Libby Beer was back to a colored knobby thing, tied with string. And Mitt was so disappointed that he could think of nothing else.

Then he came to his senses. He bent down and whispered into the cabin, "Island ahead! Come and look!"

PART FOUR

· THE HOLY ISLANDS ·

17

There were sounds of heaving and stumbling inside. To Mitt's disgust, it was Al who appeared, blinking and rubbing his bristly chin. Al glanced at the island. Then he calmly opened the locker and helped himself to the last hunk of cheesecake. Munching it, he surveyed the island again. Ynen and Hildy came out into the well. They looked first at the vanishing cheesecake, then at the island.

"That's Tulfa Island," Al said, with his mouth full.

"Are you sure?" asked Ynen. "I thought it was bigger than this." The island was no more than a great rock, surrounded by drifting seabirds that kept up a long, melancholy crying.

"Positive," said Al. "You want to turn into that mist there."

"I'll try," Mitt said doubtfully. There was little wind

now, and that fitful. He put the tiller over and hauled in the mainsail. *Wind's Road* went dipping and swinging gently toward the mist that hid the land.

"Watch out!" said Ynen. "The land's awfully close!"

It was, too, Mitt realized. It was a low green hump in the mist, only about a hundred yards off. He put the tiller hard over again. *Wind's Road* turned elegantly and leaned along outside the mist. "This must be wrong!" Mitt said angrily to Al. "There's no land this close to Tulfa. Do you know where we are or not?"

"I've a fair idea," said Al. "Turn round again."

To do that would mean tacking. Besides, Mitt did not trust Al in the least. He hesitated, and looked over his shoulder, beyond Libby Beer. And he saw a tall ship gliding out of the mist. The sun was just catching her topsails and the gold on her many pennants. Mitt turned back again. "What the—?"

The silence of Ynen and Hildy almost warned him. Al had Hobin's gun in his hand again. Mitt found himself looking into its six deadly black little muzzles. "You do what I say," said Al. He came a step closer. Mitt resigned himself to being shot. He felt, very fiercely, that it was a pity. He would never be able to sort himself out now. On the other hand, he supposed he deserved it. He was afraid it would hurt.

Then, most unexpectedly, Al hit him instead. A great blow caught Mitt hard in the stomach, and he sat down, hawking and gasping, hard on the lockers, feeling very angry, rather foolish, and quite helpless. *Wind's Road* yawed about in the douce breeze. Ynen put his hand out for the tiller and took it back again when the fat little gun pointed his way. There was no danger. *Wind's Road* simply swung and creaked and drooped, rather as Mitt was doing.

The tall ship came gliding closer. They could hear the ropes of her many sails creaking, see the dew from the mist shining in drops on her canvas, and pick out every grain in the wheatsheaf carved on her prow. She stood over *Wind's Road* like a house and took the last of the wind from her sails. Al grinned up at her tall side, highly pleased with himself.

"This has worked out wonderful," he said. He jumped up on the cabin and ran along, shouting, "Hey, *Wheatsheaf*! Hey, there! Bence! Is Bence aboard that thing?"

The tall ship turned. Her creaking sails flapped gently against the wind, until she and *Wind's Road* floated a yard or so apart. Mitt, holding his aching stomach, looked up to see a row of heads watching them, and a man on the highest part leaning over the rail to shout to Al.

"Al! Where did you take off to? There's been no end of askings and botherings and wanting to know where you were. Want to come aboard?"

Al laughed heartily. "What do you think, Bence? I'm sick of this tub. See it gets stowed in harbor, will you, and throw us a rope."

"What about them?" Bence asked, moving his head

toward Hildy, Ynen, and Mitt.

"They can come with their tub," said Al.

Orders were shouted high above *Wind's Road*. Two small, agile men came over the side of the tall ship and descended on ropes like two rapid white-headed spiders, until they landed lightly on *Wind's Road*. While she was still dipping and swinging, they handed their ropes to Al. He took hold of them and was hauled up, with a heavy scramble or so, until he reached the ship's rail, where a mass of hands reached out to pull him aboard. The tall ship turned at the same moment. Her sails creaked and filled. The air was loud with rippling for the few seconds it took her to vanish into the mist as quickly as she had come.

Hildy, Ynen, and Mitt were left bobbing in *Wind's Road* with the two small brown sailors. But they seemed to be rid of Al. They gave long breaths of relief about that, even while they were looking dubiously at the sailors. Ynen hurriedly took hold of the tiller. *Wind's Road* was his.

The sailors seemed in no hurry. They stood together by the mast, looking over *Wind's Road*, down at Old Ammet, up at the poor tattered pennant, over beyond Ynen to Libby Beer, and exchanging small singing murmurs. Quite suddenly, they came briskly to the well and swung themselves down into it.

"Will you move out and give us some room, little ones?" one of them asked cheerfully. He had a soft singsong accent, the like of which none of them had heard before.

Ynen clenched his fingers round the tiller. "This is my boat."

"Then you must continue to steer her," said the sailor.

"But you must be guided by us. The road has hazards," said the second sailor. "And will the other little ones go up before the mast to give us room?"

Mitt was so fascinated by the singing talk that he did not gather straightaway that the men were asking him to move. He got up, holding his stomach, and saw that Hildy still had not understood. Mitt nudged her, and she jumped, feeling as if she had been dreaming. They scrambled stiffly onto the roof of the cabin. The sailors settled on either side of Ynen as naturally as if they sailed *Wind's Road* every day, and gave him gentle instructions what to do. Mitt and Hildy knelt on the cabin roof and stared, while *Wind's Road* turned and heeled softly into the now-thinning mist.

They were little brown men with dark eyes and oddly light hair, as fair as light new rope. They felt safe, somehow. They were as warm and brown as the earth itself. Even Ynen felt lulled and peaceful with them. Mitt and Hildy could not shake off a feeling that they were dreaming—a good dream that they had dreamed several times before.

"This is a fine sweet boat," one sailor remarked. "Will you take in the foresails a fragment—Jenro will do it, little one. You steer left now."

Jenro, the second sailor, put his brown hand to the

ropes that led to the foresails. Ynen was a little shamed to see how much better *Wind's Road* sailed. "Very sweet," Jenro agreed. "What is the name she goes under?"

"*Wind's Road*," said Ynen.

The dark eyes of the two sailors met across him. "Is it so?" said Jenro. "Who comes sailing on the *Wind's Road*? What are the names of them?"

Ynen looked up uncertainly at the dreamy faces of Hildy and Mitt. There seemed no harm in saying. "My name's Ynen. My sister's called Hildrida, and our friend's name is Alhammitt."

Mitt blinked. Both sailors were looking at him, smiling warmly. He smiled back. They both made a little gesture, almost as if they bowed. Rather surprised, Mitt ducked his head back at them.

"This is Jenro, and I am Riss," said the first sailor. "Remember us in times to come."

"Yes. Yes, of course," Mitt said uncertainly.

Wind's Road had come gently past the green hump in the mist. The mist cleared steadily as she sailed. When Mitt looked away from the sailors' faces, he was astonished to find they were sailing among islands—more islands than he could count at a glance. Some were green and steep, with gray rocks standing above the green and trees clinging to the rocks. Some were green and low. Some were quite small. Others, in the distance, were clearly several miles long. Mitt could see houses on nearly all of them, usually near the shore, as if the sea were their road and the island their farm or garden. Sheep and cows grazed in pastures that mounted above the houses. Smoke rose from the chimneys. The sea space round them was so sheltered that it was warm and calm as a lake. Mitt could smell the salt of the sea mingling with the smell of earth, smoke, and cattle, in a close, queer mixture. He looked round, sniffing, warm and delighted, wondering why he felt so happy and so much at home, and everywhere he looked he saw the astonishing emerald green of more islands.

"Where *is* this?" Ynen said suspiciously.

Jenro smiled at him. "The Holy Islands, little one."

Hildy's head went up. The dreamy feeling left her and left her feeling strained and rather sick. She retreated to the mast and knelt there by herself, nervously clasping her hands and gripping them with her knees. She seemed to feel better like that. Ynen looked dubiously at Mitt. This was not the North. Mitt still had to get away, and Ynen wanted to apologize. He was surprised that Mitt did not seem either annoyed or frightened. Mitt supposed he ought to be. But he was entranced, smiling and sniffing. Seabirds and land birds flew over, uttering their different cries. Jenro, with a mixture of pride and politeness, began to tell Ynen the names of the islands as they passed them, while Riss softly put in a word here and there about the steering. Their voices made Mitt feel as if this was a song he had heard a long time ago, which he had never managed to learn the words to.

"That was Chindersay, and there Little Shool. Big Shool is after. Then Hollisay and Yeddersay and Farn—"

"—to the right here, then left immediately—"

"—and Prest and Prestsay. High Tross there beyond. The large one is Ommern."

"—your mainsheet out here, but with care. The wind gusts after Tross. And a sweet way to the right as you go—"

So *Wind's Road* threaded gently between tall emerald slopes and past low green humps, and Mitt listened and listened, trying to remember that song.

"Then you have Ommersay and Wittess, and we come out past lovely Holy Isle, the holiest of all. After, you will see Diddersay and Doen and the three Ganter Islands—"

Mitt thought it was not quite a song he had in mind. It was the astonishing turfy smell of the islands, or a mixture of the two. Anyway, had he not once, years ago, thought he knew this place and set out to find it? Navis came into it somehow. Mitt was so pleased to remember this much that he scrambled over to Hildy and beamed at her. "Hey, I take it all back about this place! You're going to love it here!"

He was rather hurt at the pale, haughty way Hildy looked. "This," she said, squeezing at her fingers, "isn't the North."

"Who cares?" Mitt said. "I think I'll have a go at staying here myself. I wouldn't mind—I really wouldn't mind!"

"—left now—"

"—and there is Trossaver, with Lathsay beside—"

Wind's Road slipped between long, high Trossaver and lump-shaped Lathsay and came into a wide space ringed with islands, where there was ship upon tall ship at anchor. One was just hoisting sail. Another was gliding in through a wide gap opposite, as if it were coming off patrol, but most were anchored, with bare masts. Among the anchored ships Mitt recognized the *Wheatsheaf*. She had no doubt sailed fast on wind above the islands that *Wind's Road* was too small to catch, but she was evidently so far ahead of them that Mitt suspected Riss and Jenro had sailed them on a tour of the Holy Islands. That suited Mitt, but he wondered why.

They sailed toward a long horseshoe-shaped jetty, with a host of little ships tied to it. Behind it was a small town of gray and white houses, with what looked to be the Lord's mansion rising above them at the back. The mainland was beyond again, as green and rocky as the islands, as if the town was also on an island.

"That is the Isle of Gard. The hardway to the land is behind," Jenro explained.

"And a fine fleet in harbor," Riss added proudly.

Hildy tried to unbend. "There are more ships here than in Holand," she said. She thought she sounded as condescending as her aunts. She saw Ynen wince a little. So she became angry with everyone and did not say any more.

As *Wind's Road* approached the jetty, Riss and Jenro sprang into sudden activity. Mitt had hardly had time to climb to his feet and offer to help before the sails were down, ropes out, and *Wind's Road* was quietly nudging the jetty stonework, tied up and her long journey over. Mitt and Ynen stared at one another, tired, sad, and a little aimless. Riss, meanwhile, was out on the jetty, talking to a number of large blank-faced men who were standing there.

"Will you go with these?" he said, coming back to Mitt and pointing to the men. "They are not of the islands."

They were clearly not of the islands. They were dark and heavy, like a lot of men in Holand. But since they were standing in a line along the jetty, Mitt did not see he had any choice in the matter. "I suppose so. All of us?"

"If you will," said Riss. "We shall see you." He and Jenro both shook hands with Mitt, smiled warmly, and trotted away along the jetty. Feeling rather deserted, Mitt, Ynen, and Hildy scrambled out on the jetty, too. The men closed round them to lead them away. It was alarming. But it was also very silly because for a minute or so none of the three of them could walk. When they stepped forward, the ground was either unaccountably missing, or it came up and hit them before they were ready for it.

"Too long at sea!" gasped Mitt. "You have to wait."

The large men waited, silent and impatient, while Ynen fell into Mitt, and Hildy into both of them, and Ynen and Mitt shrieked with laughter, and even Hildy was forced to smile. None of the men smiled, even when they were able to set out through the town, rolling like old sailors and giggling as they went. They were not able to notice the town much, though Mitt did see that there were fields in it, confusingly, among the houses, with cows or wheat stubble in them, and that, every so often, there was a short square-topped pillar about as high as his waist, where people had carefully laid flowers, fruit, and ears of corn. But they saw few people because it was still early morning.

They came to the mansion and were taken inside through a small door. Hildy relaxed a little. The small door meant they were probably prisoners, which must mean that nobody knew who she was. She was glad of that because she could soon put that right. Mitt was not so sure. He had simply no idea what was happening. The only thing seemed to be to wait and see.

They staggered their way up a flat flight of stone stairs to a sunny stone landing. They waited, while one of the men went to knock on a door. Then—*bang!* There was an explosion somewhere. All the windows rattled. All three of them jumped violently, and Mitt, at least, burst out in cold, trickling sweat all over. He was nearly as scared as he had been in the storm. But the large man did not turn a hair and did not pause in knocking on the door. There was a voicelike noise from beyond it. The large man opened the door.

"They're here. Shall I show them in?"

"If you like," said someone inside.

The man jerked his head. Hildy, Ynen, and Mitt trooped through the door into a long, sunlit room smelling of food and gunsmoke—as queer a mixture, though less pleasant, as the mixed smell of the islands and the sea. The food smell came from the table near the door. Al was sitting beside it, with his back to the table and Hobin's gun supported over the back of his chair. Another table was against the wall at the other end of the room. There was a row of bottles on it and cups balanced on the bottles. One bottle was smashed. Al fired again as soon as the door was shut. It was deafening. A cup jumped and shattered, and there was a great deal of laughter.

"Got the hang of this flaming gun now, Lithar," said Al.

"About time," said Bence, the captain of the *Wheatsheaf*. He was sitting on a chair by the window, eating an apple.

The third man said, "Oh, Al! I *have* missed seeing you do that!"

Lithar's clothes were nearly as rich as Harchad's, but he looked nothing like so well in them. He had a mop of fairish hair over the brown face of a Holy Islander and a long, long chin. He seemed quite well built, but he sat in a strange, hunched way which creased his clothes in all directions. When he looked toward them, Ynen, Hildy, and Mitt were uncertain how old he was, because his face was oddly lined, old and young at once. Like Mitt's face, Hildy thought, and she looked at Mitt to compare the two. But Mitt was young and undernourished, whereas—

With a horrible jolt, Hildy realized Lithar was a near imbecile. It was as if her whole future, and her whole past, too, fell away and left just herself—a small girl with untidy hair—alone in a sunny smoke-filled room. Hildy had not realized how much she had built on Lithar and the Holy Islands. She seemed to have founded on them everything which made her into Hildrida and not one of her cousins. It was not exactly her fault, but she had done the building. And it was all unreal. It had not even gone; it had just never been.

It was the same with Mitt. He took one look at Lithar, and one look at Hildy, and he knew that what was happening to Hildy now had happened to him in Holand. But he had not admitted it. Everything he had thought of as being Mitt—the fearless boy with the free soul, the right-thinking freedom fighter—had fallen to pieces there, as thoroughly as Canden in his dream, or Old Ammet in the harbor, and he had been left with what was real. And it had frightened him to death. Mitt thought his face must be as yellow pale as Hildy's. I hope neither of them are fools enough to say who they are, he thought. We better all make off North, quick.

"Who are you?" Lithar asked, with a surprised wag of his long chin.

Mitt and Ynen opened their mouths to begin on two separate false stories, but Al got in first. "Little present I brought you," he said, without turning round. "Don't you like it?"

Lithar giggled. "Well—not terribly, Al. Unless they

do tricks. Are you acrobats or something?" he asked them. "Untidy children, aren't they?" he said to Bence.

Al hitched his chair round and leaned close to Lithar, in a way that could only be described as possessive. "They're untidy because they've been at sea. Forgot to take their hairbrushes with them. But you know who they are? Who she is? She's your little betrothed. Harl's niece, from Holand. The brat with the long nose is her brother."

Hildy said, "How did you—?"

Al grinned at her. "You sit on top of the cabin, little lady, boasting for half a day how you was betrothed to Lithar, and then you ask me how I know! Be reasonable!"

"I thought you were asleep," said Hildy.

"Not me," said Al. "Too seasick. Well, Lithar? Aren't you going to thank me?"

Lithar, to help himself absorb what Al said, had put a forkful of food in his mouth. It looked like some of the tastiest sea fry Mitt had ever seen. He and Ynen looked at it longingly. They were ravenous. Lithar chewed, wagging his brown boot toe of a chin. "I suppose she'll grow," he said discontentedly, with his mouth full. "But I don't want her brother."

"Yes, you do," said Al. He went back to eating sea fry, too, but paused to wave his loaded fork to Bence. Mitt thought it was cruel. "Here, Bence," Al said. "Tell us that news from Holand you gave me on the boat." Bence raised his eyebrows and looked at Hildy and Ynen as if he did not want to say anything in front of them. Al angrily waved another forkful at him. "Get on with it!"

Bence was the ruddy, hairy kind of man who looks strong-minded but is really rather weak. He was obviously well under Al's thumb. "I just wondered—" he said. "Well, the news from Holand is that the old Earl was shot some days back, and his sons had a set-to over the earldom. Harl, the eldest son, killed Harchad, the second son, and family. And Navis, the third son, and family took fright and ran away. That's all I heard, Al."

Hildy and Ynen stared desolately at one another, while Al laughed loudly and pointed his fork at Lithar. "Understand?" Lithar nodded intelligently and plainly did not understand. "Harl," Al explained, "has come out on top. But Navis isn't dead, or not yet. You've got Navis's family here. You want the girl, anyway. She's worth alliance, and bargains and a lot of money. But you want the boy, too. He's a nuisance to Harl. Harl's got boys of his own, and he'll pay high to be rid of this one. And if the unexpected happens, and Navis comes out on top, then you've done him a favor instead, see? Don't worry about the girl. She'll grow."

"Sure to. They all do," Bence said heartily.

Lithar's lined face was riven with bewilderment, but he gave Hildy a formal smile, still with his mouth full, and Ynen a doubtful nod. Then he pointed his fork at Mitt. "But who are you? Al keeps not talking about you."

"I'm just a nobody," Mitt said quickly.

Al tipped his chair back and looked at him. "Don't be too sure of that. Murderer, aren't you?"

Lithar was delighted. "Oh? Like you, Al?"

"No—though he flaming near got in my way," said Al. "I bear you a grudge for that," he told Mitt. "Harl's going to want him, too, Lithar. He had a go at killing Hadd. It didn't come to much, but he'll make someone to blame—satisfy a crying need nicely, you might say. You offer to send him back for a price."

Lithar cocked his long face intently. "How much should I ask?"

Mitt wanted to say something, but he was in such terror that his mind was blank. How had Al known? He must have given himself away just as Hildy had, thinking Al was asleep, and his red and yellow breeches were on him to prove it.

Ynen looked at Mitt's face and knew exactly how he felt. Ynen felt bad. They had promised Mitt to take him North. Something Al had said came into Ynen's mind and combined with the way those sailors had behaved. "I don't think you should," he said to Lithar. "His name's Alhammitt."

"Half Holand's called that," Al said swiftly and loudly.

But Lithar looked at him reproachfully. "Now, Al. That isn't a name we take chances with in the Holy Islands. *You* should know that. I can't send him to Holand. I'm a god-fearing man."

"You're a superstitious ass," said Al. "You send him."

"I can't," said Lithar, and he smiled pleadingly, as if he wanted Al to forgive him.

Al's square face lost all its expression. He laid down his fork and picked up Hobin's gun again. It was empty. Al must have used all the remaining shots demonstrating it to Lithar. He grunted. Then he looked up in annoyance, because the door of the room opened. A little brown woman with white hair came in. She was a slim, upright person in a green-embroidered island dress.

"Clothing and food is prepared for the little ones," she said to Lithar.

Lithar giggled. "Little ones! A bit more respect, please, Lalla. You wouldn't believe how important they are! Shall I send them with her?" he asked Al. Al shrugged.

18

To Mitt's heartfelt relief, Lalla took them out of that dangerous room. A crowd of small brown island women were waiting for them outside, with beautiful dark faces and hair either snowy white or light-fair. No one could have been kinder or more concerned than these women. They hurried all three of them upstairs again to rooms where baths were waiting.

Hildy and Ynen, in spite of the situation, were very glad to have a bath. Mitt was hugely embarrassed. He was not used to baths. He was not used to being undressed in front of strangers. Two of the kindly women helped him, soaping and scrubbing and then drying him. Mitt was afraid he seemed unpleasantly dirty. And they kept shaking their heads distressfully over him and talking about him in soft voices almost as beautiful as their faces.

"He is too thin, this one. Look at those legs on him, Lalla. But see the shoulders, and the span on them. There is the makings of a thick man, and the flesh of a sparrow to cover him." Mitt writhed.

At length, feeling rather as if he had been put through the mangle in Hobin's backyard, Mitt tottered out into a long, cheerful room with barred windows, where Hildy and Ynen were waiting to begin breakfast. Mitt hardly knew them. Hildy had been given a faded blue island woman's dress with white embroidery down the front, which made her look grown-up and haughty. Ynen's black hair was wet and shiny and smooth. He had been given a secondhand suit so faded that it was the color of blue-green distance. Mitt became very conscious of the good suit of new bottle green they had given him to wear. He had never worn anything half so good. It gave him a feeling there had been a mistake somewhere, because it was certainly better than Ynen's.

They were left alone to eat breakfast. There were piles of smoking sea fry, new bread, crusty outside and moist within, salty butter, and bunches of green grapes, smaller and sweeter than those of Holand. As Ynen said, it made a wonderful change from pies. But Hildy simply sat looking haughtier and haughtier and not eating.

Mitt found her very annoying. "Do eat," he said irritably. "Keep your strength up."

"I can't," Hildy said, tight and toneless. "Uncle Harchad's dead. And half the cousins."

"So what? Good riddance, if you ask me," said Mitt.

"Uncle Harl's a murderer," said Hildy. "He's no better than Al."

"Well, you knew that before," Mitt pointed out, "and you didn't let it put you off your food then."

"Yes, do eat, Hildy," said Ynen.

"Don't you see?" said Hildy. "Uncle Harl has probably killed Father, too." Two tears ran slowly down her narrow cheeks. "Because we got away, people think he was with us."

Ynen looked at Mitt, appalled. Mitt sighed, rather. He felt he had enough troubles of his own, without sharing theirs. "I always thought it was wrong somewhere," he said, trying to think it out, "what you told me about when you were coming away. Looks as if your uncle Harchad may have been out to kill you."

"You mean," Ynen asked, "that when those soldiers fired at us in the West Pool, it wasn't because they thought we were you, it was because Uncle Harchad had given them orders to stop us?"

Mitt nodded. "Could be. Harchad or Harl. If you ask me, you were luckier than you knew there."

"Lucky!" exclaimed Hildy. "You call us lucky when Father's probably dead and Al's going to sell us to Uncle Harl!" Tears came down her cheeks in pulses. "Lithar's an imbecile!" she said. "And I boasted so! There's no such thing as luck. Life's horrible. I hate everything about it. I think I always have done."

"You like sailing in *Wind's Road*," Ynen said, rather hurt.

"With two murderers," said Hildy, "into captivity." She bent her head over the pale oak table and sobbed miserably.

Mitt was offended. "Stop that!" he said. "If I hadn't had to get away, you'd be lying dead in Holand at this moment, and you know it! Ynen's worse off than you, and he's not crying. All this means is that we've got to get out of here and go North. So will you stop crying and eat something!"

Tears whisked over the table as Hildy raised her head and glared at Mitt. "I don't think I've ever disliked anyone so much as I dislike you!" she said. "Not even Al!" She snatched up a bunch of grapes and began to eat without noticing the taste.

"How can we get away?" Ynen asked anxiously.

Mitt got up and tried the door. It was locked. Rather dashed, he looked over at the bars on the windows. Somehow he had not expected the island women to lock them in.

"Iron bars," said Ynen.

"Of course, stupid!" said Hildy. "This is a nursery. The bars are to stop babies falling out." Eating the grapes made her suddenly realize how very hungry she was. She began wolfing lukewarm sea fry. "Ye gods!" she said as she wolfed. "I haven't been shut in a nursery for—for some time."

Ynen and Mitt left her eating and went to look at the windows. They looked out on the mainland, rolling into green distance, and the shingly causeway which led to it from the back of Lithar's mansion. Little boats were drawn up to the causeway, nudging the shingle on either side. Immediately below them was a courtyard, with a gateway opening on the causeway. It was full of people, and people were walking backward and forward along the causeway, too.

"We could get down," Ynen said. "Next window along. There's a drain that goes right down to the yard wall. We'd better wait till there are fewer people and then try."

Mitt cautiously forced open the window over the drain and tried if he could get his head through between the bars. He found he just could. And, he knew from experience, where his head would go, the rest of him could follow, sideways on. Since he was bigger than Ynen, that meant that Ynen could certainly get through, and probably Hildy, too. So they settled down to wait until there were fewer people about.

The time came about an hour later. Mitt put his head through, turned his shoulders sideways, and shoved. He could hardly do it. He thought he must have grown. His stomach stuck. By the time he finally forced himself through onto the high sill outside, his stomach felt as if it had been pulled down near his knees. He turned round, hanging on to the bars, to help Ynen and Hildy through.

But Ynen could not get through. He was too well nourished. His shoulders were just too thick. He pushed and squirmed and squeezed, and Mitt pulled him perilously from outside, but it was simply no good. Ynen had to give up, bruised and miserable. Hildy was even worse. She was bigger than Mitt all over and could barely even get her head through. They stood unhappily against the window, while Mitt crouched outside with his knees aching from the strain, feeling both unsafe and obvious, wondering what they were going to do now.

"Do I come in or what?" Mitt said angrily.

"Could you come back up and unlock the door for—" Ynen began to say.

"Oh, ye gods!" said Hildy. "There's Father! Look!" Her face was suddenly bright red, and she looked as if she was going to cry again.

Mitt swiveled himself round on the sill to look. The man trudging along the shingle of the causeway was wearing farmer's clothes and big boots, but he was certainly Navis. Mitt knew him by the way he walked and, even at that distance, by the face that was so like Harchad's and Hildy's. "It is, too!" Mitt said. "You lot have the luck of Old Ammet!"

"It's not lucky at all," said Ynen.

"Mitt, go down and warn him, quick!" said Hildy. "Tell him we're prisoners and it's not safe for him here. Quickly, before Al sees him!"

"But he'll know me," Mitt objected.

Hildy shook the bars in her anxiety. "He can't possibly—not in those clothes. If you won't go, I'll have to shout, and someone will hear!"

"All right, all right!" said Mitt. "I'll tell him. I'll tell him to keep back on the mainland, and then I'll have a go at letting you out. Tireless Mitt does all the work again."

"Oh shut up!" said Ynen.

"And hurry up!" said Hildy.

Mitt made a face at both of them and slid down the drainpipe. Mitt to the rescue! he thought. He reached the yard wall without anyone noticing him at all. Nobody seemed particularly interested when he shot down from the wall and raced to the gate.

Navis was just about to come through it. Close to, Mitt saw that he looked tired and not very well shaved. The big boots were caked with mud. But Navis took no notice of Mitt as Mitt darted out of the gate to meet him. That encouraged Mitt. Navis did not remember him. He could only have seen Mitt for half a minute on the day of the Festival, after all.

"Hey!" Mitt said to him. "Don't come in here. It's not safe."

Mitt had reckoned without two things. Navis had been a fugitive, living on his wits, for days now. And he had Ynen's memory for faces. Or perhaps not only for faces, for he recognized Mitt mainly by his build and the way he ran. And since Navis had no reason to think Mitt would do him a good turn, he simply looked at Mitt as people do when they are surprised to find themselves addressed by a total stranger and walked past him into the courtyard.

Mitt was so annoyed by this haughtiness that he would have let Navis alone had it not been for Ynen and Hildy watching from above. He ran after Navis and took hold of his sleeve. Navis shook Mitt's hand off and walked on. Mitt was forced to trot beside him, trying to explain.

"See here, it's not safe for you here. Lithar's wrong in the head, and the fellow who shot Hadd got hold of him and made him take Hildy and Ynen prisoner. They're up there, in that room with bars. Take a look."

Since there were so few people about, Mitt risked pointing. But Navis would not demean himself to look. He trudged on, trying to decide why this murdering brat should spin him a yarn like this and taking no notice of Mitt at all.

"Father's not listening!" Hildy said, with her head pushed against the bars. "Isn't that just like him!"

"He may only be pretending not to listen because it's safest," Ynen suggested hopefully.

Mitt hoped Navis was pretending, too. "Hildy and Ynen sent me," he explained, feeling sure this would convince Navis. But Navis tramped through the main doorway of the mansion into a large stone room without appearing to have heard. The room was full of people. Mitt hung back in the doorway, wondering whether he dared follow Navis in. They were mostly island people. The singsong of their talk rang round the room. Mitt decided that it was safe enough and ran after Navis to make one more attempt.

"Do come out of here," he said, dodging about near Navis's shoulder. "They'll sell you to Harl to kill. Honest."

Navis looked at someone beyond Mitt's head and called out loudly, "Will one of you take this offensive child away, please!"

Mitt sensed a movement in the crowd and got ready to run. "Can't you *listen* to me, you pigheaded idiot!" he said.

"Will you shut your unpleasing mouth?" said Navis. "Guard! Remove this, will you!"

Mitt turned and ran. But the guard was nearer than he thought. Two big men seized him as he turned. Mitt lost his temper then. He kicked and struggled and called Navis a number of names he had learned on the waterfront.

"Oh, him again," Al said from behind Mitt. "Not to worry, sir. I'll take care of him, sir."

Upstairs in the barred nursery, Hildy and Ynen waited and waited. For a long time they were sure that whatever had happened between Mitt and their father, Mitt would come and unlock the nursery door any moment. They had great faith in Mitt's resourcefulness. But when the island women came and brought them lunch for two, even Ynen gave up hope.

"I don't think Mitt was even trying to make Father understand," Hildy said angrily. "And now he's just forgotten us. His kind are all the same!"

"I don't think he would forget," Ynen said.

"Yes, he would. He had a perfect chance to escape on his own, and he took it," said Hildy.

"I thought he felt he owed us—" Ynen began uncomfortably.

"He didn't feel anything of the kind," said Hildy. "His whole idea was that we owed him everything, because of his rotten life in Holand!"

This was so exactly the kind of thing Mitt had said himself that Ynen could not argue any longer.

Long hours later they were trying to play I Spy. Hildy was far too dejected to concentrate. "I give up," she said. "There's nothing beginning with *T* in this room."

"Table," Ynen said drearily.

The door opened just then, and Lithar shambled in. Hildy did not realize. "How was I to know it was something as stupid as that!" she snapped, thoroughly bad-tempered.

Lithar stared at her, shocked. "I don't think I want to marry you," he said.

"That goes for me, too!" Hildy retorted. "I hate the sight of you!"

Lithar turned plaintively to Al, who had followed him in. Behind Al came two of the large men, with Navis between them. "Al," said Lithar, "I don't have to marry her, do I? She's not womanly." Al laughed and patted him on the back.

"There, Hildrida. You have just received your first compliment," said Navis. "Possibly your last, too."

"Where's Mitt?" Ynen said to Al. Al laughed and shrugged. "You do know, don't you?" said Ynen. "Have you killed him?"

Al chuckled. "Say hallo to your pa like a good boy."

"Not until I've told you what a foul brute you are," said Ynen.

"He's not very nice either," Lithar complained. "Let's go away."

"After you," said Al, and everyone went out of the room again, leaving Navis standing by the locked door.

Hildy and Ynen stared at Navis. He looked tired, dirty, and depressed. Hildy felt sorry for him. She was almost certain she was glad to see him. She went toward Navis to tell him so. But she did not quite dare and stopped. Then she somehow ran at him without thinking and threw her arms around him. For just a second Navis looked surprised. Then Hildy found herself being hugged, picked up, and swung round, and her father looking more pleased and more upset than she had ever seen him. When Ynen came shyly up, Navis spared an arm for him, too, so that they all hung together in a bundle.

"Who warned you to get away?" said Navis. "How did you manage in that fearsome storm?"

"Nobody. It was an accident. Mitt and Libby Beer and Old Ammet helped," they said, and they tried to tell him about their adventures in *Wind's Road.* After a little, Navis let go of them and sat down to listen, pressing two fingers to the corners of his eyes as if he had a headache. They could not help noticing that he frowned and seemed to press harder every time they mentioned Al or Mitt.

"Why did you come here?" Ynen asked him at last.

"Was—is Al in your pay? I saw you talking to him in Holand."

Navis looked up at Ynen in surprise. "Of course not. You must have seen him the time he came to offer—for a large sum of money, naturally—to tell me of a plot against the Earl. You can't imagine how often people did that," Navis said. He sounded very depressed. "I found Al very uncongenial. But I mentioned the matter to Harchad, and, ironically, I remember Harchad telling me in return that he had put an agent in the Holy Islands to keep Lithar in line, in case the North attacked. If I had known it was this same Al, I would have stayed well away. I came because there are boats here—prepared to pay high for being taken North—and trying not to hope there might be news of you two. But it seems that Al has decided that Harl would pay more for us than I would pay for a boat—which I'm sure is true—so we are being sold back to Holand."

There was a wretched silence.

"Wouldn't Uncle Harl let us go," Hildy asked, "if we all signed something to say we didn't want to be earls?"

Navis shook his head, with his two fingers lodged hard above his nose. "He doesn't trust me. He never has. Besides, I kicked him in the stomach when he came to arrest me. He was so annoyed that he came out in the Flate after me himself, in spite of the storm. He nearly trod on me while I was lying in a ditch. By which I knew he wouldn't easily forgive me."

Ynen laughed, though he was sure it was no joke.

"But didn't Mitt try to warn you?"

He saw his father's forehead crease. "If Mitt is the boy who tried to blow up the Sea Festival—yes, he did. I thought he was lying and asked the guards to take him away. Al took charge of him after that. Is this one more mistake I've made?"

"Yes," said Ynen.

"You didn't know," said Hildy. "I never trust Mitt either. His ideas are all in a muddle. But if Al's killed him, I'm going to call on Old Ammet and Libby Beer for vengeance."

"I sincerely hope they answer you quickly," said Navis.

But when, about an hour before sunset, Al came into the nursery with a number of the largest guards, he was as sturdy and carefree as ever and rather more pleased with himself than usual.

"Up you get, sir," he said, "and you, guvnor. Bence is back from a little job I sent him on. The old *Wheatsheaf* is all ready, the tide's right, and we're going sailing again. It's not what I'd have chosen, being a landsman and inclined to queasiness, but we reckoned you'd not be able to give us the slip so easy at sea."

Navis stood up slowly. "You mean you're taking us back to Holand."

"Quick on the uptake, your pa," Al remarked to Hildy. "That's right, sir. We're taking you and the boy, and leaving the girl here."

"Why are you leaving my daughter?" said Navis.

Al looked at Hildy. Hildy wanted to hit him, to scream, to make a fuss in every way she could think of, but she felt she could not when her father was behaving so calmly. "Be reasonable, sir," said Al. "She's betrothed to Lithar. We've got to have a bargaining point. The money Harl offers has got to go up, and up again, and she'll be the reason. And if he won't offer enough, you may find we come sailing back here with you in a day or so. Look on the bright side, sir."

"Oh, is there a bright side?" said Navis.

"For some of us," Al answered genially. "I'll trouble you to step along now."

They said good-bye stiffly. None of them wanted to say anything important with Al there. Navis and Ynen were marched out by the guards. Hildy stood by herself in the middle of the room, with her hands clenched into useless fists, watching the door close behind them. She was determined not to cry till it shut.

The door opened again. Al put his head round it. "By the by, little lady," he said, "something tells me that Lithar may suffer a little accident on the voyage. He would come with us, you know. Then there'll be a new Lord of the Holy Islands for you to marry."

Hildy looked at that grinning face stuck round the edge of the door and was so angry that she shook all over. "If you mean it'll be you," she said, "I bet you have at least two wives already."

Every scrap of expression went out of Al's face.

"Someone tell you their life story, did they?"

"No," said Hildy. "I just know. You're just that kind of man."

"Then you better keep that idea to yourself," said Al. The door snapped shut, and the key grated.

Hildy went on standing where she was, too miserable and frightened even to cry now. She knew she had been very, very foolish to say that to Al. But after all that had happened, it hardly seemed to matter. She thought she might as well sit down anyway.

She was just turning toward a chair, when she noticed that the door was swinging open again. Beyond, in the dark corridor, Hildy could see one of the little island women. She thought it looked like Lalla.

"Will you come out now?" asked the gentle island voice. "It is time to be leaving, if you wish to go."

"Oh, I do wish to go!" Hildy said, and hastened out to her.

Lalla turned and walked down the passage, and Hildy walked beside her. It was so strange to be free suddenly that Hildy did not quite believe it. It felt like a dream. Dreamily she went with Lalla down some stairs and along another passage.

"Where are we going?" she asked as they came to more stairs and went down again.

"Out to the hardway. Riss is waiting there for you."

Despite her troubles, Hildy was dreamily glad. Of the two little sailors, Riss was the one she had liked best. "Where will Riss take me?"

"To the North, if you wish to go there." They came to the end of the stairs and out into the big stone room where Mitt had made his last attempt to convince Navis. It was empty now, rather cold, and seemed dim because there was such a blaze of evening light from the arched doorway to the courtyard. Their footsteps echoed softly from the stone. Among the echoes Hildy heard Lalla ask, "Will you be wishing to come back to the Islands again?"

Hildy thought about it, as they crossed the ringing stone floor. She would not have been surprised to find she never wanted to come here again. But she found she did. The Holy Islands had somehow taken her heart while she was sailing through them in *Wind's Road* into danger. "I'd love to," she said. "But not if Al's here."

"We can rid you of your enemies," Lalla said, "if you are prepared to trust Alhammitt."

"Mitt?" said Hildy. "Is Mitt all right?" Then she became embarrassed that Lalla knew how little she trusted Mitt and wanted to explain herself. "It isn't what he did. It's what he thinks and the way he's been brought up. I mean, I know I'd probably be just the same if I'd been brought up on the waterfront, but I haven't. And I can't help the way I was brought up, either. I think mostly he annoys me. I suppose I annoy him. That's it, really."

As Hildy said this, she came to the doorway and a blaze of orange sunlight. There was a bull in the court-yard beyond. It was a huge animal, almost red in the low sun. There was power in every line of it, in each stocky leg and from its tufted tail and slim rear to its great shoulders and blunt triangular head. It seemed to be loose in the courtyard, with no one to control it. Hildy stopped short and stared at it. And the bull raised two wicked horns growing out of a mat of chestnut curls, and looked at Hildy. Hildy did not care for the look in its large red eye. She turned uncertainly to Lalla.

The blazing low sun had dazzled her, but Lalla seemed taller than she had thought. In the dimness, her hair seemed not white but red, or brown. But it was the same singing island voice which said, "It was only two things I asked you. Would you come again to the Islands, and would you trust Alhammitt?"

Hildy felt the ground shake under the weight of the bull as it trod nearer. It was unfair of Libby Beer to try and frighten her. "What happens if I say no to those questions?" Hildy asked defiantly.

The lady standing in the dimness might have been a little surprised. "Nothing will happen. You will go in peace and live quietly."

Then Hildy found that it was important to her to answer both questions truthfully. She stood thinking, while the bull twitched its tail and paced heavily in the sunlight. "Yes, I want to come here again," she said. That was the easy part. "And—and I suppose I do trust Mitt really. I did in the storm. It's just when I'm angry I notice the difference between us, but I don't think that's quite the same. Is it?"

She looked up to Libby Beer for an answer, but

there was no one there. The stone room was empty. Shaken, Hildy looked out into the courtyard. That was empty, too.

"Didn't I answer right, then?" Hildy said. Her lonely voice rang round the room. Since there was no good to be done there, Hildy went out into the warm dazzle of the courtyard and walked over to the open gate. The damp scent of the Islands met her there. The sea hurried to the shingle of the causeway in myriad small ripples, setting the waiting rowing boat nuzzling at the stones.

As Hildy's feet crunched on the pebbles, Riss stood up in the rowing boat and smiled warmly. "Will you thrust on the boat and climb in, little one? We will be stirring to your ship."

Beyond Riss, *Wind's Road* was moored in the deeper water between the mainland and the causeway. Hildy could see her swinging gently in the tide. She smiled at Riss delightedly.

"I think," she said, as she kicked off her shoes on the shingle and tied a knot in one side of her Island dress to keep it out of the way, "I think I've just been talking to Libby Beer."

"That is not the name we use here," Riss said. "She is called She Who Raised the Islands."

❦19❧

Al slung Mitt into a room which was probably a store-room and left him there while he went to attend to Navis. It was a very small stone room with a skylight too small even for Mitt to squeeze out through. Mitt sat with his hands behind his head, glaring up at it and hating Navis with all his heart. All his troubles went back to Navis. He felt as if instead of kicking a bomb this time, Navis had actually kicked him in the teeth. And Mitt had only been trying to help!

"That's the last time I ever do anything for that lot!" Mitt said to himself, and fell into a prolonged and fierce daydream about what he would like to do to Navis. He imagined himself as a powerful outlawed revolutionary with several hundred seasoned followers at his back. He imagined himself conquering a town full of terrified lords and ordering them all to surrender. Out they came, with Navis among them, cringing Harchads, quaking Hadds, dozens of Hildys, and several frightened Ynens, all hanging their heads and shuffling, as the men from the North had shuffled through Holand. Mitt had them all killed, but Navis he saved till last for a truly frightful death.

It was most interesting. For years now Mitt had been too busy with other things to do any daydreaming. He found he had been missing something. He did the story over again, with a larger town, and made himself more powerful and even more merciless. He began to see that he really had it in him to become such a revolutionary. He felt considerable respect for himself. He did the story a third time and conquered all South Dalemark, pursuing Navis ruthlessly until at last he caught him.

He was halfway through killing Navis very slowly, with great attention to detail, when Al came back again. Mitt jumped up and backed into the far corner of the small space. Al's face had its most blank and unpleasant look. Because of what he had been thinking of doing to Navis, Mitt knew rather well how much Al could hurt him if he wanted to.

But Al simply leaned against the door and surveyed Mitt. "You're a real nuisance to me," he said, "and I'm going to have to get rid of you quick. How many people know where you are?"

Mitt stared at Al uncertainly. He did not know what Al thought he had done.

"Out with it," said Al. "Or do I have to knock your

head in? Navis knows you were the one with the bomb. Does Hobin know about that? Hobin must've given you that gun. I don't see you pinching one of Hobin's specials. He's too careful of them. Does Milda know where you are, too?"

Mitt shook his head and went on staring at Al. Out of the distant past came memories of Al's voice shouting that the cow had calved, and Al's square back marching away toward Holand to find work, but he could not bring himself to believe it.

"If you was anyone else," Al went on bad-temperedly, "I could send you back to Holand with the other two and good riddance! But I'm not having you tell Hobin about me. He'd have it round every gunsmith in the country, and without Harchad to back me I'd never get near a gun again. He's made it hard enough for me as it is. And all because I happened to drink a bit too much one day and let out to him how I bust up the Free Holanders. He said he was going to Holand to look after you and Milda, but I know he did it just to spite me." Here Al noticed the way Mitt was staring at him, and laughed at him. "Say hallo to your pa, then, why don't you?"

"Aren't you proud of me at all?" Mitt asked him. Al stared at him. "Chip off the old block, and so on?" said Mitt.

At this Al spit on the floor as Mitt remembered him often spitting in the dike. "Proud of *you*! I've got three kids in Neathdale, and the lot of them put together never got in my way like you do. First thing you ever did was get lost and put me under an obligation to Navis. Then you let the bull get at the rent collector. Then you hang round my neck in Holand. Then, when I thought I'd seen the last of you years before, you bob up dressed like a side of bacon and dump a bomb in front of Hadd just when I'd got my sights lined up on him! I don't know what good you thought that would do. Mind you," said Al, "I didn't know who you were then, but if I had known, I'd have said it was Milda's fault. It looked just like one of her daft ideas."

Mitt was not much given to blushing, but he felt his face going warm and red at this. "It was my idea. So!" he said. He felt he had to defend Milda to Al. "She's all right, Milda is. It's just she's not too clear about what's real. You know, always throwing her money about—" Mitt stopped. That was exactly the truth about Milda, and he had always known she was like that. Milda never looked to the future, whether she was buying too many oysters or sending Mitt to be taken by Harchad. The fact was, neither of them had dreamed what it would be like. It was very painful to Mitt, the way Al was laughing about it.

"You don't have to tell me she's got no flaming sense!" Al said. "She'd have ruined me if I'd let her. And you're just the same. Fancy making friends of Hadd's grandchildren!"

"They're not my friends!" Mitt said angrily.

"You could have fooled me," said Al. "Swap jokes on

the cabin roof with your enemies, do you? Told them half your life story, didn't you? And that Hildrida's no fool. If you say one word more to her, she's going to add it up with what I said and spoil all the plans I got for her. You finished yourself when you opened your big mouth, you did. You don't make friends with people like that. You batten on them."

There were hurrying footsteps outside the storeroom door. Someone shouted, "Al! Al, are you there? Lithar wants you."

"Coming!" Al shouted back. "I'll have to leave you to Bence to deal with," he said to Mitt. "Can't that gibbering fool manage for five minutes without me?" He banged out of the storeroom, muttering.

The bolts shot home. Mitt slid down into a heap in the corner. After a moment he wrapped his arms round his head, as if that could keep some of his misery off him. But nothing could. The horrible similarity between himself and Al was clearly no accident. Like father, like son. And as Mitt hated Al so vehemently, he hated himself, if possible, even more. He had set out to be a brute like Al, and it had not been his fault if he had failed. Worse still, everything he had thought he was doing it for turned out to be a complete sham. Al had betrayed the Free Holanders, not the other way round. Mitt felt as if his whole mind was falling to pieces, like Canden in his dream. There seemed nothing left of him at all.

"One thing you might have done, Al," he said from his corner. "You might have put me out of my misery quick, instead of running away to flaming Lithar!"

It was some hours before anyone came to put an end to Mitt's misery. By that time he was rolling groaning in the middle of the room. He barely had time to scramble up and barely time to glimpse the little brown sailor, Jenro, and another he did not know, and Bence standing in the doorway, before a large sack was pushed over his head and he was bundled head-down over Jenro's shoulder.

"Hey!" Mitt said, struggling miserably.

"Be silent, little one, and no harm will come," Jenro said softly.

"Hurry up," said Bence from the distance.

Mitt trusted Jenro and stopped struggling. The world began to bounce about as Jenro hurried somewhere with him. Mitt was uncomfortable with his head hanging down, but not badly so. After a short while he was swung up, swung down, and lowered surprisingly gently onto boards that dipped a little. Mitt heard water slapping quietly under the boards and guessed he was in a boat. He felt the boat sway, bumping as the two sailors hitched on the oars. Mitt tried to see through the sack where they were. It was a hairy, porous sack, which tickled his nose rather. He could see very little light coming through, which made him suspect that the boat was undercover somewhere and whatever was being done with him was a secret. He would have yelled, but for what Jenro had said.

The movements of the two sailors stopped. Jenro's

soft voice said, "Then, Captain, you are settled that we must be stirring out to sea to throw this little one in?"

"Yes," Mitt heard Bence say from above somewhere. "And I'm coming with you to see it done."

"Captain, there is no need to do that," said the other sailor.

"Oh, isn't there?" The boat surged heavily as Bence landed in it. "I know you lot. When you say no need, I start to get suspicious. Cast off there."

The sailors said nothing. Mitt felt the boat move. The oars began a slow, sleepy *dip-creak-splash, dip-creak-splash*. Shortly, bright sunlight fell across the holes in the sack. Mitt thought they must be out in the harbor. They went on steadily in the sun, *dip-creak-splash, dip-creak-splash*. It was so soporific that Mitt nearly fell asleep, in spite of his misery.

Then he heard the gentle voices begin again. "Captain, throwing this little one in the sea is a thing we cannot do."

"But you wait to tell me till we're past Trossaver," Bence said from the distance. "You'll do it."

"Captain, there are two of us and one of you."

"All right. You can watch me do it, then," said Bence.

"But that is a thing we cannot do."

"You'll have to put up with it," said Bence. "Al wants it done. You always do what Al wants, don't you?"

"We would not do this for Al either."

Bence seemed really astonished. "Not for Al!"

"No," said Jenro. "For this one came on the wind's

road, with a great one to guide him behind and before."

"What's that got to do with it?" Bence demanded. "You saw Al come on the same flaming boat."

"That matters not at all. The great ones contain multitudes."

"Don't you throw your religion at me!" said Bence.

The voices stopped. The oars dipped slowly and peacefully. Mitt grinned to himself inside the hairy sacking and rubbed his itching nose. He suspected that Bence was more likely to be thrown into the sea than he was. He thought Bence knew it, too. Mitt dozed off, soothed by the sound of oars and glad to forget himself. Every so often he woke up to find the argument going on again.

"What am I supposed to do when two of my best men don't do what I say?" he heard Bence demanding.

"We will do what you say," answered a gentle voice.

"Then I want this brat dumped in the sea."

"But that is a thing we cannot do."

Another time Mitt heard Bence say, "What do you think you're rowing all this way for, then? Are we just going to turn round and come back again, or what?"

"If you wish for us to turn round, Captain."

"I do not! I want this brat dumped in the sea."

"But that is a thing we cannot do, Captain."

The next time Mitt woke, Bence's nerve had broken. "I see," he was saying. "And if I lay a finger on him, it'll be me in the sea instead."

"You would not force us to that, Captain."

"Then what *can* I force you to?"

"If it is a thing that meets your mind, Captain, we can be stirring to an island and putting the little one on it. There are those where no mortal men live."

"Bother meeting *my* mind," said Bence. "It won't meet Al's."

"If you are not telling Al, we shall not be saying either."

"Hmm," said Bence. After a pause he said, "Well, it's not so different from dumping him in the sea, I suppose, provided it's uninhabited. Which island is it to be?"

"Lovely Holy Island is nearby. There is none on her but She Who Raised the Islands and the Earth Shaker."

"What's that supposed to mean?"

"No mortal soul lives there."

"I thought there was supposed to be a mad old priest living there."

"He does not live there. No mortal soul lives there."

"Oh, very well!" said Bence.

There was a noticeable increase in the creak and jerk of the oars. Mitt could feel the boat shoving through the water. After barely a minute the swing of the oars stopped. Shingle grated underneath and grated again. Mitt could hear waves rattling the pebbles of a beach.

"Hurry up!" said Bence.

Mitt was lifted and carried by two people. Their feet crunched on sand, and then his own feet were placed tenderly on what felt like turf. Jenro pulled the sack off him and smiled at him.

Mitt had a feeling Jenro was going to say something,

perhaps tell him something important, but while Mitt was blinking and rubbing hairs from the sack out of his eyes, Bence was climbing angrily along the rowing boat at the sand's edge.

"Get back here," said Bence. "Or else."

The two sailors smiled at Mitt, and Jenro certainly winked, though Mitt could not see why, before they trotted back to the boat. Mitt stood, blinking still, while they pushed the boat off, twirled it with a deft shove of an oar, and rowed smartly away, getting smaller and smaller against the green of the nearest island. He thought they were going at least twice as fast as they had come.

Mitt felt desolate. The nearest island was far too far for him to swim. Holy Island towered above him in a tumble of rocks and green grass. Little trees and heather hung far above his head. It was wild, uncultivated, and deserted. To judge from the fresh, peaty smell, there was water somewhere, but there was no food except berries. Mitt could not see why Jenro had winked. He was going to starve to death.

He tried to remember what Holy Island had looked like from the other side, as they sailed past in *Wind's Road*. He thought it had seemed lower and greener, and—though he might be mistaken—he thought he remembered that the islands were nearer on that side. It was worth going to look, anyway.

Mitt set off round the island. There was no clear path. He was forced to wander up and down, between rocks and over slippery turf, sometimes almost down to the water's edge, sometimes quite far up the high hill, and, as he went, his miseries caught up with him again. He hated himself and Al and Navis—everything—so much that he wished someone really had drowned him. He no longer wondered why Hildy had exclaimed she hated life. It was not worth living.

The sun was low. Mitt was hot and under a cloud of midges. And he found his way round the island barred by a huge block of granite. Grumbling dismally under his breath, he scrambled his way to the top of it. A green meadow spread beneath him on the seaward side, bright in the golden evening. Beyond it the sea rolled and swashed in little waves. Mitt looked out over their golden ribbing and saw that the nearest two islands were only two hundred yards or so away. He could swim that easily. No wonder Jenro winked. Then he looked down at the meadow.

There was a bull in it. It was a huge animal, almost red in the low sun. Its great shadow stretched halfway across the meadow. As Mitt looked at it, the bull raised its triangular head, armed with wicked horns growing out of a mat of chestnut curls, and looked at Mitt. Its tufted tail swung. Keeping its red eyes on Mitt, it advanced toward the rock. Mitt could feel the granite tremble under the weight of it as it walked.

Now what am I supposed to do? Mitt wondered, crouching on top of the rock.

A woman came round the rock and looked up at Mitt. "You'd better not go that way," she said to Mitt, nodding toward the bull. She was wearing a green island dress with red embroidery, but Mitt thought she could not be an island woman. She was tall, and she had long red hair which blew round her in the sea breeze. Her face was very beautiful and rather serious. "Go up that way," she said, pointing to the island above the rock.

Mitt looked where she pointed and saw a path of trodden earth climbing steeply this way and that among the rocks. He looked back at the bull, which met his eye unpleasantly. "I suppose I'd better," he said, and he stood up. Then it occurred to him that the woman was standing in the meadow, only a few yards from the bull. "Are you safe there?" he said.

The woman smiled. It reminded Mitt of the way Milda smiled, when the crease went out of her face and the dimple took its place. "Thank you. I can manage him," she said.

As Mitt set off up the steep path, he saw the woman go toward the bull with her hand held out. The bull stretched its massive neck to nuzzle her fingers. Well, rather her than me! Mitt thought.

The path went backward and forward across the hill, diving between twisted trees and making hairpin bends over rocks. Mitt climbed with the rich smell of the earth and the sharp smell of turf in his nose. In his ears the plangent plash and roll of the waves became larger, but more distant. Mitt wondered where he was going and what good it would do when he got there. Then the path went round a rock with a tree growing out of it and entered a very small hanging dell, open one side to the sea, and greener than any of the islands. Mitt stood there to get his breath. There was a great view over the islands in the golden light, islands on one side floating green-gold in blue-gray sea, and islands on the other side blue-black against the sun, floating in silver-gold, like clouds in the sunset.

Mitt, hot and breathless and miserable as he was, felt very bitter at the sight. Times out of mind, as a small boy, he had dreamed of such a place. Now he had found it, and what good had it done?

He turned away and went on into the dell. It was moist and cool. To Mitt's pleasure, there was a trickle of water running down a rock. The sack had made him very thirsty. He put his hands and then his face into it and came out dripping. He noticed that beside him there was one of those stone pillars he had seen on the Isle of Gard. It was about as tall as a sundial, but wider. On it were two small figures, one made of green grapes and rowan berries, and the other of plaited stalks of wheat.

"Hey!" said Mitt. "Here's Libby Beer and Old Ammet!"

He was stretching out a hand to give Old Ammet a touch of greeting when he felt the dell tremble under the feet of a heavy creature. He whirled round, expecting to see the bull again.

A gray-white horse had stopped further down the dell and a tall man with flying light hair was dismounting from it. Mitt hastily brushed his wet face with his arm and backed against the short stone pillar. The man was Old Ammet. He came toward Mitt, smiling a little, with his long light hair blowing and swirling about his head and shoulders as if the wind were blowing half a gale in the dell. But there was no wind at all. He had a straight, grave way of looking, which reminded Mitt a little of Hobin, though his face was nothing like Hobin's. It was like no face Mitt had ever seen. One moment Mitt thought Old Ammet was a grand old man, and the next he seemed a handsome young one. And as Mitt saw these strange changes in Old Ammet, he was more frightened than he had ever been of any nightmare. With every step Old Ammet advanced, Mitt felt another wave of fear, until he was as terrified as he had been that time in Holand when he pretended to play marbles—right up to the moment when Old Ammet spoke to him. Then it all seemed perfectly natural.

"I was needing to speak with you, Alhammitt," Old Ammet said. His voice reminded Mitt of Siriol's, though it was also quite, quite different. "I have to ask you a question."

"You could have talked to me anytime," Mitt said, feeling a little resentful. "Why does it have to be now, when I'm all to pieces?"

Old Ammet's young face laughed, and his old face answered. "Because there was no doubt till now what you would do."

"What I want to do is get out of this place and go North," Mitt said. "What's so doubtful about that?"

"Nothing," agreed Old Ammet, out of his grave old face. "The men of the Islands will help you go North." Then his face blazed young and glad and eager, and he said, "It is also quite certain that you will come back."

"How did you know that?" Mitt asked. He knew it was true. He would have to come back to the Holy Islands. "When do I come?"

"That is for you to say," said Old Ammet, young and old at once. "And when you do, it is laid down that we shall deliver these Islands into your keeping. My question to you is: Will you take them as a friend or as an enemy?"

"As an enemy to *you*, you mean?" Mitt asked, highly perplexed by this question.

Again Old Ammet's young face laughed. "We are not the stuff of enemies or friends, Alhammitt. Shall I ask this way: Will you come as a conqueror or in peace?"

"How should *I* know?" Mitt said. "What do you mean coming and asking me questions like that? What do you mean coming and pushing me around? It's my belief you've been pushing me around all the time, you and Libby Beer, and I don't like people pushing me around!"

"Nobody has pushed you around," said Old Ammet. He looked as old as the Islands. "You chose your own course, and we helped you, as we were bound to do. We shall help you again. All I needed to know was what manner of help we must give you in times to come." And as if Mitt had already told him the answer to that, Old Ammet turned away and went to his horse. The corn color of his clothes and hair caught the sun and seemed to melt into it.

"Hey, wait!" said Mitt. He felt very resentful and very disappointed in Old Ammet. He had expected more from him somehow. "Well, what am I supposed to say? You might give me a bit of help over that, at least!" he said, hurrying after the melting, hazy figure. Old Ammet turned round, melting back to a young man, and Mitt found he had to stop. "Can't you give the Holy Islands to someone else? I don't deserve to get them," he said.

Old Ammet shook his blowing hair and smiled regretfully. "I'm not anyone's judge."

"But you could be," said Mitt.

"What good would that do?" said Old Ammet. "What is your answer?"

Mitt was glad to find that he had not, after all, yet answered Old Ammet's question. He thought about it. The first thing he wanted to do was to ask Old Ammet to come back in an hour or so, to give him time to think. But Old Ammet stood there, old and patient beside the tall gray horse, and the horse cropped the cool green turf with drops of bright water falling gently from its mane, as if, for both of them, there was all the time in the world.

"I'm bad at thinking without talking," said Mitt. "I'm like Al that way. We both love to talk."

"Then why not talk?" suggested Old Ammet.

But Mitt did not talk because it suddenly came to him that he had it in him to be far worse than Al. Mitt, if he wanted, really could become the person out of his recent daydream and go round the country putting people like Navis to death. Al did what he did for himself alone. Mitt would be doing it against people. Mitt looked up at Old Ammet and caught his face as it changed to young. He looked as splendid as Mitt's daydream. Yet beyond Old Ammet was the opening of the dell, and there lay the Holy Islands spread out between the evening sea and the sky. And Mitt knew he did not want to come back to them hunting people from island to island and putting them to death. It just did not fit. But if he came back as an enemy, he would. He had Old Ammet's word for it that he would come back. And it would be like destroying his own early daydreams.

He looked up at Old Ammet's face and caught it between young and old. "It'll have to be friends," he said.

Old Ammet, turned to old now, simply nodded gravely. It was no more than Mitt expected, but he was disappointed all the same. He had hoped Old Ammet would praise him, or at least reward him, for his decision. He was a very puzzling being, and, Mitt suspected, a very powerful one, too.

"What's your name?" he said. "It isn't really Old Ammet, is it?"

"Once," said Old Ammet, "it used to be the same as yours. But people have forgotten."

Mitt thought he had known that. Old Ammet and Alhammitt did not sound so very different. "And Libby Beer," he asked. "That's a silly sort of name."

Young Ammet smiled at Mitt, dazzling him by the

heave and billow of his bright hair and the brightness on his clothes. "You can learn how to call both of us now you've decided. Go on up to our house and take what help you can from there. Remember to ask for our names." He pointed to the end of the dell. Mitt saw the path went on there, up into the rocks. While he was looking, Mitt had a feeling Old Ammet walked dazzling out of the dell, leading the horse, into the sky. But he was not sure. He was only sure he was gone.

"Well, I've met him at last," Mitt said, and he was wonderfully pleased now as he went on up the path.

It was not far, a short, steep climb through the rocks. Then Mitt came to the very top of Holy Island, into a strong breeze, and found a little gray building which looked as old as the island. Standing in front of it was an old, old island man with long white hair and a wrinkled brown face.

"Hey!" said Mitt, remembering that Jenro had said there was no mortal soul on the island.

"You've had a hard climb," the old man said in a gentle island voice. "Come and seat yourself on the bench here and be breathing."

"Thanks," said Mitt. "But I got to ask for their names first. That's what I come for."

"Sit down first. That will be needing a quiet mind," said the old man, pointing to a stone bench outside the house. Mitt went over and, a little impatiently, sat down. The old man sat creakingly beside him. "Will you eat?" he said.

"Well, I—Yes—Thanks!" said Mitt. The old man was suddenly passing him a large bunch of grapes and a flat loaf plaited like an ear of wheat, and Mitt had no idea where he got them from. "How about you?" he said politely.

"I am well, thank you," said the old man.

Mitt supposed that meant he was not hungry. He was very hungry himself. The loaf was better even than the bread they had that morning, and the grapes were sour-sweet, cold and juicy. He ate every scrap. "How about those names?" he said, munching.

"The names of the Earth Shaker and She Who Raised the Islands are strong things," said the old man, "even the least of them. Spoken aloud by the voice, they are too strong, unless the speaker has right in the heart of him. And I must tell you that the names of the Earth Shaker are cruel even then, as they are strongest. He who learns these names must never say them aloud, even sleeping, unless he wishes something perilous to follow. Will you still learn those names?"

Mitt was not sure. He did not like the idea that he might say something perilous in his sleep. He was about to tell the old man to forget he asked when he realized that Old Ammet had indeed rewarded him for his decision, and this was to be the reward. Frightening though it was, Mitt saw he would have to take it, or he would be going back on his decision. And when he thought of himself conquering and killing among the people of the Holy Islands, he knew his decision was right. "Yes, please," he said.

"And who was it sent you?" asked the old man.

Mitt answered without hesitation. "The Earth Shaker."

"Then I will be showing you," said the priest, "if you have taken enough of their gifts." He stood up as creakingly as he had sat down. Mitt brushed the crumbs off his suit and got up, too. "Can you read?" asked the old priest.

"Just about," Mitt conceded.

The old man walked to the door of the house, but he did not go in. He signed to Mitt to go inside. "Look under them in the sun," he said. "And do not speak what you read until you have true need."

Mitt had to duck his head to get into the house. When he was inside, he was surprised to find it was not dark, as he had expected, but light and warm and quiet. The late sun was streaming in through windows placed curiously low down, nearly at the floor. The red-gold light fell on the end wall, on two hollows in the stonework. In one hollow stood Libby Beer, and in the other Old Ammet. They were not as grapes and corn, but as queer old statues of themselves as Mitt had just seen them. Mitt knew that whoever had made those statues had seen them, too. Libby Beer was carved smiling as she had smiled at Mitt, and Old Ammet was miraculously both old and young at once. Mitt wished he knew how to carve like that.

Look under them in the sun, the old man had said. Mitt took his eyes reluctantly off the statues and looked at the wall under the hollows. There was a mass of cracks there, as if something had hit the wall and all but smashed it. But as Mitt looked, he found that the sun was lighting some of the cracks and not others and that the lighted parts were forming letters. The letters fell together to form words, two words under each figure, and the words were names.

Mitt had always thought he could not read without saying what he read aloud. But he dared not do that now. It was one of the hardest things he had done, spelling out those words in his head. Three of them were such strange names, too, that he was not sure how to say them. Only one—the one immediately under the hollow where Old Ammet stood—was not so strange. It was almost Ynen, or like Ynen with an extra *Yn* to it. From this, Mitt gathered, though he could not say how, that the top name in each pair was the lesser name and went with the usual figures of Old Ammet and Libby Beer, made of corn and berries, and that the names below were the strong ones and went with Old Ammet and Libby Beer as they really were. After that he found them a little easier to remember. Even so, he walked to the door with his eyes up and his mouth moving, remembering hard.

"Will you let them stay easy? They will stay in you," the old priest said kindly, seeing his trouble.

Mitt blinked at him. "They will? They seem to get away every time I stop thinking about them."

"You will be saying them when you should not if you will not leave them lie," said the old man. "Now what you must be doing is going down that way." He pointed to the rocks on the landward side of the low gray house.

"But how can I get off the island that way?" Mitt said.

"The Earth Shaker will show you," said the priest.

Mitt shrugged and looked over at the green hump of the nearest island, a good half mile away. Still, where the old man pointed, there looked to be an easy way down. Mitt turned back to thank him, and he was gone. Mitt knew he had not had time to hobble off anywhere. He was simply not there anymore. Mitt could feel that the space by the house was empty somehow.

"And he felt like a real one, too," Mitt said. "I wonder who he was."

20

Wind's Road heeled gently westward in a peaceful evening breeze, threading her way among the Islands. When the sun went red and gold behind High Tross and the misty green hump of Holy Island beyond that, Hildy began to feel chilly. Riss told her there were coats below. Hildy went into the cabin. There she found that not only had the cupboard been repaired and the water keg refilled, but the forward bunk held a pile of coats and seaboots to fit both men and boys. Puzzled by this, Hildy put on one of the coats and came out, intending to ask Riss about it.

A sweet, haunting sound came to her. It seemed to be coming from Ommern. Hildy listened, enchanted, to a tune at once melancholy and filled with joy—at once a tune and at the same time only the broken pieces of a tune. Instead of coming from Ommern, as she had thought, it came from the green hump of Wittess. But when she turned that way, the sound came from Prestsay to one side. "Piping?" she said to Riss.

He nodded. "The greeting of the great ones."

Hildy leaned over the side of *Wind's Road* listening until she thought her heart would break, but whether with joy or sorrow she could not tell.

They heard the piping aboard the tall ship *Wheatsheaf,* too, as she tilted among the islands, carrying Navis and Ynen to Holand. They were in Bence's stateroom, with Al, Lithar, and two guards. Bence was stamping about above in a considerable rage. It seemed that the *Wheatsheaf*'s sails unaccountably kept losing the wind, and they were making very poor progress.

"Can't any of you trim a sail right!" Bence roared.

"It is the wind toward evening, and the islands taking the force from it," explained a gentle voice.

"Teach your flaming grandmother!" roared Bence. "You there! Stop sleeping along that yard and trim your sail!"

The piping came to Ynen's ears very sweet and fitful, sometimes like a melting song, sometimes as a wild skirling. He could not hear it properly for the roaring of Bence. "I wish he'd be quiet," he said to Navis.

From time to time Bence fell into an exasperated silence. Each time the piping came from a different quarter. Al wriggled his shoulders at it as if it made him itch.

"I wish they'd stop that flaming piping! What do they do it for?"

"Nobody does it," Lithar said in surprise. "It happens sometimes. Always near sunset, around suppertime. Shall we have supper?"

"If it makes you happy," Al growled.

Bence's steward brought in cold meat and fruit and wine. Al did not eat much, though he drank the wine. The rest had supper and listened to the shouts of Bence and the piping in between. The steward cleared the meat away, and they were still among the islands and the piping still sounded.

Mitt heard the piping, too, as he swung down the side of Holy Island, galloping the occasional steep stretch. The sound seemed to come from the heart of the island beneath his feet. It was the wildest, most joyful music he had ever heard. Mitt felt so glad and confident that he would have sung, except that he was afraid of spoiling the music.

But when he came down with a steep rush to the shingly shore and saw the well-known elegant shape of *Wind's Road* leaning past High Tross in the haze of evening, he nearly despaired again.

"They've got away! They've gone and left me!" he said. "*Wind's Road*! Hey, there! *Wind's Road*!" He jumped and waved and shouted, knowing they were too far away to see or hear him.

A sudden wave rose between Holy Island and green Ommern and traveled swiftly to the shore where Mitt was. It was so queer, all on its own, that Mitt stopped shouting and watched it. It rushed on, one lonely peak of water, and thundered down on the shingle beside Mitt in a mass of white water and the rubbly squeaking of pebbles. Mitt scrambled hastily out of range. Then he realized that the white foam of the wave was still standing high above his head. He found he was staring at one of the lovely white horses of the storm.

"Thanks, Ammet," Mitt said, laughing a bit nervously. He had ridden a horse only when he was a very small boy, and that was a cart horse. He edged toward the horse. It put its nose down and blew salty breath at him. Nervously Mitt grasped it by its rough wet mane, which it did not seem to like, and struggled onto its slippery back. The horse shook its head and rippled the skin under Mitt, but it did not throw him off.

"Can you catch that boat for us?" Mitt said to it.

The horse surged forward, joggled him, bounced him, and then seemed to be pure movement under him. Mitt found they were galloping across the sea itself, tossing spray, tossing the horse's mane, tossing Mitt. He fell forward and put his arms round the horse's neck. There were hard muscles in it, and it felt warm and cold together, like a hot day high on a mountain. Spray dashed into Mitt's face and the dark sea raced beneath. He could only bear to watch it out of one eye. He tried peering forward for *Wind's Road*, but she had sailed behind Wittess.

Wittess was straight ahead. Almost there. Underneath him. The horse galloped straight across the island without checking. The only difference was that its hooves thudded deep and drumlike, and turf flew into Mitt's face instead of spray. Out of the corner of his eye, he saw several people, who all shaded their eyes to see Mitt against the sun. They did not seem particularly astonished.

"Must have odd things happen all the time," Mitt said breathlessly to the horse as it thudded down to the sea again. Among the sound of its hooves, he could hear the piping again, strong and wild. The sound changed to whipping water, and the horse seemed to splash wet sunset out of the sea. In the dazzle Mitt saw the deck of *Wind's Road* just in time, almost underneath him, as the horse dissolved to a wave of gray, foamy water.

Hildy turned round almost too late. She saw Riss smiling, a welter of disappearing water, and Mitt's feet landing on the cabin roof. "You're not alive!" she said.

It was not very welcoming. "I'm not a ghost yet," Mitt said gruffly. "Where's Ynen then?"

"With Father and Al on the *Wheatsheaf*," Hildy said miserably. "He's taking them back to Holand. They went hours ago."

"Oh, well," said Mitt. He was going to say it was a pity, and then forget about it, when he saw Riss was smiling at him knowingly.

"The *Wheatsheaf* will be between Yeddersay and the outer island," Riss said. "Jenro is seeing to that. They will wait until the sun goes down and the piping stops, when they will know you are not coming."

"Oh," said Mitt. This was too bad! It was not enough

to decide to come back as a friend. It seemed to mean he was expected to act as a friend, and to Navis, of all people, here and now. Ynen, Mitt did not mind. But he did not want to see Al again either. He shot a surly look at the bows of *Wind's Road*, where Old Ammet still lay, stiff and blond and bristly. It was all his fault.

But while he was looking, Mitt suddenly remembered, for no reason he clearly knew, the time when he had first seen Old Ammet in his other, better shape, standing by the bowsprit as *Wind's Road* hung on the slope of that monster wave, trying to turn over and drown them all. For a moment he felt like *Wind's Road* himself. But at that point he had already saved Ynen's life by grabbing his ankle just in time. Mitt sighed. It seemed as if it was his way to make friends without knowing he had—just as he had with Siriol, or Hobin, for that matter. Perhaps even Hildy and Navis were friends, too, deep down where it did not show.

"We better make haste to Yeddersay then," he said.

Riss looked dubiously up at the sail. He meant they were doing as much as the wind would let them.

"I'll see to it," said Mitt. He clambered sideways along to Old Ammet and gently, politely, touched the image on its shoulder. "Could you give us just a bit more wind, please?"

Hildy glowered after him. The pure annoyance on Mitt's face when he first realized what his decision meant made her feel anything but trustful of him. She saw the water ahead ruffle and darken. *Wind's Road* creaked. The sails tightened, and she heeled over with a much brisker rippling round her bows.

"Never fear," Riss said, thinking Hildy was staring at Mitt because she was afraid of him. "He has been on Holy Island."

"I wish he'd stayed there," Hildy muttered.

Wind's Road threaded among the Islands quickly now, accompanied by her own ruffle of wind. The sun was just touching the rim of the sea when she rounded Yeddersay, and there was Chindersay, and the piping came from Hollisay, loud and joyful behind them. And there, sure enough, was the *Wheatsheaf*, towering against the crimson sky, hardly moving at all, with her sails drooping and swinging about. They could have heard Bence bellowing easily on Hollisay.

"What are we going to do?" Hildy asked.

Mitt was not at all sure. "There are four things I can do, I suppose," he said. Then he had a bad moment, thinking he had forgotten those names. But, when he examined the inside of his head, they were there all right, safely stuck.

"Nothing, nothing, nothing, and nothing, I'll bet!" Hildy said scornfully. *Wind's Road* glided nearer the *Wheatsheaf*, and she saw that there happened to be two ropes dangling over her side, just where they would be within easy reach. Somebody trusted Mitt. "I'm sorry," she said. "I've been having a horrible time, you see."

"You're not the only one!" said Mitt, looking up at those ropes dangling over the steep side. Al was up there.

Mitt was afraid the sight of him was going to drive those four strange names clean out of his head. It seemed to him that it would be as well to take precautions. As Riss was bringing *Wind's Road* up alongside the *Wheatsheaf*, Mitt hurriedly leaned right over the side and came up again with his hand dripping wet. "See here," he said to Hildy, "if I get in a fix, or you do, and if I don't seem to know what to say, shout this out." And he scrawled with his wet finger on the cabin roof, big crooked letters: *YNYNEN*.

Hildy looked at them. "But that's—"

"Don't say it!" Mitt said furiously. "Just keep it in your head, will you!"

Hildy saw that if she did not trust Mitt in this, she would have lied to Libby Beer, after all. "All right. I'll remember."

"Thanks," said Mitt, and he swept his wet hand over the name, as *Wind's Road* gently scraped against the side of the *Wheatsheaf*. The ropes hung head-high. Hildy and Mitt each seized one. There was no need to climb. The ropes went up with them, hauled by a dozen men above.

"What's going on there?" bawled Bence.

One of the ship's boats went down past Hildy as she went up. Another splashed into the water beyond Mitt, as he reached the rail. As they both set their feet on the decking, helped by any number of smiling island sailors, a third boat was going down. Mitt saw Bence stare, and then make for the ladder down to the deck where he and Hildy were.

"This is your way," Bence's steward said politely.

Mitt and Hildy trotted beside him past masts and coils of rope, and past scores of sailors all busy getting down to the lowered boats, and arrived at the stateroom door just before Bence reached the bottom of his ladder. The steward opened the door for them, and they went in. Bence suddenly saw what his crew were doing and ran about shouting to them, instead.

Inside the stateroom the lamplight was not yet as bright as the sky. No one quite saw who they were until they were fully inside. Then Ynen was unable to stop himself calling out, "Mitt! Hildy, he's not dead!" Al jumped to his feet. Lithar recognized them both and said amiably, "I wondered where you two had got to."

"Bence!" bellowed Al.

"Mitt, I owe you an apology," Navis said.

Mitt nodded at him as cordially as he could. He hoped that by keeping a friendly expression on his face, he might make himself like Navis. But the one Mitt was watching was Al. Hobin's gun was in Al's hand, and Mitt kept one eye on it, with a name waiting on his tongue.

"Bence!" yelled Al.

Bence arrived in the doorway, angry and sweating. "The flaming crew have got the boats out now!" he said. "They're all rowing away."

"Bence," said Al, "how did they get here? Him particularly."

"I don't know!" Bence said, blustering a little. "They were on that boat again—*Wind's Road*."

"Then you can go by this road," said Al. He brought

Hobin's gun up, over his forearm, and fired at Mitt.

Mitt shouted out Libby Beer's lesser name as he saw Al's finger move.

With unbelievable speed, an apple from the table was in the air between Mitt and the gun. The bullet hit it. The apple burst all over the room, showering everyone with pulp, pips, and skin. The deflected bullet clanged into one of the lamps and broke its glass cover. Navis and his two guards put their arms up against a cascade of broken glass. After a stunned moment, everyone shook themselves and dusted off apple and glass.

Al looked from the gun to the broken lamp. "What did that?"

"I did," said Mitt. "And I can do it as often as you've got bullets. We came here to fetch Ynen and his father away North, and you might as well let them come. You ready?" he said to Ynen and Navis.

Ynen and Navis were already standing up. They might have left then, in that shaken moment, had not Lithar cried out. "Oh lovely! How pretty! You *do* do tricks then! Look at this, Al. Isn't it pretty?"

Everybody looked. It was irresistible. Lithar had a little apple tree growing on his knee. Its roots spread visibly over Lithar's trouser leg, sucking up the moisture from the apple pulp on it. Its leaves turned from spring green to summer dark as they looked. There was another growing on the table, and several more coming up on the floor. Lithar was delighted.

"Do another trick," he said. "These are beautiful."

Mitt almost agreed with him. Hildy agreed entirely. She leaned over the tree on the table and watched it grow in astonishment.

"Very pretty," said Al, giving Lithar's knee a cursory look as he passed. He took Hildy by her arm so suddenly and hard that she yelled. "Now get out," he said to Mitt. "You and your tricks. I give you a count of five before I break her arm, and a count of ten before I strangle her. One—two—"

Mitt could see Al meant it. He could see Hildy was too frightened to say the name he had told her. He could see Bence standing aside from the door to let him go. He could see Ynen staring at him helplessly.

"Four," said Al.

"A larger apple tree?" Navis suggested. "Heavy apples?" Mitt looked at him and saw that he was as tense and helpless as Ynen.

If he's that fond of Hildy, why does he try to hide it? Mitt thought irritably. He said Libby Beer's great name, before Al could come to five. It was a name that rang and reverberated, and became more awesome after it was said. It swelled inside the stateroom.

The result was nothing like Mitt expected. The *Wheatsheaf* shook from stem to stern as if she had hit a rock. They all staggered. There was a creaking and a hard rending. Bence, as soon as he heard it, turned and dived out of the door. The two guards hastily followed him, dragging Ynen and Navis with them. Lithar said,

"What's happening?" and ambled out past Mitt with his tree flapping on his leg. But Mitt had to stay where he was because Al, though he was hanging on to the table with one hand, still had hold of Hildy's arm.

There was a huge creaking, followed by the sound of planks snapping and splintering. The end of the ship with the stateroom in it tipped, so that Mitt had to hang on to the door.

"This ship's breaking up!" he shouted at Al, through the din. "Let go of her!"

Al seemed to forget that he intended to strangle Hildy. He dragged her to the door and stared out. He, Mitt, and Hildy all ducked back as a mast as big as a tree, shrouds, sails, and all, crashed down on their end of the ship. The ceiling above them began to cave in under it. Mitt took hold of Hildy's other arm and Hildy pulled. Al was so bemused that he let go of her. Mitt and Hildy struggled over broken decking to an amazing sight.

There was an island growing through the middle of the ship. It was a wet shiny hump covered with shells and weeds and smelling like the waterfront on a hot day, and it was growing steadily. Navis, Lithar, Bence, and the guards were all on top of it, being carried upward as the island grew. Ynen was slithering anxiously down to them. Mitt stared round, weak with awe. The poor *Wheatsheaf* was in two shattered halves, on either side of the new island, and the surge and disturbance of its growth was rocking the ring of boats where the crew sat watching.

Farther off, *Wind's Road*'s mast beat to and fro.

"What's happening?" said Ynen. "Hildy, what did he do?"

Grass was already springing on the wet hump. It grew faint and far apart at first, but it thickened as quickly as the apple trees had grown. The muddy mound grew greener as well as larger. Some grass seemed to be rooting on the timbers of the *Wheatsheaf* as well.

Navis shouted and pointed. Mitt and Hildy both turned round to find Al close behind them, in the act of grabbing for them. Hildy threw herself to one side and Mitt to the other, where Mitt sat down with a wet *smick* which reminded him nastily of the dikes by the West Pool. As he landed, he saw Al grab Ynen instead and drag him by the leg down the muddy slope. The gun was still in Al's hand. Ynen put up a useless arm against it.

"Hildy! Help!"

"Mitt!" shouted Hildy. She pointed. She meant simply to shout that Ynen was in danger, but it came out with a stammer of terror. "Yn—ynen!"

The rough water round the new island spouted up into a point. A wing shape of water whipped across Al and Ynen, knocking them sprawling. Hobin's gun was flung against Mitt. Mitt had barely time to pick it up, before the new island was a hurricane of wind and water. Huge yellow waves crashed over what was left of the *Wheatsheaf* and broke halfway up the newly green hump. One wave, sluicing down, left Ynen clinging to the grassy mud between Mitt and Hildy. Though none of them could hear, or even think, Mitt hung on to Ynen, and Hildy leaned over him screaming, "It's all *right*!" until her throat was sore.

Then it was over. The sea was rippling and calm. The island had gone on greening in spite of the waves, and it was now as green a hump as the Ganter Islands. There was little of the *Wheatsheaf* left—just a few spars floating nearby. Nor was there any sign of Al. But where he had been there was a curiously shaped patch of green corn, growing and ripening, and crackling like fire with the speed of its growing.

The crew of the *Wheatsheaf* called remarks to one another and began rowing in to look at the new island. Navis stood shakily up at the top of the mound and shouted through the twilight to know if Hildy and Ynen were there.

Mitt shook the water out of his eyes. Ye gods! he thought. What happens if you say his big name?

A desperate thrashing in the water just below him caught his eye. He slid carefully down to look. Lithar's young-old face looked up at him imploringly. Mitt knelt on the salty turf, holding out a hand, and Lithar struggled toward it.

"You should learn to swim," Mitt said, catching hold and heaving him to land.

"Never could," said Lithar. "No more tricks, please."

The nearest boat arrived then, and Jenro leaned out of it. "I will stir you over to *Wind's Road*, you and the two other little ones and their father."

"Thanks," said Mitt. "And then you take Lithar home and look after him for me." He looked at Lithar, but Lithar was not attending. He was looking woefully at his knee. His apple tree had gone. "He's a bit in the head," Mitt explained.

"We know that he is," Jenro said, without expression.

"Do what I tell you," said Mitt. "You look after him. You. And don't let anyone else get at him." Jenro still looked expressionless. Mitt was exasperated. "You've got to have someone until I come back," he said. "And he needs looking after."

"Until you come back," said Jenro. He smiled. "Very well. Will you all five climb in and I will stir to the *Wind's Road*?"

Riss leaned down to help Navis, Ynen, Hildy, and Mitt aboard *Wind's Road*. As soon as they were up, he slid down into his own rowing boat and untied it.

"I think I'd better take first watch," said Navis, rather wearily, looking at the three tired children.

"You do that," Mitt said. He felt exhausted. He had barely strength to wave to Jenro and Riss.

They waved back. "Go now on the wind's road and return sevenfold," said Jenro. The island men sat in their boats and watched *Wind's Road* lean away North in the brown tag end of sunset, carrying Libby Beer behind and Old Ammet in her bows.

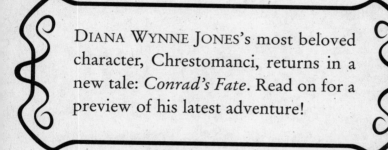

DIANA WYNNE JONES's most beloved character, Chrestomanci, returns in a new tale: *Conrad's Fate*. Read on for a preview of his latest adventure!

When I was small, I always thought Stallery Mansion was some kind of fairy-tale castle. I could see it from my bedroom window, high in the mountains above Stallchester, flashing with glass and gold when the sun struck it. When I got to the place at last, it wasn't exactly like a fairy tale.

Stallchester, where we had our shop, is quite high in the mountains, too. There are a lot of mountains here in Series Seven, and Stallchester is in the English Alps. Most people thought this was the reason why you could only receive television at one end of the town, but my uncle told me it was Stallery doing it.

"It's the protections they put round the place to stop anyone investigating them," he said. "The magic blanks out the signal."

My Uncle Alfred was a magician in his spare time, so he knew this sort of thing. Most of the time he made a living for us all by keeping the bookshop at the cathedral end of town. He was a skinny, worrity little man with a bald patch under his curls, and he was my mother's half brother. It always seemed a great burden to him, having to look after me and my mother and my sister, Anthea. He rushed about muttering, "And how do I find the *money*, Conrad, with the book trade so slow!"

The bookshop was in our name, too—it said GRANT AND TESDINIC in faded gold letters over the bow windows and the dark green door—but Uncle Alfred explained that it belonged to him now. He and my father had started the shop together. Then, just after I was born and a little before he died, my father had needed a lot of money suddenly, Uncle Alfred told me, and he sold his half of the bookshop to Uncle Alfred. Then my father died, and Uncle Alfred had to support us.

"And so he should do," my mother said in her vague way. "We're the only family he's got."

My sister, Anthea, said she wanted to know what my father had needed the money for, but she never could find out. Uncle Alfred said he didn't know. "And you never get any sense out of Mother," Anthea said to me.

"She just says things like 'Life is always a lottery' and 'Your father was usually hard up,' so all I can think is that it must have been gambling debts. The casino's only just up the road after all."

I rather liked the idea of my father gambling half a bookshop away. I used to like taking risks myself. When I was eight, I borrowed some skis and went down all the steepest and iciest ski runs, and in the summer I went rock climbing. I felt I was really following in my father's footsteps. Unfortunately, someone saw me halfway up Stall Crag and told my uncle.

"Ah, no, Conrad," he said, wagging a worried, wrinkled finger at me. "I can't have you taking these risks."

"My dad did," I said, "betting all that money."

"He *lost* it," said my uncle, "and that's a different matter. I never knew much about his affairs, but I have an idea—a very shrewd idea—that he was robbed by those crooked aristocrats up at Stallery."

"What?" I said. "You mean Count Rudolf came with a gun and held him up?"

My uncle laughed and rubbed my head. "Nothing so dramatic, Con. They do things quietly and mannerly up at Stallery. They pull the possibilities like gentlemen."

"How do you mean?" I said.

"I'll explain when you're old enough to understand the magic of high finance," my uncle replied.

"Meanwhile . . . " His face went all withered and serious. "Meanwhile, you can't afford to go risking your neck on Stall Crag, you really can't, Con, not with the bad karma you carry."

"What's karma?" I asked.

"That's another thing I'll explain when you're older," my uncle said. "Just don't let me catch you going rock climbing again, that's all."

I sighed. Karma was obviously something very heavy, I thought, if it stopped you climbing rocks. I went to ask my sister, Anthea, about it. Anthea is nearly ten years older than me, and she was very learned even then. She was sitting over a line of open books on the kitchen table, with her long black hair trailing over the page she was writing notes on. "Don't bother me now, Con," she said without looking up.

She's growing up just like Mum! I thought. "But I need to know what karma is."

"Karma?" Anthea looked up. She has huge dark eyes. She opened them wide to stare at me, wonderingly. "Karma's sort of like Fate, except it's to do with what you did in a former life. Suppose that in a life you had before this one you did something bad, or *didn't* do something good, then Fate is supposed to catch up with you in *this* life, unless you put it right by being extra good, of course. Understand?"

"Yes," I said, though I didn't really. "*Do* people live more than once then?"

"The magicians say you do," Anthea answered. "I'm not sure I believe it myself. I mean, how can you *check* that you had a life before this one? Where did you hear about karma?"

Not wanting to tell her about Stall Crag, I said vaguely, "Oh, I read it somewhere. And what's pulling the possibilities? That's another thing I read."

"It's something that would take *ages* to explain, and I haven't time," Anthea said, bending over her notes again. "You don't seem to understand that I'm working for an exam that could change my entire life!"

"When are you going to get lunch then?" I asked.

"Isn't that just my life in a *nutshell*!" Anthea burst out. "I do all the work round here *and* help in the shop twice a week, and nobody even *considers* that I might want to do something different! Go away!"

You didn't mess with Anthea when she got this fierce. I went away and tried to ask Mum instead. I might have known that would be no good.

Mum has this little bare room with creaking floorboards half a floor down from my bedroom, with nothing in it much except dust and stacks of paper. She sits there at a wobbly table, hammering away at her old typewriter, writing books and magazine articles about women's rights. Uncle Alfred had all sorts of smooth new computers down in the back room where Miss Silex works, and he was always on at Mum to change to one as well. But nothing will persuade Mum to change. She says her old machine is much more reliable. This is true. The shop computers went down at least once a week—this, Uncle Alfred said, was because of the activities up at Stallery—but the sound of Mum's typewriter is a constant hammering, through all four floors of the house.

She looked up as I came in and pushed back a swatch of dark gray hair. Old photos show her looking rather like Anthea, except that her eyes are a light yellow-brown, like mine, but you would never think her anything like Anthea now. She is sort of faded, and she always wears what Anthea calls "that horrible mustard-colored suit" and forgets to do her hair. I like that. She's always the same, like the cathedral, and she always looks over her glasses at me the same way. "Is lunch ready?" she asked me.

"No," I said. "Anthea's not even started it."

"Then come back when it's ready," she said, bending to look at the paper sticking up from her typewriter.

"I'll go when you tell me what pulling the possibilities means," I said.

"Don't bother me with things like that," she said, winding the paper up so that she could read her latest line. "Ask your uncle. It's only some sort of magicians' stuff. What do you think of 'disempowered brood-mares' as a description? Good, eh?"

"Great," I said. Mum's books are full of things like that. I'm never sure what they mean. That time I thought a disempowered broodmare was some sort of weak nightmare, and I went away thinking of all her other books, called things like *Exploited for Dreams* and *Disabled Eunuchs*. Uncle Alfred had a whole table of them down in the shop. One of my jobs was to dust them, but he almost never sold any, no matter how enticingly I piled them up.

I did lots of jobs in the shop, unpacking books, arranging them, dusting them, and cleaning the floor on the days Mrs. Potts's nerves wouldn't let her come. Mrs. Potts's nerves were always bad on the days after she had tried to tidy Uncle Alfred's workroom. The shop, and the whole house, used to echo then with shouts of "I told you just the *floor*, woman! You've *ruined* that experiment! *And* you're lucky not to be a goldfish! Touch it again and you'll *be* a goldfish!"

But Mrs. Potts, at least once a month, just could not resist stacking everything in neat piles and dusting the chalk marks off the workbench. Then Uncle Alfred would rush up the stairs shouting and the next day Mrs. Potts's nerves kept her at home and I would have to clean the shop floor. As a reward for this, I was allowed to read any books I wanted from the children's shelves.

To be brutally frank with you—which is Uncle Alfred's favorite phrase—this reward meant nothing to me until about the time I heard about karma and Fate and started wondering what pulling the possibilities meant. Up to then I preferred doing risky things. Or I mostly wanted to go and see friends in the part of town where televisions worked. Reading was even harder work than cleaning the floor. But suddenly one day I discovered the Peter Jenkins books. You *must* know them: *Peter Jenkins and the Thin Teacher, Peter Jenkins and the Headmaster's Secret*, and all the others. They're great. Our shop had a whole row of them, at least twenty, and I set out to read them all.

Well, I had already read about six, and those all kept harking back to another one called *Peter Jenkins and the Football Formula* that sounded really exciting. So that was the one I wanted to read next.

I finished the floor as quickly as I could. Then, on my way to dust Mum's books, I stopped by the children's shelves and looked urgently along the row of shiny red and brown Peter Jenkins books for *Peter Jenkins and the Football Formula*. The trouble is, all those books look the same. I ran my finger along the row, thinking I'd find the book about seventh along. I knew I'd seen it there. But it wasn't. The one in about the right place was called *Peter Jenkins and the Magic Golfer*. I ran my finger right along to the end, and it still wasn't there, and *The Headmaster's Secret* didn't seem to be there either. Instead, there were three copies of one called *Peter Jenkins and the Hidden Horror*, which I'd never seen before. I took one of those out and flipped through it, and it was almost the same as *The Headmaster's Secret*, but not *quite*—vampire bats instead of a zombie in the cupboard, things like that—and I put it back feeling puzzled and really frustrated.

In the end I took one at random before I went on to dust Mum's books. And Mum's books were different—just slightly—too. They *looked* the same, with FRANCONIA GRANT in big yellow letters on them, but some of the titles were different. The fat one that used to be called *Women in Crisis* was still fat, but it was now called *The Case for Females*, and the thin, floppy one was called *Mother Wit*, instead of *Do We Use Intuition?* like I remembered.

Just then I heard Uncle Alfred galloping downstairs, whistling, on his way to open the shop. "Hey, Uncle Alfred!" I called out. "Have you sold all the *Peter Jenkins and the Football Formulas*?"

"I don't think so," he said, rushing into the shop with his worried look. He hurried along to the children's shelves, muttering about having to reorder as he changed his glasses over. He peered through them at the row of Peter Jenkins books. He bent to look at the books below and stood on tiptoe to look at the shelves above. Then he backed away looking so angry that I thought Mrs. Potts must have tidied the books, too. "Would you look at that!" he said disgustedly. "That's a third of them different! It's criminal. They went for a big working without even *considering* the side effects! Go outside and see if the street's still the same, Conrad."

I went to the shop door, but as far as I could see, nothing . . . Oh! The postbox down the road was now bright blue.

"You *see*!" said my uncle when I told him. "You see what they're like! All sorts of details will be different now—*valuable* details—but what do *they* care? All *they* think of is money!"

"Who?" I asked. I couldn't see how anyone could make money by changing books.

He pointed up and sideways with his thumb. "Them. Those bent aristocrats up at Stallery, to be brutally frank with you, Con. They make their money by pulling the possibilities about. They look, and if they see they could get a bigger profit from one of their companies if just one or two things were a *little* different, then they twist and twitch and *pull* those one or two things. It doesn't matter to them that *other* things change as well. Oh no. And this time they've overdone it. Greedy. Wicked. People are going to notice and object if they go on doing this." He took his glasses off and cleaned them. Beads of angry sweat stood on his forehead. "There'll be trouble," he said. "Or so I hope."

So this was what pulling the possibilities meant. "*How* do they change things?" I asked.

"By very powerful magic," said my uncle. "More powerful than you or I can imagine, Conrad. Make no mistake, Count Rudolf and his family are very dangerous people."

When I finally went up to my room to read my Peter Jenkins book, I looked out of my window first. Because I was at the very top of our house, I could see Stallery as just a glint and a flashing in the place where green hills folded into rocky mountain. I found it hard to believe that anyone in that high, twinkling place could have the power to change a lot of books and the color of the postboxes down here in Stallchester. I still didn't understand why anyone should want to.

"It's because if you change to a new set of things that might be going to happen," Anthea explained, looking up from her books, "you change *everything* just a little.

This time," she added, ruefully turning the pages of her notes, "they seem to have done a big jump and made a big difference. I've got notes here on two books that don't seem to exist anymore. No wonder Uncle Alfred's annoyed."

We got used to the changes by next day. Sometimes it was hard to remember that postboxes used to be red. Uncle Alfred said that we only remembered anyway because we lived in that part of Stallchester. "To be brutally frank with you," he said, "half Stallchester thinks postboxes were always blue. So does the rest of the country. The King probably calls them royal blue. Mind games, that's what it is. Diabolical greed."

This happened in the glad old days when Anthea was at home. I think Mum and Uncle Alfred thought Anthea would always be at home. That summer Mum said as usual, "Anthea, don't forget that Conrad needs new school clothes for next term," and Uncle Alfred was full of plans for expanding the shop once Anthea had left school and could work there full time.

"If I clear out the boxroom opposite my work-room," he would say, "we can put the office in there. Then we can put books where the office is—maybe build out into the yard."

* * *

Anthea never said much in reply to these plans. She was very quiet and tense for the next month or so. Then she seemed to cheer up. She worked in the shop quite happily all the rest of the summer, and in the early autumn she took me to buy new clothes just as she had done last year, except that she bought things for herself at the same time. Then, after I had been back at school a month, she left.

She came down to breakfast carrying a small suitcase. "I'm off," she said. "I start at university tomorrow. I'm catching the nine-twenty to Ludwich, so I'll say good-bye now and get something to eat on the train."

"*University!*" Mum exclaimed. "But you're not clever enough!"

"You can't," said Uncle Alfred. "There's the shop— and you don't have any money."

"I took an exam," Anthea said, "and I won a scholarship. That gives me enough money if I'm careful."

"But you *can't!*" they both said together. Mum added, "Who's going to look after Conrad?" and Uncle Alfred said, "Look here, my girl, I was *relying* on you for the shop."

"Working for nothing. I know," Anthea said. "Well, I'm sorry to spoil your plans for me, but I do have a life of my own, you know, and I've made arrangements for myself because I knew you'd both stop me if I told you.

I've looked after all three of you for years. But now Conrad's old enough to look after himself, I'm going to go and get a life."

And she went, leaving us all staring. She didn't come back. She knew Uncle Alfred, you see. Uncle Alfred spent a lot of time in his workroom setting up spells to make sure that when Anthea came home at the end of the university semester she would find herself having to stay with us for good. Anthea guessed he would. She simply sent a postcard to say she was staying with friends and never came near us. She sent me cards and presents for my birthdays, but she never came back to Stallchester for years.

Also by Diana Wynne Jones

The Chronicles of Chrestomanci, Volume I and Volume II
Vol I: Pb 0-06-447268-X • Vol II: Pb 0-06-447269-8

The Chrestomanci oversees the magic in all the worlds. Omnibus editions of the first four novels featuring Diana Wynne Jones's most beloved characters. Contains *Charmed Life*, *The Lives of Christopher Chant*, *Witch Week*, and *The Magicians of Caprona*.

Conrad's Fate
Hc 0-06-074743-9

With the help of Christopher Chant, can Conrad figure out who is pulling the possibilities and putting his world at risk . . . and also stay ahead of his dark fate? A Chrestomanci Book.

The Dalemark Quartet, Volume 1 and Volume 2
Vol. 1: Pb 0-06-076369-8 • Vol. 2: Pb 0-06-076371-X

Omnibus editions of all four books in the thrilling fantasy epic, The Dalemark Quartet: *Cart and Cwidder*, *Drowned Ammet*, *The Spellcoats*, and *The Crown of Dalemark*.

Dark Lord of Derkholm
Hc 0-688-16004-2 • Pb 0-06-447336-8

When Derk is chosen to play Dark Lord, he is forced by the sinister Mr. Chesney to turn his country estate into a castle lit by baleful fires, manifest himself as a nine-foot-tall shadow, and lead his minions in a battle against the forces of good.

Year of the Griffin
Hc 0-688-17898-7 • Pb 0-06-447335-X

At Wizard's University, Wizard Derk's griffin daughter Elda and her fellow first-year students encounter tyrannical tutors, boring lectures, and truly terrible refectory food.

Dogsbody
Pb 0-06-441038-2

Sirius, immortal Lord of the Dog Star, is outraged when he is falsely accused of murder and banished to Earth. There he must live—and die—in the body of a dog unless he can retrieve a mysterious celestial weapon and thereby clear his name.

Fire and Hemlock
Hc 0-06-029885-5 • Pb 0-06-447352-X

Polly tries to reconcile her two sets of memories and discover the truth behind her friendship with musician Tom Lynn in time to save him.

GREENWILLOW BOOKS
An Imprint of HarperCollinsPublishers

www.harperteen.com • www.dianawynnejones.com

Hexwood
Pb 0-06-447355-4

Through her window, Ann watches person after person disappear through the gate of Hexwood Farm. Then strangeness spreads from Earth right out to the center of the galaxy.

The Homeward Bounders
Pb 0-06-447353-8

After Jamie discovers that mysterious beings are manipulating worlds in an elaborate game, they send him bouncing from world to world — until he tries to use their own rules to defeat them.

Howl's Moving Castle
Pb 0-06-441034-X

When the Witch of the Waste turns Sophie into an old woman, Sophie finds refuge in the floating castle of a mysterious man. People and things are never quite what they seem in this entrancing fantasy.

Castle in the Air
Pb 0-06-447345-7

Abdullah was content with his daydreams until the day a stranger sold him a magic carpet. This fast-paced fantasy is full of djinns, wizards, a floating castle, kidnapped princesses, and two puzzling prophecies.

The Merlin Conspiracy
Hc 0-06-052318-2 • Pb 0-06-052320-4

Roddy, Nick, and Grundo come together from different worlds in an attempt to unseat the false Merlin of Blest, who threatens the very structure of all worlds.

A Tale of Time City
Pb 0-06-447351-1

A girl evacuated from London during the Blitz is kidnapped to Time City in the far distant future, where she must help save both Time City and all of human history.

The Time of the Ghost
Pb 0-06-447354-6

A nameless protagonist doesn't know why she's invisibly floating through the buildings and grounds of a half-remembered boarding school. Then, to her horror, she encounters the ancient evil that four peculiar sisters have unwittingly woken — and learns she is the sisters' only hope against a deadly danger.

Unexpected Magic: Collected Stories
Hc 0-06-055533-5

In this riveting collection of stories, even the most routine lives are visited by extraordinary events.